New York Times bestselling author
KRESLEY COLE
and her "devilishly passionate"
(*Romantic Times*) series
The Immortals After Dark

DARK DESIRES AFTER DUSK

"The snappy dialogue and sensual tormenting make this
the best in the Immortals After Dark series."
—*Romantic Times*

"Kresley Cole is a gifted author with a knack for witty
dialogue, smart heroines, fantastic alpha males and yes,
it has to be said, some of the hottest love scenes you'll
read in mainstream romance. . . . You're in for a treat if
you've never read a Kresley Cole book."
—*RomanceNovel.tv*

Kiss of a Demon King
is also available as an eBook.

DARK NEEDS AT NIGHT'S EDGE

"Poignant and daring. You can trust Cole to always deliver sizzling sexy interludes within a darkly passionate romance."

—*Romantic Times*

"The evolution of this romance is among the most believable and engrossing I've ever read. Cole's Immortals After Dark series continues stronger than ever with the latest installment."

—Louisa White, Fresh Fiction

WICKED DEEDS ON A WINTER'S NIGHT

"Leave it to the awe-inspiring Cole to dish up a combustible mix of sorcery and passion. One for the keeper shelf!"

—*Romantic Times* (Four and a half Stars; HOT)

"Kresley Cole . . . effortlessly delivers heart wringing romance, likeable heroines, hot heroes and hotter sex . . . set against an original and exciting paranormal mythology that keeps both the story and the reader speeding along from one high point to another."

—Love Vampires

Kresley Cole

Kiss of a Demon King

POCKET BOOKS

New York London Toronto Sydney

Pocket Books
A Division of Simon & Schuster, Inc.
1230 Avenue of the Americas
New York, NY 10020

This book is a work of fiction. Names, characters, places, and incidents either are products of the author's imagination or are used fictitiously. Any resemblance to actual events or locales or persons, living or dead, is entirely coincidental.

First Pocket Books paperback edition February 2009

POCKET and colophon are registered trademarks of Simon & Schuster, Inc.

For information about special discounts for bulk purchases, please contact Simon & Schuster Special Sales at 1-800-456-6798 or business@simonandschuster.com

Cover design by Lisa Litwack; cover illustration by Craig White

Manufactured in the United States of America

10 9 8 7 6 5 4 3 2 1

ISBN-13: 978-1-4165-8094-2
ISBN-10:   1-4165-8094-8

For Gena Showalter, light o' my life.
Extraordinary writer, treasured mentor,
and dearest friend.

Glossary of Terms from
The Living Book of Lore

The Lore

". . . and those sentient creatures that are not human shall be united in one stratum, coexisting with, yet secret from, man's."

- Most are immortal and can regenerate from injuries. The stronger breeds can only be killed by mystickal fire or beheading.
- Their eyes change to a breed-specific color with intense emotion.

The Demonarchies

"The demons are as varied as the bands of man. . . ."

- A collection of demon dynasties.
- Most demon breeds can teleport or *trace* to places they've previously been.
- A demon must have intercourse with a potential mate to ascertain if she's truly his—a process known as *attempting*.

The Rage Demons

"The one who controls Tornin controls the kingdom. . . ."

- A demonarchy located in the plane of Rothkalina.
- Castle Tornin is their capital.

- Were the guardians of the *Well of Souls*, a mystickal font of power located within Tornin.

The Sept of Sorceri
"The Sept forever seek and covet others' powers, challenging and dueling to seize more—or more darkly, stealing another's sorcery. . . ."

- A breed-line broken from the enchantment caste of the House of Witches.
- Born with one innate power, their *root power*. If they lose it, they become slaves to their own kind called *Inferi*. They can trade and steal secondary powers.
- One of the physically weaker species in the Lore, they used elaborate armors to protect their bodies. Eventually they held metals—and especially gold—sacred.

The House of Witches
". . . immortal possessors of magickal talents, practitioners of good and evil."

- Mystickal mercenaries who sell their spells.
- Separated into five castes: warrior, healer, enchantress, conjurer, and seeress.

The Valkyrie
"When a maiden warrior dies with valor in battle, Wóden and Freya preserve her courage forever in the form of an immortal Valkyrie daughter."

- Take sustenance from the electrical energy of the earth, sharing it in one collective power, and give it back with their emotions in the form of lightning.
- Possess preternatural strength and speed.

The Vampires

"In the first chaos of the Lore, a brotherhood of vampires dominated, by relying on their cold nature, worship of logic, and absence of mercy. They sprang from the harsh steppes of Dacia and migrated to Russia, though some say a secret enclave, the Daci, live in Dacia still."

- Consist of two warring factions, the Horde and the Forebearer Army.
- Like many demons, vampires can *trace*.
- *The Fallen* are vampires who have killed by drinking a victim to death. Distinguished by their red eyes.

The Accession

"And a time shall pass that all immortal beings in the Lore, from the Valkyrie, vampire, Lykae, and demon factions to the phantoms, shifters, fey, and sirens . . . must fight and destroy each other."

- A kind of mystickal checks-and-balances system for an ever-growing population of immortals.
- Occurs every five hundred years. *Or right now . . .*

"With me, nothing is as it seems. It's usually much, much worse. And then—What do you mean I only get one epigraph? I get as many as I please. Only pre-eviscerated people have ever said things like that to me."
—Sabine of the Sorceri,
Queen of Illusions,
anointed princess of Rothkalina

"That sorceress might be an evil bitch, but she's my evil bitch. And I'll have no other."
—Rydstrom Woede,
fallen demon king of Rothkalina

❧ Prologue ❧

Whenever you have a sorcerer betwixt your thighs, your powers tend to disappear," Sabine told her sister as she scanned the faces of the frenzied, caged humans. "It's merely a fact of life."

"Maybe in the past," Lanthe said as she dropped the unconscious guard she'd been toting by his belt. "Things are going to be different with this one." She busily tied the man's hands behind his back—instead of breaking his arms, which had the same result and didn't waste rope. "You still haven't seen her?"

Her—the sorceress they came to release from this place—*if* she agreed to convey her powers to Lanthe in exchange for her freedom.

Sabine slinked down the darkened corridor. "I can't tell when they huddle like this." She plucked a cell door off its hinges and tossed it away, her heels clicking as she entered the cage. Up close, she could tell the inhabitants all looked very . . . *mortal*.

Naturally, they cowered from her. Sabine knew the exotic picture she presented with her garments and face paint.

As though she'd donned a mask, her eyes were kohled black in a swath from the sides of her nose to her temples.

Her clothes were constructed more of strips of leather and chain metal than of cloth and thread. She wore a metal bustier and mesh gloves that ran the length of her arms, ending in forged fingertip claws. Situated among her hair's riotous braids was her elaborate headdress.

Typical garb of the Sorceri females. In fact, if one's apparel didn't weigh more than the wearer, then one was underdressed.

By the time Sabine was exiting the next cell down, Lanthe had finished with the knots "Any luck?"

Sabine tore free yet another cage door, peered at pale faces, then shook her head.

"Do I have time to check the smaller cells in the basement?" Lanthe asked.

"If we're back at the portal in twenty minutes we should be all right." Their portal back to their home of Rothkalina was a good ten minutes away through dank London streets.

Lanthe blew a jet-black plait from her forehead. "Watch the guard and keep the freed inmates inside this hall quiet."

Sabine's gaze flitted over the unconscious male sprawled on the squalid floor, and her lip curled in disgust. She could read the minds of humans, even when they were blacked out, and the contents of this one's were giving even Sabine pause.

"Very well. But hurry with the transfer," Sabine said. "Else we'll attract our foe."

Lanthe's blue eyes gazed upward out of habit. "They could be here at any second." She hastened to the stairwell once more.

Their lives had become a droning cycle: Steal a new power, flee enemies, have power stolen by a smooth-talking Sorceri male, steal a new power. . . . Sabine allowed it to continue.

Because she'd ruined Lanthe's innate ability.

When her sister was gone, Sabine muttered, "Look after the guard. Very well . . ."

Lifting the man by his collar and belt, she tossed him in front of the exit doors. Some of the denizens grew wild at the violence, howling, pulling their hair. The ones who'd been eyeing the main exit scuttled back.

Shush the humans, easy enough. She sauntered to the guard and stepped up onto his back, opening her arms wide. "Gather round, mad human persons. Gather! And I, a sorceress of dark and terrible powers, will reward you with a story."

Some quieted out of seeming curiosity, some in shock. "Hush now, mortals, and perhaps if you are good, quiet pets, I'll even *show* you a tale." The cries and yells she'd ignited were ebbing. "So sit, sit. Yes, come sit before me. Closer. But not you—you smell like urine and porridge. You, there, *sit.*"

Once they'd all gathered before her, she crouched on the guard's back. She gave them a slow smile as she readied for her story, tugging up her skirt to fiddle with her garters, then adjusting her customary choker.

"Now, for this evening, you have two choices. You can hear the story of a mighty demon king with horns and eyes as black as obsidian. In ages past he was so honest and upstanding that he lost his crown to cunning evil. Or, we have the story of Sabine, an innocent young girl who was forever getting murdered." *Who would one day be that demon's bride. . . .*

"Th-the girl, please," one resident whispered. His face was indistinguishable through the curtain of his matted hair.

"An excellent choice, Hirsute Mortal." In a dramatic voice, she began, "Our tale features the intrepid heroine, Sabine, the Queen of Illusions—"

"Where's Illusions?" a young woman paused in gnawing her own forearm to ask.

Excellent—these were going to be narrative interrupters. "It's not *a place.* A 'queen' is someone who is better at a particular mystickal skill than anyone else."

Sabine could cast chimeras that were indistinguishable from reality, manipulating anything that could be seen, heard, or imagined. She could reach inside a being's mind and deliver scenes from their wildest dreams—or worst nightmares. No one was her equal.

"Now the ridiculously beautiful and clever Sabine had just turned twelve, and she adored her soon-to-grow light-skirted sister, Melanthe, aged nine. Sabine had loved little Lanthe with her whole heart since the first time the girl had cried for her 'Ai-bee' over their own mother. The two sisters were born of the *Sorceri,* a dwindling and forgotten race. Not very exciting story fodder, you might think. Compared to a vampire or even a Valkyrie," she sniffed. "Ah, but listen on and *see . . .*"

She raised her hand to weave an illusion, drawing from within herself and from her surroundings—the mad energy of the inmates, the lightning-strewn night beyond the asylum.

When she blew against her opened palm, a scene was projected onto the wall beside her. Gasps sounded, a few stray whimpers.

"The first time young Sabine died was on an eve much like this, in a decrepit structure that trembled from thunder. Only instead of a rat-infested asylum, it was an abbey, built into the peak of a mountain, high in the Alps. The dead of winter was upon the land."

The next scene she cast showed Sabine and Lanthe hastening down a murky stairway in their nightgowns and coats. Even as they rushed, they hunched their heads at each new batting of wings outside. Lanthe silently cried.

"Sabine was filled with anger at herself for not listening to her instinct and taking Melanthe away from their parents, from the danger they attracted with their forbidden sorcery. But Sabine had been reluctant because the two girls—though born of immortals and both gifted with powers—were still children, which meant they could be killed and wounded as easily as mortals, their injuries as lasting. Yet now Sabine had no choice but to leave. She sensed her parents were already dead, and suspected the killers were loose somewhere in the shadowy abbey. The Vrekeners had come for them—"

"What's a Vrekener?"

Sabine inhaled deeply as she gazed at the ceiling. *Mustn't murder audience, mustn't murder . . .* "Winged avengers of old, demonic angels," she finally answered. "A dwindling race as well. But since memory, in our little corner of the Lore, they had slaughtered evil Sorceri wherever they could find them, and had been hunting Sabine's family for all of her life. For no other reason than because her parents were indeed quite evil."

With a flick of her hand, Sabine changed the scene, showing the two girls stumbling into their parents' room. By bolts of lightning flashing through soaring stained glass windows, they saw the bodies of their parents, curled together in sleep.

The *headless* bodies, freshly decapitated.

In the image, Sabine turned away and vomited. With a strangled scream, Lanthe collapsed.

Another illusion showed Vrekeners emerging from the shadows of the chamber, led by one who wielded a scythe with a blade forged not of metal but of black fire.

Flashes of their huge ghostly wings appeared, and the double rows of horns on their heads gleamed. They were so towering that she had to crane her neck up to meet eyes across the room. All but for one. He was a mere boy, younger even than Sabine. His gaze was transfixed on little Lanthe, curled unconscious on the floor—one of the adults had to hold him back from her.

Sabine and Lanthe's situation grew clearer to her. This band of Vrekeners hadn't stalked them only for punitive reasons.

"The leader tried to convince Sabine to come peaceably with them," she told her audience. "That he would put the sisters upon the path of goodness. But Sabine knew what the Vrekeners did to Sorceri girl children, and it was a fate worse than death. So she fought them."

Sabine began the last illusion, letting it play to the end . . .

Her entire body shook as she began to weave her spells around her enemies. She made the Vrekener soldiers believe they were trapped in a cavern, ensnared underground where they couldn't fly—their worst fear.

For the leader, she held up her palms, a gesture of supplication directed to his mind. Once linked, she greedily tugged free his nightmares, which she then offered up in a display before him, forcing him to relive whatever would hurt him most.

These scenes made him sink to his knees, and when he dropped his scythe to claw at his eyes, she snatched his weapon from him. Sabine didn't hesitate to swing it.

Hot blood sprayed across her face as his head tumbled to her feet. Once she swiped the sleeve of her gown over her eyes, she saw that her illusions were fading, the Vrekeners able to see where they truly were once more. Lanthe had woken and screamed for Sabine to watch out.

Then time . . . stopped.

Or seemed to. Sounds dimmed, and everyone in the room slowed, all staring at Sabine, at the blood arcing from her jugular as she collapsed. One of these males had slashed her throat from behind, and all the world went red.

"*Abie?*" Lanthe shrieked, charging for her, dropping to her knees beside her. "*No, no, no, Abie, don't die, don't die, don't die!*" The air around them heated and blurred.

Whereas Sabine had her illusions, Lanthe's innate sorcery was called *persuasion.* She could order any being to do as she pleased, but she rarely gave commands— they often ended in tragedy.

Yet when the males rounded on her, Lanthe's eyes began to glitter, sparkling like metal. The terrible power she'd feared to use she now wielded over them, without mercy. "*Do not move . . . Stab yourself . . . Fight each other to the death.*"

The room was heavy with sorcery, and the abbey began groaning all around them. One of the stained glass windows shattered. Lanthe told the boy to jump through it—and not to use his wings on the way down. Eyes wild with confusion, he obeyed, the thick glass slashing over his skin. He never yelled as he plummeted to the valley floor.

When all were killed, Lanthe knelt beside Abie again.

"Live, Abie! Heal!" Gods, Lanthe was pushing, trying to command her. But it was too late. Sabine's heart no longer beat. Her eyes were blank with death.

"Don't leave me!" Lanthe screamed, pushing harder, harder . . . The furniture began to shake, their parents' bed rattling . . . More shifting . . . a thud as a head rolled to the floor. Then a second one.

The power was unimaginable. And somehow, Sabine felt her body restoring itself. She blinked open her eyes, alive and even stronger than before.

"They ran from that place, out into the world, and never looked back," she told her enthralled audience. "All that Sabine would have from that night was the scar around her neck, a tale to tell, and the blood vendetta of a Vrekener boy who'd somehow survived his fall. . . ."

Lost in thought, Sabine absently realized that the guard had awakened and was squirming under her boot heels. She reached down and snapped his neck before she got so caught up with the story that she forgot to do it.

One woman clapped her hands in glee. Another breathed, *"God bless 'n keep you, miss."*

Sabine might as well be an agent of fate for these people on this eve. Not an agent for good, nor for bad. Just serving fate—which could be either.

After all, the next guard hired might be worse to them.

"What about the second time she died?" a brazen female asked. Her head was shaved bald.

"She was fighting to defend Melanthe and herself from yet another Vrekener attack. They captured Sabine, then flew her to a height, dropping her to a cobblestone street. Yet her sister was there once more to heal her broken body, to snatch her from the arms of death."

As if it had happened yesterday, Sabine could still recall the sound of her skull cracking. *That one had been so close.* . . .

"The third time, they chased her into a raging river. The poor girl couldn't swim, and she drowned—"

"Then take it, you bitch!" a woman shrieked from downstairs, interrupting the flow of the story once more. Ah, the Queen of Silent Tongues was yielding to Lanthe.

Sabine's skin prickled as the air began to sizzle with power. The sorceress jailed downstairs was surrendering her root ability. Lanthe would be able to talk telepathically to whomever she addressed, within a certain distance.

"No, don't fret," Sabine told her antsy humans. "Have you read any of the halfpenny novels, the ones with bank robberies? That's all my accomplice is doing now. Except she's stealing something equivalent"—she made her voice dramatic—"to your *soul!*"

At that one woman began crying, which pleased Sabine because it reminded her why she so rarely took humans as pets.

"Who killed her the next time?" Brazen Mortal asked. "Vrekeners?"

"No. It was other Sorceri bent on stealing her goddesslike power. They poisoned her." *The Sorceri so adore their poisons*, she thought bitterly. But then she frowned at the memories. "It did things to the young girl's mind, this repeated dying. Like an arrowhead forged in fire, she was made sharp and deadly from constant pressure and blows. And she began to covet life as no other before her. Whenever she felt hers was in danger, a mindless fury swept through her, the need to lash out undeniable."

When some of their eyes widened, Sabine realized her pensiveness had made the cell appear to be choked with mist. She often unwittingly displayed illusions that mirrored her thoughts and emotions, even when dreaming.

As she swiftly cleared the air, another patient said, "Good miss, wh-what happened after the poisoning?"

"The sisters just wanted to survive, to be left alone, to amass a fortune in gold through just a bit of sorcery. Was that too much to ask?" She gave them an *"honestly?"* look.

"But the Vrekeners were unrelenting, tracking them by the girls' sorcery. Especially the boy. Because he hadn't reached his immortality by the time he made that leap, he didn't regenerate. He'd been broken, scarred and deformed from his injuries forever."

They'd since learned his name was Thronos and that he was the son of the Vrekener Sabine had beheaded all those years ago. "Without the use of sorcery, the girls were starving. Sabine was now sixteen and old enough to begin doing what any girl like her would."

Brazen Mortal crossed her arms over her chest and knowingly said, "Prostitution."

"Wrong. Commercial fishing."

"Really?"

"Noooo," Sabine said. "Fortune-telling. Which promptly earned her a death sentence for being a witch."

She fingered the white streak in her red hair, the one she hid from others with an illusion. "They didn't always burn witches at stakes. That's a fallacy. No, sometimes a village had burned its quota, so they killed secretly, burying a group alive." Her tone grew soft. "Can you imagine what it was like for the girl to breathe earth? To feel it compacting in her lungs?"

She gazed over her silent audience. Their eyes had gone wide—she could hear a pin drop.

"The humans expired quickly, but not so for Sabine," she continued. "The girl withstood the reaper's call for as long as she could, but felt herself fading. Yet then she heard a ringing voice from above, commanding her to live and to rise from her grave. So Sabine mindlessly obeyed, digging against others' dead flesh, blindly stretching, desperate for another inch closer to the surface."

From behind them, Lanthe's voice intoned, "At last, Sabine's hand shot up from the muddy ground, pale and clenched. Finally, Melanthe could find her sister. As she hauled Sabine out of her grave, lightning struck all around and hail pelted them—like the earth was angry to lose her catch. Since that fateful night, Sabine doesn't care about anything."

Sabine sighed. "It's not true that she doesn't care about anything. She cares about nothing very much."

Lanthe glared, her eyes shimmering a metallic blue from her recent infusion of power.

"*How amusing, Sabine,*" she said, laying the words directly into Sabine's mind.

Sabine jumped. "*Telepathy. Outstanding. Try to retain it.*" Gods, she was relieved to see Lanthe acquire another power. Her sister's persuasion had been exhausted keeping Sabine alive.

It seemed that all those deaths had made Sabine even more powerful while weakening Lanthe—in both ability and resilience.

"*That sorceress also had the power to talk to animals,*" Lanthe continued. "*Guess what you're getting for your birthday!*"

"*Oh, bully.*" One of the least sought powers of all Sorceri. The problem with communicating with animals was that there were rarely enough within earshot to be helpful. "*I can only hope a plague of locusts is milling about when I need them.*" To her audience, Sabine said, "We're finished here."

The long-haired male asked, "Wait, what happened after that burial?"

"Things got much, much worse," Sabine said dismissively.

The crying female cried harder. "H-how could it get worse than dying so much?"

Sabine dryly answered, "They met Omort the Death-less. He was a sorcerer who could never know death's kiss, and so he was instantly smitten with the girl so well acquainted with it."

Lanthe met her eyes. "He'll be wondering where we are."

"But he knows we'll always return." Omort had *controls* in place for the sisters. Sabine gave a bitter laugh. Had they actually once thought they'd be safe with him?

Just then, Sabine heard the sound of wings outside.

"They've come." Lanthe's eyes darted to the chamber's high window. "We run, run for the tunnels beneath the city, and try to find our portal above."

"I'm not in the mood to run." The building began to rock—or it appeared to—with Sabine's anger.

"When are you ever? But we have to."

Though Sabine and Lanthe were nearly as fast as the fey and were notoriously dirty fighters, the Vrekeners' sheer numbers were unstoppable. And the sisters possessed no battle sorcery.

Lanthe's gaze swept over the room, searching for escape. "They'll catch us even if you make us invisible."

With a flick of her hand, Sabine wove an illusion. Suddenly she and Lanthe both looked like patients. "We'll create a stampede of humans and run out into the night with them."

Lanthe shook her head. "The Vrekeners will scent us."

Sabine blinked at her. "Lanthe, have you not smelled my humans?"

❧ 1 ❧

A lap dance for the sexy demon?"

With a firm shake of his head, Rydstrom Woede turned down the half-clad female.

"With a lap like yours, I'll make myself at home," another told him. "For free." She cupped one of her breasts upward and dipped her tongue to her nipple.

That got him to raise an eyebrow, but still he said, "Not interested."

This was one of the low points of his life, surrounded by strippers in a neon-lit Lore club. He was on edge in this ridiculous place, feeling like the worst hypocrite. If his ne'er-do-well brother found out where he'd been, he would never hear the end of it.

But Rydstrom's contact had insisted on meeting here.

When a pretty nymph sidled up behind him to massage his shoulders, he picked up her hands and faced her. "I said *no*."

The females here left him cold, which confounded him—since he needed a woman beneath him so badly. His eyes must have darkened, because the nymph quickly backed away. *About to lose my temper with a nymph?* Getting angered at one of her kind for touching him was like scolding a dog for tail wagging at the sight of a bone.

Lately, Rydstrom had been a constant hair trigger's turn from succumbing to rage. The fallen king known for his coolheaded reason, for his patience with others, felt like a bomb about to explode.

He'd been experiencing an inexplicable anticipation—a sense of building, a sense that something big was going to happen soon.

But because this urgency had no discernible source or alleviation, frustration welled in him. He didn't eat, couldn't sleep a night through.

For the last couple of weeks, he'd awakened to find himself thrusting against the pillow or the mattress or even into his own fist, desperate for a soft female below him to ease the strangling frustration he felt. *Gods, I need a woman*.

Yet he had no time to woo a decent one. Just another conflict battling within him.

The kingdom's needs always come before the king's.

So much was at stake in the fight to reclaim his crown—from Omort the Deathless, a foe who could never be killed.

Rydstrom had once faced him and knew from bitter experience that the sorcerer was undestroyable. Though he'd beheaded Omort, it was Rydstrom who'd barely escaped their confrontation nine hundred years before.

Now Rydstrom searched for a way to truly kill Omort forever. Backed by his brother Cadeon and Cadeon's gang of mercenaries, Rydstrom doggedly tracked down one lead after another.

The emissary he was to meet tonight—a seven-foot-tall pus demon named Pogerth—would be able to help them.

He'd been sent by a sorcerer named Groot the Metallurgist, Omort's half brother, a man who wanted Omort dead almost as much as Rydstrom did. Groot was little better than Omort, but *an enemy of my enemy* . . .

Just then, a demoness dressed in black leather with cheap makeup on her horns gave Rydstrom a measuring look as she passed, but he turned away.

He was . . . curious about wicked females, always had been, but they weren't his type—no matter what Cadeon occasionally threw in his face when they fought.

No, Rydstrom wanted his queen, his own fated female, a virtuous demoness to stand by his side and grace his bed.

For a demon, sex with one's female was supposed to be mind-blowing compared to the random tup. After fifteen centuries, he'd waited bloody long enough to experience the difference.

He exhaled. But now was not the time for her. *So much at stake.* He knew that if he didn't defeat his enemy this time, his kingdom and his castle would be forever lost.

My home lost. His hands clenched, his short black claws digging into his palms. Omort and his followers had desecrated Castle Tornin. The sorcerer had set himself up as king and welcomed Rydstrom's enemies, granting them asylum. His guards were *revenants*, walking corpses, the dead raised to life, who could only be destroyed once their master died.

Tales of orgies, sacrifices, and incest in Tornin's once-hallowed halls were legion.

Rydstrom would die before he lost his ancestral castle to beings so depraved, so warped he considered them the most revolting beings ever to walk the earth.

Gods help anyone who crosses me this eve. A ticking bomb—

At last, Pogerth arrived, teleporting inside the bar. The pus demon's skin looked like melted wax and smelled of decay. The gauze he wore under his clothes peeked out at the collar and cuffs of his shirt. He wore rubber boots that he would empty outside in regular intervals, as was polite.

When he sat at Rydstrom's table, it was to a squishing sound. "My lord and master seeks a prize so rare it's almost fabled," he began without preamble. "In return for it, he'll deliver something just as fantastical." Switching to the demon tongue, he asked, "What would you be willing to do for a weapon guaranteed to kill the Deathless One?"

Castle Tornin
The Kingdom of Rothkalina

When a severed head bounced wetly down the steps from Omort's throne dais onto the black runner, Sabine casually sidestepped, continuing past it.

The head belonged to Oracle Three Fifty-Six—as in the number of soothsayers that had been in office since Sabine had come to Tornin.

The scent of blood cloyed as revenants mindlessly cleaned up the matching body.

And Omort, her half brother and king of the plane of Rothkalina, was wiping off his bloody hands—which meant he'd torn the oracle's head from her neck in a fit of rage, piqued no doubt by whatever she'd foretold.

Standing tall and proud in front of his ornate gold throne, he wore a raised armor guard over his left shoulder and a dashing cape on the right. A sword scabbard flanked his hip. Atop his pale hair sat the intricate headwear that served as both a crown and an armor helmet.

He looked suave and sophisticated, and utterly incapable of yanking a woman's head off her body.

Omort had stolen so many powers—pyrokinesis, levitation, teleporting—all seized from his other half siblings before he killed them. Yet he couldn't see the future. The lack often enraged him. "Something to comment about this, Sabine? Growing soft?"

She was the only one who dared defy him in any way, and the creatures at court quieted. Lining the halls were members of many of the factions who allied with the *Pravus*, Omort's new army.

Among them were the centaurs, the Invidia—female embodiments of discord—ogres, rogue phantoms, fallen vampires, fire demons with their palms aglow . . . more beings than could be named.

Almost all of them would love to see her dead.

"So hard to find good help these days," she sighed. Sabine could scarcely be expected to feel sympathy for another. For far too many times she'd dragged herself up from a pool of her own blood. "Which is a shame, brother, because without her we are as good as blind."

"Worry not, I will find another seer directly."

"I wish you all the best with that." Soothsayers didn't grow on trees, and already they were wading deep into the recruiting pool. "Is this beheading why you summoned me?" Sabine's tone was bored as she gazed around her. She studiously avoided the mysterious Well of Souls in the center of the court, taking in other details of the opulent throne room.

Her brother had drastically changed it since the rule of the mighty Rydstrom. He'd replaced the demon's austere throne with one made of blazingly bright gold. Tonight, blood lay splattered over the gleaming metal—from the oracle's squirting jugular.

Been there. . . .

On the walls, Omort had hung his colors and his banners emblazoned with his talisman animal: an ouroboros, a snake swallowing its own tail, to represent his deathlessness. Anything simple, he'd made lavish. And yet, this place still didn't suit the outwardly sophisticated Omort.

According to legend, the premedieval Castle Tornin had been created by a divine hand to protect the well, with six bold towers encircling it, and the central court. Though the stones that made up the fortress were rugged, they'd been placed flawlessly. Tornin was perfectly imperfect.

As rough-hewn as its former king was reputed to be.

Omort drew back his cape before sitting. "I summoned you *half an hour ago*."

"Ah, just so. I recall that now." She and Lanthe had been watching DVDs in Lanthe's solar-powered room. The sisters probably logged seven hours a day watching movies. *Alas, cable wasn't forthcoming.*

As she passed the Viceroy centaur, Sabine peeked down and asked him, "How's it hanging? Low and to the left, I see. Your left, my right." Though his fury was undisguised, he would never challenge her. She had far too much power here.

She gave him a wink to remind him of just that, then continued to Omort, "I was going to be here on time. But I had something very urgent to take care of."

"Did you really?"

"No." And that was all she'd say on the matter.

Omort stared at her in fascination, his yellow irises glowing. But when she removed her own cape, he seemed to shake himself, casting a disapproving look at her garments—a scanty bandeau top of gold weave, a leather micro-skirt, claw-tipped gauntlets on her hands, and thigh-high boots.

After raking his gaze over her body, Omort settled on her face. She'd drawn her bold scarlet eye paint in the shape of wings that spread out from her lashes up over her brows all the way to her hairline.

In ages past, Omort had wanted to make it law that females of value were to obscure their faces with a traditional silk Sorceri mask instead of mere paint mimicking one, and to cover their bodies entirely.

He'd swiftly learned how Sabine felt about that idea.

"Actually, Omort, I just came to drink my *medicine*."

"You'll get your dose later," Omort replied, waving a negligent hand.

How easy it was for him to dismiss. He wasn't the one who needed it to keep from dying a horrific death.

"For now, we have something more important to discuss—"

Hettiah, Omort's half sister and Sabine's arch-nemesis, arrived then, hastening up the dais steps to stand beside Omort's throne—her rightful place, since she was his concubine as well as his relation. She must have run here as soon as she'd heard Sabine was at court, frantic to make sure Sabine didn't steal Omort from her.

Hettiah was woefully confused on two points: Omort was Sabine's for the taking, and she would never be taking.

Omort ignored Hettiah utterly, keeping his eyes on Sabine.

"Important to discuss . . . ?" she prompted.

"My spies have long been searching for Groot the Metallurgist and monitoring the activities of his most trusted followers."

Groot lived in hiding from Omort, and was one of only two half siblings outside Tornin who still survived.

"I've just learned that he sent an emissary to meet with none other than *Rydstrom Woede*."

At last, an intrigue! "Rydstrom and Groot, our two most dangerous enemies allying. This *is* bad news."

"Something must be done. One of the spies heard the emissary promising a sword forged to kill me."

Everyone at court stilled—including Sabine.

Omort exhaled wearily. "It won't, though. It can't." He almost sounded regretful. "Do you know how many bombs, spells, spears, daggers, and poisons were supposed to have ended me?"

Indeed, Sabine had seen Omort stabbed through the heart, beheaded, and burned to cold ash. And always he rose from a dirty mist like a phoenix, stronger even than before. His very name meant *without death*.

"But Rydstrom must believe it will work," he said. "The infamously coolheaded demon was seen storming from the meeting, and heard calling his brother Cadeon as he got into his car to speed away toward New Orleans."

"Rydstrom must be on his way to meet him." *Cadeon the Kingmaker, a ruthless mercenary.* He was rumored to be able to put any king on a throne—except his brother. For centuries, the two had worked together to reclaim Tornin.

Which was now *her* home. *Get over it, demons. Not moving.*

Hettiah cleared her throat. "My liege, if the sword can't kill you, then why worry about it?"

"Because the belief is nearly as dangerous," Sabine answered impatiently. "The sword could be seen as a rallying point, used as a propaganda tool." Already little rebellions erupted over the countryside, the demons continuing to clamor for their deposed king.

Clamoring still—after *nine centuries*.

Sabine often wondered how he'd earned such fervent loyalty. "So it's clear I can't let the brothers meet," she said. "I'll intercept Rydstrom before he can reach the city."

"And then?" Omort said quietly. "What will you do with him?"

"And then I'll kill two birds with one stone," she. answered. "This is the prophecy beginning." Just in time for the Accession.

Every five hundred years, that great immortal war took place, and they were on the cusp of it right now.

Her gaze flickered over the mysterious well in the center of the court, strewn with sacrifices—bloody and unidentifiable body parts. Her future depended on unlocking its power. And the demon was the key.

When she faced Omort, his brows drew together, as if he'd thought she would balk at bedding a demon. In fact, she was eager to get this over with—and then to seize the power that was there for the taking.

At last, something to want, to *need*.

Hettiah asked, "What if the demon resists you?"

Sabine's lips parted. "Have you *looked* at me lately, Hettiah?" She turned in a circle, a move that left Omort leaning forward on the edge of his throne, and Hettiah sending her murderous glances.

Hettiah wasn't without power. In fact, her ability was neutralizing others' powers. She could erase illusions as easily as Sabine could cast them. Lanthe had nicknamed her Hettiah the Buzz Kill and Aunty-Matter.

"Don't underestimate the demon," Omort finally said. "He's one of the most iron-willed beings I've ever encountered. Don't forget that *I* faced him—and yet he lives."

Sabine exhaled, trying to keep a rein on her notorious temper. "Yes, but I have unique *attributes* that make this demon's seduction *in the bag*."

"You also have a detriment," Hettiah sneered. "You're a freak among the Lore."

It was true she was unique—a virgin seductress. Sabine chuckled at Hettiah's statement, then her expression instantly turned cold when she faced her brother. "Omort, put a muzzle on your pet, or I'll make her one from her intestines." She rapped her silver-tipped claws together, and the sound rang out in the chamber.

Hettiah lifted her chin, but she'd paled. Sabine had in fact plucked an organ from her. On several occasions. She kept them in jars on her bedside table.

But Sabine refrained from this as much as possible, because whenever she fought Hettiah, it seemed to overly excite Omort.

"Besides, *if* the demon somehow resists this"—Sabine waved her hands over her figure—"I'll have a backup plan." She always had a plan B.

"You'll need it." Hettiah smirked.

Sabine blew her a kiss, the ultimate insult among the Sorceri, who stored poisons in their rings to be mixed into drinks—or blown into the eyes of an enemy.

"Capture him tonight, and then . . . begin." Omort sounded sickened. Not only was Rydstrom a demon, which most Sorceri viewed as little better than an animal, the fallen king was Omort's blood enemy.

And the time had finally come for Sabine to surrender her virginal—hymenally speaking—body and her womb to the creature. No wonder Omort had gone into a fury with the oracle.

Part of him lusted for the power Sabine could garner. And part of him lusted for her—or for women who resembled her, like the red-haired Hettiah.

He rose then, descending the steps to stand before Sabine. Ignoring Hettiah's huff of dismay—and the warning in Sabine's eyes—he slowly raised his hand to her face.

His bloodstained nails were long, cloudy, and thick. When he pinched her chin, she said in a seething tone, "Now brother, you know I dislike it when men touch my face."

When angered—like now—Sabine's surroundings appeared to rock and explode as though from an earthquake, while winds seemed to gust in tempests. Omort hesitantly released her as the court attendees nervously stamped about.

"I have the coordinates for the road Rydstrom will be traveling," Omort said. "Lanthe can open a portal from the dungeon directly to that location, and you can stop him there. It will be a perfect trap. Unless she's already lost her thresholds power."

Lanthe could still create portals. But her ability was temporarily weakened each time, so she could only manage it once every six days or so. Sabine only hoped she hadn't burned one recently.

"Why don't you call Lanthe in here and ask her yourself?" Sabine said, making him scowl. For some reason, Omort had always loathed being near Lanthe and had decreed that the two sisters would never be together in his presence.

"Exactly how long do I have to set this snare?" she asked.

"You must intercept him within the next two hours."

"I go at once." She had little time to hatch a plot, which irritated her. She adored plotting—devising plans and subplans and contingencies—and half the fun was the *anticipation* of a trap about to be sprung. She would dream up scenarios for months, and yet now she had only mere hours.

Before she could leave, Omort leaned down and murmured at her ear, "If there were any way around your sleeping with this beast, I would have found it for you."

"I know, brother."

She did believe him in this. Omort would never willingly give her up, because he wanted Sabine all for himself and had since the first time he'd seen her. He'd said there was something in her eyes he'd never seen before—the dark knowledge of what it was like to die. Something he could *never* know.

He covered her bare shoulder with a clammy hand, sounding as if he'd just stifled a groan at the contact.

"Do—not—touch, Omort." She gritted out the words, making her plaits appear to be striking vipers until he removed his hand. Sometimes she had to remind him that she was as treacherous as the serpents he worshipped.

She turned immediately, giving him her back instead of taking three steps away before turning to exit the chamber. When she passed the well, she darted her gaze to it.

Soon . . .

"You won't fail me?" he called after her. "Rydstrom must not reach his brother."

"Consider it done," she called back with utter surety. How hard could it be to capture a demon?

❧ 2 ❧

A prize so rare it was fabled . . .

Rydstrom sped his McLaren down a deserted levee road, his headlights cleaving through the swamp fog. That crazed energy within him, the inexplicable tension, had spiked to a fever pitch.

Omort could be *killed*.

One hundred miles per hour. One hundred and ten . . .

With a sword forged by Groot the Metallurgist.

Rydstrom had waited so long for this, he had a hard time believing it was happening now. Although he didn't trust the demon Pogerth, Rydstrom trusted his ally, Nïx—the Valkyrie soothsayer who'd arranged their meeting.

Nïx had said that this campaign was a chance to kill Omort—Rydstrom's last chance. Either he would succeed in destroying the sorcerer or he would fail forever.

By all the gods, it was possible. But for payment, Groot had asked for the *impossible*. Or so it would seem.

One hundred and forty miles per hour. Though Rydstrom had hung up the phone with his brother minutes ago, he was still slack jawed. Cadeon—the most untrustworthy and least dependable being Rydstrom had ever known—had informed him that he was already in possession of the prize Groot demanded in exchange for the sword.

Cadeon had reluctantly agreed to meet Rydstrom at their customary place north of New Orleans with the payment in tow, but Rydstrom still had half an hour to reach him. There was plenty of time for Cadeon to back out—if he hadn't already.

At that thought, Rydstrom floored the gas, surging to one hundred and sixty miles per hour. *Not fast enough.* He would give his right hand to be able to trace once more. Yet Omort had bound that teleportation power in him and in Cadeon. Rydstrom had never felt as frustrated by that curse as right now. *So much at stake.*

Yes, Cadeon had already found the prize. But he would not be keen to give it up.

He'll run. Rydstrom had to get to him before he could.

Long moments passed with him deep in thought over his brother. Knowing Cadeon would let him down, he accelerated even more. *One seventy . . .*

Rydstrom would die for his people. Why wouldn't Cadeon—

Eyes stared back at him in the headlights. Not an animal, a *woman.*

He slammed on the brakes and swerved, the vehicle skidding out of control.

*   *   *

The screech of tires peeled out into the night as the demon's sports car began to spin wildly. But somehow he was righting it.

"He's pulling it back." Lanthe sounded impressed.

Sabine raised her hands and muttered, "I don't think so, demon." Just when he appeared to gain control, she shifted the vision of the road, obscuring the bridge abutment to his sight.

He sped directly into it.

An explosion of sound erupted—the groaning of metal, the shattering of glass. Smoke tendrils snaked upward, and gaskets hissed. The previously shining black car was totaled.

"Did you have to make him crash that hard?" Lanthe asked, piping her lip to blow a black braid from her face. "He won't likely be in the mood for love now."

"You were the one in my ear, yelling that he was getting away."

Earlier, when Sabine had heard the smooth purr of an engine in the distance, she'd made Lanthe invisible, then she'd cast an illusion of a vehicle on the side of the road, stalled with the hood up.

The damsel in distress. Unable to fix her own engine. A ridiculous cliché. But necessary.

When he hadn't slowed, she'd waved her arms, and still he'd continued speeding along. Refusing to let him slip past her, she'd cast forward an illusion of herself, directly in his car's path. He'd swerved to avoid her likeness.

"Besides, he's a demon," Sabine continued. "Demons are both tough—and lusty." When his door shot open, she said, "See?" But he hadn't yet exited.

"*What's taking him so long?*" Lanthe asked, switching to telepathy, biting her nails as she silently talked. "*What if we draw the Vrekeners?*" Even after all these years, those fiends continued to track the sisters' heavy sorcery.

"*We've got time yet,*" Sabine said, though she was growing impatient to see the male she'd be giving herself to—and anxious to get a glimpse of one of the most well-respected leaders in the Lore.

Of course, Sabine had read all about Rydstrom and knew details of his history. He was fifteen hundred years old. He'd had five siblings, with two sisters and one brother still living. He'd been a warrior long before he'd unexpectedly inherited the crown of Rothkalina.

And she knew details of his appearance: a large male with a battle scar on his face and intense green eyes that would grow black with fury—or desire. As a rage demon, his horns would flow back instead of jutting forward. One of his had been damaged before he reached his immortality.

Horns. And she'd be taking this demon into her body in mere moments, if her plan worked.

If not, she had her poison ring. Under a ruby was a sleeping powder prepared by the Hag in the Basement, their resident poison and potion preparer. Demons were highly susceptible to both.

Drugging Rydstrom wasn't Sabine's preferred plan, but if it came down to it, she would use all means necessary to get him into the dungeon cell they'd prepared for him—one he couldn't break free from despite his demonic strength.

It was mere feet from them.

Directly within the cell, Lanthe had created the seamless portal that opened up to the road. To conceal it, Sabine had woven one of the largest, most intricate illusions of her life, making the dungeon look just like a part of the scenery along the road.

It seemed an eternity passed before Rydstrom finally lurched from the smoking wreck. She released a breath she hadn't known she held.

And there he was.

He certainly was big—approaching seven feet tall with broad shoulders. His hair was as black as night. His horns curved out from just past his temples to run along the sides of his head, their shell-like color stark against his thick hair. Indeed, one was damaged, the end broken off.

Though he reeled a couple of steps, he didn't look *too* injured. No visible blood.

Sabine arched a brow just as Lanthe silently said, "*Your demon's just . . . fearsome-looking.*"

She was about to correct Lanthe and say, "*Not my demon.*" But the male before them would indeed be hers. For a time. "*He is a fearsome male, isn't he?*"

From his appearance, Sabine would have guessed him to be an assassin or cutthroat criminal of some sort. How odd, since he was supposed to be a bastion of reason, a wise leader who liked to solve conflicts and discover solutions to complex puzzles.

Rumor in the Lore held that a lie had never left Rydstrom's tongue. Which must be a lie in itself.

"*Are you going to try to seduce him first or just spring the trap?*"

"*Seduce him first. He might go demonic over his capture.*" She smoothed her hands down her pale blue dress

"*You look good,*" Lanthe said. "*Sweet. Nothing says 'do me!' like pastel.*"

"*That's just unnecessary, Lanthe.*" Since Sabine hadn't wanted him to know she was a sorceress, she'd worn an elegant but conservatively boring gown. She'd thought it wouldn't hurt to appear virtuous, which she assumed a good demon king would prefer.

He had *better* like her shuddersome new look. Except for her ring, not a single ounce of gold adorned her body. No makeup, either. She'd left her hair unplaited, curling almost to her waist—without a headdress. And it felt *wrong*.

"*Are you sure you want to go through with this?*" Lanthe asked. "*No second thoughts about taking one on the chin for Team Evil?*"

Eyes locked on her prey, Sabine murmured, "*Not in the least.*"

A goal, a plot, a possibility . . . all lay before her.

Once he staggered back to survey the damage to his car, crunching over glass and debris, the demon whistled in a breath at the sight, but his attention quickly turned away from the wreck.

"Is someone here?" he called. With each second that he shook off the accident, his shoulders went farther back, his chin lifting, his demeanor unmistakably *kingly*. "Are you hurt?"

Sabine didn't answer, instead letting his voice roll

over her. It was pleasingly deep-toned, with the British-tinged accent common to noble rage demons.

When he loped in her direction, he snagged a cell phone from his pocket and peered at the screen. She heard him mutter, "Bugger me." No reception out here.

He wore a dark jacket over a thin black sweater that molded over his broad chest. His clothes were simple in cut but expensive-looking. Tailored, of course. No off-the-rack garments would fit his towering build and wide shoulders.

The battle scar on his face carved across his fore-head, then jagged down his cheek. He had to have received that injury before the age when he'd been "frozen" in his immortal body—she guessed when he was thirty-four or thirty-five years old—or else it would have healed seamlessly.

The scar gave him a dangerous air that clashed with his royal bearing and rich-looking clothing, as did his horns, his fangs, his black claws . . .

"*I'd do him,*" Lanthe said.

"*Since you'd do anyone, your comment is meaningless in the definitive sense.*"

"*You're just jealous.*"

Yes, yes she was.

When he glanced back up, he met eyes with Sabine. His were the most startling green she'd ever seen.

"*Go now,*" she told Lanthe. "*Be ready to shut the portal directly behind us. Once I capture him, report my success to Omort. Loudly. In front of all the fools at court.*"

"*Will do. Go get 'em, tigress. Rar!*"

With Lanthe gone, Sabine devoted her full concentration to him. His gaze narrowed as she made the night appear dreamlike. The stars shone brighter for him, the moon seeming heavier in the sky. Brows drawn in confusion, he started toward her.

She could see him assessing her, his gaze flickering over her long hair, and over the modest gown that fortunately had grown damp in the humid night and clung to her breasts. When he peered hard at the outline of her jutting nipples, he ran a hand over his mouth.

Time to get him through the portal. When she began sauntering along the road away from him, he said, "No, wait! Are you all right?"

She turned to him but continued to step backward toward the trap.

"I won't hurt you." The demon hastened after her. "Do you have a car out here?"

"I need your help," she told him, continuing her damsel-in-distress act.

"Of course. Do you live near here?" Finally, they neared the portal's edge.

"Need your help," she said once more, ducking behind what appeared to be a willow by the water's edge, but was actually an illusion within the dungeon.

He joined her there—and Sabine sensed the portal closing. The trap had worked, and he'd never felt a thing.

"I have to get to the city," he said. "But then I can come back to help you."

Before she caught herself, her gaze flitted over the deep scar on his face—the first time she'd seen it this close.

He noticed and seemed to be waiting for her to react.

The scar didn't bother her as much as it clearly did him. She could use that against him.

All in all, he wasn't anything like she imagined. He was . . . better. And if she looked at those intense eyes long enough, she could almost forget what he was. When she arched closer to him, he drew back, suspicion in his expression.

She hastily said, "Help me *now*." Grasping one of his big hands in hers, she kissed it with smiling lips, then placed it over one of her breasts.

As if he didn't realize what he was doing, he cupped her flesh with a growl.

"This is what I need," she murmured, arching to his rough palm.

"And the gods know that I want to give it to you, right after I've settled—"

"I need it"—she took his other hand and placed it on her inner thigh—"*now*."

He squeezed her breast and leg too hard, as if he were holding on for dear life. Yet still he seemed on the verge of leaving her. She delved to read his mind, but demons could deflect her probes. She only heard his stray thoughts, and only because they were so strong.

—"*Been so long without a woman . . . can't have her . . . responsibilities*."—

Exactly how long had he been celibate? And was this brute truly thinking to deny her? *For responsibilities?*

The rejection was intriguing.

She knew that demon males loved to have their horns touched, relished having their females steering them sexually. His had straightened and become duskier with his arousal, so she raised her hands and wrapped her fingers around them.

He shuddered as if in ecstasy.

"Kiss me, demon." She gave a firm tug to lead him down to her, and he finally bowed his head. When their lips met, he groaned from deep in his chest.

—". . . connection with her, maybe the connection."—

Yes, already he sensed what she was to him. Now he'll come to heel.

He began taking her mouth, twining his tongue against hers slowly. She got the impression that he was endeavoring to be gentle for her. He probably feared he'd scare her off. But when she met his tongue and gave it teasing laps with her own, his hands landed hard on her ass to rock her against his sizable erection.

So the rumors about demon males weren't exaggerated.

When she felt him subtly thrusting that shaft against her, she thought, This is better. Once males got to this state, they ceased to think.

As she relaxed somewhat, she began to find his kiss enjoyable. He tasted good, his lips were firm, and he knew how to use them. More of his delving kisses, more squeezing and exploring her body.

But when heavily aroused, Sabine unwittingly cast illusions of fire. If he saw them, he could guess her identity. Just when she began to worry that her reaction to him might get that intense, he broke away from her.

"I . . . can't do this now. I have to meet someone. Much rides on this."

Was he serious? "Make love to me," she whispered, now sidling closer to him. "Here. Under this tree, in the moonlight. I'm *aching* for you." And that might actually be true.

"No. I have obligations." His voice was rough, his thoughts in turmoil, blasting past his own blocks.

—". . . *she's so lush . . . cock's throbbing for her . . . horns straightening . . . No! The kingdom's needs always come before the king's.*"—

Yes, Rydstrom was supposed to be patient and wise. Apparently, she could add selfless to that list.

When he backed away, her lips parted in wonderment. *He's going to deny me.* She'd offered up her body, all but begged him to take it, and he'd declined.

How surprising. The only thing Sabine loved as much as a good juicy plot was a surprise. He'd resisted her—his own female. "Then you leave me no choice, Rydstrom."

Just when he frowned, no doubt wondering how she knew his name, she began withdrawing her illusion. The road and the moonlit night gradually disappeared, revealing the sealed and locked cell. As he twisted around, his eyes narrowed with recognition.

"You're Omort and Groot's sister, Sabine, the Queen of Illusions."

"Very good, Rydstrom."

The brows-drawn look of desire from before vanished. Now he appeared disgusted with her. "Show me your real form."

"This is." She smoothed her palms over her breasts and lower. "I'm so pleased by how much it arouses you." *But it hadn't enough. . . .*

Clearly struggling to control his temper, he asked, "Why have you done this to me, Sabine?"

She motioned toward the bed now revealed in the center of the cell—the one with chains at the head and foot. "Isn't it obvious?"

❊ 3 ❊

No, it's not obvious." Rydstrom glanced from the bed back to the sorceress before him.

Thoughts ran riot in his mind—suspicions arose and were dismissed. *A bed and chains.* She'd failed to seduce him to willingly bed her. Was she now intent on *taking* what she'd wanted?

When he felt a confusing surge of lust at the idea, he realized she must already be enthralling him. Of course she was. He'd seen the road disappear, had seen the bridge abutment move. She had unthinkable power, and for some reason she'd targeted him.

He surveyed the dimly lit space. She'd lured him directly into a large dungeon cell. And one he recognized, because he'd kept prisoners here when he was master and king of Castle Tornin.

She's trapped me in my own goddamned dungeon.

When he faced her once more, she met his gaze. Her eyes were unusual—with light amber irises surrounded by a ring as dark as coffee. He couldn't seem to look away from them. "You've brought me back to Tornin, so I assume you're working with Omort."

"That's correct." Her voice was a purr.

I'm in my own dungeon, a prisoner of my worst enemy. Between gritted teeth he said, "And when will I get to face him?"

"You will not. You need not. All you need is me."

"Explain to me exactly what you plan," he demanded, cursing his reaction to her. He'd never responded so strongly to any woman before her. He'd been kissing her, lost in pleasure, actually thinking, *She might be my queen.*

Rydstrom had worried what such a beauty would think about his scar, about how much larger he was than she. For her, he'd tried to gentle his touch and kiss. All the while she'd been luring him into a trap.

"I plan," she began matter-of-factly, "to become pregnant with your heir."

His lips parted. Her very words made his shaft shoot hard as steel as every primal demon instinct inside him seemed to stir to life. This female with her plump breasts and sweet lips desired his seed, wanted to mate *with him.*

She's spellbinding me. She must be.

He'd studied Omort's family, had read about hundreds of his half siblings. Omort had murdered most of them after stealing their powers. But a few he kept close.

What have I read about this sorceress? She was aptly called the Queen of Illusions. Rydstrom had just fallen prey to one of remarkable detail. Though she looked to be in her early twenties, she would have to be centuries old.

She was reputed to be even more diabolical than Omort.

Grappling for patience, he grated, "Sabine, let's discuss this like rational beings." Rational was the last thing he felt. "What do you hope to gain?"

"With me in control of your heir, the last of the rage demon rebellions will be quelled."

The idea that the rebels amounted to even a thorn in Omort's side was heartening. Rydstrom had thought that the sorcerer's sadistic regime had broken any true momentum. "There are two flaws to your plan."

"Enlighten me, demon."

"First, my body won't . . . give up seed." A rage demon could take release in sex, but could never spill his seed until he'd claimed his female, and the seal was finally broken. "Not for any but my fated one—"

"I am yours." Her eyes held his, and he realized that she, at least, believed what she'd said. Omort had oracles, basically his own Nïx at his beck and call.

Sabine could know more than I do. . . .

Rydstrom shook his head hard, even as his mouth went dry. In fifteen hundred years, he'd never felt so attracted to another female. What if she were his? To find his queen after waiting so long? To find her as Omort's sister? "No, fate isn't that cruel."

She quirked a brow at that. "Fate is indifferent."

"What are the odds that my woman is related to my worst enemy?"

"Omort's sire lived for millennia and begot hundreds of daughters." She sidled around him. "Five centuries ago, a soothsayer told Omort that his own half sister, the Queen of Illusions, would be your fated mate, and that she would bear your heir in a time of war. After the foretelling, Omort searched for me specifically because of what I am to you. And then I merely waited here at Tornin for the right time."

"Why now? Why do this now?"

She tilted her head. "I was going to seduce you slowly. But we learned of a plot between you and Groot. I had to prevent you from joining forces with your brother, Cadeon the Kingmaker."

Did Sabine know the specifics of their plans? Tonight, Rydstrom had told his brother that should Omort learn of his quest to get the sword, he would stop at nothing to thwart them. Rydstrom hadn't known his enemy had a sorceress like this aiding him.

"What do you know about a plot?"

"More than you think," she replied. "I *always* know more than men think."

Did she know that there was at last a weapon to kill Omort? That Rydstrom had been intent on speeding to meet Cadeon so they could go barter with the psychotic Groot for the weapon? She must.

Cadeon would be at their meeting place right now, wondering where in the hell his older brother was. The brother who was never late, who never missed a meeting.

"Even if you are fated to be mine, Sabine, I'll never have you."

"Oh, you'll have me." Her lips curled in a knowing, sexual grin that made his heart pound. "Again and again until this deed is done."

Again and again. Taking her soft body, learning that perfect pale flesh . . . *No! Resist her.*

"Tell me the second flaw." She lowered herself to the large bed, sitting gracefully on the side. Her mane of glossy red hair tumbled forward, and her scent swept him up. "You've raised my curiosity."

He inwardly shook himself. "For my heir to be legitimate, you have to be my queen by marriage."

"I know." She ran her fragile-looking hand over the sheet. "We will wed."

She talked of marrying him as if it were an afterthought, while his mind was reeling.

Because he *was* drawn to her as no other woman before. And there was only one way to determine if she was truly his.

"You'll give your vow to me, demon. And I'll accept it."

The vow—the recitation that would bind a rage demon king to his queen. No ceremony, no witnesses, just a pact between two to become one. He would vocalize his claim on her, and if she accepted his right to her, then she would forever be his queen. "My people will never recognize a marriage coerced by sorcery—or a conception fueled by your notorious potions."

"Rydstrom, let's just be frank here. Considering your reaction to me"—she delicately pointed to his erection—"do you really think I'll need to use sorcery on you?"

He clenched his jaw, unable to deny what was so obvious. "Of course you'd kill me after our babe is born?"

Our babe. He'd never said the phrase in his life. Even she tilted her head at the words.

But then she slowly smiled—and it was beguiling and took his breath away. Had she noticed? "Well, I wouldn't be a very good evil sorceress if I allowed you to live."

"Then there's one thing I can assure you. You will never get my vow from me."

"Then, Rydstrom, I can't let you have me without it."

At that, everything became clear. She would tease him, sexually tormenting him until he gave up the words. Why did the thought make blood surge to his groin?

This creature taking him to the brink, over and over.

Imagining the power struggle between them, the *complication* of it . . . Fantasies arose in his mind, thoughts he usually buried at once. Secrets long kept— and forever denied. "Then all you're doing is wasting my time," he said, but his voice was roughened.

"What makes you so confident that I can't make you say or do *anything* to be inside me?"

Because so much is at stake. Never had Rydstrom been this close to all he wanted.

He had to escape to get to his brother before he did something monumentally selfish. Cadeon was a cut-throat mercenary who had just come into possession of what he'd yearned for most in the world. "You couldn't tempt me from my duty before—and I didn't even know who you were then." *Bravado, Woede.*

She stood, her shoulders back. "You haven't seen everything I have to tempt you with," she said, pulling a ribbon at her bodice. The gown slid over her pert nipples down her narrow waist and shapely legs to pool at her feet.

All that remained on her exquisite body was a sheer scrap of white silk covering her breasts and the tiniest panties he had ever seen.

His lips parted, and his cock felt like it could rip through his pants. With her eyes flashing, she raised her chin, well aware of her effect on him and prideful of it.

If this female weren't so evil, she'd be glorious.

In that instant, he decided, *I'll claim her as my war prize when I escape.*

And he would use her to get free.

❈ 4 ❈

Lanthe shuffled to court, listening to her iPod, deep in thought.

A few months ago, she'd been off-plane, sitting in an electronics store watching coveted cable. She'd caught a show about dolphins in captivity.

When the animals got lethargic and bored, their trainers would put fish into a container so that the creatures would have to work to get them, figuring out how to open it.

Lanthe remembered likening Sabine to one of those burned-out dolphins who couldn't swim freely or hunt for their meals.

Sabine had been made a killer but had no one to destroy, a survivor with no calamity to endure. Which made her a burned-out sorceress. She had been for centuries.

Yet tonight when Sabine had locked her gaze on the demon, Lanthe had realized her sister had just been given a demon-size container of fish. *Finally . . .*

To get from the dungeon to court, Lanthe had to walk outside, and the night sky above seemed to mock her, rekindling old fears—

What the hell was that? She'd thought she'd heard something *swooping* over her music.

With her gaze darting, she snatched her ear buds free, then froze for several heartbeats. Only silence. *Losing it.*

Her nerves were getting to her—that had to be it. It hadn't helped that the shuffle function had selected songs like "Don't Fear the Reaper" and Jem's "24."

"The sun's setting gold, thought I would grow old, it wasn't to be. . . ."

She'd been pensive for weeks, fearing that Thronos would find them every time they'd gone off-plane. Or, gods forbid, he'd discover a way to cross over into the plane of Rothkalina.

When Sabine had created that extensive illusion tonight, Lanthe had wondered how it *couldn't* have drawn the Vrekeners.

Though her sister responded to fear with anger, Lanthe just got scared. Something was on the horizon for her, and she sensed her outlook wasn't good.

Once she reached the main hall, she hurried toward the entrance to court. There, two revenants stood guard outside the towering double doors. As she approached, they mindlessly opened them for her.

She hated going to court almost as much as she hated staying away from it. As she passed members of the Pravus, they whispered about her behind their hands, treating her like an outcast, though she was a blood relation to Omort.

Lanthe was a princess of the realm, and one of the six great towers of Castle Tornin was her own. Still, they followed her half brother's lead in deciding how to treat her.

The Invidia—with their wild antler headdresses, whips on their belts, and star patterns over their nipples—laughed at her. The Undines, evil nymphs with paint dusted bodies, openly scorned Lanthe.

The Libitinae, four raven-winged bringers of death, frowned at her with tilted heads. For fun, they forced men to self-castrate or die. They simply couldn't comprehend Lanthe's need for male companionship.

Lanthe supposed she hadn't helped her respect quotient by doing ninety-four-point-seven percent of all the males present, excluding the revenants that lined the walls, of course. Mathematically, this meant that Lanthe was the equivalent of the high school slut.

She'd never been to high school, but she'd watched movies like *Grease*, *The Craft*, and *Varsity Blues*—and they all dealt with school sluttitude. *I'm your girl.*

She'd liked none of her ex-lovers, but she loved sex, lots of it, and well, call her crazy but once a male stole her sorcery when she was in the throes, she didn't let him hit it again.

Sabine had begged her not to sleep with Sorceri, but vampires only wanted her blood, and demons and centaurs were considered animals. The rest of the breeds here? *Creeeeeepy.*

She passed the enigmatic vampire Lothaire, who served as a general in their army, commanding a regiment of vicious *fallen* vampires. Known as the Enemy of

Old, he was a chilling sight, from his white-blond hair to his eyes that were more pink than red to his impassive face.

He was one of the few vampires she'd encountered who might actually be interested in sex in addition to blood. But he could scarcely be arsed to give her the time of day.

There'd only been one male in her entire long life who'd ever looked at her with affection and perfect acceptance. Lanthe feared—and her precious self-help books indicated—that she bedded one male after another because she ached to see that look once more.

Contrary to what Sabine believed, the night of their parents' murder hadn't been the first time Lanthe had encountered that Vrekener boy.

But Thronos had grown up to be her worst enemy. . . .

From his throne, Omort caught sight of her and glowered. Lanthe didn't know what she'd done to incur his lasting animosity, but it had become a fact of life for her. Sabine had said that he innately feared Lanthe. After all, if Lanthe could ever regain her ability, she could command Omort to lose his mind, to forget how to wield his powers.

Oracle number Three-Oh-Eight had told Lanthe that a "perilous inciting incident" would spark her persuasion once more. Lanthe waited impatiently as nearly half a millennium passed by.

"What news?" Omort said when she reached the steps to the dais. As usual, Hettiah simpered by his side—a pale imitation of Sabine. Though her features and Sabine's were similar, Hettiah's coloring was tepid in comparison to the glamorous and beautiful Sabine.

Lanthe cleared her throat. *Sabine went demon-hunting and bagged a two-pointer!* No, too blasé. "Our sister was successful," she said instead. "She's taken the demon captive."

At her words, Omort's fingers went white clutching the arms of the throne, bending the gold. Hettiah noted the reaction with a doleful look.

His eyes darted to the east wall of the throne room—which was covered with stone tablets. They were *covenants*, tablets made with the blood of those entering into any of a variety of dark pacts, with the terms inscribed in the stone for all to see.

The four main players of the Pravus had signed one, vowing allegiance to each other—Omort, Lothaire, the viceroy centaur, and the king of the fire demonarchy.

But now, Omort's gaze was fixed on Sabine's tablet. It was a *Sanctuary*—an ancient Sorceri covenant that ensured as long as she kept her body "pure," no male could "taint" it. For centuries, she'd suffered her virginity instead of any intercourse unwanted or *unnatural*.

If a tablet fell from the wall and broke, all would know that someone had violated the terms of the agreement. Omort was waiting with dread for Sabine's to break—proof positive that she was having sex with Rydstrom.

"The demon's here in my dungeon?" Omort asked absently. "For how long?"

Lanthe shrugged. "Half an hour, I guess."

"I see your sister isn't having as easy a time as she'd predicted," Hettiah said with a smirk.

"No, that's not true, Hettiah." It hadn't happened yet, but of course it would soon. "I'm sure Sabine is finding this diverting—playing with him like a cat with a winged bird. . . ."

The demon ran a shaking hand over his mouth, then seemed to catch himself doing it.

With his gaze raking Sabine's body, Rydstrom began stalking toward her with slow, menacing steps. His eyes were growing black once more, but with desire or rage or both?

She assumed that he would try to escape, would likely seek to use her as a hostage, unless she could seduce him to forget himself. She thought she still had a chance—he couldn't hide his body's reaction to her. Yet the conflict was plain on his face.

Rydstrom didn't know whether to claim her or kill her. "What do you hope to gain from this?"

"I told you."

"No, *you* personally. Your kind looks down on mine. Why would you ever want to wed a demon, to bear one a child?" He narrowed his gaze. "Is Omort holding something over you to compel you to do this? Has he imprisoned a family member? A . . . lover?"

Sabine could tell how much he hoped she was being forced into this. "No, he has no one that I hold dear imprisoned. I was quite eager to fulfill this duty." And to begin the prophecy.

Foretold centuries ago, it stated that if the Queen of Illusions bore the heir of the fallen king of the rage demons, that prince would unlock a source of inconceivable power. If she didn't, the Pravus would fall to its foes.

"*Eager?*" he bit out.

Earlier the demon had inhaled deeply, exercising more patience than Sabine had seen in a male in ages. But she sensed that with the possibility of her coercion gone, Rydstrom had just given up reasoning with her and had reached the end of his patience.

She could see him shutting down. A muscle ticced in his scarred cheek, and his eyes glowed fully black. In a flash of insight, she realized she was seeing a side of Rydstrom that few had encountered before.

"You have no idea what you're playing with," he said, his tone cruel.

"Tell me."

"You won't win this."

"No? Just imagine it, Rydstrom. I can give you whatever you want. I'll fulfill every secret desire you have."

"What do you know of my secret desires?" Had his voice roughened? Again she probed his mind but couldn't get through.

When he was directly before her, he made no move to touch her. This close to him, she felt so small next to his great height. She could perceive the heat coming off his body.

Without warning, his hands shot to her camisole, fisting the material. She stifled a gasp as he ripped it off her, exposing her breasts to him.

Collecting herself immediately, she asked in a femme fatale voice, "Do you think them pretty?"

As he peered hard at them, his brows drew together in answer.

"Won't you touch them? You've waited all your life to pet your female like this."

Just when she thought he would succumb, he wrapped her hair around his fist. He yanked her close until he was staring directly down at her.

"A little girl like you shouldn't toy with a demon like me," he said with another yank, until her hands flew to his broad chest. "You're going to lose, and when you do, I'll make you pay for this."

"Is that so—"

He cut off her words with a brutal kiss. It was so different from the first time when he'd been striving to please her. Now he seemed intent on punishing her. But she liked how bold and firm his kiss was. She liked that he didn't fear her, though many males did.

She felt herself getting caught up, lowering her defenses. When she moaned, he seemed to be losing himself as well, a growling sound breaking from his chest.

Grazing his torso with her bared breasts, she murmured against his lips, "Rydstrom, put your hands on them. You know you want to feel me once more."

With a defeated groan, he covered her flesh. The heat and texture of his palms shocked her. *A warrior's hands, callused from his sword hilt.* As he kneaded her, he took her mouth again, flicking her tongue with his.

When he pinched one nipple—hard, angrily—she gave a cry, anticipating pain; instead, pleasure flooded through her body.

What a *surprise*.

He pinched the other one until both peaks were plump and swollen. Then he grazed his flattened palms over them, up and down, his callused skin rasping her tender flesh.

He drew his head back. "Your eyes are turning blue." A timbre of pure masculine satisfaction marked his tone. "You like my touch, female."

I do. They were strangers, he knew nothing about her, but the way he stroked her was perfection.

Her breasts grew heavy under his ministrations, her sex damp. She'd waited so long for this. For him. She was so close to finally knowing what it would be like to have a man moving inside her. *"More, demon."*

He turned her so that her back was against his chest. Still fondling her breasts, he leaned in to run his face against hers, his breaths hot at her ear. When his big shaft prodded her, he ground it against her.

One of his hands trailed down her belly toward her sex. Her hips rocked up in invitation, but he teased his fingers at the line of her panties.

"Mmm. Touch me there, demon." She trembled with anticipation as his hand slowly inched inside her panties. Illusions of fire began to appear, but she extinguished them . . . barely.

Finally his fingers smoothed through her small triangle of curls. He hissed in a shocked breath to find she was shaven everywhere below it. His voice gravelly, he said, "So soft . . . will I find you wet, sorceress?"

When he dipped into her slick folds, she moaned with pleasure. His body tensed against hers, and he muttered a harsh curse. "You're ready for me."

He spread her moisture to her swollen clitoris, then rubbed it with two fingers, circling again and again. There was no hesitation—he was deliberate, but agonizingly slow.

"It wouldn't take much to make you come on my hand." As he fingered her flesh more aggressively, her eyes slid shut on a wordless cry. She was on the brink, scarcely noticing him raising the arm he held her with—

Until it was constricted around her neck in a chokehold, cutting off her air.

She dug her nails into his arm. He didn't budge. *Can't breathe . . . can't . . .*

"I can play dirty, too." He let up his grip just enough for her to catch a gasping breath. "Scream for a guard."

"Don't need to . . . one's here."

An illusion of a masked guard appeared from the shadows with his sword raised, swinging for the demon's neck. Rydstrom released her, shoving her away to defend himself.

Once clear, Sabine flipped her ring open, loosing her sleeping powder, then crept behind Rydstrom. As she let the illusion fade, she whispered, *"Behind you."*

When the demon twisted around, she blew the powder up into his eyes. "If you're going to act like an animal, then you'll be kept like one."

He gave her a blind look of pure hatred. "You little bitch!" Then he crashed to the floor.

❈ 5 ❈

"Come see my new pet up close," Sabine told Lanthe when her sister returned from court, inviting her to pull up a chair as they watched her servants stripping the demon.

Only Sabine's most trusted attendants were here, Sorceri slaves that were known as Inferi—literally "those who dwell below." She had dozens of males and females at her disposal.

"Quickly!" Sabine clapped at them. "Before he rouses." Two removed his jacket while one built a fire in the cell's grate. Still another poured sweet wine for Sabine and Lanthe. Out of habit the sisters both sniffed for poison before drinking.

"Did you tell everyone at court?" Sabine asked.

"I did," Lanthe said. "Now, what happened here? And why is he still dressed?"

Sabine summarized the events, ending with, "After he tried to strangle me, I dosed him."

"You're a mistress of deception, and he got the drop on you?"

"He's an exceedingly clever kisser," she said defensively.

"You don't seem too angry about this."

"He only did what I would have done in the same situation. If anything, I was impressed that he'd been so ruthless," she said, ignoring the measuring glance Lanthe cast her over the rim of her goblet. "This demon's a tricky one," Sabine continued. "I suspect that both his mind and desires are *complicated*."

"No way. I can almost hear him saying, *Me big demon, me lusty!*"

Sabine shook her head. "No, he's . . . different."

"Try to get into his mind. Tap into his fantasies."

"I tried. Typical demon had it blocked like a barricade."

"Does he believe you're his female?" Lanthe asked.

"I think he feels that I am but is in denial. He won't be able to deny it much longer." Which was important. Already she was running out of time. As a Sorceri female, she would repeat her reproductive cycle only every *two* months. And she was nearing the end of her fertile time.

To her attendants, she called, "Yes, put him on the bed now."

Consisting of a mattress atop a titanium platform, the bed had manacles attached by chains embedded in the solid head and footboards.

"Be careful with his horns when you lift him," she said, recalling that demons could emit poison from the points that could paralyze an immortal and kill a human. Once they'd situated him, she pointed to his feet.

As they yanked off his shoes, Lanthe said, "I still can't believe he wouldn't willingly do the deed."

Sabine took a healthy swallow of her sweet wine. "Made some mention of obligations, responsibilities."

"How could he expect you to believe he turned down sex with a nubile female who's all but begging for it for *responsibilities*? I've never heard of anything like that. Could it be you're losing your touch, old mum?"

"Suck off, fister. He just hasn't had enough enticement."

"You want me to give you some pointers?"

This was a tense subject between them. Once Sabine had realized that for centuries to come she'd never fully know a man, she'd assumed Lanthe would remain a virgin as well, in solidarity. When Sabine had mentioned that, Lanthe had laughed. Loud. More of a guffaw.

"I'm not without skills." Though Sabine was hymenally intact, she'd made up with everything but.

"Ah, yes, Sabine, the Queen of Ill"—Lanthe paused—"icit BJs."

They *were* illicit; every encounter of Sabine's was. She'd long envied couples who lazed in bed all day, but she'd always had to worry about Vrekeners overhead or Omort discovering her.

Once the Inferi stripped the demon's thin sweater from him, Lanthe whistled low. "Not an ounce of fat on him."

When Sabine crossed to the bed for a better look, Lanthe eagerly followed.

The demon seemed to be all latent strength, with rises and falls of long, strapping muscles. But he wasn't bulky—thankfully not a no-necked bruiser.

Above his corded bicep was a wide band of matte gold. The piece was permanent, and he'd likely been wearing it for centuries.

"Look at the tattoo." Sabine pointed to a spot low on his side where jet-black ink marked his flesh. "It continues on." When she shifted him to peek at his back, she found an image of a dragon that appeared to wind around his torso.

Basilisks, ancient dragons, were reputed to live in the plane of Rothkalina in a region called Grave Realm. Demons held them sacred.

Tattoos were common among demon males, but she hadn't expected Rydstrom to have one. When Sabine grazed a finger along the image, the rigid muscles beneath it flexed to her fingers.

"Your gaze looks covetous, Abie."

"So?"

"So . . . if you're his female, maybe you feel drawn to him as well. Maybe you could fall in love," she said, her big blue eyes wistful.

Lanthe was a contradiction—an evil sorceress who longed for love. Sabine had never known anyone so desperate for it as her sister. Ever since Lanthe was young, she'd seemed to be searching for it with her entire being. She read self-help books by the dozen and devoured tragic love stories on DVDs.

"The only love I'm capable of is sisterly," Sabine said. "Count yourself lucky."

If a romantic attachment hadn't happened in five centuries, Sabine didn't see it forthcoming. She'd long suspected that any part capable of loving a man had expired forever with one of her deaths.

Besides, she could never trust anyone but Lanthe, and according to popular wisdom and her sister's books, one couldn't have love without trust.

"In any case, just because I'm his, doesn't mean he's mine." The Sorceri didn't believe in fate, and so they didn't believe in a fated mate.

Still, Sabine would be cautious with her quarry. Getting attached to him, or rather to his body or his tempting kiss, would make their situation . . . *unfortunate* when she was finished with him.

"Ready for the pants?" Lanthe slapped her hands and rubbed them together. "Let's see if the rumors about demon males are true."

"Oh, they're true. In fact, I think they're underreported." Sabine bit her bottom lip. He was still semihard, and she didn't know if she wanted anyone to see him like that. To her attendants, Sabine said, "Leave us."

When she and Lanthe were alone, Sabine grasped the waist of his low-hanging pants, but paused at the button above the fly. "Maybe I'll keep these on him. For effect, when I take them off."

Lanthe's brows rose at Sabine's proprietary behavior.

"What?" Sabine said defensively. "I merely don't want him to get cold." She began chaining his wrists above his head.

"Uh-huh," Lanthe said. "I'll be monitoring this situation closely." She fastened the manacles at the foot of the bed around his ankles.

When he was secured, Sabine sidled up next to Lanthe, and they both gazed at the demon.

His broad shoulders seemed to take up the entire mattress, tapering beautifully to his narrow waist. The hair on his arms, chest, and the trail below his navel was black, but tipped with blond against his tanned skin.

"He's . . . Abie, he's *magnificent*," Lanthe breathed. "Your own demon love slave here for you to use whenever you like. I want one, too!"

"Yes, but now I have to get him up to speed with his new role."

Lanthe nodded thoughtfully. "One thing we never considered . . . what if he is the sole male we've ever encountered who continually puts his duty above his lusts? What if he keeps his promises without fail?"

"There's no such male," Sabine said without hesitation.

"I wonder. Maybe he's so firmly on the side of good that someone from the Pravus *can't* tempt him."

"Are you doubting my skill as a seductress?" Hettiah had already publicly challenged her. "How about a side wager, then?"

"I'm game. If you can't seduce him in the next week, then I get your finest headdress."

Made of the rarest blue and white golds, Sabine's most treasured headdress was winged, arching back over the ears, with gossamer strands of gold cascading over the front.

Sabine had stolen it from the Queen of Clairsentience, along with her ability to touch objects and read their history. It had been a root power, and they'd fought to the death for it. But ultimately, Sabine had given the clairsentience to Lanthe, admitting to herself that she'd truly only wanted the headdress.

The sisters didn't wager gold lightly. Their mother had often rubbed sovereigns against her face as she lovingly said, "Gold is life! It is perfection! Band it in armor over thy heart and never will thy life's blood part."

But Sabine couldn't lose this bet. She was Rydstrom's fated female. "And when I win, you have to go without sex for a year. Maybe then you'll have more sympathy for my plight." At Lanthe's disbelieving look, she said, "Yes, I said a *year*. You know that the piece is of equal value."

Lanthe cast her a pained expression, but said, "Very well, you have a wager."

Just then, Sabine's captive muttered in Demonish, his firm lips parting around each rough syllable.

"Then run along. I want to be here alone when he awakes once more."

When Lanthe had gone, Sabine climbed upon the bed beside his waist, tilting her head as she studied him up close. His horns fascinated her, how they curved back around his head and were mostly smooth, but had ridges toward the base. His thick hair could cover them almost completely, so he would be able to go out among humans, where many demons couldn't.

Recalling how much he'd loved her touching them,

she ran her fingers along them. He shuddered even when unconscious.

Next her eyes flitted over his face. He had chiseled good-looks—a strong nose and squared chin—marred only by his deep scar. The wound had obviously been severe, and she wondered how he'd gotten it.

She eased her gaze lower. This demon had a body like she'd never known.

Sabine had always preferred more dapper physiques. The men she was attracted to were almost always of the Sorceri, rarefied smooth operators. Rydstrom was no smooth-talking sorcerer—he was raw masculinity.

This didn't mean she was eager to bed him. Historically, she'd proved averse to being bitten, and demons marked their females upon claiming them. And a demon's very looks changed during sex with a mate, his features becoming sharper, his skin deepening in color, his upper and lower fangs growing.

What would it be like to have Rydstrom turn fully demonic, growling and thrusting over her? To have this powerful body working hers to orgasm? She drank deeply of her wine.

Sabine hadn't been lying about wanting his pants to remain on for effect—naturally, she planned to take his zipper with her teeth—but that didn't mean she didn't want to see him, or, rather . . . *it.*

She set her goblet on the bedstand, then slowly unzipped his pants. What was revealed made her bite her bottom lip.

A pattern of scars ran along the length of his thick shaft. Though he wasn't now, he'd once been *pierced.*

Sabine had heard rumors of archaic male rites of passage among many of the Demonarchies, but she'd thought the rage demons had done away with them eons ago.

Maybe Rydstrom had decreed it so—he had been in the position to, after all.

So the demon wore a permanent armband over his bicep, and he'd been tattooed and pierced. It seemed that Rydstrom Woede was the type of male whose outward appearance indicated nothing about what might be hidden under his clothes.

As she carefully zipped his pants back up, Sabine grinned. *What a surprise.*

❅ 6 ❅

Rydstrom woke . . . consciousness slow to come. In that dim twilight, he vaguely comprehended that he was lying on a bed.

"You're waking, after a mere half hour," Sabine said to him. "You're a strong one, demon."

Rage coursed through him with his dawning comprehension. *She drugged me.* He couldn't lift his limbs or pry open his eyelids. Though he scented her nearness, her voice seemed to come from miles away.

I'm not wearing a shirt? What the hell—

"It might be a few moments before we can resume physically, so I thought we'd talk about your meeting with Groot's emissary."

What did she know? He cast his mind back, but memories proved elusive.

"What do *I* know?" she asked, reading his mind, incensing him.

"I know why you were rushing off to New Orleans

s evening, and why you were so intent that I had to wreck your pretty car just to get your attention."

He was supposed to meet his brother tonight. Cadeon would be wondering where he was. When Rydstrom felt her join him on the bed, he slitted open his stinging eyes, but couldn't make out more than a vague shape.

In his ear, she whispered, "I know that Groot has forged a sword that you believe will destroy Omort."

He jerked from her, then bellowed at the sound and feel of chains. "You've . . . chained me?" The bitch had bound him to the bed with those manacles around his ankles and wrists.

I will kill her so slowly.

She ignored his question. "In payment for the sword, Groot has demanded the *Vessel*—a female who will beget a future warrior of either ultimate evil or ultimate good." Depending upon the father's inclination. "But wherever will you find one?"

He felt her probing his mind once more, but he had his defenses in place. "After all, demon, Vessels are born only every five hundred years."

And yet Cadeon already has one. Unfortunately, Cadeon's fated female—the one he'd spent over a year pining for—*was* the Vessel. A woman named Holly Ashwin was the payment Groot wanted.

Once Rydstrom's vision cleared, he focused on Sabine as she sat on the side of the bed, grinning at him over the rim of a wine goblet. He was relieved that she'd covered her chest. Then he frowned. Her top was white and so small and tight that he could see the bottoms of her breasts. Hadn't he ripped that one from her? *Losing my mind . . .*

"What I don't know is if you gave your tosser brother enough information to send him on this fruitless quest."

Groot had established parameters to make the trade, a system of checkpoints, with each supplying additional details about how to find his hidden lair. In their phone call, Rydstrom had given Cadeon enough information to make it to the first checkpoint and continue on the mission.

"Not fruitless," he said, but with Rydstrom missing and unable to send word, was it even *possible* that Cadeon would do what was right?

"Even if your brother somehow managed to find the Vessel and locate Groot's secret fortress, the sword just won't *work*. The Sorceri worship metal, and Groot the Metallurgist forges and enchants it. That makes him very powerful. But not enough to give death to the deathless."

As Rydstrom began to regain his strength, he struggled against his bonds.

"You can't break them. They've been mystickally reinforced."

"Release me, Sabine!"

"But I've just *caught* you," she said in a pouting voice.

His gaze darted, scanning for a means to escape. She'd trapped him in the largest cell. When he'd ruled Tornin, he'd used this jail for political prisoners. Inside were a sink and facilities, a small bed stand, a rug on the floor, and hearth tools by the fire. Nothing to aid him.

But then, he well knew . . . *No one escapes the dungeons of Tornin.*

"It looks like it's time to get back to the business at hand." She set her goblet on the bedstand.

"Business at hand? Still haven't come to your senses?"

"No, I'm even more determined than before. I don't lose, Rydstrom."

He lunged up against the bonds, snarling, "You are about to."

"Ah, here's that notoriously strong will of yours. Almost as strong as your rational mind and your sense of right and wrong. But then, was it *right* to strangle me as you did?"

"You're an enemy to me." The maddening tension from before redoubled. "An enemy I'll kill at the earliest chance."

His words were now strong, his tone lethal. Yet he alone knew how close he'd been to continuing his exploration of her, to wringing an orgasm from her responsive little body. Every inch of her had been more exciting to him than the last. "Do you have no hesitation being used like this? As a tool for Omort?"

"You seem to think me either cowed by Omort or suffering qualms about screwing someone for reasons other than pleasure or love. Neither is true of me."

"So you're just a cold, heartless bitch."

"As much as you're a self-righteous, miserable prick." Her lips curled into a smirk. "But that doesn't mean we can't have something meaningful between us."

He kicked his legs and thrashed his upper body.

"You need to understand that you're not getting

away. It's impossible." She crawled on her hands and knees toward him, giving him a view of her cleavage. She noticed his hard-eyed staring, and suddenly the top disappeared, revealing breasts that would bring a lesser demon to his knees.

The garment had been a mere illusion. And now her stiffened nipples were an inch from dragging across his chest.

In a breathy voice, she said, "Do you want our skin to touch, Rydstrom?"

When she leaned down and grazed the peaks against him, her lids went heavy, and he had to bite back a groan. He renewed his struggles, which only increased the contact.

"These chains are reinforced, as is the cell door. Accept it, Rydstrom, you're *mine.*"

"Sabine, you fucking unchain me—"

"Shh, demon." She placed her forefinger over his lips, and yanked it back just in time to miss his snapping teeth. "I know exactly what you're going to say. You'll say that I had better release you this instant, or you will throttle me or some such promise of violence. And then you'll pepper that with a threat about the future. Maybe something with a qualifier like 'when I get free.'"

She'd shushed him? "You see, my darling demon? We're so in tune, you don't even need to voice your thoughts to me." She gave him a smart-ass grin. "It's like we're already one."

"A threat about the future?" He raised his head, baring his lengthening fangs. "I won't just hurt you, Sabine. I'll kill you." *So much at stake.*

Another futile attempt to power free from the chains left the manacles cutting into his skin, blood dripping.

He was truly trapped. Which meant he couldn't get to his brother. To the sword.

To be this close to what he wanted, prevented by bonds even his strength couldn't break . . .

This sorceress had stopped him—*she*'d done this to him. She was the obstacle standing in his way. One small female would undermine centuries of toiling, of warring.

"You'll kill me?" She lightly raked her nails from his chest to his navel, then sifted them through the trail of hair running down from it. He just stifled a shudder of pleasure.

With her, his skin seemed a thousand times more sensitive, his body hungering for release like never before. And yet at the same time, he felt on the verge of rage, beginning to turn demonic.

Though his breed of demon was prone to mindless rages, he'd always kept them at bay. Now being with her was making him crazed, making him lose reason so easily. "Yes, kill you," he grated. "You Sorceri are physically easy to destroy. If I strangle you long and hard enough . . ."

"Just as you had begun to do. Know this, demon, nothing makes me more cross than attempts on my life. I have a particular aversion to being murdered."

What in the hell was she talking about?

Kneeling between his legs, she leaned over him, placing her hands flat on his shoulders. As she lowered her head, she said, "Besides, would you really want to kill the mother of your future offspring?"

"You little bi—" Her tongue on his chest silenced him, the words dying in his throat.

Inhaling deeply, he wrestled for control. He'd begun turning, his rage building in time with his sexual hunger. Never had he felt both the turning and lust at the same time.

What is happening to me?

She began kissing down his body, her silky hair trailing over his heated skin. He needed to bury his face in her long hair. Why hadn't he done that before? No, he needed to kill her.

A ticking bomb. *And she's just returned it to her lair.*

She raised her gaze to his but continued to dip licking kisses to his torso, like a creature drinking from a pool. Then her hands were on his pants.

As they stared at each other, she slowly lowered his zipper, the sound so loud in the silent chamber. Against his will, his hips rolled with his need.

"You felt how wet I was," she whispered, giving him another lick. He could feel her breaths hot on his skin, traveling lower. "Wouldn't you want to sink *this* into me?"

Just as she was baring his cock, he bucked his hips. "Release me!"

Scenes of things he wanted to do to her flashed in his mind. *Pin her to the ground and shove into her.* Pumping his seed into her pale body again and again. *Till she begs me for mercy.* More fantasies, more rage tangled in his mind.

Her eyes widened at his shifting visage, at the demonic changes he could feel. She finally drew back.

He twisted around, driving his horns into the chains over his head, gouging his arms in the process.

"Calm, demon," she murmured, her mesmerizing voice washing over him. But he fought her pull—

She took his cock in her firm grasp; he jerked in surprise. He'd been getting himself off for so long, the softness of her hands stunned him.

She began working him steadily, and thrashing his body only made his cock shove in and out of her fist.

Fighting, twisting, *hating* her, even as she continued stroking him. Blood poured from new wounds at his wrists and ankles—

Like a lightning bolt, a shock of pleasure shot through him, *unfamiliar* pleasure. Dazed, he lowered his eyes.

Moisture had beaded on the swollen crown, and she'd blown on it, cooling the hot pre-semen that had collected there.

When his shaft pulsed in her hand, seeming to strain toward her parted lips, she stared with eyes shimmering once more. She was excited, her breaths panting, reminding him again of how aroused she'd been before, how she'd wet his fingers. "I can *see* it throbbing, demon."

He believed her—he had never felt this kind of aching pressure in his entire life.

Confusion welled, because he craved feeling her gaze on him, wanted her to lust for what she saw. He wanted her to desire him, even as he needed to kill her. The conflict within him grew stronger.

She dabbed her tongue to her bottom lip. "I think you want me to lick you there. To close my mouth over the head and suckle you."

As he groaned at her words, his cock jerked, and another bead arose. When he arched his back from the astonishing pleasure, she murmured, "Only your female can bring forth your seed. Have you ever been this close?"

I . . . haven't.

❧ 7 ❧

"Are you beginning to believe I'm yours?"

As he'd done a few times before, the demon met her gaze steadily with his inscrutable obsidian eyes, but he said nothing. Sabine realized he did this when he was tempted to lie. Most people looked away in the same situation, but his eyes challenged hers.

She leaned forward. "I can't imagine how frustrating it must be not to spill your seed. Sex must be so diminished. I bet you constantly wonder what it would be like to mount a soft, writhing female and pour your seed into her."

At her words, his brows drew together as if in pain, his lips curling back from his fangs.

"Now you can stop wondering. Say a few words, and I'll climb atop you and feed you into my body. I'll ride you so hard, demon, until you can't come anymore." She wanted to—she was nearly as aroused as he was.

To know this at last . . . she'd never imagined that he'd deny her this final step.

The crown was now slick all over. As they both stared, she was finally able to read one of his thoughts, because he was silently commanding her.

Run your tongue over the head! hit her mind like a blast of heat.

"Do it, *tassia*," he rasped aloud.

"What does that word mean?"

"*Wicked female*, because that's what you are. Now taste what you've wrought from me."

"I want to," she murmured in truth as she leaned down, lower, closer. Her breasts ached, her nipples swelling into tight points. "I will."

She knew exactly when he could feel her breath on his flesh; his every muscle tensed in anticipation.

"Say the words, Rydstrom. Make me your queen."

"Lower . . . put it in your mouth!"

He's going to bloody do it again. Deny me. She drew back and coldly said, "Your vow, demon. Or I go."

"*Never!*"

As she rose up, releasing him, she snapped, "You can't win this—you only waste my time!"

His hands fisted above the manacles. "Finish me!"

"Just a few words away!" She cast an illusion over herself of the dress she'd worn earlier. "Maybe next time."

He reverted to his demon tongue, which she didn't have to understand to know he was cursing her vilely. No matter. She turned for the door, leaving him digging his heels in the bed and thrusting that great shaft into the air.

Outside, her ubiquitous assistant was waiting, ready to take direction. Sabine just called her "Inferi." She called all of them Inferi.

Though Sabine was still humming from her encounter with her captive, she attempted to sound calm as she gave out instructions.

She ordered that he be sedated once more, then made to clean himself and see to his needs for the night. After that, he was to be secured to the bed with a collar at his neck, and then have his wrists bound behind his back—just in case he decided to release any steam.

Sabine figured that if he got aroused enough, even a "little bitch" like her would begin to look like a Pollyanna.

Deep in thought, she left the dungeon, trudged to her tower, then began the six flights of stairs to her room. She knew she should be more alert to danger—Omort had cornered her on her way to her room often enough—but she couldn't get her mind off Rydstrom's body.

She'd never expected to be so affected by him. She'd been taught to think of herself as better than demons, and had seen this "breeding" as a mere play for power.

But aside from his inexplicable bent toward good—and the fact that he was their blood enemy—Rydstrom called to her. He was so different from the men she'd known and fraternized with that he intrigued her.

How had he gotten the scar on his face? And the ones along his shaft? Now that she'd seen most of him, there was no erasing the vision of his chest and those long, brawny arms. She'd run her greedy gaze over his large sex. . . .

Sabine sighed. Tonight, she was going to have to make a date with B.O.B.—her battery-operated boyfriend.

Once she crossed the threshold to her chamber and bolted the door behind her, she relaxed marginally and cast off the illusion of her dress. She was tired, but then, she was getting home from a full day of work.

She gazed into her gilded mirror. Her career was everything to her.

Plots and subplots. Sabine was notorious for them, and she was in deep with one right now.

Omort, Sabine, and Lanthe alone knew the real truth behind Rydstrom's capture. The demon's heir wasn't needed to quell rebellions but to unlock the mysterious Well of Souls in the center of Tornin's court. Sabine didn't know how the prince would release the power of the well. Only that he would.

But what Omort didn't know was that Sabine would see that her son unlocked it for her—alone. She was going to usurp the power from the Pravus. From Omort himself.

Sabine planned to take the kingdom of Rothkalina and turn it into a queendom.

By capturing the demon, she'd finally seized the means to do so. Now if she could just get him to bed her.

Rydstrom had never known such a pain existed. His cock was still in agony. He tried to ignore the pressure within it, tried to ignore the chains that bound him, but the manacles cleaved into his skin.

The indignity of this burned him inside like acid.

His mind was in turmoil, questions surfacing endlessly. Would she return tonight? How long would she leave him bound? How had Sabine learned so much about Groot's bargain?

How long had this capture been planned?

He had to get free—but how? *No one escapes the dungeons of Tornin . . .* He'd need to use Sabine as hostage. Unless she could be turned against Omort. How much loyalty did she have for her brother?

The benefits of winning a sorceress like her over to their side would be incalculable.

He tried to remember what he knew about the Sorceri in general. He recalled that they were greedy for wealth, merry hedonists who lived their lives in pursuit of pleasure—and gold. But they were also secretive and paranoid, suspicious of strangers who arrived at their doorstep. Most tended to live in the farthest reaches of the earth.

Yet they weren't an inherently evil race. *You're just thinking this way because you want her.* Maybe, but the fact remained that it was a possibility. Right now, it was the only one that seemed viable.

He was still in disbelief that she possibly was his. The Accession often brought pairs together, seeding families. He'd secretly entertained the faintest hope that maybe he could find his other half during this one. Over the years, he'd fantasized about his female constantly, wondering if she'd have a throaty laugh. Smooth skin. A body he could lose himself in.

Rydstrom struggled to recall a single thing he'd change about Sabine physically. Her skin was glowing, her cheeks rosy. Her glossy hair had shone in the firelight. Not a single mark marred her skin.

When her eyes had shimmered a bright metallic blue with her desire . . . she couldn't feign that. Nor her body's reaction. Her sex had been wet, the soft lips *bare*. His claws sank into his palms.

After the last few weeks, this was just fuel on a blaze. There were too many conflicts within him. His mind simply didn't work like this. Usually potential decisions unfurled in precise tree diagrams, with clear choices and predicted outcomes. Normally, he was rational, and liked things straightforward, *needed* them to be so.

Yet now little was as it seemed, or if it was, it was utterly *wrong*. He had returned home but as a prisoner. He might have found his fated queen, but she was conniving, cutthroat, and amoral. Until he could escape, his fate and the fate of his people rested in Cadeon's hands—and that was a tenuous position to be in.

Especially now, when Cadeon had with him the woman he'd once drunkenly called "the highlight of my existence."

Rydstrom had been there the first time Cadeon had seen Holly Ashwin, and he had sensed an energy between them. Yet Cadeon had been unable to attempt her because he'd thought she was a human.

Now Cadeon had learned Holly was actually a Valkyrie. So nothing stood in Cadeon's way of having her.

How could Rydstrom expect his brother to not only deny himself his female but also to turn her over to Groot, a psychotic murderer who only wanted to breed with her?

The last time the kingdom had needed him, Cadeon had turned his back on Rydstrom and their family. Why would this time be any different?

Thinking of Cadeon and Holly made another suspicion creep over him. The two of them were complete opposites. Cadeon, a slob and a cold-hearted mercenary, had found his woman in a glasses-wearing, genius mathematician with a fixation on cleaning.

The obsessive-compulsive scholar and the rolling-stone soldier of fortune. A completely unexpected and absurd pairing.

Rydstrom was known as upstanding and good, Sabine as treacherous and evil. It didn't seem to matter. He couldn't ignore how his body had reacted to the sorceress. Instinctively he knew that should he sink into her, the seal would be broken. He would at last know the feeling of releasing his seed, and would be able to forever after.

Recently, he'd consulted the soothsayer Nïx about his future. She'd replied with a grin, "It's a doozy." She'd seemed secretly amused, as if from some kind of irony.

Nothing could be more ironic than Sabine being Rydstrom's queen. This situation was precisely what Nïx would find amusing. The Valkyrie worshipped fate like a religion.

And they were the first to admit that fate was a fickle bitch.

I can deny it. . . .

The cell door groaned open and servants entered. "We're to get you ready for this eve." Again powder stung his eyes.

❈ 8 ❈

When Sabine shot awake, she found her bed was sitting in the pouring rain and muddy field she'd been buried alive in all those years ago.

She blinked her eyes, realizing this was a chimera scene from a dream. She'd always cast illusions when dreaming or in the grip of a nightmare. As she absently ran her fingers over the scar at her neck, the illusion faded, her bedroom revealed again. . . .

This tower room was once supposed to have been the private chambers of Rydstrom. It was in the west tower, the one closest to the water, and had wall-size windows that she kept open to the ocean breezes. She'd redecorated it with flowing banners in scarlet and black that whipped in the wind.

She knew going back to sleep would be impossible, since she'd scarcely managed to drift off the first time—

"You didn't dream of your prisoner," a voice intoned from the shadows of her chamber.

She jerked back to the headboard when she spied Omort's yellow eyes glowing in the darkness.

After hastily covering her scanty nightgown with an illusion, she made the room appear to blaze with fluorescent light.

This was why she could never sleep through a night. Omort could have bound her wrists behind her back, a simple move that would have blocked her ability to cast illusions—her only defense. "You've crossed a line by coming into my room, brother."

"Wasn't that just a matter of formality? One soon to be done away with?" He was sending his mental probes out like sonar, but she'd learned to block them completely. He often demanded others open their minds to him, but never Sabine—as if, deep down, he didn't really want to know her feelings about him.

"What does that mean?"

"With Rydstrom's capture, we are one step closer to . . . the inevitable."

How much longer can I put Omort off? His trespass in her room boded ill. Once she surrendered her virginity to the demon and bore the child, she would have no sanctuary to protect her. She hadn't thought he'd be waiting like a vulture, especially not with Hettiah to tide him over.

When he approached the bed, she kept her demeanor composed. Barely. "What do you want?"

"Your covenant is still intact on the east wall. It doesn't go well with your captive?"

"He is as determined and strong-willed as you said."

"Maybe I should go see—"

"No! That's not possible. He doesn't need to be reminded of our connection," she said, then hastily asked, "How goes the search for an oracle?" They were caught in a vicious cycle, locating weaker and weaker soothsayers. Each one invariably made mistakes and was executed. Then an even weaker oracle replaced the dead one. "Finding any talent?"

He gave her a look that let her know he'd allowed the change of subject. "I've selected one and dispatched fire demons to collect her."

To collect her. Oracle Three Fifty-Six had been a volunteer instead of an "acquisition" of Omort's. Some females stepped up for the position, no doubt thinking they'd be smarter, better, less expendable. They never were.

"It's critical that we have one in place as soon as possible," she said in a measured tone. Sabine had to tread carefully with this subject, for it was a potentially enraging one for Omort.

He'd once stolen the gift of foresight from an oracle but had no talent for interpreting the visions he received. It had made him even more deranged before he'd been forced to relinquish the ability.

"And we shall," he said absently as he crept around her room, inspecting her things, pausing to pick up a book here and there. Hundreds were stacked all over. Most were histories of this kingdom, of Rydstrom. She'd been studying him for years.

"I hadn't known you were so well versed on my enemy."

"I take this seriously—my opportunity to garner power for the Pravus."

"Yes, I have studied him much as well. Rydstrom has long fascinated me." He carelessly flipped through an ancient tome, then tossed it away. "Does he believe you're his?"

"I think so."

Omort smiled, revealing flawless white teeth, but the expression never reached his cold eyes. "How disappointed the demon must be." He sat down on the bed beside her.

Calm . . . calm . . . distract him. "What happened that night you faced him? When the kingdom fell? I've read what's been recorded, but the details are hazy."

"I'd made a secret pact with the Horde king, Demestriu. He aggressed Rydstrom, depleting his armies, then launched a surprise attack. Rydstrom was forced to journey away to defend. That's when I captured Tornin. The castle was unprotected because Rydstrom's heir Cadeon refused his summons to defend the holding."

"Why would he do that?" From everything she'd heard about the mercenary Cadeon, he was fearless.

"Who can understand demons? I find great pleasure in knowing that Rydstrom blames Cadeon for turning his back on his kingdom. What Rydstrom doesn't understand is that I well knew the importance of Cadeon's presence in the castle. That's why I had five hundred revenants waiting to ambush the prince. If Cadeon had obeyed his brother, he and his guard would've been slaughtered."

Interesting. "And you personally faced Rydstrom."

"He's the only being I've ever fought that lived. Instead of merely burning him to ash, I played at honor, facing him in a sword duel in one of his strongholds. He beheaded me—the blow was true, and deadly for any other. But I rose. He used his brute strength to topple the roof, trapping me inside, and was able to escape."

Omort's hand was inching closer to her covered ankle. "Sabine, how much can I trust you?"

"Probably not as much as you can Hettiah. Shouldn't you be with her now?"

"She doesn't understand things as you do. And as much as I will it differently, she is a pale comparison to you. A dim shadow to your light."

"Did you come into my room just to state the obvious?" Her brother's attraction to Sabine wasn't fueled only by her looks. She believed Omort secretly hungered for death. In lieu of that, he hungered for her, a woman who knew death so intimately.

When he grazed his forefinger over her covered ankle, his eyes slid shut and drool collected at the corner of his lips. Stifling a shudder, she hastily rose, then crossed to the seaside balcony.

This place always calmed her, like a balm for her mind. During most of her sleepless nights, she stood out here, watching the sea.

Omort moved behind her, not touching her, but standing far too close. No warmth emanated from him. He was cold and deadened like a corpse.

Rydstrom had been all inviting heat.

"You should go, brother. I have a challenging day tomorrow. I'll need to be on top of my game to be the first to break the iron will of Rydstrom."

"I'm glad that you've ceased underestimating him."

When she could feel his cold breaths on her neck, she whirled around, hastening to her chamber's drink service. She poured sweet wine—only for herself—then held up her goblet to Omort. "Brother, do be a dear and poison me."

Every month, Omort gave her and Lanthe the *morsus*, literally the "stinging bite poison." The power of the morsus was that it didn't cause pain upon ingestion but upon withdrawal.

Weaning from the poison was supposed to be so excruciating that she and Lanthe were considered perpetually "condemned." Without an antidote, the pain would be so great they'd eventually die from it.

The morsus kept them from leaving Omort and from rebelling. For the most part.

He exhaled as if she were putting *him* out, then rotated the thick ring on his forefinger. As he snapped open the jeweled covering of his poison cache, she stared at the ring. It held so much significance for her. It was the source of life, the enforcer of her obedience.

And the ring told her when Omort lied, as he'd unconsciously rotate it.

When he poured the black granules into her wine, a hiss sounded and smoke tendrils seeped upward. But once it settled, it would be odorless and tasteless to those who weren't trained to detect it.

Ages ago, he'd slipped the morsus into their wine before they'd learned to identify potions by smell and taste—and before they'd learned to create their own to counter him.

Sabine nonchalantly held up the goblet. "*Slàinte.*" She drained the contents. "Now, I really need to get some sleep. Remember, Omort, I'm doing this *for us.* And I know you want us to succeed."

"Very well, Sabine." With a last lingering gaze, he finally exited, but not before she heard him murmur, "*Soon.*"

Alone once more, she returned to the balcony. As she surveyed the tumultuous sea and breathed deep of the salt air, she mused over her current situation.

Plots and subplots. She wanted Tornin for herself and for Lanthe. Yet after tonight, she suspected Omort would try to force her to surrender before she ever even got a chance to make her play.

She shivered. He'd been emboldened to come into her room, bringing with him coldness and misery hanging over him like a cloak. She felt pensive, unclean.

For the first time ever, Sabine's gaze wasn't held fast by the sea. She turned to the south, toward the dungeon tower.

The demon was such a force of nature, she imagined herself getting lost in him. Ultimately, she found her feet taking her in his direction, her heart aching for . . . *something.*

❦ 9 ❧

Without a word, Sabine climbed into bed with the demon.

Though she sensed his instant tension, she lay on her back beside him, not touching him, but close enough to feel the heat from his big body.

For long moments, they lay side by side in silence, as if they'd called an uneasy truce. They both stared at the ceiling, so she made it appear to fade away, revealing the night sky.

He tensed even more. "Your power is great." His voice was rumbling.

In the dark, she seemed to feel it. "It is."

"Is this all illusion or did you make the ceiling disappear?"

"My vanity tells me that you're impressed with my goddesslike gift and curious about it. Experience tells me you want to learn my strengths and weaknesses so you can kill me."

"I'll spare your life, if you free me now," he said.

"You've served me ill. But you've done nothing irrevocable yet."

"Demon, give me time." How could he be so warm? Unbelievably, she felt herself growing relaxed. "To answer your question, all is illusion. Optical and auditory."

"You can't make others feel things?"

"I have no tactile illusions. Not yet. Which is a shame because I could decimate an army with arrows I imagined. But I can make others feel things, just the same."

"Like what?"

"I can make you see your worst nightmares or your most coveted dreams. And I can control them."

"Do you have other abilities?"

"Dozens," she lied. The only other one was Lanthe's birthday gift from so long ago—communicating with and mesmerizing animals. "I wield many."

He seemed to take that in. Finally he asked, "Have you thought about what you seek to do? What it would be like to bear and raise a demon child?"

In truth, she hadn't thought much about that whatsoever. She didn't allow herself to imagine her pregnancy, delivery, or the upbringing of a demon prince. If she ever began wondering what their halfling would look like, she forced herself to think of something else.

The agenda had been set, the plot hatched. The rest was just details.

But Omort's visit was throwing a kink in her plans.

She answered the demon's question with one of her own. "How do you know that I don't already have a litter of demon children?"

"Do you?"

"No, I have no offspring."

"What if you bore a female? The kingdom of Rothkalina is patrilineal."

"Don't remind me. You know, in the Sorceri sept, females can inherit the crown. Morgana is the current Empress of all Sorceri." Sabine turned on her side, and he did as well, his arms still chained behind his back.

"The people wouldn't accept a female here. I wonder if I'd be kept alive long enough for another go?" A lock of his thick black hair fell over his forehead, but he could do nothing to move it from his eyes.

"I'm fated to conceive and deliver a healthy boy for your heir."

"A *son*." Had his voice roughened? "One I'll never see if you have your way. Never to teach or protect."

She fell silent. Contrary to popular belief, Sabine didn't *relish* hurting those who'd never done anything to her. But she didn't rule the world—yet—and so she couldn't change the outcome of this situation. For her and Lanthe to be safe at last, a demon was going down. This demon beside her.

He was collateral damage that couldn't be helped.

"Wait . . . if you know you're going to have a healthy boy, then you could assassinate me as soon as you find out you're pregnant."

She'd camouflaged her face and expression with an illusion, so he never saw her glance away.

"I won't leave behind my child to be raised here, in blood and hatred. I've heard the rumors of depravity going on in Tornin. Blood sacrifices and perversions. In *my* home."

"Omort does so enjoy his blood sacrifices."

The demon's lips parted. "Listen to yourself! You're so inured, you can't even realize how sick your world is."

She narrowed her eyes. *Just because I don't flinch doesn't mean I'm blind.*

Sabine knew how sick it was all too well. That was why she was determined to get above it.

"You'll never get my vow, sorceress."

"I won't stop until I do."

"Are you going to keep me chained the entire time? I know better than most that this cell is inescapable."

"Security isn't the only reason I'll keep you bound. I want to be certain you don't release any steam we build together, so you'll be in a bad way." When she traced a finger down his chest, the muscles in his torso contracted in response. "But it occurs to me that if you're so adamant about not wanting your offspring here, then you must be accepting that I am yours."

"Have you ever thought about what that would have meant for you? If you hadn't resorted to this?"

"You mean if we'd met under different circumstances? Would you have been good to me? True to me?" Her tone was amused. "If I hadn't been called to capture you this eve, I'd thought about setting myself up as a waitress at your favorite restaurant. I would have been the winsome but down-on-her-luck *Lorean*, who wears dresses with floral patterns and who needs just one little break to beat the rat race—or a male to save her." She chuckled at that. "I'd planned to serve you pie and let you peek up my skirt."

"If I hadn't known differently, then, yes, you probably would have found yourself with an honorable male who would've been true and good to you."

"They say a lie never leaves your tongue."

"You sound disbelieving."

"Because I am. I've never known a male who didn't use the truth as it suited him, bending it and changing it at will."

"I don't."

"Then tell me, am I everything you'd hoped for physically?"

He did that silent challenge thing with his eyes, then said, "Morally you're not. I hadn't expected to be saddled with one of the most evil females in the Lore."

Omort's words from earlier resonated within her. *How disappointed the demon must be . . .*

"One of the most? Not number one?" She pouted. "Well, everyone needs aspirations. Interestingly, I've never considered myself *eeevil*. Just because I occasionally steal."

When he scowled at that, she amended, "Or kill someone who gets in the way of my stealing."

"Why do you have to steal?"

She blinked at him. "How else would I get gold? Join the typing pool?"

"Maybe you could do without."

"Impossible. You must have gold." *Gold is life . . .*

"You're hated by more than can be imagined."

"Do you hate me?" she asked.

"I don't yet, but I believe that it's inevitable."

She laughed softly. "Hating me is like hating a

sharp sword that cuts you. It can't help the way it was formed."

"A sword can be refashioned, shaped anew."

"Only after it's broken down. Imagine how painful the forge fire and hammer blows would feel—as terrible as when it was first fashioned. Why repeat all that pain?"

"To get it *right* this time."

She let that drop. "Tonight, you called me *tassia* when I was in the midst of exquisitely fondling you. If it means wicked female, is there no male equivalent?"

"You don't know this? You can't speak Demonish?" he asked, incredulous.

"It's considered uncouth to learn that language, and it's forbidden to be spoken in the castle. I already know five other languages, anyway. Five is my limit; the slate is full."

"So you didn't understand me when I was cursing you?"

"Not at all. But you've called me evil and bitch enough times in English that I can glean—"

The castle bells tolled then, ringing out in the distance.

"They ring at midnight and three now?" His tone was laced with disgust. "Why three? Does that mean you have a malevolent god to go worship? One greedy for those blood sacrifices?"

"Should I worship reason? Like you do?"

"You could do worse."

"Do you want to know a secret, Rydstrom?" she said. "I worship Illusion."

"What does that mean?"

She reached for his forehead, stroking his hair to the side. "Illusion is Reality's coy lover who cheers him when he is grim. Illusion is cunning to his wisdom of ages, sweet oblivion to his knowledge. A bounty to his lack. That is what I hold sacred."

"You see *yourself* as Illusion?"

She gave him a slow grin. "Do you want to be my Reality?" When his piercing green eyes dipped to her lips, she said, "Are you musing about our kiss, demon? I hope so, since I keep thinking about it. I liked the way you kissed me."

The line between his brows deepened. "Why did you come here tonight?"

To dilute the disgust Omort makes me feel. "To warn you. I'm going to be taking off the gloves for our next encounter." Or, rather, putting them on. "I will show you no mercy the next time I come here." She couldn't, since every day that passed made it more unlikely that she'd conceive.

The Sorceri simply weren't a prolific species like others in the Lore.

The demon was studying her face, intently, as if trying to delve beneath the mask of her illusions. "Sabine, I don't believe you're as bad as you seem."

"With me, nothing is as it seems. It's always much, much worse."

"No. I don't think you truly want to do these things to me, or to my people."

"Do what things? Make a bid for power? Capture a demon?" When he didn't answer, her tone grew cold.

"You think you can change me, don't you? Into someone who's *good*? Maybe *rehabilitate* me?"

"In my circumstances, I have to believe that. You can be made to see things differently. I can teach you—"

As she rose, the room appeared to rock from her fury. Above them, in the illusion of sky, a cascade of shooting stars blazed. "I beheaded the first male that tried to turn me toward good." At the cell doorway, she added, "I was twelve."

❦ 10 ❧

When Rydstrom caught Sabine's sultry scent, he briefly closed his eyes in pleasure, then cursed himself for his weakness.

What would she do to him tonight? Her attendants had left him unclothed and chained to the bed by his wrists and ankles, a single sheet covering his lower body.

For two days she hadn't returned. Hour after hour had crept by, the dungeon seeming to close in on him, the manacles continually cutting into his skin.

All rage demons knew tales of those among their kind who'd turned fully demonic, but never reverted. They lived like animals—a hellish idea for someone like Rydstrom. To forestall that rage, demons of his kind took release multiple times a day.

Sabine had denied him even that.

She'd asked him if he hated her. At the time, he hadn't, but the seed had been planted. It grew every day she left him in the bleak cell.

"You are angered by your treatment, and now you're sulking," she said airily as she entered and stood behind the bed. "But I plan to make it up to you."

More torment. More teasing. His growing hatred warred with need. He cursed his shaft when it rose in anticipation beneath the sheet.

Why in the hell had she remained away so long? He'd had no idea where she was or even if she would ever return.

"Not interested in what I have to offer?" She reached over the headboard. "Just as I warned, I've brought a stocked arsenal today, demon."

He felt cold metal against his skin and gazed down at her hands on his chest. She wore full-length gloves made of metal mesh that ended in silver-tipped claws, razor sharp and glinting.

Gauntlets? Unease built in him.

"I'm going to use all my unique talents to seduce you. Won't even look at your female?"

He'd have to crane his head around to see her. He refused to show her how curious he was.

Don't look . . . don't do anything she wants you to.

When she began to knead his muscles, he tensed, but she knew how to work those claws so she didn't pierce his skin.

"As I lay in the dark the other night, it occurred to me that just because you had denied yourself, I shouldn't have to."

Did she mean she'd taken another into her bed? Was that what she'd been doing all this time? His fangs grew in his mouth.

She leaned down to murmur at his ear, "So, I fantasized about you . . . while I pleasured myself."

He didn't have a second to bite back his rage—and relief—before she asked, "Do you want to see what I was imagining?"

Still leaning over him, she turned her hands up and put them side by side in front of his face. The air above them blurred and heated. An illusion began to play on the far wall, like a film on a movie screen.

He parted his lips at what she'd conjured. The scene showed her naked on all fours, with him behind her, clutching her hips as he took her hard from behind.

His lids grew heavy, his jaw slackening. He couldn't look away, instead gazing on for long moments as his shaft stiffened with each beat of his heart. The hatred he felt toward her was being drowned out by wanting inside her body.

If I could just slake myself, relieve the pressure, then I could think . . .

To imagine claiming her was one thing, to witness it was another. When he saw his shaft buried into her sex, Rydstrom groaned, unable to hold it in. "You toy with things you don't understand. I will lose all control. I could kill you as easily as claim you."

She ignored him. "Would you like to see what I thought of when I climaxed?" The idea of her masturbating her pink bare flesh till she came on her own fingers . . .

Suddenly, the vision changed to show Sabine on her knees before him as he stood. He had his fist in her long red hair, guiding her head as she sucked his shaft. He bucked into her mouth, clearly on the verge, his head thrown back. She'd imagined this?

She sauntered in front of him, in front of the illusion still playing. He lost his breath; time seemed to slow.

"Sabine?" She was clad in Sorceri dress, the same the ancients of her kind had favored ages ago. She wore an elaborate headdress in gold and silver that might easily have been the crown of a queen. Her hair was in wild plaits, spilling out all around it.

A mask of jet-black kohl made her amber eyes glow, and her lips were painted blood red. The metal of her top barely covered her breasts. Below her short skirt, her hose were like fishnet but made with threads of gold, climbing to her mid thighs.

He'd always thought the traditional dress for the Sorceri females had the potential to be mind-numbingly erotic. He'd never seen it on the right woman.

Until now. Rydstrom hissed out a curse. *Deny it all I want . . .*

The Lore held that they'd dressed like this because they were among the physically weakest of all the species. They had no claws, so they mimicked them. They were vulnerable to injury so they protected their heads and their torsos with metal. The masks disconcerted their stronger opponents.

If she'd been nigh irresistible to him before . . .

She was now his fantasy made flesh—standing framed by an illusion showing his legs nearly buckling as she sucked him so deep.

Mine. She turned in a leisurely circle so he could see her from the back. As he beheld her pert ass in that skirt, he thought, *I'm undone.*

"I've decided we should get to know one another," she purred, facing him again. "Perhaps you've been reluctant to wed me because you haven't seen what a winning personality I have." She let the illusion behind her fade.

"Winning personality," he repeated dumbly. Now she wanted to talk, when he was doing his damnedest not to rock his aching shaft against the cool sheet.

"I'm curious, demon. What do you enjoy sexually?"

He'd been trying to figure that out for most of his life. He knew he enjoyed her dressed like this. It made him fantasize about spending hours divesting her of wicked garments.

The puzzle of unfastening each complicated piece ... the time it would take, the *anticipation.* The knotted leather laces on her metal top alone ...

"It's rumored that you're attracted to good girls, to virtuous women."

After an inward shake, he said, "I want a good queen for my people."

"But that's not what you need in bed."

"And how would you know that?"

"By the way you've been eye-fucking my body in this attire and tenting your sheet. Do you know what I think? I think that deep down, you've always wanted a wicked girl. Fate knew it, and that's why I was given to you. I think you've been taking virtuous women—

self-sacrificing, boring, virtuous women—only because that's what you were taught to do."

"You have no idea what you're talking about."

"I know everything about you, Rydstrom. I've studied you for years, devouring unauthorized biographies of the very old kind. And over the last two days, I've reviewed all the texts on your family's history, on *your* history. I've been working to reconcile what was written with what I know about you personally."

Sweat beaded on his brow. How much could she have learned?

"For instance, I'd read that you attempted your first female on your thirteenth birthday and your second the day after. I believe this to be true."

It was. For a demon prince, attempting females was critical. He'd bedded one after another, trying to find his consort. Rydstrom had taken more females in the first century of his life than he had during the fourteen that followed.

She continued, "They were all older than you and they were 'ladies,' which is code for 'sexually ignorant.' Did they simper? Did they call that your penis instead of your cock?" she asked, pointing a claw-tipped finger at it. "And were they too gentle with it?"

Yes to all those questions. He hated gentle. He wanted to take a woman over a long night and feel it the next day. When he'd been a young male, he'd had a friend who would show off the claw marks down his back from his latest abandoned conquest. Rydstrom had envied him bitterly.

"How awkward that must have been, taking one stranger after another. You had so many. And you were so very young to be handling that kind of pressure. The repeated disappointment."

His bed partners had always been nervous, each one inwardly hoping to break the seal, to become his consort. Sex had begun to be an ordeal, one embarrassing mating after another. *"I am sorry that I pulled thy hair"*; *"'Tis fine for you to do so, my liege."*

He grated, "I did what was necessary for the kingdom." His older brother Nylson and their father had found their females in neighboring kingdoms. "We had every reason to expect that I could find my female—"

"In a virtuous demoness who would be as selfless as you," she finished in a disgusted tone. "And instead you found your queen fifteen centuries later in *me*—a deceitful, thieving, gratuitously violent sorceress."

"That remains to be seen."

She gave him an amused expression, a victorious one. "You took so many to your bed. Did you please them all?"

Not even close. He answered honestly, "I haven't had any complaints." Because they wouldn't dare. And that was a problem. For all his life, women had treated him like a king in bed. And though it might sound good, it left him cold.

"But then you've never been with a Sorceri female before." She sat beside him. "We tend to be more exacting than your average demoness."

"You think I've only slept with my kind?" He had, figuring the queen of the rage demons would at least be of the demon breed. He'd never imagined he would be matched with a sorceress. *No, it isn't certain.* Not until he was inside her could he be sure.

Deny it all I want . . .

She ran those metal tips over his stomach, and his muscles dipped and tightened. "You're a dominant, virile male, and a king as well. Perhaps you'd be tempted if I were wicked—and submissive."

Never. He wanted a greedy female, aggressive, one bordering on selfish. He'd had enough selfless females to last even an immortal lifetime.

She drew back the sheet, then ran a claw along his shaft, lightly but enough to sting. His eyes rolled back in his head.

"A shame, because you're not going to get submissive. Not with me."

Good. My queen. I can't deny it . . . Then protect her. From himself.

"Sabine, if I turn, I will lose all control. Instinct will take over, and if you're the focus of everything the demon in me wants and needs, then gods help you. Is that what you want?"

"It's what I'm counting on."

"It won't be gentle . . . you can count on that as well."

"Maybe I wouldn't want gentle, demon. Maybe we fit together more than you can imagine." She tapped a claw to her chin. "So let me get this straight. You crave hard sex with wicked girls, but you don't want a submissive?"

"Stop putting words into my mouth." He could never explain it to her, didn't really understand it himself.

Even as he wanted to master her, he hated the idea of her as acquiescent. He needed her to struggle against him, to give as good as she got. He craved power plays between them, mental games.

But ultimately he did want to dominate her. At the end of a night with her, he would know he'd won when she pleaded with soft words in his ear to let her come—or, gods willing, when she clawed his back as she begged.

When his shaft pulsed, her eyes widened. "What are you musing about that has you reacting like this?" She raised her opened palms to him. "Let me into your mind. Let me see your fantasies."

"Why in the hell would I ever do that?"

"We could see your most secret desires, could watch them together. You know I can make all your wildest dreams come true if you let me into your mind."

She took his shaft in her gauntleted hand, making him hiss in a breath. "Still not convinced? Then ask me for a boon—within reason—and I'll grant it if you do this. There must be something you want from me . . . ?"

boon?" He narrowed his gaze, the black irises intermittently flashing with that piercing green.

"Yes." *He really does have the most divine eyes I've ever seen.* "Just ask me." *How painful it must be for such a mighty king to have to bargain for things he wanted.*

"This can only help your agenda."

When she released the thick flesh pulsing in her palm, he seemed to bite back a groan. "It's true that I could become clearer on how to satisfy you and tempt you even more." *And you could become clearer, too. Because I don't think even you know what you want.* "So make two requests."

"There's nothing you'll actually grant me worth the disadvantage. You could see more than my fantasies."

"Rydstrom, if I wanted whatever's in your mind, I could easily drug you with a truth serum. Besides, this isn't mind reading. Consider it more of a mind *expedition*. And I'm going to display everything I find."

"If I was considering this, I'd want a night with you, where I was unchained. And I'd want to be free within the cell when you're not here. And clothed."

"What if you tried to release some steam when you were alone and unchained?"

Again that lock of hair fell over his forehead. "I'd vow not to."

"And you never break your vows?"

"No, Sabine. I don't."

"Very well, demon." She raised her palms to him.

"No! I didn't—"

"Expect me to agree? And yet, I did. So you'll feel a drawing sensation. Just relax. I'm told it's not unpleasant, but definitely palpable. You'll know I'm inside your head."

She began to pull from his mind.

"I said no!"

"Too late." She turned to the side and blew against one of her palms. A scene arose against the wall, drawn from his own thoughts. . . .

In the vision, Rydstrom was free with her in this chamber, leisurely divesting her of her stockings, rolling them down her legs with infinite slowness. By the time he'd unhurriedly slipped her full-length gloves from her arms, she was visibly trembling.

"You want to see me quiver in anticipation?"

He said nothing, just watched himself leisurely unfastening her top before stripping her to her thong. He left her choker, yet in his imaginings, it looked more like a collar.

The scene flickered and changed to show Sabine facing the wall, with her wrists bound and hanging from a peg above her head. "You want me in bonds?"

She looked away to gaze at the real Rydstrom. He was staring in seeming awe, but more, he appeared surprised by what he was seeing, as if he'd never truly allowed himself to entertain thoughts like these. In the bed, his cock was harder than it had ever been, standing erect as he rolled his hips.

She took him in hand once more, fondling his length from base to head, as the Sabine in the vision struggled against her bonds. "Am I to *want* to escape you?" When he shook his head, she said, "Then what?"

She'd been stroking him until he was shuddering with pleasure, but since he wouldn't talk, she stopped.

He finally bit out, "I've kept you on the brink for hours." His horns were straightening, his sweat-slicked muscles corded with strain, sheening in the firelight. "You're desperate to touch me, or yourself, anything to come . . . it's all you can think about."

In the fantasy, he roamed his hands all over her body, pinching, cupping, palming her bared breasts. Then he kicked her legs apart and yanked her thong to her thighs, stretching it taut around them. When he pressed a finger into her sex from behind, he groaned through clenched teeth in both the vision and beside her in the bed.

She murmured, "So this is what my demon likes." Sabine found herself secretly flattered by this. Of all the fantasies a male could have—multiple women and men, fetishes, or even deviancies—his dreams were centered only on *her*. Only her.

She was also surprised by how erotic *she* found these scenes. The idea of being tied up by an enemy should infuriate her—not *arouse* her. In her past liaisons, the males had always been Sorceri, which meant they'd been potential enemies, out to steal her precious power. Showing weakness with them was dangerous, letting go was out of the question. If they'd feared her—and many of them had—she'd done nothing to dissuade them.

In Rydstrom's fantasies, he didn't fear her. He acted as if he *owned* her, which was strangely exciting to her. With him like this, there simply wouldn't be a *choice* of whether to let go or not. He'd demand it.

Still lazily thrusting his finger with one hand, with his other he pressed her head down, gathering her hair forward off her nape so he could brush his lips there. He murmured how much he wanted her, rubbing his face against her as he rasped how beautiful she was. . . .

Her breath hitched. "Have you ever tied a woman up?" When he didn't answer, she let the illusion waver, threatening to take it away.

He grated, "I haven't."

"But you want to tie one up, you *need* to."

He stretched against his manacles to rub his horns along her arm. As if he couldn't stop himself, he bit out, "You, *tassia*."

The *lust* in his voice . . . She swallowed, easing down to lie beside him.

In his vision, he turned her so she faced him, then knelt in front of her. After tearing away her panties, he pull her leg over his shoulder to spread her to his mouth.

"In *your* fantasies, you go down on me?"

He turned to rumble at her ear, "Until your thighs quiver, and you drench my tongue."

She just stifled a gasp as the scene changed once more to show him greedily licking and sucking between her legs. When he drew back to blow on her, she cried out and shamelessly undulated her hips.

But in the fantasy, he still wouldn't let her come.

Unable to stand it any longer, Sabine took control of the scene and changed it. In *her* vision, she'd managed to loop the binding off the wall peg so she could grab his horns. She used them to writhe and grind her sex to his tongue until she could climax with a scream.

In the bed, he yelled out, bucking hard into her fist, thrusting for relief. Whatever she'd just done had hit the bull's-eye with this male's desires.

"Make me come, tassia!"

"Make me yours, demon. As your wife, I'll do anything you want me to. I'll give you anything you need to be pleasured beyond your wildest imaginings."

When the sorceress dipped her other hand to cup him, hefting the weight of his ballocks, he groaned in fresh agony.

A kingdom's at stake. And still he struggled to remember exactly why he couldn't have this creature. *Mine.* Just a taste of her. "If you can make me hunger to come like this, how do I know you haven't given me some potion to make me feel drawn to you? You could deceive me into thinking you're mine."

She released him, going up on her knees, then leaned forward until their faces were inches apart. "Look into my eyes, Rydstrom. See me clearly. You *know* it's me."

Gods, her kohled eyes were stunning, her red mouth glistening.

"Do you still deny I'm yours?"

"I can't know . . . not without attempting you."

"That answer was a perfect way for you to get out of saying that you don't deny it." As her gaze focused on his lips, she licked her own. "I'm going to kiss you now. And if you bite me, demon, I'll cut off your cock and feed it to the ravens."

No simpering female here. She'd never say, "'*Tis fine for you to do so, my liege.*" Never.

But then, just to throw him once more, she kissed his lips *tenderly,* licking and coaxing until his head swam from sensation.

Ah, gods, mine.

When she drew back, her eyes were glowing metallic blue. "I heard your thought loud and clear. You know it's me. You've accepted that I'm the one you've waited so long for."

She'd read his mind yet again. "And you?" he snapped. "Have you 'waited' for me?"

Her tone grew cold. "Do you expect me to be a virgin when you were out furiously attempting every skirt in your kingdom?"

"How many males have come before me?"

"I'm five hundred years old. Use your imagination. Does it bother you? The idea of other men petting my body, tasting it, *penetrating* it?" He felt a muscle tic in his scarred cheek, and she saw it. "Oh, it does!"

"Just *finish* me."

She gripped his shaft, stroking him once more. "Say the words, demon, and I'll do anything you want me to. How many times do you think you'd want me this first night of our marriage? Ten times? So many positions to try."

He gritted his teeth to stifle the vow he was tempted to utter. The pressures battling his resistance were nearly overwhelming. Could he deny the sight of his fantasies? When unsatisfied need had built for weeks even before he'd met her? The air seethed with tension.

"And then there's your bondage fetish to explore—"

"I don't have a fetish!"

"Why do you deny it—or me? What male could be expected to resist this?"

Chin raised, he bit out, "*I* would be. Others would count on me to deny myself for the greater good."

"To what end? How does denying yourself help anyone else?"

"The sooner I do this, the sooner I die."

"What if I told you I wouldn't kill you—I'd keep you as my pet?"

"I'd opt for death."

"Then I need to make it so that you want me so much, you don't even care."

"It's good, Sabine," he rasped, trying to catch his breath as she expertly stroked him. "It's *really* fucking good. But it's not that good."

Her eyes narrowed. The chamber seemed to rock once more, and wind from nowhere blew her hair. "Then you won't miss *it*, stubborn demon. When *it* goes away."

She removed her hand and rose from the bed. "I'll keep doing this every night. I'll do it until you lose your mind from lust. You might have an indomitable will, but mine was forged in fire! You'll find it's more than enough to break yours."

"You're not going to leave me like this!" He swore once more for the vilest, cruelest revenge on her. Each second that passed, he hated her more and more. She was going to leave him throbbing in pain, his shaft thick with semen, his claws biting into his palms. "Come back here and finish me!"

"I can play these games over and over, demon. As a matter of fact, I think I enjoy them."

Gods help him, he might, too.

Once I turn the tables.

❦ 12 ❦

"You still look unsullied," Lanthe said when she and Sabine met upstairs.

Sabine hated that word. She hated that it was never used to describe males and that she couldn't get herself sullied quickly enough. "Yes, Lanthe, I'm still *pure*."

"Round two went that well?"

For the first time since she was a young woman, Sabine experienced total bewilderment. "I've waited all this time to have a purpose, to gain power, my life on hold for centuries." She remembered wanting nothing, aspiring to nothing. *I care about nothing very much . . .* Now was the time to act, yet she couldn't. "I never thought he would resist me."

She shivered to recall the way his green eyes flickered black when he'd looked at her with utter lust. And still he'd denied her. He'd resisted not only the call of a female to a male but the call of his mate.

"What if I'm *not* his? What if the prophecy was wrong?" Oracles didn't usually make mistakes, but those interpreting their words did. "I don't get it. I'm sexually attractive to a remarkable degree—"

"And humble."

"It's not bragging if it's true. And I'm *his*—which means, this is *in the bag*. Or should be." Though most of his kind searched their entire lives for their other half, Rydstrom hadn't. Once he'd lost Tornin, he'd been obsessed in his quest to reclaim his crown.

Now that the worst of her pique had passed, she reflected on all she'd learned. To please him as he truly needed, she would have to surrender the reins—or appear to.

Sabine was so strong on the outside, always having to be on her game, never revealing any vulnerability. There'd been times that she'd actually wondered what it would be like to lie back and just surrender to a man.

If she trusted him. *If* he was worthy. *The demon would never seek to steal my powers. . . .*

"I knew he was complicated." But she'd never guessed to what degree. "The levelheaded, upstanding king has a wicked side." And one he'd obviously long denied.

Lanthe's eyes went wide. "Do tell!"

"He craves *total* control, but he doesn't want me to give it to him. He wants to win it."

"That sounds kind of exciting."

It *was*. Gods, that demon's masculine heat was addictive . . .

"When you were with him, did you feel more drawn to him? " When Sabine frowned, Lanthe said, "Just tell me—if this was another place and time, and you were just two ordinary beings, would you see him again?"

He wants to kiss my neck and tell me that I'm beautiful. . . . "Our kind considers demons hardly better than animals."

"That's not what I asked."

"I . . . maybe," she muttered.

Lanthe's face brightened. "Oh, Sabine! This is wonderful. You could fall in love—"

"Always with your talk of love! Do you know what I love? Life. And romantic love is a distraction that makes staying alive more difficult. Besides, we're *not* in another time or place."

And still Sabine glanced over her shoulder toward the dungeon and felt a tinge of . . . *something.*

When she turned back, she found Lanthe preoccupied, gazing up at the sky.

"A karat for your thoughts," she said. "It's Thronos, isn't it?"

"*What?*" Lanthe cried.

"You're worried he will find a way to this plane. But, Lanthe, he *can't.* And even if he could, we're not the same scared girls we used to be. We'd hang him by his own entrails."

"Yes, by his entrails," Lanthe repeated in a weird tone.

"How about we go watch some of your DVDs?"

Lanthe had quite the collection of films. Every month, she opened a portal from her room directly to a Best Buy, and then they ordered their Inferi to make like an ant line to the movie section. "We'll watch a horror movie and drink wine every time a blonde trips on her own feet."

"Sounds good," she said without enthusiasm.

"It'll be great. We'll get merry and raise hell."

Suddenly Sabine felt the tiny hairs on her nape rise. Great, Lanthe had gotten *her* spooked. She glanced up, but found no Vrekener.

Instead, she spied Lothaire atop the rampart, his trench blowing in the sea breeze, his thick white-blond hair stirring. The general of the Fallen Vampires within the Pravus army was watching them.

Lothaire was one of the most complicated males Sabine had ever encountered. His eyes were pink—not clear of blood, but not red with it either. He was considered fallen, and yet he prevented himself from making those last few kills that would send him over the brink.

Whenever Sabine made herself invisible and moved about the castle, she would catch Lothaire spying on others, an analytical, cunning look on his face.

His interest in her and Lanthe boded ill.

Without breaking his watchful gaze, Lothaire disappeared.

Thoughts growing darker. . . .

Rydstrom twisted in the chains, chafing against the heavy metal collar around his neck. *Darker with each hour.*

At the end of this night, he'd still resisted the sorceress, even with his fantasies projected in a vision. But the pain was becoming too much to withstand. His cock throbbed to be inside her, aching so much that Rydstrom was unable to reason. Unable to just *think* clearly.

He had to escape. *Play along. Let her think she's seduced you to do what she wants.* A dangerous ploy, because he feared she could. He was greedy for her, would give almost anything to have her.

But he wouldn't give up his kingdom.

Before, he'd burned to get free so that he could bring Cadeon in line and trade the Vessel to claim Groot's sword. Now he burned to get revenge against Sabine.

He imagined all the ways he'd make her pay once he was free. He'd make her beg for him between her thighs. He'd make her plead as she writhed in the chains he bound her with.

The visions she'd shown him tonight had shocked him in more ways than one. Until Rydstrom had seen them, plain and bare, he never would have admitted that was *exactly* what he would like sexually.

Knowing that was true meant recognizing that he had spent his entire existence since his thirteenth birthday merely attempting. He'd been careful choosing each woman he'd been with. Every sexual encounter had been an investigation to find his mate—or rather, to rule out that the demoness of that encounter was *not* his mate.

Again and again, he'd experienced meaningless, noncommittal nights, where he expected disappointment and was glad to be done with it.

With Sabine—he wanted to keep her beneath him for days.

Deny it all I want. He'd never hungered for another female a fraction as much as he did her. Though these encounters with her ran contrary to his desires—*she* should be chained in *his* bed—they were still hotter than any reality he'd ever experienced.

And soon she would be in his power. She'd given her vow that he was to be left free the next time she came to him. Now that he was more familiar with her ability, he could predict it, could withstand it, and capture her.

Once free of the castle, he could take Sabine into the forests surrounding Tornin and remain hidden there for some time. But to get back to his brother, Rydstrom would have to escape this plane.

The fact that Omort monitored all teleportation off Rothkalina was well known. Yet so long as beings didn't enter the plane, Omort hadn't cared overly much about them leaving.

Rydstrom had long heard rumors of secret smuggling portals in Grave Realm, the most perilous area in the entire kingdom. If they reached a portal, they could escape completely. Omort was rumored to be weak away from the well, and he wouldn't likely give chase himself. Rydstrom could easily handle anyone else he sent after them.

But whenever Rydstrom planned how the night of his escape would unfold, he feared his own will, was disturbed by his fantasies. Because he didn't see himself capturing her and escaping.

He saw himself throwing her to the bed and covering her, fucking her with all the strength in his body.

❧ 13 ❧

"My demon is cross with me," Sabine told him the next night. "I figured you would be fuming when I didn't keep my promise to free you." Instead, she'd ordered him chained to the bed again with his wrists above his head.

She could tell he was already on the razor's edge toward rage—his eyes were no longer green, just constantly black—but that hadn't stopped him from growing erect beneath the sheet.

He *should* be hard for her, since merely descending the steps up to his cell had made her primed for him, her body tingling in anticipation.

As he lay bare-chested, straining against the manacles, her appreciative gaze flickered over his brawny arms and broad shoulders. Her eyes followed each rigid sinew of muscle along his torso and across his stomach. She forgot to breath as she stared at the dusky trail of hair descending from his navel to the edge of the sheet—the sheet that continued to rise and pulse from his shaft.

The demon king truly was *magnificent.*

"You made a vow to me, sorceress."

She gave herself an inward shake. "Did I?" she asked blithely. "But really, you should know better than to trust someone like me. So it's your own fault for being gullible."

His eyes went dark with menace. His fangs lengthened in warning. In their situation, how could he appear so dangerous? As if he were the one in control?

"I was naughty to break my word. I think you should punish me." Her lips curled. "Doesn't *your* type of male like that sort of thing?"

When she sat on the side of the bed, he leaned up, stretching the chains taut. "I will punish you, Sabine." At her ear, he rasped, "When I get free, the first thing I'm going to do is turn you over my knee. I'm going to whip that exquisite ass of yours until your pale skin is heated and throbbing from my palm. I'll chain you down in my bed, and I swear to you, I will make you beg."

"Then I'll be sure not to free you."

"It won't do you any good. Eventually, I'll get loose. You've drugged me. Tormented my body over and over. Held me against my will. You'll be punished for these things. And you'll pay in kind."

"I *can't* free you, Rydstrom. I know you plan to use me to escape. I don't intend to lose you this eve—and I don't intend to be captured." When he was still baring his fangs, she said, "Tell me you hadn't planned to escape, and I'll free you."

He did that steady eye-challenge thing, but he didn't

deny it. Though she wanted to view his unwavering honesty as a weakness, he didn't look weak ... he looked in control. Masculine and fierce.

"Rydstrom, do you think I *like* chaining you up and using you?" At his scowl, she said, "Very well, I like it a little bit. But I'd prefer to make love to you normally. Or at least as much as your fetish would allow."

"I don't have a *fetish!*"

With a flick of her hand, she made the dungeon appear to be her room, with breezes rushing in, the red and black banners whipping.

He frowned in confusion. "This is my room."

"Now *ours*. I've been sleeping in your chambers, awaiting you."

When he took his eyes off the room, he raked his gaze over her body.

Sabine had dressed much as she had yesterday, except the clothes were even more intricate. Her top was made of gold and silver, twisted and knotted to circle over her breasts, then climbing up around her neck. Her eyes were kohled with a purple so dark it was nearly black.

"You're doing that eye-fucking thing again—would you like to see all of me?" she asked. "I could strip for you."

At length, he gave a curt nod as if he couldn't stop himself.

She slipped her full-length gloves from her arms, then tossed them negligently onto the floor behind her. The top took long moments for her to unlace, and his eyes were riveted on her fingers unknotting the ties. Each second seemed to excite him more.

"Did you choose that top because you thought I'd like it?" He was breathing harder.

"Yes, to please you."

When she began stripping her skirt, he ordered in a husky voice, "Slower, female." His eyes were burning, his expression so hungry. He seemed unaware that he was subtly rocking his hips.

She eased the skirt to her ankles, kicking it away, leaving her black lace thong and thigh-highs.

"Now those," he bit out, jerking his chin at her panties. She inched them down, teasing him to a fever pitch.

Once she'd gracefully stepped from the thong, he grated, "Stop there." Only her headdress, choker, and hose remained. "Now turn around."

As she did, she said, "Is this the body of a queen, or what, Rydstrom? Come on, demon. Admit that you like me." She faced him again. *Hungry eyes, dangerous expression.* Shivers danced over her.

How could a *look* be so arousing to her?

She held his gaze as she sauntered up to him. "If you cooperate with me, I intend to kiss your body from your strangely erotic horns to your toes." She climbed over his waist, and when he bucked, she grabbed his horns, stilling him. "That's not cooperating, my darling." She leaned forward and rubbed her face over the smooth surface of one.

With a groan, he turned his own face to reach for one of her nipples, nuzzling it. But once he tugged the swollen tip between his teeth, she had a moment of alarm. He could bite her . . .

Instead, he sucked her nipple into his mouth, his tongue swirling, making her moan. To reward him, she ran her lips over his horn. His massive body shuddered beneath her, rattling the chains.

When he groaned against her breast, her eyes went heavy-lidded. Fires began to light the perimeter of the chamber, stoked with each of his feverish licks around her nipple.

With the faintest smile, she let the flames burn.

Sabine pulled back, then brushed her mouth against one of his ears. "Demon, I would be a good lover to you." One of her delicate hands was smoothing over his chest. "I'd give you everything."

Right now he had no doubt of that. "I don't understand you. The last time you came in here, you were hard-bitten, like you were going to battle. Now this . . ."

No longer was her touch impersonal. It was tender, desiring . . . like he'd imagined his own female would touch him.

"Do you still deny I'm yours?" There was an edge to her voice.

"I deny it no longer." He blinked, shaking his head to clear his vision. "Sabine, there's a fire—"

"It's only illusion, demon." In his ear, she whispered, "It's unconscious. The flames come from me when I get extremely aroused."

Extremely aroused? And the fire was growing. When he comprehended that she was in desperate need like him, the driving instinct to sate her raged inside him.

This seduction was too powerful, like she was using magick. The fire, the sweetness of her touch . . . "You're weaving some kind of spell."

"There's no spell. I just desire you."

Even as she soothed and whispered her words, he grew more frenzied, turning more demonic.

"Accept me as yours. Claim me." She cupped his face, giving him a tender, coaxing kiss like she had the last time she'd come to him. When she kissed him like this, his resistance melted away.

Once she broke the kiss, she leaned down to trail her lips across his chest, her shining hair sweeping over his skin. Her breasts swayed, her hard nipples glancing over him. She'd been working him into a lather with her seeking kisses and her silken hands grazing all over his body. And now she dipped down his torso, her destination unmistakable.

When she rubbed her soft face against his shaft, his head fell back. He raised it a second later.

"Typical male," she murmured, "wanting to watch. Well, watch this . . ." She teased the crown, licking the slit until he yelled out.

"Demon, you taste so good . . ."

He gazed at her in disbelief. "*Tassia*, suck it between your lips."

Her hand clasped the base, her lips closing tight over the swollen head. "*Ummm*," she moaned around it, sending vibrations along his shaft.

"Take it deep for me!"

She did, pumping her fist and sucking him without mercy, working in concert to pleasure him. A helpless groan broke from his chest when he saw her fingering her sex. Not a selfless woman but a greedy one expecting her pleasure. *Good.*

"You . . . like this? Are you wet?"

In answer, she raised the hand she'd been using to pet herself toward his mouth. When he realized she expected him to taste her, his cock jerked in her mouth, and he quickly leaned down. He sucked her slick fingers, snarling in bliss, his seed palpably climbing.

The night began to grow hazy. He was going more demonic with a female than ever before. The need to have her lashed at him.

He released her fingers only when his back bowed. *So close.*

She dug her nails into his torso, marking his body in her abandon, whipping him to a frenzy. "I have . . . to take you!" With his wrists chained behind him, his arms straight back, he gave a furious thrust between her lips.

She stopped and pulled back.

"*No!*" he bellowed.

Gazing up at him with her deeply kohled eyes flashing metallic, she clutched his shaft, still wet from her tongue. Between panting breaths, she said, "Give me the vow, demon. I'll make your eyes roll back in your head."

The throbbing pain was too much . . . goading him to give in to her.

"Rydstrom, I want this. Did you never think that I need you, too?"

Need me? "Sabine . . ." He trailed off when he heard a yell coming from the main tower. "What was that?"

"Nothing, absolutely nothing—"

Someone pounded on the cell door.

"Ignore that, demon," Sabine said. "What were you going to say to me?"

"Abie!" a female called from just outside. "Quickly!"

Sabine made a sharp sound of frustration, then leaned her forehead against his shaft, pressing it against his stomach.

Rydstrom bit out, "Finish this, Sabine. I need you to finish this!"

She eased up over him, lying atop him with her head on his chest. As they fought to catch their breath, she was shaking—he was shuddering.

But even as he was in agony, she felt so damned right against him.

Mine. He needed to have his arms around her, to clutch her tighter, to keep her by him.

"Let me in!" the woman called. "I'm not leaving until you open up."

Sabine sighed, then pressed a kiss to his chest. "Your heart is so strong," she murmured, sounding impressed. When she lifted her head, she met his gaze. "I wonder if it could beat for both of us."

He rasped, "If I thought I could have more of you like this, it'd be yours."

Her lips parted. Another shout sounded from the main part of the castle.

"Abie, I will create a portal into that cell if you don't come out!"

Sabine glanced away, and when she turned back, he briefly saw something in her eyes that wasn't there before. For a heartbeat's time, she'd appeared . . . fearful. The fires dissipated in a rush.

Rydstrom knew how deadly the beings here were. His alarm for her cooled the worst of his lust. *My female.* His instinct was to protect her. But she *was* one of the deadly beings here—he had to remember that.

Instinct had never warred with his reason this much. He was torn inside, the conflict taking its toll. "Are you in danger?"

"What would you do if I said yes?" She smiled, but it didn't reach her eyes. "Would you keep me safe?"

"Yes," he answered without hesitation. "Free me, Sabine, and I'll protect you with my life."

"Why? Only because I'm your female?"

"Protecting you is what I was born to do."

"I have to go."

"Then kiss me," he said, the words leaving his tongue before he'd even thought.

She cupped his face in her small hands and leaned down. She kissed him—differently. He cracked open his eyes to find hers squeezed shut, her brows drawn. As if she were desperate to lose herself in the kiss.

He soon did, his lids sliding shut. Lost in the way her lips trembled against his, lost in the rightness of his female needing him.

❧ 14 ❧

He'd been just about to say the vow, Lanthe!"
Sabine had barely been able to redress she'd been
so affected by Rydstrom. "So help me, this had better
be the coming of the *apocalypse*—"

"Yep, fairly much. We're kind of under attack."

"Acutely or chronically?"

Lanthe answered, "Nothing at this *exact* moment.
Of course, something could have come up since I came
to the dungeon. In any case, Omort summoned you—I
figured you wouldn't want him coming to search for
you."

Sabine turned to one of her Inferi. "You. Come
here." She'd promised the demon that he could be free
to move about the cell and clothed. And she was feeling just guilty enough to allow him a pair of pants and
some limited freedom.

As the attendant ran off with her instructions,
Sabine and Lanthe hastened to court.

"Your eyes are still glowing, Abie. You might want to camouflage that before you see Omort."

Sabine wove a new illusion over her face. "It was ... nice with Rydstrom. Unexpected." *A demon lover with eyes like night—who looked at her as if nothing else existed for him.*

"Are you falling for him?"

"Could there be a more doomed relationship? It is ridiculous even to contemplate." *His husky voice . . . the way his smooth skin tasted.* "He's just so ... so *good.*"

"I think that intrigues you," Lanthe said. "He's a male as strong as you, and one you can't defeat."

"Can we talk about this later? Perhaps after you tell me what's happening here?"

"Pravus patrols are returning with reports of small uprisings, increasing in number and intensity. Some of the rage demons even attacked the patrols."

"They've never dared before."—

"They know we have their king. And evidently they also know Cadeon has undertaken the quest for the sword. Just like you'd said, it's become a rallying point."

"Can there be anything else?"

"Absolutely! I also heard that Omort has dispatched four fire demons to acquire not just a soothsayer, but the most powerful one in existence."

Sabine said, "Nïx."

The notorious Valkyrie oracle called Nïx the Ever-Knowing, or Nucking Futs Nïx, was rumored to be three thousand years old and exceedingly insane.

But her foretellings, when she deigned to give them, were always accurate.

"It seems she keeps eluding the fire demons," Lanthe said. "Oh! Almost forgot—we've heard word that vampires are converging in the forest outside the castle to take Tornin."

"Lothaire's?" Was that why he'd been studying everyone, because he planned some kind of treachery?

"We don't think so. His covenant is still intact."

When they reached the grand double doors of the court, a snickering group passed the sisters on their way inside. "What in the hell is going on?"

"They know you haven't been able to seduce him."

Her face fell. "The covenant." Actual evidence that she was still a virgin was available for all the world to see.

Now everybody would be waiting for the tablet to break. The Sorceri males she'd been sexual with—the ones who could never talk her out of her virginity—would think it great fun that she couldn't even give her virtue away to the one she'd supposedly saved it for.

"There are betting pools," Lanthe muttered.

"Betting pools. And what are the odds?"

"You don't want to know. But we could make a mint if you can put a lock on this."

Everyone in the castle knew she was failing in her bid for power. And she was about to enter court—a ruthless jungle of backbiting and betrayals. Not only would this be damaging for her ego, but if she lost face badly enough in the power-worshipping Pravus, her very life could be in jeopardy.

Sabine heard more snickers. Hettiah and her coterie of worthless Sorceri friends strolled past the sisters on their way into court. Their mocking glances made it easy for Sabine to see she would have to strike out.

Lose face, lose life. This was her world. She hadn't gone through the effort of surviving in it this long just to be killed when she was on the cusp of something more. "I'm going to have to fight in there if challenged."

Though she and Lanthe had no battle sorcery, they both were scrappy and had become fair swordswomen. In battle, Sabine used her illusions to make them invisible, allowing them to run around the field, decapitating merrily.

It wasn't very valorous, but then, only stupid people held valor over life.

"I know you'll have to," Lanthe said quietly. "And I can't be there with you."

"Hey, don't worry." Sabine held up her gauntlets. "I just had my claws sharpened." She rapped the metal together, and the smooth ringing tone was pleasing to the ear—

Without warning, Lothaire traced in front of them, peering down at them from his towering height.

Sabine raised her hands up to him, ready to draw his nightmares. "I've heard friends of yours plan to visit?"

"I'll trace away before you madden me, sorceress," he said, his words laced with a thick accent. Some said he hailed from Dacia, and had been a true Transylvanian.

Sabine's lips thinned, but she lowered her hands. He hadn't threatened her, and she wasn't *supposed* to attack Lothaire. Technically, he was part of the New Pravus.

One of the inner circle. His blood was in that tablet that hung on the east wall.

He said, "Just to be clear, I have no friends. And *my* soldiers are in the bailey downstairs."

"Then who lurks in our forest?" she asked.

"One of the splinter factions breaking away from the Horde since the old vampire king died. My spies indicate they'll attack tomorrow night."

Tornin had protections in place—basically a mystickal moat—so the vampires wouldn't be able to trace directly inside. At least, *not for long*. "What do they want?"

"The well."

The Well of Souls. Armies always sought to control it, because each faction of the Lore had its own legends surrounding it.

The Lykae believed it cured the madness that accompanied the transformation to werewolf. The vampires believed it allowed them to be daywalkers and to turn human females into vampires for their potential Brides. The House of Witches believed it gave them the abilities of all five of their castes.

In truth, Sabine didn't know what the hell it did. Even Omort vowed he didn't. All they knew was that the well's power would be unimaginable—and unlocked only by Sabine's son.

"Who leads the vampires?" Lanthe asked.

"They have no true ruler, because they won't accept a commoner like myself."

The Horde was notorious for following only those born in the royal line. "Yet you lead the ones who've joined the Pravus."

"I might have mentioned to them that the well will resurrect the old Horde king to rule them once more. As soon as the Pravus wins."

Devious vampire. He rose another notch in Sabine's opinion. "What about Kristoff?" He was the old king's nephew and should be the true ruler, being of royal lineage, though not a drinker of living blood.

Lothaire shook his head. "They know he will make them abide by his laws. They have been lawless for so long, they won't be brought to heel that easily. Plus, they like the taste of human flesh." Had he licked his fang for a shot of blood? "This is a mere fraction of the army that will gather. In the next two nights, more will come. Many of them know this land from fighting the mighty demon king in ages past."

Everyone knew the tales of Rydstrom riding out in his fearsome black helmet, beating the Horde back from Tornin. His battles were legendary. "One would think you'd be able to persuade them to leave."

"Would one?"

"Sabine!" Omort yelled from inside. He was glassy-eyed, but when he saw her at the doorway, he seemed to rouse. Then he spied Lanthe beside her. "Be gone, Melanthe!" he ordered. "Back to your tower."

"*One day . . .*" Lanthe said telepathically, slinking off. "*Good luck.*"

As Sabine sauntered inside toward the throne, all eyes were on her. When she separated from Lothaire—lest others suspect them of a secret alliance—the vampire murmured, "Noted, sorceress."

Once she reached the dais, Omort was fiddling with

his poison ring. Sabine would give anything for the antidote to his morsus. Each poison was individual, and since Omort's was prepared by the Hag in the Basement, she was the only one who could cure Sabine.

But the Hag had entered into a covenant never to surrender the antidote to another. . . .

"Cadeon the Kingmaker continues after the sword," Omort said.

In as soothing a tone as she could manage, Sabine said, "Yes, brother, but it could take him years to find the Vessel."

"Cadeon already has her!"

Sabine's lips parted. "Are you saying the Vessel is on her way to Groot?" With a male like him, that female would bear another ultimate evil. The world couldn't withstand another like Omort. "Send fire demons to assassinate her," Sabine said coolly.

"You think I haven't?" Omort yelled, spittle coating his bottom lip.

He disgusted her. Earlier, when Rydstrom had realized she was going to leave him, he'd inhaled deeply, visibly in pain. And then he'd gained control of himself. Who was more powerful, the quiet demon king she kept in chains or the mad sorcerer who could destroy the world but couldn't keep a single castle in order?

Omort snatched up a goblet, dashing it against the wall. "Those demons continue to fail us."

"We'll think of something," Sabine said. "I'll go after her myself if I need to. And I never fail you."

"You are failing me right now! You've been in the demon's cell again and again!" He slammed his fist on the throne arm. "We've been waiting days for some kind of progress—why can't you get him to do this?"

"Was there a time limit to my task?"

Hettiah said, "We've heard word that you go and do nothing but talk."

Once! "Your pet's making sniveling noises again, Omort. Shut—her—up!"

"I think you're not committed to this cause!" Omort snapped. "Perhaps I should withhold the morsus to spur you on."

Sabine's eyes narrowed. The chamber appeared to rock. "You keep threatening me with that, and you will *not* like the outcome."

"You dare—"

Four fire demons traced in front of the dais, just to her side. The court fell silent in shock.

The demons were beaten, bloody, and *handless*. Pinned to the shirt collar of one was a folded note stamped with an *N* in a black wax seal.

Nïx. The Valkyrie had sent them back with their hands lopped off—rendering them powerless.

Omort stormed down the steps to them and ripped the parchment free, tearing it open. As he read, a vein bulged in his forehead. "That bitch! She'll know my wrath and will learn to fear it!" he yelled, crumpling the letter and throwing it away. "I go for her myself!" In an instant, Omort raised his hands and smote the four to ash.

Stepping around the charred remains, Sabine scooped up the note, smoothing the paper to read:

Dear puss,
  Is this all you've got? Why don't you strap on your big girl panties and come face me yourself? Unless you fear that the Nïxanator will spank Omort's wittle bottom.
  By the way, you've taken one of the most respected leaders in our army. We're going to want him back. Especially since Sabine can't break him.

Bringing it,
Nïx the Ever-Knowing, Soothsayer Without Equal,
General of the New Army of Vertas.

Sabine whistled out a surprised breath. The Valkyrie truly was crazed.

Then she frowned. *Can't break him?* Again, was there a time limit? Style points?

And what was this Army of Vertas? Sabine had heard rumors that Nïx was placing factions together—the Lykae, the Forbearers, the noble fey, the House of Witches, a mix of Demonarchies, and many more. Had they all struck an alliance?

Perhaps they were using this letter to lure Omort into a trap. Sabine knew the other side had mystickal prisons, entire islands that were inescapable. Could *they* capture the deathless one?

Sabine stared at the script, her thoughts racing.

"Bring me the rage demon!" Omort commanded. "I'll send Rydstrom's arms back to the Valkyrie!"

"No!" Sabine cried, her heart in her throat. Omort would butcher him. Rydstrom would regenerate the limbs, but the pain . . . "You will not—"

The sudden hit took her across the face, blood spraying out from her mouth over the marble.

Hettiah had attacked her? That cold, pure fury Sabine knew so well swept through her. Then came the bile, the nausea, that could only be allayed with violence. *Self-preservation, survival.*

A red haze covered her vision; Sabine spat more blood as Hettiah's friends surrounded her.

❧ 15 ❧

Rydstrom was disgusted with himself. One blow job and he'd been ready to capitulate everything. Yes, it was the best one he'd ever received, but still . . .

He shook his head. It wasn't just *what* she'd done to him, but *how*. She'd been everything he'd ever dreamed of. And when the room had gone ablaze, letting him see the intensity of what she was feeling . . . ?

What male wouldn't be tempted to do *anything* to have her?

So close . . . He'd almost broken down. If Rydstrom surrendered his will in this, he could impregnate her. And then, what if he couldn't escape before she killed him?

His child would be raised by her and by Omort, used as a pawn. They wouldn't understand a demon child's needs. As if they'd care. He would never subject a child of his to the hell on earth they promised.

She wanted a vow Rydstrom would not give.

For a rage demon king to marry, he would make a claim and a vow of self: *"I claim the honor of protecting and keeping you. You are mine—my consort to touch, to guard, to cherish. You will rule beside me and create our dynasty. Accept my claim, and it will be so, now and ever after."*

If his female accepted him, then they would be wed forever. But Rydstrom couldn't pledge his life to another under this kind of coercion. He would do it when he was ready.

And when she was worthy.

He heard footsteps, not hers. The attendants had already been here, leaving him free, clothed—

A guard of five vampires materialized in his cell. One was Lothaire, the Enemy of Old. He'd been a Horde general, but Rydstrom had never engaged his troops.

Rydstrom snarled, "What do you want—"

They attacked as one. No matter how hard he fought, he couldn't repel them with only his horns and fangs, couldn't keep them from shackling his wrists and ankles together.

When they traced him, he found himself in the court at Tornin. What Rydstrom saw there made his stomach clench.

The well, that purest power, was strewn with grisly body parts. The most evil beings in the Lore were gathered around it, dozens of breeds—the Neoptera, winged insectlike humanoids, the Alchemists, eternally old men with long, straggly green beards, the Cerunnos, ram-headed snakes. . . .

In my home.

Omort sat upon a gold throne, smirking. When Rydstrom lunged forward, fangs bared, the vampires held him fast. *Can't break free . . .*

"Welcome to my court, demon. The mighty Rydstrom doesn't look so legendary now."

"Fight me, you fucking coward!"

Omort strode for Rydstrom, but then he stopped, turning his attention to the center of the court, as if helpless not to.

Rydstrom's breath left him in a rush. Sabine! She was surrounded by females, bleeding from her mouth. Every protective instinct within him flared.

When he grappled against the vampires, Lothaire gave him a sharp kidney punch. "Easy, demon," he muttered, his accent thick.

One of the lackeys with Lothaire said, "Hettiah will just erase Sabine's illusions. I'll bet twenty sovereigns on her."

"A fool and his money," Lothaire sighed. "Sabine will thrash her. That one burns rage like kerosene."

Sabine's eyes did look glazed with a mindless fury. "What is this?" Rydstrom demanded.

"A mere feminine row. Hettiah—the one who vaguely resembles Sabine—and her friends intend to murder your female. They see her failure with you as a weakness. They'll keep attacking her." Under his breath, Lothaire added, "Demon, you're killing her."

"Release me so I can guard her!"

"Keep watching."

There were too many of them. She couldn't hold

off a dozen. One snuck behind her with a dagger. "Sabine!"

Like a shot, she dropped down, dodging the blade, sweeping her leg around to take out the female's feet. Once the woman fell to the ground, Sabine snatched the knife, then raised her booted foot to crush her enemy's face with the heel.

She quickly turned to Rydstrom—looking shocked that he was there—before she made her face a mask. Their eyes met. Hers held a silent warning. He could do nothing to help her.

In an instant, she made her body appear to dissipate into hundreds of flying bats as she cloaked herself in invisibility. Hettiah raised her hands, seeming to wipe out Sabine's illusion. But it was too late; when Sabine was visible once more, she already had her claws dug into Hettiah's scalp.

Holding her in place, Sabine drew back her other gauntlet, made a metal fist, and punched Hettiah's nose. Bone crunched and blood sprayed with Hettiah's screams.

Sabine kept her hold, twisting her slim body as she dodged Hettiah's blows. With her other hand, she aimed her palm at the rushing opponents, exactly as she had with him when she'd pulled secrets from his mind.

The women shrieked in terror, clawing at their own eyes. She'd loosed their nightmares?

Then Sabine spun around with a kick, connecting her boot with Hettiah's jaw. The woman's body flew back, leaving a huge piece of her hair and scalp in Sabine's clawing grip. She tossed it at Hettiah's unconscious body on the ground, then went invisible again.

The foes still standing darted glances but couldn't see her. One's throat suddenly gaped open. When another was stabbed in the temple, she dropped to her knees, then slumped facedown on the ground.

When all were felled, Sabine revealed herself. Rydstrom gaped at her, as did everyone at court, except Lothaire, who was busily collecting coin.

She was sprayed with crimson, out of breath—and smiling. Until she caught sight of Omort storming for Rydstrom, yellow eyes wild with rage.

Rydstrom gave a roar, lunging forward against the vampires' hold. The sorcerer laughed—with one flick of his hand, Rydstrom was thrown back against the wall, pinned there by the throat.

With a shrug, Lothaire and his vampire guards traced away.

"Does Nïx seek to capture me?" Omort tightened his hold on Rydstrom's throat. "Tell me what her weaknesses are!"

What in the hell had Nïx done now? Rydstrom gritted his teeth as bones fractured in his neck. He couldn't move to defend himself.

"Answer me, demon!"

The pressure began to lessen. "Fight me!" It increased once more. Black spots began obscuring his vision.

"*What are you doing?*" Sabine screamed as she swept through the crowd. She was like a furie in her wrath, with her bloody face and hair. Her eyes glowed like hot blue metal. Rydstrom focused on her. *Stay alive . . . stay alive.*

"Questioning my prisoner," Omort replied over his shoulder. "Before I take his arms for the Valkyrie."

With another snap of bone, Rydstrom's spine was severed. *No feeling below my neck.* Omort would keep squeezing until his head was forced from his body.

This is how it will end. His skin began to tear, and scenes from a long and wearying life flashed before his eyes. No woman, no offspring. His only legacy was . . . failure.

"*Release—him—now!*"

Omort faced Sabine. After a moment, Rydstrom plunged to the ground.

He lay paralyzed, his body motionless. As his vision began to clear, the court appeared to pitch and rumble, with winds rushing in. Sabine's wild hair tangled all around her head.

The beings within ran for cover.

"He's *my* prisoner, brother. And is under *my* protection." Though so small compared to Omort, the sorceress gazed up at him without fear. "I didn't want him hurt this way."

Omort took halting steps toward her, fascination plain in his rapt expression.

Omort . . . wants her? As a lover?

"Leave this court." She ordered Omort out, refusing to look at him. And the sorcerer was actually turning to leave.

There had been rumors of incest, tales that Omort loved one of his sisters unnaturally. *Not her. No, don't let it be her.*

But Rydstrom couldn't deny what was so obvious—Omort wanted Sabine.

Between gasping breaths, Rydstrom laughed bitterly, crazed. *My court, my home . . . my woman. Everything is wrong, twisted.* He rasped, "That has to sting, knowing a demon will be claiming your possession . . . knowing she'll always crave me over you."

Sabine's eyes widened. Omort twisted around. With another flick of the sorcerer's hand, an invisible force punched through Rydstrom's torso, ripping it wide open.

❦ 16 ❦

Rydstrom had no idea how long he'd been in and out of consciousness. He cracked open his eyes. He was on the bed in the cell? Pain as he'd never known assailed him, but only above his neck—below it, he couldn't feel anything.

"Bring the Hag!" Sabine ordered someone unseen. "Quickly!"

Who knew how much later, an old woman crept into the cell, carrying a roll of bandages and a dripping burlap bag. She sat beside him on the bed, scooping a thick paste of strong-smelling herbs from the bag, stuffing his wound with it. He perceived nothing.

As "the Hag" worked, Rydstrom watched Sabine pacing with his eyes slitted so she wouldn't know he'd awakened.

"How long will it take for him to regenerate?" Sabine demanded.

"Two days," the old woman answered, "until you can steal his seed."

Sabine didn't seem surprised by the woman's temerity.

Another female rushed inside. "The castle's abuzz! I heard you were screaming at Omort." She had black hair and was furiously biting her nails. Her features were similar to Sabine's. *Another sibling?* "Damn, Abie, do you want to end up like the oracle?" She swept a glance toward the bed. "Oh, your demon! No wonder you got so riled."

Sabine began pacing again. "Give us the cure, Hag. I know you can make it."

"I pledged my covenant." The woman began unrolling the bandages. "If I broke it, I'd be killed and you'd be given a new concoction."

"What would it take for you to give it to me?" Sabine asked in a lowered voice.

"One of those who entered into the covenant must release the other. Or die."

"There must be another way."

"You dream, sorceress," the woman muttered. "And dreams belong in slumber."

"I *plot*. And plots belong in every minute of every day."

The two stared at each other. What was happening here? Rydstrom blinked his drawn lids, and for a split second, the old crone appeared to be a young, elven brunette. *What the hell?* Sabine didn't seem to have noticed anything.

A choking sound broke from his throat, interrupting the tense moment.

Sabine whirled around to face him, approaching

the bed. "Don't look down, demon." Sabine, in all her fury, had prevented his death. For now. But did she not realize that Omort would return, would come after him again and attack like the coward he was?

She easily read his thoughts. "I will keep you safe. This won't happen again." She brushed his forehead tenderly, then frowned at her hand. She dropped it, hastily glancing around to see if anyone had caught her. "Sleep, demon."

He couldn't keep his eyes open any longer. *"Don't read my mind,"* he thought. *"Do not . . ."*

"I won't," she said.

"Give me your vow!"

"You have it." She murmured, "Now sleep, demon. And dream. Dream of what you need most."

His eyelids slid shut. And he did.

From a chair beside the fire, Rydstrom gazed at his wife in their bed. Flickering light shone over her face as she slumbered peacefully. Their beloved son slept in a crib in their chamber.

Outside, an ocean storm boiled, whipping against the castle; inside, they were warm. Rydstrom watched over the two, protecting them.

Nothing had ever felt so good.

The pup sounded hungry, so Rydstrom crossed to the crib. Gently cradling him, he brought him to his mother's breast. Half-asleep, Sabine held their babe lovingly and murmured Rydstrom's name.

My family . . .

His eyes flashed open. *I need that most. And she is the key to it all—*

At once, pain assailed him, agony stabbing at him all over with each breath. *My spine's healed.* How long had he been out . . . ?

Sabine swept into the cell just then. She was dressed in a different metal top than before, and her eyes were painted a navy blue. How much time had passed? "I can't stay long, just coming in to check on my colossally stupid demon."

He could tell she was on edge, the affectionate and soft Sabine of before gone. "How long was I out?" he asked with effort. He lay in bed with only one ankle shackled and his arms free, not that he could lift them yet.

"A day. Your body has been mending rapidly. Your spine and neck are already healed, as are your battered lungs if you can speak once more."

When he peered at the bandage wrapped around his torso, she said, "Your skin hasn't closed over the wound yet, but it will soon. You're lucky you weren't harmed worse. Why in the gods' names did you have to taunt Omort like that?"

"Because it felt good . . . to finally do so."

"If I hadn't been there, you would've died."

Sabine's power and cunning had been indescribable. She was as powerful in her own right as Omort—more so even, because the sorcerer wanted her.

But did she return his feelings? Had they slept together? More disgusting things had happened within their numbers. Maybe that was why she allied with him.

Or was it because she couldn't quite kill him? Without Omort's deathlessness, could Sabine defeat him? She might be plotting toward it right at that moment.

What if Rydstrom convinced her that the sword would work? Would she make her move?

The queen on the chessboard, waiting for her moment to strike.

Rydstrom could give it to her. What did he have to lose?

Sabine crossed her arms over her metal top. "I suppose you feel no need to thank me for saving your life. You're a very ungracious demon, in addition to being colossally stupid."

He'd never been more certain that he was about to die, and she'd prevented it. *But* . . . "It's because of you and your trickery . . . that I am here in the first place!" Pain erupted from his wound.

"It's because of me that Omort has spared you all these years. Have you never wondered why he hasn't pursued your assassination?"

Rydstrom had wondered, especially since he'd settled in New Orleans, staying for months in the same place. He liked his home there. It sufficed until he could reclaim his kingdom. Until he could take back Tornin—*and scour it clean.* His eyes briefly closed against the memories of what he'd seen last night. "Are you sleeping with Omort?"

"I am not sleeping with him. I'm sleeping with no one. There's an heir to be had, and I'd rather no one question its parentage."

She hadn't denied that she'd *ever* slept with Omort, but he sensed she hadn't. Or maybe he merely refused to believe it—because that would put her forever out of his future.

"Why did you fight Hettiah?" he asked. Each word was coming more easily now.

"She attacked me. She's been looking for a way to get revenge on me for centuries."

"Why?"

"Probably because I made a wreath out of her intestines in front of the entire court. And I've plucked out her organs a few times. And I might have kept them in jars on my bedside table."

"You . . . you do not." *And the vampire had said I was killing her?*

"Yes, indeed. I'm missing her appendix and spleen." She rose, crossing to the table where a plate of food was laid out. "And on that note, are you hungry?"

He cast an irritated glance at the plate, filled with fruits and vegetables, with no meat to be found. "Now, sorceress, how do you expect me to heal . . . when you feed me twigs?"

Over the last week, Sabine had yet to provide for him meat and demon brew—a potent fermented drink. The Sorceri drank sickeningly sweet wines and brandies, calling demon brew a *crude concoction.* He couldn't stomach their sugary creations.

"I keep forgetting that my pet's a carnivore." She set the plate down. "Here, I'll make you more comfortable." With a wave of her hand, she suddenly made the cell appear to be his old room here.

But this time, she added a sea storm outside. How would she know . . . ? "You read my mind, didn't you?"

"I did," she said, her tone absent, although her expression was one of interest.

He'd suspected that she concealed her expressions. In the future, he wouldn't scrutinize her face, he would watch her hands, the tensing of her slim shoulders. "Do you often break your vows?"

"Constantly." She nodded. "I'd go so far as to say uniformly."

The fact that she'd broken her word to him was infuriating—her lack of shame made it that much worse. "No reservations about being known as a liar?"

"It's not my fault the truth and I are strangers—we were never properly introduced."

"And what did you learn when you hacked into my head?"

She seemed keyed up, listening for something from the outside. Again she didn't look anxious, but she paced. "You used to be lulled to sleep by the sea storms here, and have long missed your room in your tower. You have a contentious relationship with your brother that disturbs you greatly. You resent him for losing your kingdom."

Everyone thought he blamed his brother Cadeon for losing his kingdom. He did partially—was he supposed to act *pleased* with him? But Cadeon also lied, cheated, and he warred for profit. His life had no meaning.

And yours does . . . ?

She continued, "You've two sisters, Mia and Zoë, who you barely speak to. They have their own lives, and you wonder if maybe you should have involved them more in your quest. You're ashamed because you found yourself envious of a friend of yours who'd finally found his mate. A Lykae. I think his name is Bowen MacRieve?"

Rydstrom met her gaze, though he was discomfited by what she'd seen. Because he *was* envious, and he considered that a weakness. A good man would be happy for a friend.

But Rydstrom was one of the oldest in the Lore, and over the long years of his life, it seemed that one at a time, each of his comrades had found their females.

All of them had experienced something he could only dream of . . . something so vital, they'd each begun to pity him for the lack.

His mien was stoic, but she could tell he was unsettled by all that she'd discovered. "Anything else, sorceress?"

"Lots and lots." The demon was a solitary male. He had friends but was too obsessed with his mission to enjoy them. He didn't approve of his disreputable brother or his brother's crew of mercenaries, so he didn't spend unnecessary time with them.

Sabine had taken him from no lover.

"Mainly," she said, "I saw that you are . . . lonely." And his loneliness had called to her—which mystified Sabine, only adding to her general state of vexation. Last night, when she'd imagined the pain Rydstrom would feel to have his arms hacked off, she'd been so consumed with *something* that she hadn't even heard Hettiah approaching to attack. Feelings made people stupid, vulnerable.

And more, she'd been *embarrassed* by what Rydstrom had seen at court. She'd never forget the revolted look on his face when he'd surveyed what used to be his.

For some reason, she didn't want him to think that just because she lived here, she was like them.

Just because I don't flinch doesn't mean I'm blind.

"You had no right to be in my head!" He twisted in the bed, his lips thinned in obvious pain. "And then you made me dream of . . ."

"Dream of *what*, Rydstrom?" She'd missed it. "I bade you to dream of what you needed most. I'd meant *healing*. Did your mind supply other particulars?"

His expression grew closed. "It's none of your concern."

She let that drop. For now. "I've also seen that you want to take me over to your side. That would be quite a coup. One thing though—I'm not likely to align myself against the most powerful sorcerer ever to live."

"I saw your power. You're stronger than he is."

"Don't play to my considerable vanity, demon." She examined her nails. "It will gain you nothing."

"Ally with me and seek asylum within our army."

"Asylum? Where? In your castle? Oh, I forgot, you haven't one. At least with Omort, I'm kept protected from your kind."

"Become my kind, and no one will ever hurt you again."

She sat at the foot of the bed. "That's the difference between me and you. I won't try to convert you. Do I like that you never lie and esteem things like valor? Of course not. But I don't try to rid you of those traits. Why does your kind forever seek to change ours?" That was what she hated most about them—not their odd, counter-intuitive beliefs *per se*, but that they would force them on others.

"Because we live more contented lives. We have loyalty, fidelity, honor—"

"All three are overrated. The only chance you have to demonstrate any of them is to deny yourself something or someone that you desire."

"Then in the same vein, what about your *loyalty* to Omort? Have you been tempted to align with his enemies?"

"Never," she lied. She was *constantly* tempted to betray him. Even more so now that he was cracking under the pressure of the uprising rebels, the vampires waiting at the castle walls to strike at sundown, the taunting of a foolish Valkyrie.

The idea of Sabine with a demon. . . .

But in truth, Sabine could have been steadfast to Omort. She recalled when he'd first come to find her. He'd seemed gallant as he'd saved her and Lanthe from an attack by ignorant humans. When he'd brought them to live in a plane with no humans or Vrekeners, the sisters had finally felt safe, protected in Tornin.

Until the first time Omort had laid his hand on Sabine's thigh.

Of course, they hadn't believed he was their half brother simply because he'd *said so*. But they had known that their mother, Elisabet, had committed some sin that made the noble family of Deie Sorceri disown her. Some transgression had made her feel so unworthy that Sabine and Lanthe's worthless father had seemed a good catch.

From Omort they'd learned that Elisabet had been the Vessel of her own time—and she'd given birth to an ultimate evil—*him*. . . .

Rydstrom interrupted her thoughts. "Omort can't fight off the alliance the Valkyrie Nïx is forming. Not alone."

"Ah, yes, your Vertas. That's what Nïx called it."

"You're talking to her?"

"*Corresponding* more like. She's utterly unhinged, by the way. You'd trust a madwoman to lead your army?"

"There's a method to her madness," he said dryly, but she caught the undertone of respect in his voice.

Luckily, Sabine didn't want his respect, so she wasn't jealous of the Valkyrie. She could earn his respect any time she wanted—*if* she wanted.

"Besides, Omort won't be alone, demon. You saw members of his army." Members that they would be losing if Omort didn't get control of himself soon. "This Accession should be a good one."

"And it doesn't bother you that we'll be on opposing sides."

"You act as though we haven't always been."

"Maybe so, but we will *not* be any longer."

"Then you'll have to join the Pravus, because I plan to be on the *winning* side." Yet for the first time, she wondered. Omort was proving useless against the threats surrounding them. Without him at the helm, the army was rife with rumor and instability. Already covenants were breaking as smaller factions defected from the Pravus.

This evening, with the coming dusk, Sabine and Lanthe would have to risk their lives in battle because he couldn't rise to the challenge. "Demon, you have to understand—Omort truly can't be killed. There's simply no way to defeat him."

"What if there were?"

"And still, you believe in Groot's sword." She gave him an indulgent expression. "It's a fable, Rydstrom. Even if it would work, and even if you were free, you'd never get close enough to Omort to use it."

"It *will* work. Nïx has vowed that it will. She is never wrong."

"She must be . . ." Sabine trailed off when a yell sounded from outside. Soon the din of bridled horses and marching soldiers followed.

Sunset. The vampires were attacking. "I have to leave. I won't return for some time."

"Why? Where are you going?"

To try to shore up the cracks in my brother's sanity. And if unsuccessful . . . "To the battlefield."

❊ 17 ❊

"O*mort's still comatose?*" Lanthe asked telepathically as she sidestepped a stray centaur arrow.

Sabine swung her long sword at a vampire's neck—from behind—slicing clean through. "*No, not comatose. Just descending further into madness.*" She scooped her steel-toed boot under the vampire's severed head, punting it away. "*Omort's glassy-eyed, sweating, demanding sacrifices.*"

Just hours ago Sabine had gone to his tower again—and she *loathed* going there—to implore him to decimate the converging army. She'd found him sitting on his bed, petted by the still-healing Hettiah, screaming for another sacrifice. "Something young!"

"*We can't win this without him,*" Lanthe said. "*Even if we can only be seen by our trail of headless bodies.*" Invisibility had its merits.

"*You're right.*"

The revenants were decent enough fighters, but they were mindless. Though the Libitinae prowled from the night sky, and were cunning killers, they played with their victims.

The centaurs had their poisoned arrows, but they were at a disadvantage with tracing vampires because they were such big targets—multiple vampires would launch themselves onto a centaur's back, then haul him to the ground, draining him all the while.

Lothaire's vampires were cutting a swath, yet there were only so many of them. Sabine spied him far across the battlefield, engaging others of his kind, slaughtering with a wild grin on his face, the first time she'd ever seen him smile. His hair was braided on the sides of his face, berserker style, the thick strands dark with blood.

Sabine tilted her head. He was as tall as the demon, but not as muscular. *Why am I thinking about the demon now?*

With an inward shake, Sabine thrust her sword at an unwitting vampire. Once she'd felled him, she watched Lanthe gut a leech, yanking her sword up through his body.

Lanthe was normally so pensive and thoughtful, but in combat she was vicious. A dozen times already, Sabine had wanted to call out, "That's my little sister!"

"*Sabine!*" Lanthe suddenly cried. "*Why are vampires looking at us?*"

Sabine peered around them. She and Lanthe were . . . *visible?* She flicked her hand to cast another illusion, to no avail.

Only one person could extinguish her power like this. "*Hettiah.*" She'd made them visible. "*Can you do a portal?*" Sabine asked as she and Lanthe put their backs together, circling, swords raised as they searched for escape.

"*Already tried and got nothing,*" Lanthe answered. They were surrounded, vampires edging closer and closer.

"*I think we're dead.*"

"*I think you're right.*"

They were now both powerless, two little Sorceri females in the middle of the vampire Horde. Sabine scanned the distance for Lothaire but didn't see him—

One leech dove for her with his fangs bared, grazing her skin until he hit her breast plate. She was able to duck under him and fell him with a backhanded hit. But more were advancing.

Hundreds more.

Strangely, at a time like this, Sabine found herself wondering how the demon would feel about her death. Would he mourn his female?

Lanthe whispered out loud, "Abie?"

Sabine heard her, even over the clamor of the battle—hooves thundering, bowstrings singing, swords clashing.

Closer . . . What to say to her sister? How to protect her?

The end was coming . . . vampires rushing forward . . . almost reaching them . . . until the attackers became . . . *ash.*

Their forward momentum sprayed the soot over the sisters' boots.

Power sieved all around them. Sabine twisted toward the castle. Omort stood on the ramparts, with his mouth open, eyes maniacal, and palms raised. He had smote them all.

Like all the warriors of the Pravus still standing, Sabine stared up at Omort in shock.

Sudden silence reigned on the torn and bleeding battlefield. Wind blew her braids around her face, and she could hear nearby trees rustling in the breeze. Night birds sang in the distance.

The ash scattered. . . .

Omort turned that murderous gaze on Hettiah. She fell to her knees, weeping.

Lanthe stood by Sabine's side. *"That's the being you want us to take on?"*

Sabine had told him she was going *to the battlefield*.

He wanted to prevent her from riding out to meet those who would kill her. And to prevent her from slaying them—most likely his own people. He suspected that they'd learned of his capture and were rebelling.

She is out there, unprotected. He wrenched his arms hard against his manacles in frustration, the healing muscles in his torso screaming in protest. Now that he was able to rise from the bed, they'd begun chaining his hands behind his back once more. Though the skin on his uncovered chest was newly mended, raised like a new scar, he still suffered pain whenever he stood or moved suddenly. He paced, willing her to return.

I can change her. I can make her understand right from wrong. Once I escape . . .

He was talking himself into the impossible, because he wanted his mate *beyond* reason. He recalled that dream of his. That perfect peace. He craved it like nothing before. He wanted the Sabine from their last night together, the woman who'd set his blood on fire.

She's mine. For better or worse, she's my woman.

Don't die . . . don't . . .

When he caught her scent, his eyes briefly closed. Shortly after, she entered the cell, standing before him. She was out of breath, her breastplate rising and falling. She wore a spiked headdress connected to a collar, metal hose, and full-length gloves with razor-sharp claws.

Her eyes were dilated and blue, and she bled from the corner of her lips. She'd come to him straight from the fray? He narrowed his eyes. *She's shaken.* Rydstrom knew what a soldier who'd had a near miss looked like. *And she's come to me.*

When blood trickled to her chin, she swiped her forearm over it.

So beautiful. So deadly. Mine. In an instant, he grew hard for her. *No! How can I want her when she's fresh from a battle—with my own people?*

Yet when she ran for him, nothing could have stopped him from lunging forward for her. Her hands shot up to cup his face as she stood on her toes to kiss him. Her lips were so soft, trembling beneath his.

He'd been out of his mind with needing to see her safe again, and showed her how much with his kiss. *Relief.* He took her with his tongue, savagely slanting his lips over hers, until she was clutching his shoulders. With a groan, he finally broke away. "What happened tonight?"

Panting, she said, "Close call." She drew one glove down her arm, then the next, tossing them away.

"I feared you were going to die."

She unlaced her breastplate at the sides. "At one point, I was sure of it," she said, dropping the piece to the ground.

Just when he felt her hard nipples brush against him, her hand began traveling down his body.

"Unchain me, Sabine." His cock was straining for her touch.

"I can't."

"Let me protect you."

"Kiss first; talk later . . ."

He shuddered when she dipped into his pants and brushed her fingers over the slick head. She took him in hand, rubbing the pad of her thumb over the crown in mind-numbing circles.

Over. He inhaled sharply, groaning against her lips as he set back into their kiss. He was going to have her one way or another.

Their breaths grew ragged, frenzied. He was dimly aware of the illusions of fire spreading around the cell.

With her free hand, she unzipped his pants, giving them a shove so they fell to his ankles.

Then she tugged on his cock, leading him to the bed.

Still kissing as if their lives depended on it, both of them went tripping toward the mattress. With his wrists bound, he couldn't catch himself. At the last minute, he twisted so that he didn't crash on top of her.

Between kisses, they maneuvered until she was on her

back beneath him. Ignoring the pain, he levered himself up onto his knees. Yet then frustration rose in him. He couldn't shove her skirt up, couldn't rip off her panties, couldn't pet her . . . "Take off your skirt for me."

Seeming dazed, she loosened the knotted ties on the side of her skirt, and it fell away.

"Now those." He gave a nod at her black thong.

She worked it down to an ankle, then kicked it away, leaving her clad only in her hose and headdress. Her eyes were heavy-lidded, glowing metallic blue amid the kohl.

"Between your thighs," he rasped. "Show me."

As she eased her legs open for him, he thought she whimpered. A rough sound erupted from him as he gazed at her copper curls and glistening flesh. "Touch yourself there. Let me see you. . . ."

Her hand eagerly obeyed, and her delicate fingers began gliding over her sex. He hissed in a breath. *No awkwardness. No hesitation.* For the first time in his long life, he would have the type of woman he secretly desired.

She was glorious beneath him with her braids spread out over the bed, her flames reflecting in her eyes, her body quivering as she masturbated.

"Give me your vow, demon. Make me your queen."

Queen of the very people she killed? But then he frowned at two lines of blood running parallel down her neck to her chest. "What is that mark?"

She waved it away—literally, disguising it with her illusions. "A vampire tried to sink his teeth into me. But my armor stopped him short."

"Why a vampire?"

With a huff of irritation, she removed her hand and leaned up on her elbows, blowing a plait out of her eyes. "We're *at war*—he's not going to crayon me to death."

Not killing my kind? "You're at war with the vampires?"

"With some of them. What had you thought?"

"I . . . not rage demons?" She'd risked her life against a mutual enemy.

"*What?* You thought—"

"Sabine, just give me a minute." *Just let me think. . . .* "You can't fight against them anymore."

"You can't stop me. I love slaying leeches."

"We have that in common. But they are deadly foes. Just remain within the castle walls."

"There's only one way I would stop engaging them— the possibility of conception."

Vampires had taken the lives of his father and brother. Rydstrom would be damned if they took his queen's. *The only way to keep her safe is to impregnate her.* Which meant he'd have to wed her, unless he could win this battle of wills between them. He would make her lose herself, so she'd receive him—without the vow.

"And why would I go after *rage demons* anyway?" she asked in a scornful tone. "That's like hunting sheep—"

"Will you shut up?" he snapped. "I'm considering giving you my vow."

She blinked up at him. "Oh." As she gave him a slow grin, she transformed the spikes jutting from her headdress into delicate golden leaves, with streaming vines twining in her hair.

"I'll do it—as soon as you release me from the chains."

"I'll release you once you've done it."

He lowered himself until his cock rested directly on her, flesh to flesh. Hers was hot and ready for him. His throbbed so hard, he would be surprised if she couldn't feel it. But when he tried to enter her, his shaft slipped along her slick folds.

She cried out, "Rydstrom!"

He tried once more, and again he thrust over her. "*Ahhh.*" Sweat covered his forehead from the desperate need to plunge into her core. "Need my hands, love."

"Give me your vow."

"Feed me inside you." With his jaw clenching, he grated, "And I will."

With her other hand, she grasped his length, but instead of placing him at her entrance, she ran the crown along her wet sex. He shuddered when she circled the swollen head against her clitoris. "Marry me, Rydstrom." And all the while her heavy-lidded eyes held his. He felt as if he were losing himself in them. "I need you, demon. All of you. Can't you feel how much so?"

"Inside you, *tassia*. Need inside . . ." He yelled out when the crown briefly breached her tightness. Desperate to sink into that heat, he shoved his hips forward, but she still held him firmly, aiming his shaft up. He hissed in pain from the movement. *Give anything to pin her hips down.* "Damn you, sorceress. You're mine—I want what's *mine*."

"Then take me. And feel me come for you. Say the words."

Protect her from the battle, any way you can. She'd been teaching him the rules of her game, and now he would play to win. He would make her his. But he'd do it his way.

"Sabine, I have to have you." He tried to thrust inside her one last time, but he only ground against her sex, making her head fall back. "Look at me when I give you this vow."

When Sabine met his gaze, he uttered words in harsh Demonish, "*I will never wed you, Sabine. Not until there is trust between us. And I vow to you, I will have my revenge against you.*" He finished by saying, "Do you accept?"

❈ 18 ❈

The demon's eyes were so steady, so compelling, her heart seemed to stutter with feeling.

"I do, Rydstrom. I accept you. But how do I know you said the vow?"

"Because I never lie."

She stared at him for long moments, until he grated, "I've waited fifteen hundred years for this. Don't make me suffer any longer."

With a hard swallow, she pressed the broad head to her entrance.

"Take more." The rumble of his voice had turned to a husky rasp. "Now!" His sweat-slicked muscles bulged, his features turning sharper.

She shivered, then worked more of his shaft into her. "You're . . . too big." It was uncomfortable, stretching her.

"Then I want you even wetter. Arch up to me."

"Yes!" She did. With heavy lidded eyes, she watched him brushing his lips all around her nipples. "Rydstrom, suckle me."

At her words, he shuddered. "This will be over . . . before it begins." Finally he dragged his tongue over one of her straining peaks. When his lips greedily latched onto it to suck it hard, she cradled his head, holding him to her as she moaned in bliss.

Her free hand dipped down to finger her clitoris, and soon the fullness inside her started to feel necessary, even essential—as if she'd die without it. She was getting so close. . . .

He released her nipple. "Deeper, *tassia*." He tried to thrust, but she scrambled back. "No! Take more of my cock." He wasn't even halfway inside her.

She noticed the injured muscles in his torso were twitching. He wasn't yet strong enough to lean forward without his hands, couldn't force his hips forward. He couldn't take her as he obviously needed to.

"I'm . . . trying," she said. "I'm too small for you, demon."

"Roll your hips up."

"You're too big. Just give me a second like this." As they were, she was on the verge of coming. "Another second—"

"I *can't*." He stilled, his brows drawing together. "*Losing control.*" He began to pull back.

"But I'm close!"

"Don't want to hurt you—"

She sank her fingernails into his ass.

He roared with pleasure, his back bowing with it. "Don't do . . . that! Not *that*."

So she did it harder. It was like spurring him, like lashing a beast with a whip. He began to go fully demonic, his skin darkening, sheening in the firelight. The sight of him in this state unnerved her—and *aroused* her. Even more.

Gods, she wanted to lick every inch of his beautiful skin. The tone of his voice was different, his bearing changed. His upper and lower fangs had grown, and his gaze was riveted on the spot where her neck met her shoulder.

A demon wanted to bite her, to place his claim on her for eternity. And still she was about to go over the edge with this male. . . .

Between panting breaths, Sabine cried, "Oh! I'm going . . . to *come!*" Flames erupted as she arched her back, her nipples jutting.

And then he felt the unmistakable clenching of her sheath. Her body was squeezing the head of his cock like a little fist.

"Sabine!" He was about to ejaculate inside her. *At last.* He felt a savage thrill at the thought of spilling his seed into his woman, the seed he could finally give her. "Need to . . . mark you." *So long I've wanted her.*

"You're turning *even more?*" she said, alarm in her eyes.

"Lean up—"

"No! Demon, don't do this. I'll fight you if you mark me!"

"*No?*" he snarled. She'd told him *no?* He could scarcely hear her—*too far gone.* "Then you'll take more of me!"

After days of torment, that building pressure was about to be released.

His demon strength soared through him. *Need deeper inside her. Shoot my seed so deep.* He leaned his forehead on the cold headboard, finally balancing himself to thrust. Positioned like this, his hips shot forward uncontrollably, forcing his shaft up inside her.

So tight. Too tight? He thought she'd cried out as she writhed, pinned on his length. But all he could hear was his heartbeat thundering in his ears. Was she trying to shove him away? Screaming for him to stop?

Virgin.

The thought vanished when the pressure in his shaft became pain. She dug her nails into his shoulders—and he loved it.

He gave a brutal yell as his come shot from his cock for the first time.

The heat, the force. "Ah, gods, Sabine!" At the feel of that first hot jet pumping into her, his eyes rolled back in his head.

He mindlessly thrust, spending until he was emptied, until the ache receded at last. When he opened his eyes, her head was whipping toward his nose. *Crack.*

"What the hell?" he roared.

"I waited five hundred years for *that?*" As she squirmed from beneath him, her illusion briefly wavered before the mask was back in place.

Her eyes were watering.

Inhaling deep breaths for control, he said, "You were . . . a virgin?" Damn it, he'd warned her about going demonic, because he'd known he might hurt an *experienced* woman—but this . . . "I never wanted to hurt you, Sabine. Why did you let me believe you were experienced when you were pure?"

Whatever he said was the exact wrong thing. "I *am* experienced, and I am *not* pure!" As she cloaked herself in invisibility, he felt the biting slap of her palm across his face. He'd hurt her, and his fierce sorceress had hurt him back.

Once she'd gone, he stared down at his still semihard shaft, wincing at the blood and seed. Undeniable signs of her pain, and his pleasure—which had been stronger than he'd ever dreamed it could be.

But the guilt for hurting her wouldn't recede.

Neither would the knowledge that the vow he'd given her was for revenge.

❧ 19 ❧

"That good?" Lanthe asked when she found Sabine sitting on the side of her bed in a bathrobe, with her head in her hands. Though the fire was stoked, she was shivering.

"Why did I even expect anything different? He was *awful*. If I had to decide right now, I'd say I never want to do that again."

"It's only because he's a big demon, and it was your first time."

"Maybe demons and Sorceri truly don't belong together. Maybe their kind is just too strong for us."

"He probably just lost control of himself during his first claiming of you. I mean, you had been building up some serious steam, and—"

"He ended up blowing in a big way. Lanthe, he wanted to mark me with his huge fangs." And when she'd told him no, he'd shoved inside her with all the strength in his body. She shuddered. "You should have seen the way he looked. He's truly a *demon!*"

"I can't believe you had *bad* sex, and now I'll have *no* sex. For three hundred and sixty-four more days. That'll teach me to wager against you."

Sabine didn't crack a smile. With a sigh, Lanthe sat beside her, wrapping an arm around her shoulders. "Look, I think maybe we've been hurt so often that even if someone harms us accidentally, we're blind to see it that way."

"Do you really believe that?"

"Yes. I think . . . I think that not *everyone* is out to get us or to use us." When Sabine only made a scoffing noise and kept her head in her hands, Lanthe added, "Granted, every being we've come into contact with in the last five hundred years has, without fail, tried to screw us over. I don't know, though. Maybe the demon's truly an honorable guy. What if he's one in a million? What if he would take back the hurt if he could?"

Sabine peered up. "One in a million?" If Rydstrom was, then Sabine might not have been *completely* in the right with her actions. He *had* warned her about how he would lose control. Still, how was she supposed to know what would happen? She'd never done anything with a demon before! "He didn't know I was a virgin," she admitted.

"Oh, Abie, no."

Maybe I shouldn't have head-butted him, or slapped him, or . . . "And I left instructions for him to be punished." Her infamous temper had gotten away from her yet again. "For him to be bathed. Thoroughly. It might not be too late to take it b—"

Without warning, the door to her chamber opened.

Omort entered. "Leave us," he told Lanthe. "At once!"

She had no choice but to hurry out, casting Sabine a fearful expression before she left them alone.

Sabine sat upright, apprehensive to be anywhere near him after that earlier show of power.

He paced the room, his cape snapping. "Your covenant . . . broke." When he faced her, his brows drew together. "I feared you would enjoy it. With him."

"Do I look like I enjoyed *that?*"

"I am sorry you had to go through it. You will not again."

She exhaled with impatience. "We can't be sure I'm pregnant."

"The demon's seal is no more?" When she hesitantly nodded, he said, "Then another female can breed with him."

As Rydstrom's fated mate, Sabine was the one female who could bring forth his seed the first time. But now that that seal had been broken, Rydstrom could impregnate other females.

"You will not return to him," Omort said. "Lanthe or Hettiah will take over your duties—once she has healed."

"Hettiah shouldn't be alive right now. She almost got both of us killed."

"She has been punished accordingly."

"Why would Hettiah do this with the demon, anyway?" Yes, he could get her with child now, but . . . "The *heir* has to be mine. *I* am Rydstrom's queen." Saying that out loud shook her. *I'm* the *true* queen of this castle. And *he's my . . . husband.*

Omort gazed away. "The child only has to be of his blood."

"The rage demons won't recognize any but a legitimate heir."

"I might have . . . misspoken about the prophecy. The boy need only be born from him."

Misspoken? "What exactly do you know about how he will unlock the well?"

Omort studied her face with those eerie yellow eyes. "I want to trust you. I need to. These hours have been agonizing to me."

"You plan for us to rule together, but you tell me nothing."

"I didn't want to put undue pressure on you." He twisted his ring. *Lying to me.* "The fact is that Rydstrom's son will be sacrificed."

"What did you say?"

"His firstborn child will be given to the well—"

"You mean *cast* into it?" She wove an illusion over her face as her eyes darted for a waste bin in case she vomited.

Sabine hadn't particularly wanted a demon son—the only reason she would ever have done this was for the power—but she'd be damned before someone harmed her offspring. Demon halfling or not.

"This is why I didn't tell you. I didn't think that you'd understand what had to be done. You're not as . . . *strong* as you act."

Not as *evil.* He was assessing her reaction. If she was somehow pregnant from that debacle and became proprietary about the child, Omort would just punish her, and still kill her son. Any sign that she might care for her babe would be seen as weakness.

"What makes you think that Hettiah will have an easier time seducing him than I did?" Sabine didn't even bother mentioning Lanthe in this context. She would never do this.

"The demon will be given an aphrodisiac."

Over my dead body. "Because the heir doesn't have to be recognized."

"Exactly. Sabine, open your thoughts to me."

"Never, Omort. I'll *tell* you what I'm thinking. I couldn't care less about what I had to do to get the power from the well," she lied, meeting his gaze without hesitation. "But I am infuriated that you didn't believe you could trust me with this. Why?"

"Sabine, everything hangs in the balance."

"Tell me."

He stood to pace once more. "Cadeon has taken up the charge. He has the Vessel and proves unrelenting. I wasn't going to worry about him since Cadeon has failed in every attempt to redeem himself. But in this, he continues to succeed. Because the very Vessel he's to deliver to Groot seems to be aiding him in her own doom—"

"Rydstrom said that Nïx has vowed the sword *can* kill you. Is this true?"

Omort fiddled with his ring, even as he met her eyes. "No. Of course the sword won't work. Nïx isn't infallible."

He's lying! Breathe . . . breathe . . . "You're not being truthful with me."

His eyes skittered over the floor. "It is . . . possible." This explained why he'd been so unstable! "I need to trust you. Can I trust you?"

Never! "Of course, brother." *He can be destroyed!*

"This is one of the reasons I seek Nïx in particular," he said. "So I could question her about the weapon."

To disguise her excitement, Sabine acted indignant. "Why didn't you tell me this? You keep critical secrets like this from me? This is a vulnerability we can't afford—especially not now. Especially since Cadeon might actually succeed."

The ne'er-do-well brother of Rydstrom was that close to having the means to give death to the deathless. How to use this information? How to exploit this vulnerability in him?

"I should have confided in you." Omort stopped in front of her, then reached for her face, murmuring, "I love you."

She jerked back. The last of her temper—gone. "You don't *love* me. You don't know what that is!"

What was worse, Sabine didn't know if she had a grasp on it either.

If Omort had been sleeping with one of his sisters, it hadn't been Sabine.

She'd been a virgin for Rydstrom. After all these years, she'd remained untouched.

What if I impregnated her? Rydstrom gazed up at the ceiling of the cell he had gotten to know too well. It was absolutely possible for her to have conceived.

Conceived my child. He found himself wanting it to be true—even as he knew the clock would begin ticking down on his life. If she was pregnant, they would have no more use for him. More than ever, he had to escape. *Take my female, take my child, return for my kingdom.* . . .

Rydstrom needed the sorceress here. He'd hurt her, and he wanted the chance to make it up to her. But he was uneasy over more than the pain he'd given her. Though he'd taken Sabine, she wasn't his wife, and he hadn't completely claimed her as his mate.

He needed to mark her to satisfy his demon instincts.

Rydstrom tensed when he heard loud footfalls sounding down the dungeon steps. Shortly after, three large males entered the cell, all clearly Inferi slaves. He recalled Sabine's fury—had she left orders for him to be beaten?

The largest one began unchaining Rydstrom. Which meant a chance to escape. He stilled in readiness. Three Inferi could never control a demon—

Again a powder stung his eyes. *Gods damn them* . . . Yet this time Rydstrom remained awake, seeing.

Only he couldn't move.

There was something in the men's eyes as they gazed at his prone body. Once Rydstrom recognized it, his heart went cold.

Lust.

When they strung him up in the shower and stripped his pants from him, Rydstrom couldn't move a muscle to fight them. As they washed his deadened body, he was impotent to do anything but stare at the ceiling as a scalding hatred blazed inside him.

She'd done this to him. Sabine had ordered this, knowing how much he would despise it.

Once he escaped, he'd humiliate her in front of a thousand demons, he'd *give* her to them to use. As soon as the thought arose, rage erupted in him, possession burning hot. . . .

He lost himself in that rage, going awash in it, again vowing for the cruelest revenge. An exact reprisal to her, for every wrong she'd dealt him.

I won't rest until I've made her pay.

❧ 20 ❧

"Didn't get a chance to call off the, uh, bathing?" Lanthe said telepathically, able to sip from her goblet and communicate at the same time.

"Alas, no," Sabine said, modeling an outfit in front of her oversize mirror, readying for another night with the demon. "And it went . . . badly."

"Tell me."

"The Inferi's powder wore off, and Rydstrom attacked with his poisonous horns."

The trio hadn't intended to do more than bathe him, but he'd gone insane, fighting them like a beast.

"He temporarily paralyzed one of my poor Inferi before they contained him," Sabine said, selecting another top from the collection recently forged for her. "I mean, I knew he wouldn't like being touched by three males—that's why I ordered it. But to react like that? The thought of being bathed by strange women merely sounds titillating to me."

"And you're going to him just three nights later?"

"*I don't have a choice.*" Unfortunately, she wasn't pregnant. The Hag could divine such things within days, so this morning, Sabine had descended into the bowels of the castle to consult the old crone. Rumor had it that she'd once been a beautiful elven maiden who'd met with some kind of curse.

Sabine couldn't see it.

The Hag's basement laboratory was squalid and disturbing with all the butchered animals—Sabine had had to bathe twice to get the odor of fried batwings off her body.

The woman had taken her blood and told her the news—a blow to Sabine because she was nearing the end of her fertile cycle.

Out of curiosity—and for no other reason—Sabine had asked the woman if Rydstrom would have been poisoned by the morsus if he'd bitten her neck. The Hag had glared at her with aged opaque eyes. "Not unless you were in the full blown throes of the poison. So there's no excuse for you to deny the demon male something he *needs* to do. No excuse other than your own selfishness," she'd said, demonstrating her customary insolence. "You take his seed and give nothing. . . . "

Now Sabine told Lanthe, "*Tonight it has to be business as usual.*" Hettiah wouldn't be out of commission much longer. "*I have to conceive so that Hettiah doesn't bear my husband's child.*"

Lanthe winced. "*That sounds really messed up.*"

"*Because it is! Over my dead body will that be happening. And you know I don't say that lightly.*"

"*Have you thought any more about Groot's sword?*"

Once Sabine had told her about it, the two of them had been antsy, wanting to plot, to act, to do *something*.

Outcomes and possibilities. Actions and reactions. Although plots usually came to her easily, Sabine was having to work for this one.

Plus, the memory of Omort's wrath on that Vampire army weighed heavily on them as well.

"*I'm staying the course with the demon.*" Sabine had ultimately decided the prospect of the sword was too up in the air to even consider a plan of action.

"*I thought you'd sworn off sex.*"

"*I'm going to give it a second go,*" Sabine said as she donned a top that had metal cups shaped like actual paws, with claws flared. Knowing the demon would like it, she laced up the leather ties on the sides.

"*You're softening toward Rydstrom, aren't you? Can you look me in the eyes and tell me you feel nothing for him?*"

"*Lanthe, you know perfectly well that I could look you in the eyes and lie,*" she said. "*But I won't. Honestly, I'm drawn to him.*"

Sabine's head had been filled with thoughts of him. She craved his warmth against her body, his scent surrounding her. She'd lain in bed, staring at the ceiling as sea breezes rushed in, wondering what it would be like with him here in her bed. Could he touch her slowly at first?

"*I keep thinking of him as my husband. It's silly that a few words should affect me like that, but the idea makes me possessive of him.*"

"*You don't seem too broken up about having to bed him again.*"

"*Upon further reflection, I've realized it wasn't all bad.*" The time leading up to the pain had been incredible. She wanted more of that excitement, was aching for it. She was a born hedonist, a Sorceri who craved her pleasures. The demon could give them to her.

Last night, she'd woken to a chimera of Rydstrom slipping into bed with her, that intent look in his eyes and handcuffs dangling from his fist. . . .

"*The demon Cadeon is still going strong?*" Lanthe asked.

Sabine gave herself an inward shake. "*From what I understand, he had four checkpoints to get through, and he and the Vessel have already completed three.*" She settled a new headdress over her plaits, clasping the back of it to her collar. "*But even if he gets the sword, he'll never get close enough to use it.*"

"*We could. If given the chance, could you personally take Omort out?*"

Sabine's eyes went cold. "*In a heartbeat.*" She smoothed her finest metal fishnet hose up to her thighs, securing them in place with tight leather garters. Then she covered much of the hose with wicked steel-toed boots that climbed up past her knees.

"*You still won't consider uniting with the rage demons?*"

Sabine shook her head. "*Omort would kill us before we even had a chance. How quickly we forget his power.*" Over her short skirt, she draped a belt hung with a dozen blue-gold tassels. "*Besides, if we united with them, we'd have to turn around and kill them.*" When Lanthe raised her brows, Sabine said, "*Or we'd be out a castle. And I'm not keen on sharing.*"

"*Not even with your husband?*"

There was that word again. She hesitated, then said, "*Think of what Rydstrom would demand from us—obedience, lawfulness. Yes, it would be better than with Omort. But it couldn't be better than if we ruled.*"

"*That's true.*" Lanthe rose to head back to her room. "*Try to get some information tonight. Maybe they have a plan of their own.*"

"*I'll see what I can find out.*" After Lanthe left, Sabine finished at the dresser, drawing her face paint in blurred streaks of black and gray that covered her eyes and fanned out toward her temples.

She checked her reflection. Was she alluring enough to tempt him from his certain ire? The mirror said *yes*.

But then she had the most startling thought. More of an impulse, really. And one she readily checked. She gave a nervous laugh, glancing around the room.

For a second there, she'd thought about telling him she was . . . sorry.

Though he burned with rage toward her, Rydstrom wanted her with him.

Being separated from her like this wasn't natural—it went contrary to his demon instinct.

He hungered to have his mark on her, his scent on her skin. He needed to run his horns all over her.

His fists clenched. *Damn it, when will she return to me?*

A male materialized in his cell. Lothaire. *Kill.*

"Don't look at me like you'll rip my throat out," the vampire said in accented English. "I can aid your escape." He held up a key in one hand and a pack in the other. "Your freedom. And supplies. I can trace you to Grave Realm, but not off-plane."

"Why aid me?" Rydstrom demanded, wondering what his game was.

"I want something from you. You'd have to make a vow to me."

"A vow to do what?"

Lothaire said, "When I ask you for something in the future, no matter what it is, you must give it to me."

"*Fuck—off.*"

"Think about it. Your options are limited at present."

They were. And in his current state, Rydstrom couldn't think of anything that Lothaire could ask for that would be worse than what he'd forfeit if he remained prisoner here—his female, his child, his kingdom, and eventually his life. "Why help me now?"

"Because at this moment, Sabine's sister Hettiah is limping her way here to drug you with an aphrodisiac. And that won't do."

"Not by Sabine's leave?"

"I would seriously doubt that."

"What you ask for is too steep, vampire. I'll resist the sister and her potions—"

"Not if you're unconscious."

"She could do that?" At Lothaire's nod, Rydstrom grated, "Even if I escape, I'll be found before I can get us off-plane."

"Us?"

"Sabine. I'm not leaving without her."

The vampire shook his head sharply. "Come back for her—we'll be discovered, and Omort will never let her go."

"Wherever I go, Sabine goes. It will be this way from now until I'm dead."

Lothaire gave him an appraising look, then nodded. "You have a few days before the sorcerer can manage to get all the illegal portals sealed. Especially since I'm in charge of that security measure. Now Hettiah nears."

The idea of that woman drugging and using him while he was unconscious made Rydstrom shudder with disgust.

"Make the vow, demon. I know much about this kingdom. And I know much about your intended new prisoner. How to render her *completely powerless.*"

This time Rydstrom didn't hesitate. "I vow it. Now tell me."

Lothaire nearly smiled, a mean expression on him. "She can't purposely cast her illusions with both hands bound behind her back." He began unlocking Rydstrom's chains. "Her tower is the west one."

Heart thundering, Rydstrom said, "I *know.*"

Lothaire clasped his wrist and traced them into her room.

Sabine was admiring herself in the mirror, the most beautiful creature Rydstrom had ever seen. *Mine.*

"*Hello, princess.*"

≋ 21 ≋

Sabine's breath left her when she spied Rydstrom in her mirror's reflection, with his eyes wild. And *Lothaire*, too? The vampire was working with him? That traitor!

She raised her hands to cloak herself, but Rydstrom lunged across the room and captured her wrists behind her back. Did he know that would prevent her from casting illusions? She shrieked once before he covered her mouth with his other hand.

Would it be enough for the Inferi outside to call for the guards?

While Rydstrom tied her wrists with a length of cord, Lothaire traced over to help him. She fought the two as the vampire secured a gag around her head.

With muffled curses, she berated the traitor. He *shrugged*.

Shouts sounded as the castle raised the alarm. Seconds later, guards burst into the room with swords raised, a mix of revenants, Sorceri and fallen vampires. The latter nodded at Lothaire and *traced away*.

Rydstrom tossed her behind him, sending her tumbling to the ground, then faced off against at least ten guards. His horns flared ominously, the color of his skin deepening in his rage. His muscles expanded and flexed before her very eyes.

She watched in awe as the demon launched himself at the guards, slashing with fangs and claws. That dragon tattoo seemed to come alive, snaking its movements over sweat-slicked flesh.

Lothaire casually stood beside her place on her floor, drawing a knee up and resting his boot on the wall. "We could simply trace," he said, "but then, you'll likely want him to work some of this out of his system. And I'm hungry."

She cursed him again behind the gag, but his attention was fixed on the melee.

Rydstrom was tearing the soldiers apart with such a ferocity, that even she was stunned. *And that's my husband.*

Lothaire himself quirked a brow, glancing from Rydstrom to Sabine and back again, linking the demon's savage reaction to her. He muttered, *"Noted."*

Two Sorceri guards charged her and Lothaire. The vampire pushed away from the wall and fought them, seeming to enjoy the battle, easily dodging their swords with his tracing.

He slew one, then clasped the second's flailing body tightly to his own, piercing his neck. His blonde brows drew together with pleasure. Between his and the demon's brutality, Sabine stared in horrified fascination.

She shook herself, scrambling to her feet to escape them. Almost to the door . . . But the demon was clashing with two more revenants, and the three barreled toward her.

Out of the corner of her eye, she saw a sword hilt rushing toward her head.

When she cried out in pain, the demon roared with fury. Then . . . nothingness.

His thoughts were dim—any part of him that was rational was muted. His demon instinct was ruling him.

Take my woman . . . get free.

More shouting soldiers charged up the stairs. With Sabine draped across his shoulder, Rydstrom hissed, "Trace us, vampire!"

Lothaire dumped the guard he'd been draining, then clutched Rydstrom's wrist once more. "Hold her tight."

After an instant of blackness, Rydstrom saw mountains soaring in the distance. The moon glowed off the sand of a barren plain. The vampire had traced them to Grave Realm.

Rydstrom was free—and Sabine was in his possession. He drew her from his shoulder into his arms. She looked innocent, but it was a false face. She'd tormented him again and again.

His mind was burdened with confusing hatred, his body with aggression and primitive need.

My woman. So pale and perfect. *To use as I please.*

He bent down to lay her limp body in the sand, then checked her head. A knot had risen, but nothing her immortality wouldn't rapidly shake.

"A blade," he grated as he untied the cord he'd bound her with. When Lothaire handed him a dagger, Rydstrom cut lengths that he tied around her wrists like cuffs, then he secured the two together with another line.

Once he'd finished, Lothaire tossed Rydstrom a black tunic and the pack. "There's a canteen of water and supplies to camp for a few days." From his waist, he unfastened a sword belt. "And a weapon—to defend against the beasties," he said, seeming amused by that.

Rydstrom drew on the tunic, then strapped the sword to his waist.

"You've got a week at the most to locate a portal. Strike out due west from here—you'll likely begin to find rage demons, refugees who will know the way."

Rydstrom lifted Sabine once more. "What will you ask of me?"

The vampire's pale-eyed gaze locked on Rydstrom. "Something that will be worth what I've lost here by breaking my pact with Omort."

"When?"

"When the time comes. In a week, a decade. Maybe a millennium."

"You're still my enemy," Rydstrom said. "I could simply hunt you down and kill you."

"I'd expect nothing less. You're an honest king, but you're still a ruthless one. Now go. The clock ticks."

When Sabine woke, the moon had not yet set.

She was greeted by a pounding pain in her head, and since the demon had thrown her over his shoulder, each of his long strides was increasing that ache. Her hands were still bound behind her back. Which meant . . .

I'm powerless.

Glancing up through her braids, she could see they were in a different region of Rothkalina—gone from the seaside castle and verdant forest to a desolate plain. There was only one region in Rothkalina that wasn't replete with green forest—the aptly named Grave Realm.

Where the wild things are . . .

She was out in the middle of a perilous territory with a madman, Lanthe must be out of her head with worry, and Sabine had no morsus—if she didn't get back to the castle, to Omort, she truly would be condemned.

All of this was because of that traitor Lothaire! And the bastard had traced them to Grave Realm. She'd stake him herself!

Sabine could only imagine how Omort was taking this betrayal . . . or who he was taking it out on. She believed Lanthe would be safe, but she hoped her sister would protect their Inferi.

Gradually, one head-pounding stride of his at a time, the plain gave way to a gnarled forest of petrified wood. Shadows from the moon slithered over the ground. Unseen things scurried in the dirt.

More alarming, her skirt was riding up to her waist, leaving her ass in no more than a thong. The hand he used to pin her to his shoulder now covered her curves completely, and he'd begun kneading them.

What will he do to me? She didn't want to have sex with him again, especially since he was in this agitated state. For one thing, her plan was foiled. For another, the pain was too fresh. When she'd decided to return to his cell, she'd had every intention of being on top. . . .

Rydstrom abruptly halted and dropped her to her feet. In the waning moonlight, his crazed eyes held a look of expectation, his lips drawn back from his fangs.

Steady Rydstrom had snapped.

Apparently, Sabine had grabbed a tiger by the tail. And she'd just become its prisoner.

Not for long.

"Rydstrom," she whispered.

"What?"

She whispered more faintly. When he leaned in, she butted her headdress against his nose, then launched her steel-toed boot between his legs—

He caught her by the ankle and flipped her onto her back. He was on top of her in an instant. "You're a vicious little female." He crushed his face into her hair, inhaling. "Treacherous."

When he began kissing her neck desperately, she frowned up at the sky—he was kissing her as if he'd *missed* her. Just as his loneliness had called to her, now his yearning did.

"But you won't be for long."

He was already erect, and when he ground his shaft against her, a shock of pleasure jolted through her. She was getting caught up, his excitement fueling her own.

Wait . . . What did he mean by *won't be for long?* Planning on converting her to his side, changing her? *Always wanting to change me!*

He took her mouth, his firm lips crushing hers.

Before she got lost in the frenzy of his kiss, she nipped his bottom lip hard.

He hissed a curse as he bolted to his feet. Grabbing her by the waist, he hauled her over to a flat boulder. When he sank down on it, he laid her across his legs.

"What are you doing?" With her hands tied, she could do nothing to prevent him.

"Keeping my promises." Just as she realized what he was talking about, he shoved her skirt up to her waist.

"Rydstrom, just wait!" She wriggled when he yanked her panties to her ankles. "Demon—"

He brought his palm down with a loud slap. It stung, but it sounded worse than it felt.

This was his revenge? Would he mind if she slept through it? "Is that all you've got, demon? Was that punishment or affection? I'm confused—"

Whap! She whistled in a breath on that one, writhing over his lap. Another slap, followed by stinging pain, then another. His other hand was kneading her thigh. He was excited by this, heaving his breaths.

And something began to happen to her. To her amazement, she was growing aroused. What was it about the demon? Would there *ever* be a time when he couldn't make her want him? Maybe like right now, when he was spanking her ass and seemed a razor's edge away from throttling her?

But she was hyper-attracted to strength, and the demon was the strongest male she'd ever encountered. She'd never forget him fighting those guards—the ferocity within him. . . .

With his next slap, her cry turned to a moan, bewildering her. Even he hesitated.

She was a true daughter of the Sorceri—a hedonist who would take her pleasure where she found it. Here she was in the wilds of the realm, captive of a demonic being, receiving blows—and her illusions of fire were already lighting the night.

What a surprise, she thought, with the faintest smile.

She maneuvered over his lap, easing her knee to the side, spreading her legs. His body grew still. His hand hesitated in midair. All she could hear was his ragged breaths.

Then he gave a harsh groan as he leaned back to see between her legs. *"Touch you . . ."*

She nodded. At the first contact, she cried out, then moaned when he delved one of his big fingers inside her. Had he just freed his shaft? She could feel that he'd begun stroking himself beneath her.

In and out went that seeking finger. "Getting so *wet*," he rasped. *"Sorceress, you drive me . . . mad. . . ."*

✖ 22 ✖

Rydstrom was deep in that twilight between reason and instinct, where nothing made sense. He was losing control with her and couldn't savor it more.

He'd escaped with her. *At last.* Just thinking of her as his prisoner—his possession—made him want to bellow with triumph.

With her wild plaits flowing down her back and the metal adorning her body, she looked as wicked as she acted, taking the slaps—and raising her ass for more. And now she needed to come, badly. Her fires were already burning.

This is ecstasy.

He worked a second finger inside her hungry sheath. "So tight. Hot." Her flesh glistened, gripping his fingers. "And virgin no more."

With his other hand, he worked his fist up and down his shaft, until it throbbed to release its seed. He let his fingers slide out of her only long enough to turn her over so he could see her face.

There was no shame and no fear. With her eyes half-lidded, she lay across his lap, tilting her hips up, wantonly using his fingers. *So beautiful . . . so fierce. Mine.*

That still-unfamiliar pressure within his shaft mounted, the sensitive crown rubbing against her ass. *Pleasure so extreme it's pain.*

His muscles tensed, his body readying to come. He roared to the sky, beginning to ejaculate against her ass. On and on it continued while he yelled, pumping hard jets, his hips jerking uncontrollably beneath her.

She gasped, then moaned low. The sound of that drew forth from him a last explosion that landed between her spread legs. Even marked like this, she was writhing, moaning, about to come . . .

But he removed his hand to refasten his pants, then set her on her feet.

As she blinked up at him in bewilderment, he ripped the bottom of his tunic to wipe his seed from her.

"What are you doing?"

"I'm finished." *Don't push me . . . don't enrage me.* "You've three nights you owe me. Three nights where you'll know what I went through. Then we'll have parity between us."

When he swiped her skin, she bucked against him. "I'll kill you for this!"

In the moonlight, he could see her ass was bright red. *How hard did I slap her?*

"*Very* hard, you oaf!" she answered.

"Stay out of my goddamned head, Sabine!" He tossed the cloth away, then yanked up her scrap of underwear with so much force she rocked up on her toes.

"Or what? You'll spank me? Do you often strike women?"

"Never." Not once in fifteen centuries.

"Ah, that's right, you're King Rydstrom the Good. You don't seem so good now."

"You wouldn't recognize a good thing if it was spanking your ass." He wrenched down her skirt so hard, the material ripped.

"Am I turning you bad, demon? Shattering that upstanding façade?"

"That could've been much worse." He took her arm, propelling her forward as they journeyed on. "It didn't have to be like this. You started us on this path. Do you remember the time I *asked* you to release me? Do you recall my pain as I lay in that fucking bed, with my chest ripped open wide and my spine severed? Day after day, I was trapped in that goddamned dungeon—*because of you!*"

As if she'd heard none of that, she squinted up at his horns. "Hey, are you going to be like this for long?"

He released her, confounded by this female. *Gods, she's got me twisted inside.* He resumed walking, not turning back as he spoke into the night, "You'll follow me now. If you don't, you'll be eaten alive out here."

"Where are you taking me?" she asked, trailing after him. "What are you going to do to me? Besides taking out your fetish on me?"

He stopped and rounded on her, making her crane her head up at him. "Woman, why would you possibly push me?" His eyes narrowed. "You're taunting me because you like it when I lose control."

She gazed away for a split second, then said, "Not likely. How else should I act with someone who's taken me prisoner? Pleasant?"

"If you had any sense, you'd *avoid* provoking me." Done with this exchange, he turned to resume their trek. The harsh sun would soon be rising, and the terrain was only going to become more grueling. . . .

With each mile, she badgered him about where they were going and how long they'd be gone.

She'd complained about the heat of the sun, the furious pace, and his rationing of their dwindling water supply.

Other than to feed her sips from the canteen, Rydstrom ignored her, his thoughts in turmoil. Part of him felt triumphant. He was free, and had Sabine as his captive. He'd already begun his revenge and had been greatly rewarded, coming so hard his legs had been weak afterward.

Another part of him felt guilt for his treatment of her. Anytime that guilt arose, he would remind himself of all she'd done to him. The humiliation of those men bathing him. . . . The memory of that alone had him turning to her with his lips drawn back from his fangs.

Because of her behavior, he would feel free to do with her whatever he wanted.

But how long could he go without claiming her? If he hadn't done it already, he didn't want to impregnate her. Yes, he wanted his son, but not yet, not when there was so much danger. Not when he knew Sabine would run back to Omort at the earliest opportunity.

When they trudged up a steep incline, she tripped and fell forward onto her front. Spitting out sand, she snapped, "I've put up with this long enough! You've got to free me, else I can't keep up. At least free *one* of my hands. I need both to work illusions. Rydstrom, I can't keep going like this."

He clutched the front of her metal top and yanked her up with it.

"Omort will come for me! You'll never get away with this."

"Another word, and I'll gag you."

Against his warning, she said, "And Lothaire will be burned to ash . . ." She trailed off when he tore another length of cloth from the bottom of his shirt. "Rydstrom! I'll be quiet—"

He wrapped the cloth around her head, tying it tight like a bit to gag her. "I *know.* . . ."

For another hour, he left her like that, gagged as they covered more ground. He could *feel* her glare on his back, but he didn't want to hear any more of her complaints or demands.

He finally glanced back at her. She'd straggled farther behind, the journey taking its toll. She was sunburned, her knees bloodied, her legs cut. Her ass was probably still on fire.

He wanted to feel nothing but satisfaction over her suffering—and couldn't. It went against his instinct.

Damn that sorceress. Got me so twisted. He cast her a black look over his shoulder.

She straightened and assumed her haughty expression—then stumbled once more. Though he could have continued for days on end, he obviously had to stop for the night for her.

When he found a freshwater lake in a protected canyon pass, he dropped his pack near the shore and crouched down to unpack the contents: a small bottle of wine, bread, chicken, cheese, a knife and flints, bedding.

Sabine sagged in relief, dropping to her knees, then wobbled over on her hip.

After he started a fire, he ate his share of the food, then leaned over to yank her gag down.

She swallowed repeatedly, working her jaw out. "Is it as sweet as you'd hoped?" she asked. "Your revenge?"

"It will be. We're just beginning, princess. There will be parity for everything you did to me. Three nights you came to my cell and tormented me—"

"It wasn't three nights. You have no idea what I would have done the night you were injured. If I hadn't been summoned to court, I might have gotten carried away."

"Though you hadn't before?" He gave her some water from the canteen.

When he brought the chicken up to her lips, she turned her face away. "You know I don't consume meat."

"You knew I did."

"I won't eat it."

"Go hungry." He finished the food, then arranged the bedding under a leafless tree near the fire he'd built.

"I need you to free my hands, so I can wash off." She twisted around to peer at her backside. "I seem to have gotten demon seed on myself!"

He jerked his chin toward the lake. "There's the water."

"What do you expect me to do with my hands bound?"

"Ask me to bathe you."

When she only glared at him, he stripped off his sword and clothes, then dove into the deep water from a low ledge. The temperature was cool and soothed his battered body.

He surfaced to see her carefully stepping on the slippery rocks at the edge of a dropoff, several yards above the one he'd used. Just when he was about to point out a sandy shore for her to go to instead, she slipped and tumbled into the water. In an instant, she disappeared.

Her hands are tied behind her back, the metal like an anchor, weighing her down.

With a surge of panic, he dove for her.

❧ 23 ❧

"What are you going to do about my sister?" Lanthe demanded of Omort. Only her concern for Sabine gave her courage with the monster before her.

He didn't even seem to be a man any longer, just personified wrath. Hettiah knelt at the foot of his throne, with her head bowed, constantly shuddering as if with cold.

Over the last several hours, he'd killed again and again, Inferi, revenants, even rage demons abducted from their towns.

But nothing could appease him. Bodies had piled up all around the well, with sightless eyes and tangled limbs on a canvas of blood. The stench and flies were becoming unbearable.

"You've got to send the fire demons after her. They can teleport—"

"You think I haven't considered that?" he yelled. "Rydstrom will have taken her to Grave Realm—there are ways off-plane there. And none of the fire demons or vampires have been there before!"

Demons and vampires could only trace to places they'd previously been. Lanthe didn't know if Omort was aware of this, but whether or not the *vampires* could teleport to Grave Realm was irrelevant. None were allied here any longer.

The covenant tablet between the factions had broken, and when Lothaire's legion disappeared, it had become obvious who had betrayed Omort—and Sabine. The fire demon king remained allied, but for how long?

Truthfully, Lanthe wasn't worried about Rydstrom hurting Sabine. In fact, she believed he would protect his female with his life. What she was worried about was Sabine's morsus. "Omort, if we can't find her, when will the poison hit?" Lanthe asked.

He gave a humorless laugh. "A week before she expects it to."

"You lied to her about that?" she cried.

"It matters naught," he said. "You'll open a portal to Grave Realm. The revenants will scour the area and retrieve her this eve."

Lanthe swallowed. "I don't . . . have a portal to give you."

When Omort had called for Sabine's Inferi to torture and kill, Lanthe had made a command decision, opening a threshold to save the servants under her and Sabine's protection. Lanthe honestly believed her sister was safer with the demon than any being inside Tornin. And the sisters had made a pact that if anything should happen to one, the other would provide for and protect her Inferi.

Omort faced her with confusion in those yellow eyes. "What are you saying to me?"

"I can't generate a threshold for several more days." When he shot to his feet, storming toward her, she scuttled back from him. "If you do anything to me, you'll never get Sabine back."

"Or, I could take your power." He raised his palms, sinister heat rising above them. "And butcher your useless body. . . ."

Sabine flailed and coughed as the demon lugged her to a beach.

"It took you long enough!" She'd thought she would drown again, was sure of it, until she'd felt his hands clamping her sides.

"I dove straight down!" Glowering at the metal as if it were to blame, he took hold of her headdress, unlocking it from her collar.

"No!" she cried.

But he tossed the piece over his shoulder toward the camp. Once he'd removed her choker and spun it away like a Frisbee, he clutched her ankles. Before she could react, he'd snatched her feet out from under her. When her back met the sand, he was already yanking a boot off.

"Stop this, demon!" Fighting him was futile, but she still tried. She kicked out, aiming for his recently injured chest, connecting a couple of solid hits.

He didn't even seem to notice them, flinging her boots away. "You're my captive. My responsibility. I'll make sure you're clean."

After her spanking, Sabine had noticed that Rydstrom had calmed, that wild look diminishing—but in no way disappearing. Now it was back full force. His very voice was altered, his language and bearing decidedly *not* kingly. He'd held himself rigid and aloof before. Now there was a fluidity in the way he moved.

Glaring up at him, she said, "And I suppose I don't have any say in this?"

He shook his head slowly, his attention already on her bustier. He stood, hauling her to her feet. With his brow furrowed in concentration, he began unlacing the intricate knots of her top, unraveling the swollen leather ties.

He was getting aroused once more, that thick shaft rising. His movements became unhurried, as if he relished this task and didn't want it to end.

Once he'd removed the bustier, his gaze was transfixed by her breasts, rising and falling with her hectic breaths. He seemed to give himself a shake, then worked her skirt down her sandy legs.

"Enough!" She bucked against him again, thrashing her body, but he looped an arm around her waist to still her.

With a slap on her still burning ass, he gave her a look of warning so menacing, she decided she might heed it. "Stand here. Do not move." He tugged down her panties and mesh hose, tossing them into a pile.

After he'd stripped her completely, he began unbraiding her plaits. His countenance was fierce, but he handled her hair with infinite gentleness.

When he'd finished, he pulled her into the water up to her knees. There he laid his hands on her shoulders, pressing her down to kneel, putting his jutting shaft right in front of her face.

Just when she thought he was going to try to force her to take him with her mouth, he knelt before her.

Once he'd rinsed the sand from her, he began investigating her body. He traced her collarbone with those big demon hands, his eyes following his movements, then his lips. When his gaze dipped to her breasts she knew what would follow. He grazed rough palms over them, kissing her nipples with the merest brush of his lips.

Somehow, he was being gentle with her, his caresses so out of place with the anger she could feel still seething inside him. His touches were . . . *tender.* Consolatory. But did he want to console her over what he'd done—or what he was about to do?

He scooped water over her chest, licking it from her breasts, sucking drops from the tips. He used his teeth to nip at her straining peaks, then he drew back to stare at them. His eyes were riveted on them, as if he was fascinated with this part of her.

She cursed her body for responding once more. But she was unfulfilled from their earlier encounter, and from nights of yearning for him even before her abduction. Her lids grew heavy, her earlier alarm and rancor ebbing.

He ran his lips over her ear, nuzzling it as he said, "I've waited a long time for my female. Fifteen centuries, I've gone without her." He gently ran his horns against her neck. "Without *you.* No longer."

He clasped her shoulders and turned her so he could drag his lips down her damp back. When she shivered, he rasped, "You still like my touch." He drew the backs of his dark claws across her sensitive ass. "You always will."

By the time he'd turned her to face him once more, his kneading and kissing had put her in a daze of lethargic arousal. When he eased his hand between her legs, cupping her, she rested on him, pressing herself into his palm, leaning her forehead on his shoulder.

A *daze . . . do what you will . . .* She didn't care. Until he raised his other hand to her face.

She stiffened and scrambled back. In a deadly tone, she said, "Don't ever touch my face, Rydstrom."

Nine times out of ten, when a man had his hand raised in the vicinity of her face, it was either to cow her or kill her. In her five hundred years of life, this had proven true.

"I do as I please with you." When he grasped her chin, she flinched, and damn him, he noticed the weakness.

"You don't have any right—"

"You gave me that right with your treatment of me."

He ran his other palm lightly over the front of her neck. When he frowned as if he'd perceived the raised scar that was still invisible, she fought to get free, but he held her tightly. She had only so long before her illusions faded. Soon he'd see the white streak in her hair, the scar at her neck. She'd never imagined she'd be powerless near him.

"Are you going to want sex with me now?" she hastily asked to distract him. "Because I already gave at the office—"

"No."

"—and it was a debacle . . . what did you say?"

"I'll make the same deal that you offered me. You'll concede something to me before I'll take you. Something you'll never want to say."

Parity for the wedding vow she'd forced him to give her.

"You'll say: 'I beg you to claim me. I need you as my master and surrender my will to yours.' And when you do, I will reward you."

"So, then . . . *never*."

"I vow to you I won't take you until you say these words to me. And I won't let you come until you either beg me for it or until your three nights have passed."

"If you're not going to demand sex from me, then you're keeping me only because of your revenge?"

He stared down at her with eyes dark like night. "And because I keep what's mine." With his hands clasped behind her head, he rubbed his thumbs over her cheekbones, then leaned in to kiss her.

Their last real kiss had been frantic, maddening. Like a drug to her. Now he licked her bottom lip before tugging it between his teeth.

When he finally took her mouth, he slipped his tongue in, tempting her to meet him.

She soon did, lapping at him, making him groan. His shaft prodded against her belly, and her hips began rocking toward it. Her back arched to get her nipples against his warm body.

But he broke away, leaving her breathless. She was still blinking for focus, dizzy from his kiss, when he swept her up in his arms, lifting her from the water.

"What are you doing now?"

Without a word, he carried her to the pallet beneath the tree, then laid her on it, still wet, with water drops trickling down her sides.

He untied the rope between her wrists—but only to lead it toward the trunk. "Wait . . . No, demon!" But he forced her arms over her head, binding her to the tree.

Then he knelt before her. "Spread your legs."

"Go to hell."

With his big palms covering her inner thighs, he forced her legs open, then gazed at her for long moments.

She wanted to look away, but she couldn't draw her eyes from his compelling face, his scar lit by the fire.

"Do you know how bad I've wanted to taste you?" When he licked his lips, she almost whimpered. "*Mouthwatering*," he rasped. "*So beautiful*." Again, his voice sounded unfamiliar.

He bent down and nuzzled her curls, making her cry out. Then he brushed his mouth against her sensitive lips, his breath hot on her.

She drew her knees up around him. "Rydstrom! Ah, gods . . . do it!"

"Do what?" He spread her flesh with his thumbs.

"Taste me . . . kiss me," she breathed.

When his tongue first dipped to her, he groaned against her so hard, she felt it. She moaned with abandon.

Pressing his mouth to her core, he delved his tongue, licking her deeply, thoroughly. He was making her melt for him . . . exploring her with his lips, his fingers— nothing was sacred.

Never had she been kissed like *this*.

"Your taste . . . drives me mad," he snarled with a firm lick over her throbbing clitoris. His tongue snaked over it again and again, without mercy, until she was helplessly undulating to his mouth. *Getting close . . . so close.*

She could see he'd begun pumping his fist over his shaft, the gold band on his bulging bicep glimmering with his movements. The rhythm grew more furious with each flick of his clever tongue.

The demon was wild with her. The corded muscles of his body visibly tensed for his orgasm. He growled against her just before his semen began lashing over her hip.

"Hot. It's so *hot,"* she gasped, on the brink of release herself.

But once he'd finally finished spending, he drew his head up from her. She gazed at him, realizing he was pleased that she'd watched him come, excited by that.

With a satisfied groan, he collapsed onto his back. As she watched his penis still pulsing over his rigid stomach, she hungered for it, shamelessly rolling her hips for it.

Had she actually wanted to forego sex? Now she was desperate for another try.

As soon as he'd caught his breath, he said, "Back to the business at hand," repeating her words from the first night she'd captured him. He leaned down to her once more. "I could do this all night. *Think I will . . ."*

"Yes!" He began devouring her again. *"More,"* she moaned, going out of her head. Just when she was about to come, he pulled back.

"No, no, no." She stamped her feet. In a gasping voice, she said, "You are seriously . . . making me . . . want to kill you!"

"Uh-huh." He leisurely grazed the backs of his fingers all along her body, making her shiver. Just when her breaths had calmed somewhat, and she'd closed her legs, he said, "Wider."

Gritting her teeth, staring at the branches above, she let her knees fall open.

For hour after hour, Rydstrom kept her on the brink. He'd come twice more, but then he'd begun to pace himself, determined to outlast her.

He'd never seen a woman in this kind of frenzy. Her head thrashed, her mane of red hair drying and spreading out over the blanket. Her nipples strained up to the sky as her back arched.

Illusions of flames burned all around them.

Withholding her pleasure was punishing for him as well—it took all his will to disobey the driving instinct to sate his female. But her reaction also excited the hell out of him.

Yet she wouldn't break. Though he ached to mount her pale body, to ride her relentlessly, this was a battle of wills, and he simply didn't lose them. . . .

By the time the moon had begun to set, she was panting, her body sheening with sweat. Her nipples were puckered and swollen.

As he lay beside her, she earnestly gazed into his eyes, whispering, "J-Just hold me, demon. I can move against you."

The image her words conjured made him want to groan. Him clasping her little body tight, with her rubbing her sex against his shaft—until she quivered in his arms. . .

He bent down and swirled his tongue around one of her nipples, murmuring against it, "Beg for me, sweet. And I'll make you come till your eyes roll back in your head."

"Never!" She thrashed her head, crying, "You don't understand—"

"Don't I?" he grated, sitting up.

Arms still tied above her, she collapsed over on her side, her small body trembling, her knees drawn to her chest. While he watched, her eyelids fluttered closed as she finally passed out in exhaustion.

It was still dark when she woke. She was alone on the pallet, with no idea how long she'd been out. She frowned down at her body. He'd released her from the tree and cleaned her?

When she glanced up, she found him naked, leaning back against a boulder, his arm on his raised knee. He was watching her with an inscrutable expression. Though he was still demonic, it was fading, his obsidian eyes not so frenzied.

She'd never forget the possessiveness in his gaze tonight. Shivers coursed over her skin when she recalled the pure masculine pride on his face when he'd realized she'd watched him spending.

He stood then, a magnificent male in the flesh—with a body made for sex. The demon belonged out here in the harsh wilderness, a being from myth, a male from legend.

And he was her husband.

When he joined her on the pallet, her body was *still* aching, but she was too exhausted even to contemplate release. He drew her to his chest, then wrapped his arms around her, pulling her tight against him.

She stiffened at the unfamiliar embrace, realizing he meant for them to sleep *together*. Like this.

But when he rubbed his face against hers, her eyelids grew heavy. He was shockingly warm against her as he kissed her neck, her ear. His touches were tender again. It was as if he regretted that she hurt, even as he was the one punishing her. Gods, the demon confused her!

Though he hadn't released her hands, she could still cast scenes from her dreams. Right now, she would give her finest headdress for a stay-awake potion from the Hag. The idea of Rydstrom knowing her private thoughts, her memories. . . .

Sabine worried what this demon would think about her past if it were laid bare for him to see. She didn't want him judging her, or worse *pitying* her. Her mother used to say, "Gods give me *anything* but a good man's pity."

Yes, Sabine was anxious, but her muscles were sore, and his body felt so incredibly good against hers. Warm, hard . . . safe.

Don't dream . . . don't dream. . . .

Sabine drifted off once more, and then she slept like the dead.

❈ 24 ❈

"Heat it, stroke it, beat and grow it. Rub it, twist it, love and kiss it . . ."

Rydstrom shot upright, woken by a woman's eerie chanting.

He gazed over at Sabine, but she slept still, her eyes darting behind her lids. He was forced to leave her as he sprinted toward the sound.

"*Gold is life . . . it is perfection,*" said the woman. Her laughter followed.

When he seemed to reach the source, he swung his head around.

No one is here. A decoy? Had he been tricked into leaving his female? He charged back to Sabine—

She was sleeping just as he'd left her, with her long lashes against her cheeks. Exhaling a relieved breath, he lowered himself beside her. As he gazed down at her stunning face, he realized that his rage and lust had faded enough so that he could reason once more. But he could come to no conclusions when it came to Sabine and his confusing emotions.

Last night, his demon nature had demanded revenge, a reprisal to placate his wrath. Yet at the end of the night, the demon in him had ached to see his mate in pain.

He didn't know what to think about her, or about himself. Because he was actually considering breaking his vow for revenge. The one that had sustained him in that dungeon, had kept him from fully succumbing to rage.

He was in an impossible situation. If he gave her another two nights of torment, then he was no better than she'd been to him. But if he didn't, he would break his vow—and again, he'd be no better than she was.

Maybe he should accept her rationale that she'd only denied him for two nights total . . . yes, then he'd only have one remaining.

His gaze narrowed on her long mane of glossy hair. Among her red curls was a strand of shining white that he'd never seen before. He grasped the lock, brushing it between his thumb and forefinger. She'd hidden this— why?

The lock fell, forgotten when his eyes settled on her neck, on the scar that collared her. His lips parted as comprehension came. He clutched her shoulders, yanking her upright to inspect her skin.

"What?" She blinked against the rising sun. "What's wrong now?"

"What is this scar? Some kind of operation?" he asked, praying that it was. "Answer me!"

Her eyes briefly slid closed as if she were embarrassed. "Yes, Rydstrom, an operation."

"You're lying again!"

"No, I'm not," she said, her tone deadened. "It was an involuntary one, intended to amputate my head."

His mouth went dry. "You were *young*. How old?"

"What does it—"

"How old?" he bellowed, the sound echoing through the nearby canyons.

"Twelve, demon." She met his gaze. "I was twelve years old the day a soldier from the army of *good* slit my throat from ear to ear."

"Tell me what happened."

"A clan of the Vreken killed my parents. When I fought back, they tried for me. And before you say anything—yes, I did *have* to fight. You have no idea what they do to children like us."

He shook his head. "The Vrekeners adopt you, take you into their families."

"And separate siblings so their minds are more easily turned. They *brainwash* the females of our kind to be like theirs—biddable and grave, the exact opposite of our true nature. They brainwash us to think like *you*!"

"How could you have survived this wound?"

"It doesn't matter. Just that I did."

"You'll tell me!"

She thrashed, but he held her firm. "My sister, Lanthe used to be able to give mystickal commands. I was dead—my heart was still, and there was no blood left in it. But she somehow commanded me to live and to heal."

"Is that why your hair turned white?"

She gazed away. "I won't talk about this any longer." She struggled to get free again. "I don't understand what the big deal is." When he gaped at her, she gave him a look of disgust. "Demon, do you think that was the only time I was murdered?"

No amount of railing would get her to tell *him* the story of her deaths. The demon didn't deserve to know. He wouldn't *understand* it, not as he should, because he'd been conditioned to think differently than she'd been.

She glared up at him, and whatever he saw in her expression made him release her.

He ran a hand over his mouth. His appearance was almost back to normal, but he seemed a hair-trigger from turning. "We need to get going," he muttered.

Get going . . . Farther away from Tornin, from her morsus, from her sister. Starting on another interminable day.

Her arms were asleep, pinpricks dancing from her shoulders to her wrists as she clenched and released her fists. Her breasts were aching, her unfulfilled desire from the night before hitting her body as hard and as alien as an illness.

And she'd slept for at least five hours. That hadn't happened since she was a girl! Which meant for all those hours, she'd been vulnerable, her safety completely in Rydstrom's hands.

She resented that.

"I heard something this morning—a woman chanting," he said as he doused the remains of the fire. "But when I went to investigate, no one was there."

"I didn't hear anything." Evidently, she'd been dreaming, but she couldn't remember of what. At least he hadn't *seen* her dream.

"We have to make good time today." As she watched in horror, he took his sword and lopped off the heels of her boots.

"Don't you think it's time you filled me in on the details of our situation?"

"I'm taking you with me to my home in Louisiana." He pulled her up to her feet. When she stood naked to his avid gaze, his jaw clenched, but he didn't touch her.

His manner brisk, he tugged her skirt up her legs. "We have to meet up with refugees who are going off-plane."

"Omort can tell who comes and goes."

"Not this time."

"You're taking me to one of those illegal portals, aren't you? How long will we be walking?"

"A few more days."

"He'll find us before you can reach it," she said, making a muscle tic in his scarred cheek.

Once he'd redressed her in her metal bustier and altered boots, she said, "What about my hose and panties?"

"You won't wear them when you're with me."

She bit her tongue. "If you won't free me, then I need you to go fetch my collar and headdress for me."

"Go *fetch?*"

"I didn't mean it like that."

"Not a chance, princess."

"But you have to!"

He stormed over to both, swooping them up. "What is so bloody important about them? They almost made you *drown!*" He twisted around to lob them into the water.

She shrieked, *"No!"* But it was too late. They were gone.

Her breath left her, and she rocked on her feet. *Gold is life . . .* The smooth water surface had erased them from the earth, like they'd never existed. Her bottom lip trembled, but she could do nothing to hide it, not emotionally, not mystickally.

"Come, then," he said, his voice gruff.

As he took her arm, she gazed over her shoulder. "I can't believe you did that." Losing gold to another was one thing, but to throw it away . . . ? *Incomprehensible.* "There's no excuse. None."

"It's worthless out here."

"Not *worthless*, you oaf! Those pieces protected my head and neck!"

"Then you'll have to depend on me to do their job!" When he drew her along, she trudged forward in stony silence. . . .

After that, hours passed without event. She found his green eyes constantly on her. He was becoming more attentive, helping her over rough patches in the terrain, holding her arm to steady her. But he still wouldn't release her bindings.

And any time she tried to convince him to let her go, he threatened the gag. She wondered how real that threat was, because he clearly wanted to talk to her today—but only about one topic. He kept asking her how many times she'd died.

Finally she said, "Why do you care? Does it soften you to know terrible things were done to me when I was a girl?"

"I . . . don't know. Do you want my sympathy?"

She shrugged. "I don't deserve your sympathy." Though this could have been a maudlin statement, she said it as if it was a fact of life. Because it was.

"The strand of white in your hair. I've heard of that occurring when someone knows fear so bad, it shocks their system. What happened to you, Sabine? Did Omort hurt you?"

"He's never hurt me." *Physically.*

"You are still loyal to him?"

She couldn't tell the demon as much as she wanted to, or needed to. She couldn't tell Rydstrom how she hated her half brother, or how much she agreed with Rydstrom—that Omort had to be killed. Anything she said now could be seen by Omort later when they were recaptured. Her brother would force the demon to open his mind. *And my betrayal would be there, plain for Omort to see.*

"He's protected Lanthe and me for many years," she hedged. "And besides, should I be loyal to you over him? You keep me bound, risking my life in this dangerous place. At least he cherishes my life. He'll be coming for me."

"I look forward to that."

"Speaking of loyalty—why would Lothaire betray

Omort for you anyway? Had you two been working together all this time?"

"The vampire wanted something I could give him, and we bargained for my freedom."

"He's the one who traced us out here?" At Rydstrom's curt nod, she said, "When would he ever have had a reason to be in Grave Realm before?"

Rydstrom shrugged. "He said he knew much about the kingdom."

"Is that so? Then maybe he could've gotten us closer to a portal instead of making us tromp through this gods forsaken place."

"The portal openers move constantly. Suck it up, sorceress."

When she stumbled once more, she said, "Demon, come on!"

"Unless you can tell me another way to render you powerless, the bindings stay."

"What if I vowed not to use my power?"

"Your *vow*?" He gave a cruel laugh. "You'd be gone in seconds."

"You said there'd be parity, but it's not like I tortured you. I never physically harmed you, yet you're killing me out here."

"Under your *care*," he sneered the word, "I had my spine severed and a hole punched in my chest."

"That wasn't my fault—I saved your life." Her expression lit with realization. "You're most upset about the three who bathed you, aren't you? I'd thought you might like it!"

"No—you—didn't."

She nodded easily. "Okay, that was a lie. But I didn't think you'd *hate* it, per se." When he narrowed his gaze, she said, "Yes, yes, that might be a lie as well."

"How would you feel if I had three women bathe you?"

She quirked a brow. "Like I was on a date gone well. And actually, according to your parity rule, you *have* to arrange for it. And they have to be ravishing, because I sent you choice Inferi—and they were all volunteers, believe me."

He snapped, "This is exactly why I will *not* do that to you—if it's not punishment to you, then it won't be like for like." He increased his pace.

"What exactly does your parity involve again?" she asked, hurrying to keep up. "I'm unclear."

He stopped and turned so suddenly she almost ran into him. Gazing down at her, he said, "You will have one more night where I am going to make you scream with need—unless you beg me to ease you. After that I won't take you again until you say, 'I beg you to claim me. I need you as my master and surrender my will to yours.' And Sabine, I can wait as long as it takes. You will lose if you match swords with me in a battle of wills."

"*As long as it takes?* Exactly how long are you planning to keep me? When will you release me?"

He gave her a strange expression—part possessive, part aggressive. His eyes turned sharply from green to jet-black. "I *won't.*"

❧ 25 ❧

Over the long day, the landscape gradually transformed again. The thickening underbrush tangled at their feet, and wind-whipped trees filled crowded groves. Rivers carved through plateaus, with cliffs overlooking all.

He and Sabine continued to ascend, crossing one shallow stream after another.

She glared at every bramble, glared at the sun blazing overhead, glared at him whenever he helped her drink from the canteen.

Rydstrom couldn't stop thinking about what he'd learned this morning. Where had he been five hundred years ago when Sabine had been unprotected and tortured?

Maybe if he'd been able to let go of his quest for the crown and had searched for her instead, he could have spared her this. *My female, slashed like that as a mere girl.*

Had she been afraid? Had she known what was about to befall her?

She'd said that wasn't the last time she'd been murdered, and, in this, he believed her. So how many deaths had she suffered? Exactly how else had she died? How old was she each time?

No wonder she held life in so little regard.

He'd yelled at her this morning, shaking her to get her to tell him. And something had happened. She'd gotten a look about her, and her eyes had darted. Her swagger had vanished.

As he'd suspected, whenever she was discomfited, she camouflaged her expressions with an illusion of either amusement or patronizing indulgence.

Now there were no illusions. And she was so used to mystically hiding her expressions that she didn't remember to school them.

Angry, sarcastic Sabine had started *blushing* today, as well. Whenever she'd caught his gaze on her strand of white hair or her neck, a pink flush colored her high cheekbones. She acted as if he now knew a flaw in her character that she'd tried to keep hidden.

Sabine had become an open book. And what he was reading disturbed him greatly.

She'd asked him if the knowledge of her past had softened his anger. He almost felt numb to that anger, as if his confusion about her had overwhelmed it. At every turn, she confounded him. Like the most complicated puzzle he'd ever encountered.

This situation reminded him of when his Lykae friend Bowen had been trying to win the pretty witch Mariketa. The two had gotten off to a rocky start, since he'd trapped her in a tomb of Incubi and hadn't rescued her for weeks.

Rydstrom remembered being perplexed by his friend's confusion and weird aggression. Rydstrom had been so smug, calmly advising Bowen to reason the situation out. He recalled Bowen snapping that he was going to enjoy it when Rydstrom found his own woman. *She'll make your horns go ramrod straight every time she saunters by.* Bowen had been eager to see her shake Rydstrom's unflappable demeanor.

Was I once unflappable? It seemed a lifetime ago. *Now I comprehend what Bowen had gone through.*

But the Lykae had ultimately used his head to figure out how to win the witch. Once they'd been wed, Bowen had told him, "I learned a lesson—with a mate, *do nothing irrevocable.* There are lines not to be crossed with a female, ones you can never come back from. And *never* for an immortal would suck in this case."

Do nothing irrevocable. But by leaving Sabine bound, Rydstrom was earning her hatred. While he took his revenge, was he doing something she could never forgive? It didn't matter what actually was wrong or right or fair—only *what she believed was.* . . .

As he helped her across another stream, she said, "Why do you even want this kingdom back so badly?"

No one had ever asked him that specifically. Weeks ago, the Valkyrie Nïx had asked him, "Which would you prefer to have? Your queen or your crown?" He often thought back to that night. He'd answered his crown, a choice made so easily.

"It's my birthright," he finally answered. But it hadn't always been. Rydstrom hadn't been raised as the heir of Rothkalina. And as the second son of an immortal king, he'd had no reason to think he'd ever be the ruler.

Fate had had other plans, and Rydstrom had changed his out of necessity. "I want to see my people prosper once more."

"Why?"

"Because I'm their king. Their well-being is my responsibility."

"At least you're honest and not spouting nonsense like 'Because I love them as a father loves his children.'"

Rydstrom feared that he *didn't* love his people—not enough. Sometimes he *resented* them, resented that he was trapped in a never-ending struggle to win a crown that should never have been his.

His older brother, Nylson, and their father, the great king, had gone to battle the Horde. They'd disregarded the custom to separate the king and heir in times of war, and they'd both died.

Leaving Rydstrom as a bewildered young ruler.

After that, he'd burned to get his brother Cadeon, his own successor, out of harm's way, fostering him with another family as soon as he was old enough. Which Cadeon took a nine-hundred-year exception to. . . .

"I also want my home back," Rydstrom added. "To restore it to its former glory." *And to scour it clean.*

Never had he felt at ease like he had at Tornin in ages past. He'd always held on to memories of his family there, of Mia and Zoë playing hide-and-seek with

Cadeon when he was just a pup, of laughter echoing in those great halls.

But once Cadeon was grown, he had ignored Rydtrom's summons to return to the castle and hold it against their foes. Cadeon had chosen to remain with his foster family. Tornin had fallen. . . .

If Rydstrom could win the kingdom back, then maybe some of the strain would fade between him and his siblings.

"Do you think you deserve this kingdom?" Sabine asked.

"It's mine by right."

"Might makes right," she countered. "In any case, were you such a great king that it would be *right* for you to have it back?"

"I believe I was." Of course, he'd only been ruler for very few years.

"You left this kingdom mired in the past. No advances even for the time. No roads, no tolls, no permanent portals connecting Rothkalina with other provinces."

"I didn't have time! I'd been at war with the Horde from the first day of my rule." When that crown had first sat so heavily on his head. "And you forget—many of my kind can trace. Beings shape their world by necessity. There wasn't a need for clunking metal contraptions or blowing up mountains to build roads."

"If you keep the kingdom without arteries, then only those who can teleport can prosper. I'll bet you're feeling the sting of that right now since you can no longer trace."

"Because of Omort," he grated. In the past, Rydstrom had been able to effortlessly trace from Rothkalina to other planes and civilizations. Now he was in his own kingdom, traversing Grave Realm—*by foot*.

Just another reason to slay Omort. With his death, Rydstrom and Cade's ability to trace would be restored.

Sabine continued, "And what about other non-demon beings who might want to make Rothkalina home? You're hardly attracting them to settle here."

"Like the Sorceri?"

"Maybe." She raised her chin. "We're not without talents."

"Rothkalina has a dearth of wine drinkers and slave keepers."

She ignored his sarcastic comment. "Not that they'd want come to this medieval plane anyway. We're merry and the rage demons are stodgy and stuck in old ways."

"Then what's your excuse for wanting to remain?"

"Here there are no Vrekeners and no humans. Demon, even an evil sorceress needs a safe home to call her own."

If you accepted me, I'd give you one. . . .

"It's not like Tornin is a premium castle though," Sabine continued. "Don't you really want to get back in Tornin because of the well's power?"

He tensed. "Do you know what it does?" Because Rydstrom . . . didn't.

"Maybe I do. But don't worry, I won't tell. I like that everyone's imagination runs wild. Some think it's a mystickal prison, a power base, a wish granter. Oh, and that it resurrects the dead. Do *you* even know?"

"I know that my breed of demon was created solely to protect that well. Tornin was constructed to house it. It's my duty to safeguard both."

"And you *always* do your duty. Doesn't it ever get boring? I think that's why you're so attracted to me, because I've shaken your reasonable, rational, ordered life. I'd wager that you've felt more excitement with me in the last week than in centuries."

That hit far too close to home. "And I think I've never known anyone as egotistical as you."

"Egotistical? Try self-confident. Should I be meek instead? Would you like me better then?"

"No. I've never wanted a meek woman for my own. I've wanted a queen—"

"And now you have one."

They carried on in silence as the terrain grew more punishing, leaving him to mull over her words. Even with their history, the fact remained that he had *her*.

The one he'd longed for. . . .

She began lagging behind again. Fortunately, the brush opened up just ahead, revealing a scene below them. The sun blazed down on a clear green pool fed by dozens of cascades.

"Do we have to cross this water, then?" She rubbed her forehead on her shoulder, trying to keep the sweat from her eyes. "I can't swim. Even *if* you released my hands."

He opened his canteen and helped her drink, then took a healthy swallow. "All Lore creatures can swim. It's instinctual."

She gave a bitter laugh. "I can't tell you how wrong that statement is."

"Have you drowned?"

"I don't know how to swim. Never learned. An out-doorswoman I am not."

"Have—you—drowned?" he snapped.

"More—than—once?" she snapped back, her eyes growing blue with anger.

Obviously, this was a sensitive subject with the sorceress. "I'm weary of this, Sabine. You give me hints of what you're like, about your history. Am I supposed to spend the rest of the day wondering if you've drowned? Or why you don't like people touching your face—"

"Sorry I don't feel chatty just now! I'm out of breath and need to rest!"

He shook his head. "We press on—"

"We have to stop! I'm *hurting* here. My arms have been asleep for twenty-four hours. And when was the last time you wore metal against bare skin? There is one reason for this top—to look fabulous. Not to trek through the wilderness. Out here it collects sand, which rubs against my breasts. And they are already far too sensitive because you were forever kissing and sucking on them last night!"

Memories of the night before flashed in his mind, and he stifled a groan. Throughout the day, he'd been recalling with pleasure all the things he'd done to her body—and planning with anticipation what he'd do to her tonight.

The most excitement in centuries? She was right.

"Demon, are you listening to me? This isn't parity. I never kept you in pain or hurt your flesh."

"You're immortal. You'll be healed by sundown—"

"Just take a look at them! They'll be pink and tender. Oh! And I'll bet my face is getting more sunburned!"

It was, which made her freckle across the bridge of her nose, which meant she looked even less like an evil sorceress. *Damn her*. Her body was so fragile, not like other females of the Lore. A Valkyrie or furie would be laughing at a hike over this terrain.

"You want me to fix it?" He unfastened her top, then yanked it off her, dropping it to the ground.

If he'd expected her to gasp and stammer, he'd have been wrong. Instead she sighed, flexing her back and rolling her head on her neck.

Her breasts *were* pink and looked tender. The tips budded right before his eyes. His mouth watered to lick and suckle her—

"Oh, don't you even think about it, demon!"

"You dare act angered with me?" Angered over his desire for her? The very need she'd stoked to a blaze?

Sabine stormed over to him, bare breasted, her hair shining like fire in the sun. "Yes, I *dare*!" She kicked his shin with the metal tip of her boot.

He gritted his teeth. "Do that again, sorceress, and you will not like the outcome."

"I'm beginning to wish I'd ordered more boy-on-boy shower-time for you."

His eyes went wide, then narrowed. "You're aching for your next spanking, aren't you? Keep this up, and I'll oblige you."

"You'd love that, wouldn't you? I think the reason you don't want to release me is because you'd have to part with this anger, and then you couldn't treat me like your sex slave each night. It's so good for you, you can't stand the thought of letting it go."

He cupped her nape. "You might be right."

"Of course I am!" Her eyes were blue, her lips parting around panting breaths. She was so damned sexy, too much so.

He dragged her into his chest. Had she gone up on her toes?

And then they were kissing each other, crazed, frenzied. Like the night he'd claimed her. Taking her trembling mouth was a madness, an addiction. Wringing those little moans and breathless cries . . . he could kiss her forever.

When she subtly arched her back, he groaned, raising his hand to gently pet her tender breasts—

Her stomach growled. Loudly.

He broke the kiss, leaning his forehead to hers as they caught their breath. "We'll stop here for the night, sweet." He took off his tunic, draping it over her front like an apron, then tying the sleeves around her back. "Looks like I need to hunt for my woman."

She rolled her eyes. "I don't need you to hunt, demon, I need you to *gather*."

❧ 26 ❧

"Drop it, Sabine!" Rydstrom bellowed from a lower plateau.

Earlier, he'd set up camp on a high promontory, settled her by a fire, and finally threaded her arms into his tunic—retying her right after, naturally. Then he'd gone all he-man, marching off to snare the unwitting creature he'd just been dressing. Though he'd kept her in sight the entire time, he'd eventually gotten far enough away for her plans.

"Drop—the—wine!" He started charging for her. "Bloody now!"

In response, she maneuvered the bottle neck in her mouth's grasp, tightened her lips, and turned it up, gulping the contents.

"Damn it, Sabine!" he yelled as he ran.

When he reached the campsite, she dropped the emptied bottle with a gasp and took in the sight of him.

His bare chest was heaving, and sweat trickled from his neck. Her eyes followed a bead as it slid down his torso over the ridges of muscle. *Magnificent demon.*

Then she frowned—he was holding a skinned animal of indeterminate species. Take away the animal carcass, and this would be one of the sexiest sights she'd ever seen.

"Do you know what I went through to get the cork out?" she asked him, turning to muffle a lady-like burp against her shoulder. "Then you expect me to go unrewarded? Besides, I can't face the upcoming trial of ritualistic animal abuse without wine."

He sank down on the opposite side of the fire, spitting the poor creature on a stick.

As he secured the little carcass over the flames, she studiously surveyed the scenery. Rydstrom had made their camp high up on a large jutting cliff. Below them the falls trickled into a pool of the darkest green—the color of his eyes. Other cliffs surrounded the water on three sides, and as the wind rushed in, white blossoms danced on the swirling air.

In minutes the smell of roasting meat was pervasive. After the day's arduous journey, she was starving, and the scent wasn't as bad as she'd thought it would be. In fact, it was . . . appetizing.

"It smells *good*, doesn't it, sorceress?"

She turned up her nose. "I won't eat it."

"Just look at it."

Before she could stop herself, she did. Her mouth watered at the sight. It was so succulent, it dripped, making the fire hiss. *No, I'm more refined than this. I don't eat animals!* "You are fully aware that my kind doesn't consume meat."

"You will now."

"Now what? Now that you're the boss?"

His gaze flickered over her belly.

"Ohhh, now that you think I might be carrying your babe. Will you force me to eat it?"

"I didn't cause this situation. Remember that." His tone made her raise her brows. "If your plan worked, and you've gotten yourself pregnant with a demon, you'll need meat to feed it."

"Do you not think that it would make me sick to eat something I never have before? Something I find revolting? Perhaps you should have ascertained if I was high-maintenance before you abducted me."

When her stomach growled again, he rose and snatched up the empty pack. "Do not move, princess. I'll be back with something you might deign to eat."

A short time later, he returned with the pack full, dumping the contents on the blanket. She quirked a brow at a selection of berries. "A male trying to poison me. How . . . novel."

"They aren't poisonous." He scooped up some and popped them into his mouth.

"Not to demons, but they're toxic to me. Because we're not of the same *species*."

"You make it sound like we come from different planets. We're not that different."

"No?" Her gaze flickered over his horns.

He ran his hand over one, then glowered at her. Strangely, she seemed to be exasperating him—but not *angering* him.

She gave a nod at a dirt covered root. "I'm not a bunny, Rydstrom. And is that *bark*?" With a laugh, she said, "Good gods, you brought me bark to gnaw on!"

"How am I supposed to know what you'll eat? You pass up perfectly good food—"

"That animal is not *food*. The Sorceri are too refined to eat other living things."

"You care about animals more than you do about other people."

"You see, that's the thing—cows never try to steal my sorcery and chickens rarely try to murder me. *Why* this is so—I do not know. Just that it is."

"Is there anything here that you can eat?"

"The other berries aren't poisonous." When she gave a nod to indicate them, he rinsed them off with water from the canteen, then returned to sit beside her.

As he fed them to her, she took her time eating. He should be forced to wait for her, since he wouldn't allow her to feed herself.

But he didn't seem to mind her nibbling one berry from his palm at a time. In fact, he seemed to enjoy it. "My new pet's an herbivore," he said with amusement in his husky voice.

Disconcerted by the hint of a smile on his face, she gazed around her once more. "It's cooler up here. Why did we have to go so high?"

"Because most creatures don't."

"You wouldn't have to worry about that if you freed me—I can talk to animals."

"Uh-huh."

"Demon, I'm being quite honest about that. I can speak to them, and they understand me."

"In any case, you won't need that ability. I'll protect you from any threats."

"Threats." As they'd gone deeper into Grave Realm, she'd caught him inspecting paw prints in the clay. She'd seen him rest his hand on his sword hilt. "We're in danger. Great. You've taken me to the most hazardous place in the entire kingdom—home of R.O.U.S.'s and the like—then bound me so that I can't defend myself."

"Rodents of Unusual Size? I don't think they exist."

Her lips parted. He'd quoted *The Princess Bride*.

"Don't be so shocked," he said gruffly. "At the local coven of witches, that movie plays twenty-four-seven. They drink every time they hear *my darling Westley* or something. It's hard to miss."

"Are you often at that coven? Visiting with *the witches?*" She could just imagine how those little magick mercenaries would fawn over the towering demon king. Sabine disliked witches, was wary of them.

"You sound condescending. Aren't the Sorceri related to the witches?"

"Distantly." Though they might have shared ancestors and a love of revelry, and some of their powers were interchangeable—and stealable—the Sorceri were a unique culture, far distinct from the earth-worshipping witches. "So answer my question."

"I've been by a few times," he said. "As you might have seen when you were hacking into my brain, my good friend Bowen is wed to Mariketa the Awaited."

Sabine had heard of that female, but then most in the Lore had. She was the most powerful of the witches, so talented with mirrors she'd achieved the status of Queen of Reflections.

To steal her powers would be a coup. But going up against a strong witch or a coven of them was dangerous. A witch could steal a Sorceri's power—if she killed her. "Ah yes, I remember seeing Bowen. He's the one you're jealous of."

"I wasn't jealous of him—I was envious that he'd found his mate."

"But now you have, too."

"At last, I have."

"Yet you won't release her?"

"She'd run at the first opportunity. Possibly taking my child with her. Both are far too valuable for me to risk losing."

Should I tell him I'm not pregnant? It would only anger him yet again. And now he seemed relaxed for the first time since she'd known him. Even that first night before he'd discovered who she was, he'd been on edge.

She decided she'd keep that knowledge secret for now. The Sorceri weren't known as being guarded for nothing.

When he leaned over and kissed the bridge of her nose, she asked, "What was that for?"

"Your freckles are gone. I told you everything would be healed by sunset." His gaze briefly dipped to her breasts.

She was indeed healed, and the sun was setting, closing another day. She gazed out at the horizon at the last glimmers of light. This meant she had one fewer day until the morsus would strike.

Though she had almost two weeks left, the worry had begun to prey on her.

Contrary to what she'd told the demon, she didn't believe that Omort was coming to save her anytime soon. Rydstrom's escape would rock the Pravus, further jeopardizing the strength of the alliance. And then there was Lothaire's betrayal.

Factions would be bailing left and right, leaving fewer behind to come after her. If the fire demons and vampires weren't available to trace or had never been to this place, then only Lanthe could get to her out in Grave Realm.

But, as Sabine had discovered over the last two days—it was a *big* realm. The odds of Lanthe opening a portal nearby were slim.

And if Rydstrom took Sabine off-plane . . . ?

She was almost spooked enough to consider telling him why she was in danger. But she could just imagine explaining the morsus to him.

"By the way, I'm going to have to take a U-turn and run back to Omort, your most hated enemy, because I've been poisoned. By whom? Oh, Omort himself. Once I find a way to get back to my brother, I'm going to beg him to give me even more of the poison I've been taking. Is there any proof of my poisoning? Outward signs? Um, none. Not until I have an epileptic-like seizure and begin vomiting blood. And no outwardly identifiable marks, not until I am officially

dying. Then you'll see a red X somewhere on my body. But by that time, it will be too late."

The demon wouldn't likely believe her, and she couldn't think of a vow he'd accept as true. Perhaps breaking hers so routinely when she'd first captured him hadn't been advisable.

But how was I supposed to have known to act like my word was good?

The only thing she could do would be to create a clay covenant between them. But she didn't see a kiln or an oven forthcoming in Grave Realm.

Exactly how bad was his mistrust? She'd make a foray to see. . . . "Rydstrom, if I were to tell you something that sounded crazy, and asked you to believe me, could you possibly—"

"No."

"You don't even want to think about—"

"No."

"What would it take for you to trust me? A vow? Some kind of promise?"

"It will come, Sabine. I believe that. But only with time."

Time that I don't have.

Even if she could eventually convince him, she didn't have *eventually*. Her only hope was to get him to untie her—and to run, to try locating Lanthe in this place. If the sisters got close enough to each other, they could communicate telepathically.

Which was a good thing, since Sabine had zero sense of direction. She frowned. But so did Lanthe.

She mentally waved that detail away. They'd figure something out.

So the first step was beguiling Rydstrom to free her. That shouldn't be a problem. Sabine was an enchantress. She could seduce him to do her will.

The scene was set: the stars were feverishly bright and the moon heavy. Small ripples in the water below them caught the moonlight, reflecting in patterns of emerald shimmers.

Yes, I can be seductive. The demon wouldn't know what hit him when she turned on the charm. . . .

Once he'd eaten his catch—with exaggerated relish—and cleaned up the food, she waited a bit, commenting on the night and weather, then said, "My arms ache, Rydstrom." She flexed her fists for effect. "They've been asleep for so long."

When he gave her an appraising glance, she probed to read his mind, but he had those blocks firmly in place.

"I have a deal for you," he said. "If you answer any questions I ask, I'll free your arms for an hour."

She just stopped her lips from curling. *Well, that was easier than I'd figured.* "You have a deal, demon."

❧ 27 ❧

This wasn't part of the deal!" the sorceress screeched when Rydstrom waded into the pool. "You didn't say anything about water!"

Though he cupped her ass, holding her up, she'd locked her legs tightly around his waist. Gods, she fit into his palms like she'd been made for him to hold her like this.

He was headed to a rock island he'd spied from aloft. Situated in the middle of the pool, it had a shallow bar circling it and was surrounded by deep water. "I won't untie you anywhere else. This way you won't use your illusions to escape me—unless you want to swim back by yourself."

"Swim! I've told you I can't swim! I don't like deep water!"

"Exactly." Earlier, when he'd told her his intention, she'd tried to fight him, tussling against him as he'd stripped her. But to no avail. He had an agenda and wouldn't be moved from it.

This morning, he'd realized that to win some kind of affection from the sorceress, he would have to change his tactics with her.

When he'd gone hunting, he'd recalled that dream of his yet again. And he'd mused that if Bowen had used his head to win his witch, Rydstrom would do no less for Sabine. He would figure out how to make it work between them.

But first he had to understand her to determine the right way to garner her affection. To do that, he needed to earn her trust.

The puzzle of her . . . the challenge of *them* . . . Rydstrom was up for it—and he was committed.

Once he'd waded in up to his chest, she cried, "Go back, go back! What if you slip?" She was quaking.

"I won't slip, sweet. Look, we're here." The pool grew shallow again. At the island, he set her to her feet in knee-high water.

Her gaze darted all around her. "You can't understand how horrific I find this."

Probably as horrific as I'd found my court.

"Sit there." He pointed to a long, low rock. When she reluctantly did, he sat behind her, untying only the line that went between her rope cuffs. He set it beside him, keeping it within easy reach.

At once, she stretched her arms above her head, turning them this way and that. "What about these?" she asked, scratching at the rope still on her wrists.

"They stay."

"What? They itch like crazy!"

"They—stay."

She seemed to bite her tongue against a sharp reply, instead saying, "As you wish."

To reward her cooperation, he began massaging her shoulders. She moaned, and her head dropped forward, her long hair parting over her neck. When her pale nape was left uncovered, he was helpless not to kiss it.

Her breath hitched in, and she shivered.

He kneaded her upper arms all the way down to her fingertips, then continuing back up. "Better?"

"Hmm? Oh, yes, better."

"Then it's time for questions."

"Ask me, then."

"How many times have you died?"

She tensed beneath his palms, but answered, "Over a dozen."

"What's it . . . like?"

"The most terrifying, wretched feeling you can imagine."

"Tell me about one time."

"A Vrekener had flown me high above a village, then dropped me. I was lying on a cobblestone street with my skull cracked open." Her tone grew distant. "You can feel your blood seeping out. Without the blood, the body gets so *cold*, but then, if it pools around you, it's like a warm blanket, for a few moments at least."

He couldn't be hearing this . . . that she'd been *thankful* for a pool of blood.

"Rydstrom," she murmured. His hands were squeezing her too hard.

He let up the pressure. "Why would they hurt you like that?"

"Because I killed their leader. The Vrekeners were responsible for many of my deaths. Including one of the drownings."

"One of the . . . ?" He shook himself. "When we get off-plane I will seek them out and inform them that you and your sister are under my protection. Any move against either of you will be considered an act of war against my kind."

She turned to kneel before him, laying her delicate hands on his knees. "You'd do that?"

"You're my female—I will never let anyone hurt you." He brushed her face, and she scarcely flinched. "Since your sister helped keep you alive, I'm indebted to her as well. Is she the black haired female who was in the cell after my injury?"

"Yes, her name's Melanthe. She's got to be so worried about me."

"If there's an avian messenger among the refugees, we'll send word to her that you are unharmed."

Sabine looked confused by him, then she smiled—a genuine, heart-wrenching smile.

It made his chest tight with feeling. "You couldn't be more beautiful."

She sighed, "*I know,*" making his lips quirk. Then she added, "You're not too shabby yourself. In fact, I think you're the most handsome male I've ever seen."

He exhaled. "Why do you always have to lie?"

"All right, you're not *the* most handsome. But you're in the top ten. Maybe even in the top three."

"As long as I made the podium."

"I do love your body. You're an exceedingly well-made male." She began touching him as if she was seeing him for the first time, sweeping her soft palms over his chest, shoulders, and neck.

When she brushed kisses along the scar on his face, she said, "How did you get this?"

"From a sword fight. When I was young, I was a brawler. That's how I broke my horn, too."

"You weren't always so calm and steady?" When he shook his head, she asked, "And the tattoo?"

"It was part of my rite of passage, to be marked with the image of a beast."

"And the scars down . . . here?" She grazed the backs of her fingers along his shaft.

Her touches were setting his blood on fire, but he strove to keep control. He had an agenda, and he was playing to win *everything* from this woman.

His voice was hoarse when he said, "Another part of the ritual. All demon males who reached a certain age had to complete it. Until I denounced it."

"Why did you?"

"Because it hurt like hell."

"I could have kissed it better." She grinned. The wine was definitely hitting her.

"I think I like my sorceresses drunken." It made it easier to get the puzzle pieces he needed most, for example, "How is it that you were a virgin?"

"I was saving myself for you," she said easily, but he was beginning to better detect her lies.

"No, you weren't."

She shrugged. "I claimed *sanctuary* on my body. It's a Sorceri covenant that holds that if I remained virginal, then no man could force me into having sex with him."

"Like Omort?" he bit out, his horns beginning to straighten with rage.

"I don't want to speak of him tonight. And my reasons are my own." She gazed at his horns, then glanced her fingers along one. "What it's like when you start to go demonic?"

He let the subject of her virginity drop. "I don't like it."

"Why? Your body has so much more strength—"

"And it's diverted away from my brain. It's as if I'm burning on pure instinct, like a rabid animal. I can't think. I can't reason. Thoughts come more randomly." He ran his hand over his jaw. "I hear my heartbeat drumming so loudly that I can't hear a conversation nearby. And yet I can detect a leaf crackling a half a mile away. Nothing makes sense. Which is really difficult for me."

"Because you're such a slave to reason?"

"Exactly. You could be telling me something perfectly logical, but if it went counter to my instinct, my brain would discard it." He tapped his temple to emphasize his point. "And, Sabine, you seem to keep me on the edge of it. That's a very uneasy place to be."

"Why do I?"

"I took you, but I didn't mark you. Which means I haven't truly claimed you. The demon in me is not *satisfied*."

"What would it be like if you marked me?"

"If I got to that state, I would be completely turned, which is rare for our kind. Once I was inside you, I'd sink my fangs into your neck, and it would stun you."

"*Stun* me?"

"Some say it's to keep the female steady while the male comes in her."

"Oh," she said, her voice breathy. "And if you did that to me, you would be less likely to get *unreasonable*?"

"It would help. But still, I feel no bond coming from you. As much as I would like you to feel more for me, I know that you don't."

"What if I told you that I've decided to stay with you?" She gave him one of those tender, coaxing kisses that made him wild for her, but he forced himself to pull away.

Rydstrom knew what she was doing. *Seduce the demon to that mindless state.* To get him to do what she wanted. But what she didn't understand was that he expected these games from her.

And he liked them.

"Kingly Rydstrom, holding yourself off from everyone and everything," she said softly. "But you won't with me. I've decided to willingly go with you."

"Have you, then? Why's that?"

"Because, lonely demon, you need me so much. And because you're my husband."

He stifled a wince. Not her husband. *But I will be.* "You say that only so I'll leave you untied."

"Yes, I want that." She took one of his hands and rubbed her silky cheek against the palm. "But that doesn't mean what I'm saying isn't true."

Her words made him again remember the dream of them sharing their lives, sharing a bed, raising a son. If she was pregnant and escaped . . .

He didn't want to admit it even to himself, but part of the reason he kept her bound was because he *had* started to believe they might have a future. *Another conflict within me.* Because he couldn't keep her tied forever.

"I want to stay with you," she murmured, her lips inches from his.

She was playing him. Rydstrom knew it. Yet that didn't mean he didn't enjoy hearing this. "Say it again."

"I want to be with you."

"Again."

"I don't want to part from you. Take me to your home, the place where you live off-plane. I'm not going to try to escape from you. I wish to remain with you."

He stared into her eyes, needing to trust her. But he couldn't. Not yet.

"I brought you out here for another reason," the demon said.

"What's that?" Sabine asked lazily, gazing at him. Had she been one of those women who sighed, she would have now.

His black hair was tousled, his green eyes rapt on her face. His skin was damp and sheened in the moonlight. *Such a gorgeous male.*

And he was surprising her again and again. His promise of protection not only for her, but also for Lanthe affected her so much. She believed he would give his life if necessary to fulfill his promise.

Regrettably, he couldn't save her from the morsus. Only two people in the universe could—

"You need to learn how to swim," he said.

"What? No way! I panic in the water. This is the calmest I've ever been—"

"Then this is a good time to learn." He stood to swoop her up in his arms, then waded in deeper.

"Rydstrom, no!"

"Just trust me, Sabine. All I want you to do is get used to the water. Just float."

Maybe if she acted as if she trusted him, he might extend the courtesy? "What do you want me to do?"

"Stretch out on my hands." Even with her body stiff with tension, he maneuvered her easily. Soon she was lying flat on his palms. "Let go . . . trust me."

"I *can't*."

"You can—you're already doing it."

"I'm . . . floating?"

"I'm not holding you up, just in place. That's it, just breathe easy. Good girl." His voice was soothing, his big hands her anchor. "Relax."

That peculiar watery silence surrounded her. Above her, blossoms swirled in the moonlight. Her hair tickled her shoulders. He continued caressing her back, and soon she did relax.

Her lids slid closed. *Peaceful. Perfect.* . . .

When she opened her eyes, she found him studying her face. The possessiveness in his gaze made her breath hitch. "My naked body is spread out before you, and you're looking at my face?"

"I'm trying to figure out how your mind works. If I can do that, then this"—he trailed his fingers between her breasts and lower—"will always be mine to enjoy."

"Do you really believe that?"

"I have to, Sabine." When she shivered, he said, "Time to go in." After easing her back to the shoal, he helped her to her feet, then reached for the rope he'd left on the rock.

"What are you doing? You're not going to retie me?"

He snagged her wrists. "Of course I am."

"Why? I thought we'd come to an understanding." He was unbending, even though she resisted. "Rydstrom! How long will you keep me bound like this?"

"Until I know you won't run."

"You're bull-headed, unreasonable—"

"Cautious."

She was livid that her plan hadn't worked. "And now you're getting that look in your eyes! Oh, I know what's coming! If you torment me for another night, I will hate you!"

With his gaze narrowed, he nodded. "I know how that feels, wanting to hate, drawing on it. The only thing that got me through my own rage was vowing revenge. Did you never think I'm able to be gentle with you now because my wrath is placated in other ways?"

"All this was a sham!"

He gave a humorless laugh. "Of course it was! I'm well aware that you were playing me—"

"No, a sham on *your* part! You cajole me to give you my trust, but you won't even consider giving your own!"

"Give *you* my trust? How easily you forget all that you did to me. By keeping me from my brother, you might have destroyed my chances of ever reclaiming Tornin, my home. I vowed revenge, Sabine. I need it, I need you to surrender to me!"

When he lifted her from the water, cradling her to his chest, she kicked at him, squirming, but his hold was like a steel cage.

"Demon, don't. No more of this *tormenting* me!"

He ignored her, ferrying her to shore, then started the ascent to their camp—heading to that pallet, where he would do *things* to her all night.

Once they reached it, he let her slide down his naked body. He grasped her upper arms, keeping her in place as he kissed her neck.

She just prevented her head from falling back. "Demon . . . don't make me weak . . ."

"You make *me* weak." Against her damp skin, he rasped, "Surrender to me, and we can end this. Sabine, I want you so bad." She could feel his hard length pressing against her.

"Not bad enough to break your word."

"One day, you'll be glad you have a man who keeps his word. You gave me unbearable nights. You'll get them as well. I vowed—"

"Save the explanation—you *like* this. You're keeping me tied just because it turns you on!"

"I've explained that I can't risk losing you."

"You're taking fifteen centuries of denial out on me!"

"Maybe what you're saying is true in part. I do like having you at my mercy. I crave driving you mad, as you were last night. Do you know what that does to me to see your eyes go blue with lust—for me? To see fires burning all around us?"

He rubbed his face against hers, inhaling her scent. "I've never felt things like this, and I want *more*," he growled at her ear. "You are my obsession, Sabine. I've heard every male has one in his life. And you are mine."

"Release me!"

"*Surrender to me. . . .*"

Between gritted teeth, she said, "If you don't let me go, I'll hate you. I vow I'll kill you!"

He dragged her down to the pallet. "Ah, but my beautiful captive doesn't keep her vows."

❧ 28 ❧

"Would you care for any child of ours?" he asked her when he had her clasped in his arms, ready for sleep in the chill night. His hand slipped under the tunic and inside her skirt to rest on her flat belly. "Demon or no?"

She drowsily murmured, "Unless he was a miserable tool like you." Then she drifted off.

Miserable tool. What if he were killing something between them with each of his actions? *Do nothing irrevocable.* And yet tonight she'd screamed, "*I hate you. . . .*"

Over the long hours that he'd teased her, keeping her on the brink of release, she'd never surrendered to him.

She'd been out of her head, her body writhing in a frenzy. She'd rolled her hips, enticing him to break his vow. When he'd beheld her beautiful sex, glistening to be filled . . . nothing had ever excited him more.

But now the two nights were done. Tomorrow, he'd get her to surrender completely, and he'd take her once more. Then he would get control of himself. He had to.

Troubled and plagued with uncertainties, he finally fell asleep.

Toward dawn, Rydstrom blinked open his eyes and found himself deep within an illusion. Sabine was casting chimeras in her sleep. Were these her *dreams*?

"Heat it, stroke it, beat and grow it. Rub it, twist it, love and kiss it," a woman chanted as she ran a fistful of gold chains against her cheek. This was the female voice from the night before—now he could see her.

She wore a silk mask around harried blue eyes. Her headdress stretched out behind her head a foot on each side, the extensions like wings, each crammed with sapphires. Her jet-black hair was tangled beneath it.

"Gold is life. It is perfection. The element exists solely for us." Once she dropped the chains into a laden chest on her dresser, she dug her hands down into piles of coins, letting them pour through her fingers.

When she turned to the mirror, Rydstrom could see two girls in the reflection, one with red hair, and one with black. They were Sabine and Melanthe, both so young, watching her in wide-eyed fascination. This woman was their mother. And she was clearly mad. . . .

"Band it in armor over thy heart, and never will thy life's blood part. Gild your hair and face and skin, and no man breathes that you can't win. Never too much can a sorceress steal, those who defend"—her face went cold—"she duly kills."

The Sorceri worship gold, Sabine had told him. He'd thought it had been an excuse for greed, but she believed it was more. Recalling her look when he'd thrown her headdress into the water, he ran a hand over his mouth.

I will buy her new ones, buy her thousands of them . . .

When Sabine's eyes darted behind her lids, and she made faint cries, Rydstrom reached for her shoulder to wake her, but drew back his hand as a new scene appeared.

A nightmare. Literally.

On a blustery night, Sabine was standing at the edge of a pit, with women lined up on each side of her. She looked to be merely fourteen or fifteen.

A male in black robes stood before her, flanked by followers with pitchforks. He asked her in Latin to recant her evil ways.

Donning the smirk Rydstrom knew so well, she spit in his face. The man backhanded her, hurtling her into the pit—no, a grave.

My gods. The followers stabbed the other women with pitchforks until each one had fallen atop her. Shovelfuls of earth began to build, the weight crushing her. She couldn't get enough air. . . .

An eternity seemed to pass before a dim voice called from the surface. Her sister. "Rise up, Abie! Climb and heal!"

Bile rose in Rydstrom's throat as Sabine mindlessly dug past the bodies, blindly climbing for that voice, until her sister could pull her free of the grave.

No wonder Sabine was so hard. He'd only thought about her treacheries, never comprehending that she'd been dealt with in kind.

If she hadn't been hard, she would be . . . dead. And

then he wouldn't have her with him now. Would he curse the very traits that had kept her alive to be with him?

No. No longer.

In the illusion, the rain poured as she fell to her knees, vomiting earth. Lanthe knelt beside her, rubbing her back. When the rain washed away the filth from Sabine's hair, Lanthe picked up the new white lock and wept. . . .

His fists clenched as a seething fury rose in him. He needed to fight for Sabine, to defend the girl who would grow to be his woman. *I would give anything to go back and spare her that—*

Suddenly, his ears twitched at an unidentifiable sound. He inhaled the night air and caught foreign scents nearby. He finally heard footfalls rushing toward them, but when he scanned the area, all he could see was her dream. "Sabine!" He shook her. "Wake up!"

He was blinded to reality by her illusion. "Sabine, damn you, wake—"

Sabine woke to a roar as a battle hammer connected with Rydstrom's skull.

The demon flew back, blood spurting from his head. At least seven armed Teegloths were attacking, grotesque half-man, half-beast beings with protruding bottom fangs and reptilian skin.

She lunged to reach Rydstrom, but one tossed her across the clearing. Dazed on the ground, she rubbed her eyes on her shoulder, blinking repeatedly. She was completely vulnerable, couldn't protect herself with her illusions. Couldn't help Rydstrom . . .

He was still conscious! As he struggled to rise, one told him, "We take the female now." He spit the words.

"Not while I live." Rydstrom had maneuvered closer to her. "Get behind me."

She rose unsteadily, tripping toward him. She didn't reach Rydstrom before they descended on him.

As he dodged their swinging battle hammers, they drove him back to the cliff's edge. A cudgel connected with his arm, crushing it. The pick end of another hammer slashed over his thigh.

When his leg buckled, and his knees met the ground, the edge began to crumble, the rock splintering beneath him.

Just before it collapsed, he caught her eyes. *"Coming for you."*

In a rush of dust and spraying rock, he disappeared.

"Rydstrom!" she screamed, rushing to the edge. *Oh, gods! Too dark . . . can't see him!*

But she reminded herself that he was a formidable demon—not a Sorceri. He could live through this and more.

She rounded on them. "Why did you attack us? Have you been sent for me?" Maybe Omort had posted a bounty?

"Our land. You trespassed," one said, as he began ransacking Rydstrom's bag, stealing goods, taking his sword. He was the largest, which meant he would likely be the leader. "You to slave market."

Slave market? They didn't know she was one of the Sorceri—she wasn't demonstrating powers, nor was she dressed like one. She had no jewelry, and the blue tassels on her belt didn't necessarily look like gold.

Do I tell them I'm a princess of Omort's realm or the queen of the demon king?

She had better do something fast. The Teegloths weren't just slave traders. They were trophy collectors, with the body parts of their enemies affixed to their crude leather vests. Fingers and scalps adorned them. One had only ears on his vest, and he was staring at hers with intent in his beady eyes.

"I'm sister to Omort of Rothkalina. By law, you must ransom me."

"Ransom—sell as slave. Naught different," he said, his speech pattern primitive.

She'd heard about the slave markets, the ones Omort had allowed to proliferate, for a percentage of the gold. "That was King Rydstrom you just attacked, and I'm his wife. He will find me. And when he feasts on your throats, I will pat him on the head."

Another asked, "Ties up wife?"

"It's a game we play. I couldn't expect something like you to understand it."

He slapped her.

She staggered, her mouth filling with blood. When she spat at him, he struck her twice as hard, until her vision wavered and she reeled on her feet. He hauled her up, tossing her over his shoulder. Dawn was just breaking as the pack set out. . . .

Hours later, Sabine still had seen no sign of Rydstrom—or of any other beings who might aid her.

Why wasn't she succumbing to that cold fury she knew so well? Where was the nausea, the urgency? When she recognized what was happening, she was disgusted with herself.

I expect Rydstrom to save me.

With her bound hands, she reached for the back of her belt, plucking a gold tassel, dropping it for him to follow. She hoped he appreciated that she was shedding gold for him. *But the do-gooder probably wouldn't!* He'd tossed away her headdress like an apple core!

By dusk, she was convinced that every ounce of blood in her body resided in her head. She'd also accepted the fact that Rydstrom might not be coming for her. His injuries had been severe—*before* he'd fallen.

Now, fear threatened to overwhelm her. And that fear wasn't only for herself.

In the dying sunlight, sand gave way to rock as they neared another mountain. Ah, gods, they took her *inside* it, down into a pitch-black mine.

For hours, she could see nothing, could only hear their breathing and grunting words as they continued deep within.

At last, the Teegloth dropped her on her ass in the dark, and she heard them scuttling about around her.

They started a fire, and as soon she could see once more, she almost wished she couldn't. While they tore into their dinner—bones and bloody meat—they eyed her with renewed interest.

She surveyed the area, searching for any means to escape. They were in a central terminus of mine shafts, an area where three corridors ended. This mine looked just like what she would imagine, with beam ceiling supports and track laid out.

But there were no leftover picks or shovels for her to run her bindings against. And Rydstrom's sword was out of reach, lying among their belongings haphazardly pilled at the edge of the camp.

Once they'd finished eating, the leader wasted no time, dragging her off to the side, then yanking her beneath him. She couldn't fight back—already bound for them.

More powerless than I've been since I was a girl.

A ropy line of saliva hung from the corner of his deformed mouth, inching toward her face as he ripped her tunic to shreds. . . .

❧ 29 ❧

Rydstrom came to in a rush, grappling to free himself from the rocks that had fallen over him. Once loose, he lumbered to his feet, every movement grueling.

Staggering with dizziness from his head wound, he scented the night air for her while assessing the damage to his body: severed muscles in one leg, broken ribs and collarbone. One arm fractured. Skull possibly cracked—

He caught a hint of her scent to the south.

Like a shot he sprinted in that direction, favoring his good leg, ignoring the pain as he began the most important pursuit of his life. For miles Rydstrom charged ever closer to her.

He hadn't known if the Teegloths had been sent by Omort to return her, hadn't known if she would willingly go with them. But the way she'd screamed his name when he'd fallen . . .

And then he'd begun finding gold tassels each time the Teegloths crossed water, or traveled in creek beds.

When Rydstrom realized she wanted to be found by him, his excitement was quickly extinguished by dread. If the Teegloths hadn't been sent to find her as a bounty, then they would feel free to use her.

They were taking her toward a chain of mountains, likely to the mine shafts within. Their habitat.

He wiped blood and sweat from his eyes, somehow increasing his speed. Sheer will forced his muscles to obey, and soon he'd reached an entrance to the mines. He charged inside, descending into the core of the mountain.

Suddenly, her shriek echoed in the dark. His heart dropped even as he bolted in the direction of the sound. . . .

With a furious scream, Sabine head-butted the Teegloth. He slapped her, leaving her gasping on her side, her eyes watering.

And that was when she caught a glimpse of Rydstrom stealing out from the shadows. He'd lived!

As he stalked closer, his horns flared with aggression, his muscles seeming to grow before her very eyes. At the edge of the firelight, he silently collected his sword.

When the leader pawed her, rolling her over once more, she hissed, "Teegloth, you're going to pose a question, and get beheaded before it's answered."

He roared, *"What you talk of?"*

She only smiled as Rydstrom swung his sword.

"You took the wrong demon's wife," she told the severed head as she clambered away from its corpse.

With the death of their leader, the others howled with a furor. Rydstrom put himself between her and the pack. "Stay back!"

When they attacked, sweeping those hammers at him, he used his sword and claws against them. One tried to take him from behind, but he threw his head back, poisoning it with his horns.

He took hits that would have felled trees, but still he remained standing. Even injured, he was too strong for them to defeat. She watched in awe as the ruthless demon fought, lit by fire and cloaked in shadows from the mine.

Husband. Gods, he was amazing. *He's fighting for me.* No one but Lanthe had ever fought for Sabine, never, no matter how much she'd needed them to—

One slammed Rydstrom's massive body into a roof support. The shaft seemed to quake all around them. She couldn't scramble up swiftly enough with her hands behind her back.

When the immense beam began to splinter, she screamed Rydstrom's name.

With a roar, he took her by the waist and tossed her out of the way—just as the ceiling of the mine collapsed, boulders plummeting around him and the remaining Teegloths.

Nothing but dust. Again she was helpless, coughing, only able to wait. Would he make it out?

Waiting . . . Heartbeat, heartbeat. *Damn it, stupid demon, don't die! Don't—*

Rydstrom lurched out of the haze. He was bleeding freely from dozens of injuries, his breaths ragged. Brows drawn with feeling, he dropped to his knees before her, still demonic, staring into her eyes.

She was overcome with relief that he'd lived and with gratitude that he'd saved her.

Then she remembered that she was one of the most powerful Sorceri ever born.

This damsel in distress could have defeated this entire pack in moments. Except her husband had bound and tied her and made her *vulnerable*.

He clasped her in his arms so tightly, she almost cried out. She *felt* when a sound was wrenched from his chest—part growl, part groan.

Warm . . . safe . . . *furious?* She futilely resisted him, cursing him. He said nothing, just clutched her, cupping her head to his chest, keeping her there with his big palm.

She was infuriated that any of this had happened at all when it could have been avoided. By keeping her tied, he'd risked her life.

But was she more angry that she'd been jeopardized—or because *he*'d been?

He finally drew back, his gaze flickering over her, assessing her injuries. His eyes darkened at every bruise. When he eased her skirt up, his Adam's apple worked in his throat as if he dreaded what he might find.

"They didn't rape me. No thanks to you."

He took deep breaths, wrestling for control, and his demonic visage receded.

When he smoothed blood from her lips, she flinched from his hand.

"Sabine, I'm here—"

"And I'm *beaten*. Trussed up like a present for their convenience."

He took a swath from the ripped tunic and tied it over her breasts, then he scanned the camp for their belongings. He left her side only to retrieve her boots. "If they intended to sell you as a slave, they wouldn't have struck your face, unless moved by anger."

"Yes, I taunted them. Therefore, they had every right to hit me! Right?"

He returned with her boots, then pulled them on her. "*Why* did you taunt them?"

Without looking at him, she muttered, "Because it felt good," repeating his own answer when asked why he'd goaded Omort.

"More might come." Rydstrom helped her to her feet. "We have to leave this place."

"You're not going to free me?" There was a hysterical note to her voice.

"You are angry that you were vulnerable. I should have been more vigilant."

"Damn you, Rydstrom, you won't release me even after this? I was defenseless! You saved me, yes, but you put me in this situation in the first place. Just like when I saved you from Omort, after bringing you into Tornin. Are you happy, demon? To get your parity once more?"

"Happy?" he snapped. "If anything had happened to you. . . . Damn it, I will be more watchful. I won't sleep."

"The Teegloths aren't the only threats out here," she said. "There are beasts from legend. As you know, I could drown."

"I also know that you'll run away from me at the earliest opportunity." When she shook her head to deny it, he said, "There's not a doubt in my mind! Every word you've said about wanting to stay with me was a lie. Now we don't have time for this. I won't be moved from my decision—and we need to get out of these mines before more come."

His tone brooked no argument, and when he grabbed her arm to hasten her from this place, she let him lead her.

They continued on, limping through the murky tunnel for what seemed like miles, until they reached the surface at last.

A new landscape greeted them. High bluffs overlooked green hills that were dotted with trees. The late afternoon sun blazed above them, and the wind gusted. More terrain, more stumbling, more misery.

Enough. She yanked her arm from his grasp. Sabine—never a patient person in the best of circumstances—had hit her limit.

She simply . . . stopped.

"Come on, keep up. We're near them. I can sense it."

"Enough, demon."

"What?"

She sat, then drew her knees to her chest. "I'm sunburned, bruised, hungry. I've been sexually tormented for two days. No metal guarded my hair, neck, or chest during a *mine collapse*. You took down my braids so my dusty hair continually blows into my eyes. And I can't move it! On top of all this—I was kidnapped by monsters to be sold into slavery!"

And I'd feared for the demon's life, at times more than my own. What was happening to her?

"I'm not going any farther, not until you free me."

"Sabine, get this through your head. There's no way I'm letting you go. If for no other reason, you could be carrying my babe!" Had his shoulders straightened? Proudly?

"That's impossible."

"Yes, we were together only once, but it could happen."

"There is no babe—I'm not pregnant!"

"How can you know?"

"I knew days after," she said. "The Hag can tell that quickly."

"And you let me think you might be carrying? Another lie!"

"Why *wouldn't* I let you think that? I had no idea what your plans for me entailed!"

"Every day you teach me not to trust you."

"You know what? You had better keep me bound, because if I get free I—will—take—you—out! I am *done.* You're going to have to carry me because I'm not moving."

"You think I won't?" He yanked her up.

"I'm sick of you!" she yelled in his face. "Sick of being treated like this! And to think I'd worried—" She bit her tongue.

"To think you'd done what? Ah, sorceress, were you worried about *me?*" he asked in a scoffing tone. Then his eyes narrowed as he studied her face. "You *were.*"

"Ha! I was only worried about my own skin," she said, but she'd darted her gaze. *Damn him, he knows I'm lying.* So she kicked him. "Now let me go!"

He tangled his hands in her hair, grasping the back of her head. They were both still out of breath. She was staring at his lips, licking her own. When she took her gaze off his mouth, she found his eyes were focused on her own lips.

They were about to do that frantic kissing thing again, and she didn't know if she was strong enough to fight it—

"*Hello!*" a voice called from a distance. "*Is someone out there?*"

The refugees had found them.

❊ 30 ❊

Rage demons were *everywhere.*

By sunset, she and Rydstrom had followed a pair of demons—camp guards—until they'd reached a bluff overlooking a sea of tents spread out below.

When the guards had come upon them earlier, the two had wanted to know what they were doing outside the boundaries "when there are beasties about."

Rydstrom had merely demanded to be taken to whoever was in charge. He'd been shirtless and still had blood on him, but he was outwardly—if not calm—then at least *stable.*

Now, as she and Rydstrom trailed the guards down into the camp, through a crowd of what must be hundreds, Sabine stared around her.

The demons stared back. Whispers sounded, females glaring at her lack of clothing. The women here apparently favored excessive clothing—unnecessarily long sleeves and skirts.

A lesser sorceress would have been discomfited by

the fact that she wore a swath of cloth, a micromini, and sand—and had her hands tied. Sabine glanced around, her demeanor bored.

When males leered at her body, Rydstrom's hand fisted on her arm, his horns already straightening.

As she surveyed her surroundings, Sabine had to exhale in exasperation. *Medieval castle, and kingdom, and people.* Why should she be surprised that this place looked to be straight out of a Renaissance fair?

The "housing" consisted of pavilion tents, each with elaborate valances hanging from the roofs and topped with pennants flying aloft. She recognized several of the noble families' colors. These demons had come from all over the kingdom.

The guards took them to a sizable round pavilion. Inside, well-dressed males milled about, clearly noblemen.

One asked Rydstrom, "What were you doing outside the boundaries? Everyone has been informed of the dangers of this place."

"We aren't part of this group. We came from outside."

"Well, we've no more room here," the man said. "We can barely feed everyone as it is."

"Make room. I'm Rydstrom, your *king*."

Instant silence was followed by an uproar.

—*"Rydstrom hasn't been back to this plane in centuries!"*

—*"But the scar . . . ?"*

—*"There were rumors he'd been captured by a sorceress."*

Sabine said, "Only *a* sorceress? Try *the* sorceress—"

"I *am* your king," Rydstrom spoke over her. "And I grow weary of this."

"It's true," a woman's voice said from the back. "He's Rydstrom." A demoness strode forward. She was beautiful, with long chestnut brown hair and petite horns that shone with health. Ah, but she was a pastel-wearer. She was forever dead to Sabine.

Rydstrom narrowed his eyes at the female. "Do I know you?"

She seemed taken aback. "I . . . yes, you do. I'm Durinda. I was a lady-in-waiting to one of your sisters at Tornin." A young demon boy of maybe six years peeked out from behind her too-long skirts. "And this is Puck." She ruffled his blonde hair. "He was my best friend's son."

Puck was missing a baby fang, and he stared at Sabine with owl eyes. Which seemed to distress this Durinda, because she sent him outside at once.

Sabine had just become the pink elephant in the room. When their gazes fell as one on her, Rydstrom said, "My prisoner, Sabine. From Castle Tornin."

Jaws dropped, and another uproar sounded.

—"*Omort's sister?*"

—"*The Queen of Illusions?*"

—"*She'll kill us all in our sleep!*"

Sabine jerked her chin up at Rydstrom. "So now I'm only your prisoner? Why didn't you introduce me as—"

"*Silence.*" His grip on her arm made her wince and keep her mouth shut, for now.

Rydstrom asked the apparent lead noble, "Is this where the portals off-plane will open?"

"Yes, my liege," the man answered. "In four days."

Sabine noticed then that Durinda seemed spellbound by Rydstrom's muscular chest. There was something in that demoness's eyes that made Sabine step closer to him, leaning her body into his so much that he frowned down at her.

Sabine might not be keeping her husband, but for now, Rydstrom was *hers*, and Sabine had never learned how to share.

Durinda said, "I'm sure you're fatigued from your journey, my liege. You can have my tent, and we'll find a place for . . . *her*."

"She stays with me," he commanded.

Durinda's face paled at his fierce tone. "O-of course."

Sabine said, "Durinda, we accept your hospitality." *As our due*.

Though the demoness's shoulders stiffened, she showed them to a spacious tent. The canvas was colored a subdued blue with a steel gray fringe on the valances. Tracery scrolled over the sides. The effect was striking—and denoted wealth.

Inside, the color scheme continued. A pallet in the corner was gray, with lush quilts in blue. Paper lanterns decorated with matching tracery hung from the roof supports.

Sabine's pavilion would be bold crimson and jet with a gold fringe. *Real* gold. *Because I'm worth it*.

The demoness removed some bags, then hesitated at the entrance flap.

In her crispest tone, Sabine said, "That will be all, Durinda."

With an indignant huff, she whirled around.

As soon as the flap closed, Rydstrom said, "Do you have to act like that?"

Sabine rounded on him. "Yes. As a matter of fact." *She was ogling my husband!*

"She's doing us a kindness by letting us sleep here."

"No, she's *not*. They believe you're their *king*, which means that this tent and anything in this camp and in the whole bloody kingdom is *yours*. Since I'm your queen, that means all is mine as well. Why would I show gratitude to people for giving me what's already mine?"

When he began dousing the lanterns, she said, "And why didn't you tell them I'm wed to you?"

After all she'd put up with, he wouldn't even acknowledge her as his queen? She couldn't help recalling Omort's words. *How disappointed the demon must be. . . .*

Was Rydstrom shamed to claim her as his wife? "People will find out. You might as well admit that we're wed."

"Sabine, we're both injured and exhausted," he said, capturing her hand and dragging her down to the bedding. "We'll speak of this tomorrow."

Sabine was out of sorts in every way. They'd been less than four hours from reaching this place; maybe they could have done without her meltdown. No, she *should* still be furious with him over her treatment and her continued captivity—

Damn it, is he embarrassed of me?

She'd noticed two things when she'd slept with him during the last couple of nights. When he wrapped his arms around her, he clasped her as tightly as he would his most treasured prize. And whenever he did that, she fell into a deep numb sleep.

Sabine welcomed it now. The heat from his body was so palpable, it seemed to stroke her in the dark. The world soon fell away. . . .

She woke in the night, blinking her eyes to find him watching her, his face so weary.

"No more bad dreams, love."

Had he seen her dream? She didn't remember it—

He pressed his lips to her hair. "You're safe, now." He eased his hand to her face so slowly, touching her cheek with the softest caress she'd ever received. It was almost as if he'd practiced how not to startle her.

Her last thought before sleep claimed her once more: *If I'm not careful, I could get used to having a demon husband. . . .*

❧ 31 ❧

"Retro-Amish. How . . . charming," she said when Rydstrom brought her changes of clothing the next morning. He was relieved to see that her face and body had healed overnight.

Though she'd just awakened, he'd already bathed in nearby hot springs, dressed in new clothes, and met with the head noblemen, who were all too eager to turn over the governing—and the problems—of the camp to him.

They'd been rife with curiosity about Sabine. *Was she the king's concubine or prisoner or both?* Rydstrom wouldn't volunteer anything, just commanded that while she was not to be freed, she was to be shown the utmost respect—and that everyone here be apprised of that order.

Sabine gave a nod at the clothes. "Let me guess—from Durinda?"

"Yes, they're courtesy of her." After Rydstrom's meeting, the demoness had guided him around camp, with the boy Puck following. He was an orphan that Durinda hoped to foster in the future. Though the demoness clearly knew Rydstrom, he couldn't seem to place her. But she was friendly enough, and the boy reminded him of Cadeon at that age. *The exact age my brother was when I sent him away.*

"Durinda—and many others—noted your lack of clothing last night. They favor more conservative garments."

Since last night, word of Sabine and Rydstrom's identity had spread to the entire populace. The people were uneasy about the sorceress within their midst, even as they gazed at him with . . . hope. They thought he was going to make their lives better.

The responsibility weighed on him. Everywhere he looked he saw work that needed to be done. And food was growing scarce here. All the game in the area was depleted, and hunters were having to go farther afield, which put them at risk for other dangers.

He wished he had someone to speak with about this. He wished he had *Sabine* to speak with. But they'd had only had one real conversation.

"Conservative garments, Rydstrom? Don't you mean *stodgy?*"

"Call it what you will."

"You don't seem as angry as you'd been last night," she observed. "Not still bristling about the baby—or lack thereof?"

Rydstrom had repeatedly mulled over the night before. At the time, he'd thought she was worried about him. Now he suspected he'd heard and seen things that weren't there, wanting her to be anxious for him, to give a damn about him. "I wasn't angry about that, but about the deception. And I've since become glad that you aren't."

"Is that so?" she asked, her tone disbelieving.

"I know little of children or of the starting of families, but I figure there should be no hatred between the parents."

"Rydstrom, I don't *hate* you."

"You did last night."

"Last night I was furious. Look, whether I deserved the last two days or not, they've still been very difficult for me. And your female is not mild-tempered in the best of circumstances."

Rydstrom frowned, absently saying, "Maybe a hot bath would be welcome." She'd just sounded so *reasonable.*

And he hated that his first thought was, *What's her game now?*

"*Ruffles?* Your revenge is devilish and hateful, Rydstrom." Once she'd bathed, he'd dressed her in an ankle-length flowing skirt and a long-sleeved blouse with—she shuddered—*flouncy things.*

A plain corset and pantalettes served as underwear. Soft slippers covered her feet. She frowned down at them. "How am I supposed to kick with these?"

"You're not."

"Have you ever seen pictures of cats dressed up by humans? That's how ridiculous I feel right now."

"Good. Maybe this will curb your ego," he said as he led her back to the tent.

"Doubtful. It burns too bright, demon. So do you agree that women should dress like this? Are you old *and* stodgy?"

"I think women should dress as they please. Within reason."

She was about to grill him on that last bit, but she noticed that people were stopping what they were doing to spit on the ground after she passed. "My popularity here, well, it's just embarrassing how they fawn."

"I can't blame them for how they feel."

"What?"

"They're among the hardest hit by Omort's regime— hence their determination to risk Grave Realm to escape his rule."

"And I'm to be hated for what Omort has done? Have you heard of any specific account where *I've* gone out of my way to hurt any of the people here?"

"No, just as I've never heard any where you've gone out of your way to help them."

"Of course not. I will *never* aid someone, not unless there's something in it for me. Because I have a brain in my head. Demon, you want things from me that I simply can't give. And you hope to see things in me that just aren't there. I will always lie, cheat, and steal—"

"And duly kill anyone who defends their gold."

"You saw my dreams."

"I did. I saw your mother. And I saw when you were buried."

She swallowed. *Don't you pity me. Don't you dare.*

"You're strong, Sabine. If you could temper that strength with—"

"Compassion? Kindness? Mercy?"

"Why not?"

"Rydstrom, I wouldn't even know where to begin. . . ." She trailed off as they passed Durinda. The pretty demoness smiled winningly at Rydstrom. He gave her a wave.

Sabine didn't like this little exchange at all. She recognized that she was feeling jealousy. She'd experienced it before Rydstrom, but for *things*—objects others possessed that she didn't.

Now she felt as if Durinda had just taken a grab at her gold. Wondering how her gold would feel about that, Sabine gazed up at Rydstrom. "Do you think it's possible to desire another after you've found your female?"

"I think it depends on how badly one wants his female."

"Then it's a good thing you're obsessed with me."

"Why? Are you concerned that I might desire another?"

She was saved from answering when a tussle broke out among boys nearby.

Durinda hurried over to snare Puck from the fray. He'd been fighting with much bigger kids—which meant that Puck was scrappy and marginally worth a second of Sabine's attention. For a juvenile demon male, she'd seen *less* cute.

He'd probably been teased about his name. "What kind of parents would name their kid something that rhymes with f—"

"*Dead* parents," Rydstrom said quickly. "They're both dead, Sabine. And he's having difficulties because he's an orphan who hasn't yet been fostered by another family."

"What about Durinda? Why isn't she his new mother?"

"Because she is . . . unwed."

"The demon made his first funny." He was *serious?* "It is impossible that you just said that."

He only ran his hand over the back of his neck.

When Durinda spoke to Puck in Demonish, Sabine said, "What is she telling him?"

"That fights solve nothing."

"Are you . . . are you *jesting?*" Before Rydstrom could steer her away, Sabine called, "Don't listen to her, kid! Fights solve *everything!* Just be sure to win them!"

"Enough! The boy doesn't understand English like the others. He was raised in a small farming village and only speaks Demonish."

"You agree with that twit about fighting, don't you? My dark gods, the world's gone mad! Tell me you wouldn't teach our child that, because it would be a deal breaker."

He stepped close to her, gazing down at her. His voice was gravelly when he said, "I didn't know you were still in negotiations."

Sexy demon. She swallowed, again wondering if there would ever come a time when she wasn't affected by him. *Inward shake.* "Our negotiations fell through *before* you brought me to this gods forsaken time warp." She turned from him—

The hits came out of nowhere. She gawked down at her ugly blouse, which had just gotten uglier.

Some teens had thrown rotten tomatoes at her, splatting them over her chest. She stared in disbelief. If this had happened at any other time in her life, someone would be about to die.

Through gritted teeth, she told Rydstrom, "Untie—me—*now*!" Her nails were digging into her palms, drawing blood.

He swept a menacing glower in the offenders' direction, and the parents came forth to apologize abjectly.

Rydstrom told them, "I will return to finish this matter." Then he began squiring her back to the tent.

"That's all you're going to do? Not good enough, Rydstrom!" She struggled against him. "Untie my bloody hands!"

"Why? So you can kill some misguided children?"

"No, I'll just give them nightmares for the rest of their lives." The way people were staring at her eyes, she knew they were glowing blue with fury.

Once they were back inside, he dragged her over to the bedding in the corner. She was dismayed to see that while they'd been gone, someone had driven a stake into the ground. Attached to it was a length of cord. *No, the demon wouldn't dare . . .*

He fetched her a towel from the dressing stand, dipping it in the washing bowl. After he stripped her shirt, he rubbed her clean, then redressed her in another awful blouse.

"How are you going to punish those little punks?"

"I'm going to tell their parents that you bade me to be lenient with them."

"Well, aren't you a cunning demon? Already working

on my image among them. Too bad that will be a *lie*. And Good King Rydstrom doesn't lie."

"By the time I leave this tent, it won't be a lie."

"Never! Not on your—"

"Then I won't arrange for you to write a message to your sister. Even though I'd found a messenger here who thinks he can get a letter to Tornin."

"Truly? Oh, fine. King Rydstrom, will you be lenient with the poor, misbegotten sons of curs who threw rotten vegetables at me?"

"I'd be glad to convey that." Was he eyeing that long line attached to the stake?

"Don't even think about it!" When he bent down to tie her ankle, she kicked out with those useless slippers on her feet.

But he seized her leg, holding her in places as he knotted the line. His task complete, he started for the exit.

"Where are you going? You can't leave me like this!"

He stopped with one hand on the flap and faced her. "You stir up ill-will when you're out. There's much I have to do, and I can't watch you constantly."

"Then *free* me."

"Not a chance." He pointed at her ankle. "There's enough line for you to reach the guard outside."

"Guard?" she cried. "Do you think I can escape . . . ?" She trailed off. "He's for *my* protection. Again you leave me defenseless."

"The guard won't let anything happen to you."

"But what will I do?"

"Sit in here. Contemplate why others might feel moved to throw things at you."

As he ducked out of the tent, she yelled, "You leave me tied up like a dog? Then you had better remember that this bitch bites!"

And then he was gone.

An hour inched by before the tent flap opened once more. Surprisingly, it was the boy, Puck.

"What do you want?" Sabine snapped, sitting up on her haunches, scouting for vegetables on his person. "Come to throw tomatoes?"

As he entered, he pulled a blade from his pocket. *Excellent.* She was going to be shanked by a pup barely out of diapers.

Yet then he drew a piece of wood from his other pocket and plopped down beside her, beginning to whittle.

Oh. "Can you make me an eye-socket-size stake? For Rydstrom?" Puck frowned, not understanding English. "Or better yet, you can use your little knife to cut through these bindings."

He grinned with total incomprehension.

Sabine didn't care for children, and after repeated failed attempts to communicate his role in her escape plot, his presence swiftly began irritating her. "Shoo, then. Get out."

He didn't budge.

In an exaggeratedly cheery voice, she said, "You've shown me what a good wittle whittler you are!" Her tone normal once more, she said, "So go *the hell* away. I've important things to ponder."

Nothing. "Oh, I get it! You're doing some kind of cute orphan stunt. Trying to make me like you so you might get a new mommy because I *am* wed. Of course, your taste is to be commended, demon boy person. Alas, you've got the wrong mark here. I've got nothing to bring to the mommy table."

He only tilted his head at her. Then he solemnly held out his hand as if he wanted to give her something.

Sabine *did* like to be given things. "What is it? Let me see." She rolled her eyes. "I'm tied here, clueless—I can't hold out my hand."

He laid something on her knee, something tiny and white. Sabine had noticed that he'd been missing his bottom fang. Not *missing* anymore!

And he'd obviously been saving it for a *long* time. "Oh, that's just not right." Her face screwed up into an expression of distaste, and not just because it was disgusting. "Don't you know you can get gold for that tooth? What's *wrong* with you?"

❧ 32 ❧

Rydstrom had never thought he would be so happy to see a female's jealousy. *Sabine* was jealous of *Durinda*. Over the past two days, she'd displayed it repeatedly.

This was an indication that his female might truly feel something for him—an indication he'd *never* expected.

Again the puzzle deepened.

Rydstrom did spend most of the days with the demoness since she helped him organize the upcoming portal crossings. They were arranging groups based on destination. Most would go to one of a few Lore-rich cities like New York or Savannah. For extra money, one could give the portal keeper exact coordinates.

There were difficulties inherent in assimilating so many Lorekind into human societies. If a thousand demons suddenly showed up in Savannah, someone was bound to notice.

As he worked with his people, preparing them for this new world, he grew shamed that he'd resented them, resented his responsibility. He found them to be industrious, hardworking, and down to earth.

Durinda was an invaluable help as they readied for the exodus, but Rydstrom also enjoyed her company. She was someone from his past who shared memories of Tornin from better times. He liked talking to her about the castle, recalling it in its glory, trying to erase what he'd witnessed of the court just days ago.

They also talked of Mia, Zoë, and Cadeon. Durinda said one of the reasons she was so protective of Puck was because he reminded her so much of Cadeon at that age. He did Rydstrom as well.

He remembered his brother as a towheaded little boy. His new horns had driven him crazy, itching as they grew. He'd run them against everything, even against the walls of the castle, leaving little gouges, all three feet high.

Rydstrom had never thought he'd miss Cadeon, but he did. Through the centuries, they had battled against others together, and routinely against each other. Before Sabine, Cadeon had been the only one who could provoke Rydstrom's ire. He gave a laugh. The two of them would get along perfectly.

But even with the contention between Rydstrom and Cadeon, they rarely separated. They were so often together that many in the Lore simply called the two of them *The Woede*. Cadeon presently lived in his pool house.

Today Rydstrom had learned that many rebels were rallying because of his brother's continued success in his quest for the sword. He was proud of Cadeon— shocked—but proud. . . .

Rydstrom and Durinda shared another commonality. She was reluctantly journeying off-plane to marry a male she refused to believe was hers. "At least *he*'s convinced we are a pair," she'd said. "I'm not certain at all. We have absolutely nothing in common. I don't think two more dissimilar beings could be paired."

Durinda had no idea.

Rydstrom and Sabine were nearly complete opposites. But now there was no doubt that Sabine was his. Although Rydstrom burned to bed his sorceress again—and for her to carry his mark—he would take things slowly, earn her trust.

Rydstrom was in this for no less than eternity.

Every day she was here, Sabine grudgingly grew more attracted to the demon.

Now as she watched him readying to go out, she realized she hadn't truly seen him as a potential mate until he was out of his chains. She respected power, was attracted to it, and he'd been powerless. Now he was so commanding, so delightfully in charge. People gazed at him in awe whenever he went out.

Yet even when he was among many, he still seemed . . . lonely. *Kingly demon, holding himself off from everyone.*

Unfortunately, Sabine's increased attraction wasn't mutual.

Each day Rydstrom spent more time with Durinda, leaving Puck behind to irritate her. They must figure that the boy would be safe from her influence since he didn't speak English. And she couldn't get the little punk to leave. He would shyly enter her tent, bringing her a "gift" each time. One day she received the husk of a dragonfly, the next day, a rock.

Rydstrom still took Sabine to the hot springs each morning. When they passed Durinda and her clique— draped in the same stupid long skirts that they'd forced on her—the demoness acted very familiar with Rydstrom, which made Sabine bristle.

And each night, he still held her tightly in bed. Because she was sleeping five or six hours a night, she had multiple nightmares. Whenever she woke, he was there, tenderly stroking her hair.

Last night, he'd rasped, *"Shh, baby. I've got you."* That made her toes curl every time she recalled it.

But he'd made no move to get sexual with her again, even though she'd felt him erect, pressing against her back. His self-denial disconcerted the hell out of her, and she wished she could talk to her sister about his behavior. Lanthe was a love guru. She would understand what Rydstrom's game was.

Gods, she missed her sister so much. They'd never been separated for this long. But just as Rydstrom had promised, he'd arranged for her to write Lanthe.

That second night, the demon had brought Sabine a piece of parchment and a *quill*. Though if she'd thought she would have an opportunity to get free, she'd have been mistaken. He'd released one hand and pinned the other behind her, glancing over her shoulder as she wrote.

"Just tell her I'm taking you off-plane," he'd said. "This won't get to Tornin until after we've gone."

"She'll know you're going to New Orleans. Omort will send assassins there."

"Yes," he'd said simply.

When she'd finished and Rydstrom had retied her, she'd said, "I was almost moved to hug you for this, Rydstrom, but alas, armless hugs lose a little something. So instead, I'll do you a favor. I'll help you with your brother."

"Cadeon and I are beyond a sorceress's help. Besides, I did this for you because you were cooperative about the teens' punishment. Then for you to grant me a boon back? I don't want us to get into that habit."

"Why not?"

"Because you and I are . . . we're *together*."

She recalled thinking, *Are we together, and what exactly does that mean?* She had zero experience with relationships. "Oh, no matter, then," she'd said airily. "I was just going to tell you something that might lessen your resentment over the past."

He'd gruffly said, "Tell me, then."

"The fall of Tornin would've happened regardless of Cadeon's actions."

"All my brother had to do was answer my dispatch, journey to the castle, and remain within its walls until I returned from the front line against the vampires. Instead, he turned his back on me, choosing to remain with his foster family. I know you won't understand the importance, but there needed to be a royal presence there."

"Oh, I do understand the importance—whoever controls Tornin controls the kingdom. Omort did as well. That's why he had five hundred troops, lying in wait to assassinate Cadeon."

Rydstrom had grown still. "What did you say?"

"It didn't matter how many guards you'd assigned to Cadeon. If your brother hadn't ignored your dispatch, he never would've made it to the castle alive."

"How do I know you're telling the truth?"

"Why would I lie about that?"

When he'd left her, he'd looked like he'd just been clocked with a gauntleted fist. . . .

Now he was readying to leave her yet again. The demon was wearing a dark green tunic that brought out the color of those remarkable eyes of his. The woven material hugged his broad shoulders and defined chest. His jet-black hair was as tousled as ever.

Had Sabine been one of those women who sighed, she would have right now.

"Where are you going this time?" she asked.

"Hunting."

"Uh-huh. With whom? Durinda?" She sounded like a scorned housewife. All she was missing was a cigarette stuck to her bottom lip and a squalling kid on her hip.

He strapped his sword belt around his waist. "That's right."

"You mean females are allowed to ride horses here?" She blinked in feigned amazement. "Can they touch weapons, too? Or will they be banished from the Clan of the Cavebear like Ayla?" When he wouldn't rise to the bait, she asked, "What is so interesting about that demoness anyway?"

"I like that she cares about others above herself," he said. "I admire that she's noble minded and virtuous."

Sabine gave a scoff. "I could be virtuous, if I wanted to be."

In an incredulous tone, he said, "You don't know the meaning of virtue!"

"Of course I do—it means your thong must be white."

He gazed upward, inhaling for patience, then said, "Look, I enjoy merely talking to her, actually having a conversation that doesn't devolve into fighting."

"Ah, you like her *conversation?*" Sabine walked on her knees over to where he stood. "Then I'm sure with enough of it, you'll forget what *I* did with my mouth." She gazed up at him. "Dialogue always trumps exquisite oral sex. You'll hardly remember how hot my mouth was and how hungry I'd been for you." She licked her lips.

He swallowed, growing erect right before her eyes. "Sabine, I do remember. I think about it *constantly*. But there's a lot to be said for comfort with another, for ease and companionship. If I could have all that with you . . ."

"Companionship?" Her eyes narrowed. "You've slept with her!"

"No, I haven't! Why would you say that?"

"Because of the way she looks at you. And at me."

"What's bothering you most about this situation? How quickly the boy is growing on you or how much I'm enjoying spending time with another female?" As he exited, he said, "I'll be back near sunset."

Excellent. She'd sent her husband off aroused and angry on a date with another woman.

She had nothing to do but stare at the roof of the tent and ponder her situation. What would she do if she could escape Rydstrom? The tales of the beasts that lived in Grave Realm and her recent Teegloth abduction definitely gave her pause about setting out on her own. But she wondered if anything could be worse than facing the morsus withdrawal?

If she somehow made it back to Tornin, with no pregnancy and no demon, Omort might prey on her at once. He could even withhold the poison until she surrendered to him.

Yes, that would be the reason why she would hesitate to flee from the demon—*not* because she was growing attached to him. And not because she thought about kissing him nearly every time she looked at his firm lips.

It took another hour before Puck, the demonling, entered the tent. And he'd brought her another present.

"A lizard. Just what I've always wanted."

When the creature leapt from his hand into her hair, Sabine gave a cry and shook her head violently until it hopped away.

Puck laughed, and it wasn't like that weird high-pitched giggle she'd heard out of children before, the one that begged the question: why would one possibly tickle a child just to elicit that noise?

He had a real chuckle, and she kind of smiled in response. He began scampering around after the lizard, continually glancing over his shoulder with a little wave at her, as if giving her reassurance that he *would* catch her gift again.

She frowned. *He's the only one here that's nice to me.*

At Tornin, her Inferi were always fawning. Courtiers kissed ass for concessions. *Everyone here openly hates me.* Luckily that didn't bother her. At all.

"Hey! Just sit, kid. You're making me dizzy." He hesitated, so she gave a deep nod at the floor beside her. "Sit." When he plopped down, she said, "If you're to be my only friend in this gods forsaken place, I need to get you working for me. And I was only half kidding about the shank."

Incomprehension. He shyly began speaking in Demonish, or, as she liked to call it, Gibberish.

"Blah, blah, blah. Demon boy, I can't speak that language. Furthermore, I don't want to pollute my brain by learning it. So it's time for you to learn mine. First lesson—I'm *Say-been*. I'm oft described as *byoo-tee-full* and *mah-jest-ick*."

"Ai-bee," he said.

She stilled. *My name the way my little sister has always said it. The sister I'm missing like a lost limb.* "Don't you call me that again!"

His eyes went wide. Great, she was about to lose her only entertainment. "Ha-ha. Sabine was kidding."

The little demon tilted his head. She waited for him to bail. . . .

But he didn't. And she frowned to realize she'd actually been holding her breath.

❧ 33 ❧

"Ah, gods! It's going to kill them!" someone screamed a few hours later.

Whatever *it* was, Sabine wished *it* all the luck in the world. She was stewing, the demon's words going round and round in her brain. *How much I'm enjoying spending time with another female. . . .*

Bastard.

Rydstrom had gone off with Durinda hours ago, and eventually Puck had left to eat dinner with others.

The sun had set, gloaming heavy upon the sky. And Rydstrom still wasn't back. The moon would be beautiful tonight. Romantic even.

"Someone help them!"

With an irritated exhalation, Sabine worked her way to her feet, then butted her head against the tent flap to exit. She might as well watch the show—

Her lips parted. A crimson-scaled basilisk was chasing demons all over the place, swatting tents up into the air. Its enormous tail pummeled the ground as it roared. The sound drummed in her ears and shook the night.

Sabine's guard was gone, convening with others, who looked like they planned to attack it.

The dragon cornered a group in a canyon pocket, tensing to pounce, its forked tongue darting into the air.

When it finished with that course, Sabine would be a sitting duck, tied to a stake—with no guard! While Rydstrom was out playing Romeo with the twit.

She caught sight of a noblewoman, a demoness in Durinda's clique who'd turned her nose up at Sabine. She was running back and forth talking to herself.

"Hey, demon lady person," Sabine called. "If you untie me, I can save them all with my goddesslike powers."

She slowed, hesitating, wringing her hands.

Hand-wringing and pacing, Sabine thought in disgust. *Repetitive actions—way to take action, woman!* "Do you *want* them to die?"

"Th-the males are defending the females and children." Demons with torches were preparing to rush the beast. "They will save us—"

"Thanks. I think I just vomited a little in my mouth." This society needed to be *rewritten*—completely! "The torches those guys are planning to use to scare him away will do nothing but make him feel friskier. So, the ties . . ." She twisted around and held up her bound wrists.

"If I freed you, King Rydstrom would be incensed—"

"Well, he's not here now, is he?"

* * *

"Your mind is occupied with other things," Durinda said quietly to Rydstrom. After a successful hunt, they'd slowed their lathered horses on the way back.

"I apologize," he told Durinda. "I've much to mull over just now." He couldn't stop recalling earlier when Sabine had gazed up at him with those amber eyes. She'd been merry, having fun, teasing him . . .

Yet another facet of her.

Learning about Sabine was exactly like arranging jigsaw pieces—sometimes they didn't fit.

For instance, she was a female who killed viciously, and yet she'd befriended—in her own way—a friendless demon boy. She was a sorceress who was so cold and hard that she kept a woman's tongue in a jar, but she'd begun turning to Rydstrom trustingly in sleep, nuzzling his chest.

He'd decided that Sabine needed someone to always be there to soothe her nightmares, the ones he'd witnessed. By the gods, he would be that man.

"Your thoughts are filled with the sorceress."

"Among other things." His musings weren't only on Sabine. What she'd told him about Cadeon—if true, and he suspected it was—meant that he had to rethink nine centuries of strife.

And now Cadeon was making him proud, pursuing that sword. But could he really turn Holly, his true mate, over to Groot? If Cadeon did, he'd hate Rydstrom forever.

"Sabine is clearly more than a concubine to you," Durinda said.

Rydstrom didn't deny it. "She's my female."

"You . . . you *attempted* her?"

He nodded sharply, not liking her tone.

"I had wanted—and expected—so much better for you," she said in her halting way. "In fact, I don't see how it could get worse."

Rydstrom didn't either. He'd never met anyone as self-absorbed as Sabine. She lied, stole, cheated, and killed. Aside from Puck, every one of his subjects loathed her.

And I'm still falling for her. He couldn't help it—each time she clutched at him for comfort from a nightmare, or revealed glimpses of her sly sense of humor, his feelings for her grew. "It isn't like I had any choice in the matter."

"Why do you keep her bound in your tent?"

"She would likely run from me at the first chance." Even if Sabine was becoming more attracted to him, growing to trust him somewhat, she belonged to a different world—one in which she was rewarded for all her vices. A world he was certain she wanted to return to.

Durinda said, "You can't keep her tied up forever."

"I'm hoping once we get off-plane I can win her affection." *If she's even capable of it.* No, she had to be.

"I just can't believe with all the demon females you attempted, you could never find one among our own kind."

"No, it didn't happen. And not from lack of trying." He gave a humorless laugh. "Just be glad you weren't among them."

A pause, then: "Rydstrom, I-I was."

❈ 34 ❈

"You can save them?" the hand-wringing woman said.

At Sabine's earnest nod, she finally freed her hands and untied her ankle.

Sabine massaged her wrists with a mean smile. *Idiot!* At once, she stripped off the ridiculous blouse but left the corset, using her power to make it look like a metal breastplate. She imagined a bold headdress and collar, weaving the image over her, then used illusions to paint her face and plait her hair.

"Sabine, you must hurry!"

"Must I?" She stalked up to the woman. "Don't you ever call me by my given name again! I'm Rydstrom's queen—*your* queen. We're married whether he wants to admit it or not." She started away from the commotion, saying over her shoulder, "All the best with that."

The demoness hurried after her, with her eyes watering. "B-but you said . . ."

"Look, is it really my place to save the lives of people stupid enough to run into a canyon and get cornered by a dragon? Yes, I'm egotistical, but who am *I* to challenge natural selection?" It wasn't her fight—

"Ai-bee!" a small voice echoed in the distance.

Sabine stilled. Puck was among the trapped demons. The little punk, who didn't have the sense not to be dragon food, had just called her name.

Which meant he'd just made her situation into one of two options: self-loathing if she risked her neck to save him *or* a bad day if the punk died. She exhaled. Maybe even worse than a bad day.

Turning toward the chaos, she muttered to herself, "I can't believe *I'm* doing this."

The woman clasped her hands to her chest. "Oh, thank you!"

In answer, Sabine lunged at her and snapped her teeth. "In *no* way am I doing this for *your* thanks." Then she carried on. *So stupid . . . so bloody stupid.*

Yes, Sabine had the ability to talk to animals.

But what if the big bastard didn't *want* to chat?

"I . . . didn't remember," Rydstrom told Durinda. *And I still don't.* But Sabine had voiced her suspicion of exactly this, and he'd vehemently denied it. Which meant he'd unintentionally lied to her.

"Well, this certainly is uncomfortable." Durinda stared straight ahead. "It was centuries ago, and I understand there were . . . many."

Had the demoness been trying to rekindle an affair? He'd assumed she'd just been kind to help him familiarize himself with the place. He'd thought she'd merely enjoyed reminiscing. "It was indeed long ago."

They rode on in onerous silence, but when they reached the rise over the camp, he found a scene that defied description.

In full Sorceri regalia, Sabine appeared to be muttering to herself as she shoved people out of her way while storming toward a *dragon*. The beast was poised to attack a cornered group—with Puck among them.

Drawing his sword as he spurred his horse, Rydstrom charged down the hill toward her. He'd never reach them in time.

When Sabine neared the beast, she yelled for its attention. Rydstrom's heart dropped when it rounded on her in a rippling flash of muscle and crackling scales.

"*No!*" he bellowed. "Get away!"

The beast hissed, darting its forked tongue. Yet she faced it with her chin up and shoulders back, raising her palms. Heat blurred the air above her hands. When it swept its paws, she leapt over them, then ducked under its swatting tail. "Hey! That was close! Stop this *now!*"

The beast slowed its tail, seeming to glower in confusion.

Rydstrom dismounted his horse in a full run. As he closed in on them, he could hear her talking to the dragon. She'd said she could speak to animals. Could she hold it off?

"That's better. You don't want to feed upon me," she murmured. "Though I *am* the tenderest, I'm also poisonous." She chuckled as if at an inside joke. "Don't be cross with us, great one." She cautiously reached up and petted its gleaming scales. It jerked back, yet then allowed another stroke. "We didn't know this was your home." The beast chuffed air.

Sabine glanced at Rydstrom, her eyes glowing bright in her mask of kohl. "Do you think it could eat me in one bite?"

"Move away from it!"

"So you can strike this exceptional fellow down?"

"To protect you, yes!" Rydstrom hated the idea of killing one such as that, but he readily would.

"I've got this. Luckily, one person here had the sense to free me—against your orders."

Could she control it? He didn't want her in jeopardy, but she looked as if she was having . . . *fun*. He motioned for those cornered to begin slipping out.

The beast tensed. "Keep talking," Rydstrom muttered to her as he helped Puck and another away. Almost everyone had escaped.

Sabine continued, "Confession time, dragon. One night last summer, when my sister Lanthe and I were really bored, we almost sent all the creatures from Grave Realm through a portal to a place called *Times Square*. We've since seen why that would be hilarious only to *us*."

The creature's eyelids were growing heavy, as if it were mesmerized. When all the people were a safe distance away, Rydstrom lowered his sword.

Instead of escaping when she'd been freed, Sabine had voluntarily waded into a *dragon's* way to save others. She'd told him she'd never help another if there was no benefit to herself. Yet now she *had* . . .

"*Cwena*," he murmured, his chest tight with pride. *Little queen.*

The way she was interacting with the beast was the most remarkable thing he'd ever seen—it looked powerless not to be enthralled by her.

We've that in common, dragon.

"Would you allow us a night or two longer here?" she asked the dragon.

In answer, it chuffed hot breath at her again, then turned its immense body to stalk off into the night.

People cheered. At once, Puck ran for Sabine in that headlong way the young did.

Yet she didn't kneel and open her arms to embrace the boy. She snatched him up by his belt and carried him like an accessory, berating him for not fleeing from things that have fangs bigger than his body. And the child looked as if he couldn't have been happier.

All around her, people rushed forward to express gratitude.

She negligently waved her free hand at them, muttering, "Yeah, yeah. Say it with gold."

Even Durinda thanked her as she collected Puck.

When Sabine approached Rydstrom, he was at a loss for words.

"If you think about binding my arms again," she began, "I'll call my big friend down here once more, and he will go off his newly restricted diet." She continued on, ignoring him.

Sabine had told him, *"Lonely demon. You need me so much."*

He feared she was right.

❧ 35 ❧

For two days, his female had free run of the camp, wreaking utter havoc.

The once reviled sorceress could do no wrong in the eyes of the demons here—and she was taking full advantage of that fact.

When a group of young females had asked her what one should name her horse, she'd answered, "I like the sound of Fellatio."

When Rydstrom had confronted Sabine about it, she'd said, "Do you know how priceless it was to hear that demoness sigh, '*I love my Fellatio*'? Even gold can't buy moments like that!"

At his unbending look, she'd rolled her eyes. "The *young* female was nineteen. And if she doesn't know what the word means by now, then she has bigger problems than what to name her pony." She'd added, "You ridiculed the fact that I remained purposely ignorant of your language because my kind finds it uncouth. But isn't that exactly what the females of your kingdom do about sex?"

He opened his mouth, then closed it, unable to deny her reasoning.

And she'd made many *decrees*. For the vintner to mix a sweeter wine for her. For the smithy to begin work on her crown and new breastplate. For a cook to prepare vegetarian dishes.

Puck followed her everywhere. Luckily, he couldn't understand her when she said things like, "Is it still behind me? Why won't it stop following me? It's looking at me again, isn't it? I can *feel* its little eyes on me."

Though she acted as if she didn't care for Puck's company, Rydstrom had spied her sit on a bench and pat the space beside her for the boy to sit. He'd also seen her brush Puck's hair out of his eyes.

Each time, she'd seemed to startle herself, glancing around guiltily—as if her kindness was improper. In her old world, it would have been.

As for Rydstrom, he couldn't spend enough time with her—literally. She avoided him.

She'd demanded her own tent, refusing to share his. The night of the basilisk's attack, he'd found her in the bluffs high above the camp to thank her for saving the lives of his people—and to indicate that she was still to sleep with him.

She'd told him, "My subjects have provided me with a new place. Now, if you don't mind, I've had a taxing day saving all of these refugees, my subjects and all—

since I am their queen, even if you let them think I'm a lowly sex slave."

"They don't any longer."

"I deduced that when they started with the obeisance and gifts and all. They adore me. Coins will be minted with my face on them. It's in the works."

Sabine had refused to budge. Rydstrom allowed this because she remained here. If she stayed, he thought they might have a future.

Did Rydstrom go out of his way to see her? Every damned minute that he could. He was searching for her this very afternoon. She wasn't at the hot springs, nor at the particular bluff where she liked to sit.

But from that height, he spied her playing dice down in the camp, gambling with others. When Rydstrom sank down to watch her, something sharp jabbed him. A basilisk scale? He peered around him and found more strewn about. Had she been sitting up here *with* the dragon?

He ran a hand over his side, over the tattoo. All those years ago, Rydstrom had been marked with the image of this beast, never knowing that a sorceress would captivate both a dragon—and a demon.

Now she was laughing as she played dice, likely saying outlandish things. But her companions always thought she jested. They were awed by her beauty and mysterious air, by the illusions of gold that gleamed on her and the bold paint that masked her face.

They simply thought she was a merry queen—that one did not *ever* want to anger.

As Sabine could make the dice appear to be anything

she wanted, she was doubtless bilking others of their gold. He suspected Sabine was stockpiling her winnings in a secret location—

He heard someone approaching . . . *Durinda*. They hadn't spoken more than a couple of words since her revelation, and he grew tense.

"They love her now," she said, sitting beside him. "Amazingly. You know she still calls the children *spawn* and uses the pronoun *it* when referring to any of them." She made her voice like Sabine's—condescending and unamused—as she said, "'*It* smells fusty . . . If *it* wants to give me your family's savings, then who are you to naysay?'"

Before Rydstrom could defend Sabine, she said, "*But* she is actually behaving like a queen. An unorthodox one to be sure, but a queen just the same."

"*You* believe that?"

Durinda nodded. "Sabine had the power to fend off a dragon, and made the choice to protect these people. And she's told the girls—the ones that she confused terribly about horse monikers—that she would give an educational class on . . . things of that nature. Yes, she did ask for gold in return, but one could argue that was merely *taxes* for government services. If given authority, she would enact social change."

He recalled what Sabine had said about the ignorance of the women, the medieval state of Rothkalina, the lack of infrastructure.

"And she's right about the fighting," Durinda continued quietly. "It *can* solve problems. We lived in a genteel society where we weren't as strong as we could have been. And when we were defeated, we were wholly unprepared for centuries of tyranny." She met his gaze. "Do you think Sabine would rest if she perceived her kingdom to be vulnerable?"

Never. He couldn't ask for a fiercer queen.

"You know, it's given me hope," she said. "If two people as unlikely as you and Sabine can be mates, then maybe the male I'm journeying to wed is the right one. I am optimistic."

This relieved Rydstrom greatly. He felt himself relaxing around her once more. "Do you think your new husband will allow you to keep Puck?"

"I do hope so. Because if not, your queen has offered to take him."

His brows shot up. "What?"

"She told me, 'I'll be taking that demon boy person.' When I reminded her that Puck wasn't her pet, she rolled her eyes at me and said, 'Hellooo, that's what I'm trying to *remedy.*'"

He felt his lips quirk.

"Interestingly, Puck found gold under his pillow in exchange for his tooth. I suspect she made herself invisible and slipped in our tent, though she vehemently denied involvement and called me a name I won't repeat here. Puck is beyond ecstatic."

Rydstrom had already accepted that he needed Sabine. He hadn't dared hope his kingdom would embrace her like this.

Maybe she was exactly what Rothkalina needed. Fate *had* gotten it right.

There were only two problems. First, Sabine wasn't truly his queen. And after she learned that he'd deceived her, she wouldn't be likely to forgive him. Secondly, Rydstrom planned to slay her brother at the earliest opportunity.

He'd considered talking to her about Omort, the future, and the fact that there would soon be a war—Rydstrom anticipated striking this spring. But for now, he'd decided it would be better just to get her to New Orleans, back to his home before she could bolt.

"I also came here to tell you that the portal keepers have begun arriving for tomorrow," Durinda said. "They come with information—the Lore is abuzz with tales of your brother claiming the sword from Groot the Metallurgist. Our Cadeon has succeeded."

"Any word of how he's done this?"

Durinda shook her head. "Not yet."

Two weeks ago, Rydstrom wouldn't have given a damn *how*. But now he feared Cadeon had turned over his own woman for it.

Rydstrom had expected his brother not only to betray his female, but to hand her over to a madman bent on breeding with her—and Cadeon might actually have done it for the sake of the kingdom.

Rydstrom's gaze was transfixed on Sabine. *If so, he's a stronger man than I am.*

Sabine had an urgent decision to make.

For the past two nights, she'd adored sitting up on the bluff, keeping time with the dragon, gazing out at her sleeping subjects, and watching the silhouette of Rydstrom as he paced in his tent for her to return.

But the portals were opening at noon, mere hours away, and she still hadn't decided if she was going with him.

As she gazed down at him readying his people, with his shoulders back and looking so *kingly*, Sabine debated her course of action. She was free and could easily escape. But those same worries about traversing Grave Realm and what she could expect from Omort plagued her.

And more, she was only a day away from getting into Rydstrom's house, into his life. By all accounts, Cadeon was ever closer to the sword. Maybe Sabine should journey with Rydstrom just in time to collect that sword for herself? Lanthe would get her message and come for her in Louisiana, providing her escape well before the morsus was supposed to hit in twelve days. And ultimately, the sisters might have their queendom . . .

Or maybe she and Lanthe should ally with Rydstrom? Sabine had told him she'd always be on the winning side, and now the tides were turning. Rydstrom *looked* like a warrior king who could defeat Omort. If the rage demons could get the sword, the balance could swing decidedly in their favor.

But if Sabine allied with Rydstrom, there would be more to deal with than mere war and destruction. The demon wanted her . . . affection.

He wanted a future with her—her *entire* future. This eternity idea had her spooked. She hadn't even been out on a real date, had never seen the same male twice, and now she was supposed to promise her eternity to a demon she'd known for only weeks?

There were actually times that she'd been tempted to. When she recalled those interludes in the wild when he'd caressed and licked her body, teasing her to a fever pitch again and again, she no longer grew outraged—she grew aroused. She longed for him to touch her, even to bed her again.

And then, over the last two nights when she'd woken alone, sleepily hunting for his big warm chest, she'd thought, *Why not try whatever he was offering?*

So what to do? What to plot?

Just then, Sabine realized that Rydstrom caught sight of her. As if he sensed she was considering running, he'd had his gaze on her all morning. His brows were drawn, a question in his eyes.

In answer, she gave him a lewd hand gesture. He grinned.

Oh, my. Sabine had never seen him smile. And it was *divine.* She frowned down at her chest. *What was that?* Why, that might have been a tender feeling.

He started toward her, and she couldn't say she was broken up about that. When he reached her on the bluff, he sat beside her. "It will soon be time to leave, Sabine," he said. "I never formally asked you before, but will you come with me to my home—our home—in Louisiana?"

"Do you have gold there?" she asked.

"No, but I could get some."

"Are you rich?"

"In that realm, if you're an immortal, you'd have to be an idiot *not* to be."

"Is your house nice and big?"

"*Our* house is a showplace, a mansion built centuries ago in a district known for its gardens. I've always taken pride in it—it's one of the most expensive and coveted in the city." He seemed eager for her to see it.

"You're not used to having to ask for things," she observed. "Is it difficult to ask me to come with you?"

He shook his head. "It might have been. If I didn't want you to so damned badly."

Sabine had once heard that Cadeon was the smooth talking brother of the two, but she thought Rydstrom's gruff admissions were much more intense and meaningful than any smooth talking could be.

"*Why* do you want this so badly? Because I'm fated to be yours?"

"No, because I know we can have something more between us."

She gazed into his green eyes and saw honesty—and desire. He wanted her, and he wanted her to see how much. She couldn't seem to look away.

"If you come with me, you won't regret it."

And if she *didn't* see where this could lead with Rydstrom, she might wind up regretting it for the eternity he wanted from her.

"I will, then," she finally said. "But I have some conditions." When he waved her on in that kingly way of his, she said, "The parity is done. We start this as equals."

"Agreed. As long as we start this."

"And I will only commit to six days with you. After that we'll reconvene."

"Why only six days?"

"Six is my favorite number," she lied.

"No, it's not."

"You're right. But it's still my condition."

"Anything else?"

"We never speak of Omort during this time."

After a hesitation, he nodded, then said, "I have some as well. You'll have to be honest with me."

"I will be, as much as I can."

"Sabine . . ."

"Look, that's a really big concession for someone like me to make."

He exhaled. "You have to give this thing between us a fair try. Can you do that, *cwena*?" He stroked his thumb over her cheek.

Sabine frowned just as he grinned. She hadn't flinched.

❧ 36 ❧

New Orleans, Louisiana

We have to walk?" she murmured, exhausted from the rough crossing.

The coordinates Rydstrom had given the portal jockey hadn't gotten them directly to his house.

"It's not far. Just six houses down."

She could tell he was anxious for her to like his home. She admired what she'd seen of the posh neighborhood, but she was too tired and chilled to be excited for him.

The portal they'd just come through had felt as if it had been hacked through space. Compared to it, Lanthe's thresholds were seamless masterpieces. No wonder she could only create one every so often.

"Are you sad about Puck?" he asked.

"Just tired." In truth, she might like to see the little punk again. He'd been bawling for her. Which shouldn't have shocked *anyone.*

"Chin up, demon boy person," she'd told him with an awkward pat on his head. Then she'd given him a note that she'd had translated into Demonish. When he'd read it, his eyes had lit up, and he'd nodded gravely.

"What did the note say?" Rydstrom had asked.

"It said that if he is bad enough, they will send him to come live with me."

Rydstrom had given her that look—the cross between perplexity and bewilderment, the one she believed he used only for her. The one that said, "*Surely, you're kidding. I really want you to be jesting.*"

"Here it is," he said when they came upon an estate with towering wooden gates and stone walls covered with ivy.

The grounds were immaculate, the mansion stunning with its Corinthian columns and wraparound veranda. The effect as a whole was opulent but tasteful. The sultry air was redolent with the scent of gardenias.

"How big is this place?"

"Plus or minus twenty-thousand square feet." At the front entrance, he said simply, "I want you to like it here."

"I'm sure I'll love it if the inside is anything like the outside." *So tired.* Sabine shivered.

He held her hand as he opened the door. At once, the smell of sour beer and cigars wafted over them. She put her free hand over her mouth.

"What in the hell?" he muttered as they journeyed deeper inside.

In the sitting room, beer-soaked Playgirl magazines lay over clearly expensive antique furnishings. Cartons from drink mixers were strewn over a wooden floor. Two empty kegs floated in barrels of melted ice—atop luxurious oriental rugs.

She followed Rydstrom's gaze up. Above them hung a resplendent *bronze d'ore* chandelier with chains of rock crystal gracing filigree arms. From one of those arms dangled a . . . *thong*.

He was growing more and more furious. "This looks like Cadeon's pool house."

Sabine didn't care what it looked like. She just wanted a bed—in a place that didn't smell like this.

Surveying the destruction, he absently said, "Maybe Rök did this?"

"Who's Rök?"

"Cadeon's roommate."

When they heard laughter outside, Rydstrom stormed toward the sound, dragging her along to a terrace that overlooked manicured grounds—as well as an oversize pool that was chock-full with dazzling females. They were all clad in bikinis. Or less. Topless chicken fighting was currently underway.

"Your friends visiting?" she asked archly.

"I don't know half of them. Looks like Valkyries and witches."

Witches? Usually, she'd be on guard around a group of them, but these females were tanked. Out of habit Sabine probed for their powers, not finding anything there she'd get out of bed for.

But Rydstrom's attention had narrowed on one woman—a petite beauty sitting on a chaise longue, smoking a cigar and talking on a cell phone.

She wore a red string bikini, stilettos, and a tiny T-shirt that said, *"Heels Tall . . . Bikini Small."* Her hair was as black as night, shining in a glossy mane over her shoulders.

Sabine could hear her say, "No, we're not paying for him!" A pause. "Because you sent him to the wrong house! He stripped for the elderly widow next door. From what we understand, she's keeping him *and* his plastic nightstick." Another pause. "Do I sound like an anatomist? How should I know— Hello? Helloooo?"

"Who is *that?*" Sabine asked Rydstrom.

"Going to bloody kill her," he muttered.

Before Sabine could ask again, the female caught sight of Rydstrom. "Demon! You're back." She tossed her cigar into the pool, hurrying over to them. "And you poached the sorceress from Team Evil. I knew you could do it!"

When she drew her sunglasses back to rest on her head, she revealed pointed ears—and vacant golden eyes. But Sabine still sensed great power in this female.

To Sabine, she said, "I'm Nïx, the Ever-Knowing, Soothsayer to the Stars." She extended a hand.

Sabine raised hers, ready to fight the notorious Valkyrie. "Rydstrom, what in the hell is this? You know we are enemies."

"Nïx won't do anything. I promise you."

"Won't I?" Nïx asked, her expression deadpan. Then she smiled, flashing small but noticeable fangs. "I'm in no mood to kill the demon king's love today!"

"Kill me, Valkyrie?" Sabine scoffed. "I can make you see things that will turn your brain to soup."

"*A-gain,*" Nïx sighed, unfazed by the threat.

Sabine probed the Valkyrie's mind, finding easy access— With a stifled gasp, Sabine just as rapidly withdrew her probe. *Chaos, utter chaos.*

"Welcome to my world!" Nïx said with an exaggerated wink. "Now, sorceress, I'm trying to win you over, so let's not quarrel. And let's not speak of you-know-who. I'll even grant you a boon, a foretelling." Nïx briefly gazed at the sky, then back at her. "Your sister will receive your avian-dispatched message in two hours. Though covered in pigeon poo, it will be legible."

The Valkyrie knew about the message! "Is Lanthe worried? Is she safe?"

"She's safe," Nïx said. "As of right now. That's a real-time quote and might not be applicable to the future. Is she worried? Lanthe senses you're safe with the demon—she doesn't believe Rydstrom will harm you in any way."

Sabine experienced so much relief, she almost felt like she owed Nïx.

"Wow. You sorceress-es-eses always had the most enviable garb," Nïx said. "And the makeup!" She ran a forefinger under her eyes and then down her cheek.

In response to the compliment, Sabine said, "I thought you'd be . . . *bigger.*"

Rydstrom stepped between them. "Nïx, do you want to explain to me what the—"

"A dorseri!" the Valkyrie suddenly exclaimed. "Yes, yes, of course!"

"What's that?" Rydstrom asked, as if he were used to interruptions like this from the soothsayer.

Nïx nodded sunnily. "That's what we should call a Sorceri and demon halfling!"

Sabine cast Rydstrom a look askance, but he shrugged. "Yes, Nïx that sounds about right, but for right now, I need to know what's happening here."

"We heard that the folks were going to be gone for a bit," she explained. "And by folks, I mean you, Cadeon, and Rök. We don't have a pool at Val Hall, and they don't have one at the Animal House of Witches." She hiked her thumb over her shoulder at the swimming witches. "So we moved in."

"Then move out! And get my house cleaned up."

She gave him a military salute, then snapped her fingers at a pair of witches, sprawled on nearby loungers. "You two. You can do a cleaning spell."

One slurred, "But Nïxie, I'm really pre-hungover."

Nïx's eyes went wide. "Do it, or the photos go live!"

The witch shook her fist to the sky, crying, "Damn you, Valkyrie! Damn you and your digital ways!"

Nïx turned to the rest of them and called out, "Party's over, because the demon king's lame. I mean *home*. The demon king's *home*!"

The crowd grumbled, most of them unsteadily filing out of the pool. A buxom dark haired witch strolled by topless. "Hiya, big guy," she purred. "You remember me? Carrow? Mariketa's best friend." She ran her finger over his chest as she passed.

The only reason Sabine let "Carrow" live was because Rydstrom didn't turn to ogle her from the back.

As soon as the cleaning witches started chanting, power surrounded them. Sounds drifted from the house.

The grounds grew immaculate, the litter vanishing. In minutes, the pair was done. They went for a high-five and missed.

"There, all better now," Nïx said as she turned to Sabine. "Dearling, you look peaked. You should rest."

"Yes, I'll show you to our room." Rydstrom put his hand on Sabine's lower back. "Nïx, I'll be back," he said over his shoulder as he whisked Sabine inside.

Now that the odor was gone and the mess cleaned, Sabine noted other details of the mansion, like the rich wood paneling and high ceilings throughout. Fans lazily circled overhead. The demon had taste.

When they reached a spacious room upstairs, he said, "This is ours." It was so large, it had a sitting area. A balcony overlooked the pool.

The bed was immense, and she eyed the rich beddings hungrily. When she sat at the edge of it and removed her boots, he strode to a chest of drawers, pulling out an undershirt.

"Here's something for you to wear for—"

By the time he'd turned back, she'd already stripped and crawled under the covers, half asleep.

When Rydstrom returned, he told Nïx, "She didn't need this commotion, Valkyrie. *I* didn't need it." He ran a hand over his horn.

The crossing had been grueling. And he didn't think Sabine would admit it, but he suspected she'd been upset by Puck's teary good-bye. She'd frowned and said, "*This is . . . uncomfortable. The demon boy makes me uncomfortable.*"

"Dirty Rydstrom, you wore your sorceress out!" Nïx appeared as mad as ever. "She's not like your typical demure demonesses, you know."

"I know this." Gods, he was glad of it. "Damn it, Nïx, some of your *guests* are still in the pool."

"I've got this." To the others, she called, "Hey, witches, did you see that redhead who was just here in the wicked cool clothes?"

One called back, "The one dressed up like a sorceress?" while another declared, "I'd do her."

"Well, she's a *real* sorceress. She's *Sabine* the Queen of Illusions—"

That got them surging for the sides of the pool, some of them crying out: "The bitch will gack our powers!"—"She'll make us insane!"—"Where is my intoxibong?"

With a contented sigh, Nïx said, "I think Sabine's introduction into New Orleans Lorekind will be fraught with moments like these."

"Is Sabine safe here? When will Omort strike?"

"Well, there actually was a benefit to our invasion of your home—the witches put a protection spell on the perimeter. Something about a probation officer coming after Carrow." She shrugged. "Anyway. No one but those who live here can enter your property without invitation."

He'd been planning on setting traps. This was better. "How long will the spell last?"

"As long as you don't cancel the credit card I found in your drawer."

He inhaled for patience.

"I also had them put a spell on your weapons armory so that it can't be broken into. You know, getting ready for the arrival of The Sword."

Rydstrom had a sizable stone armory in his study. It had been lockable. Evidently, it was now *invulnerable*. "Then my brother is on his way here. Is he safe?"

"Yes, yes, enough with your abject thanks, Rydstrom. I already know my help is priceless, and that you should name your firstborn daughter Nïx. To answer your question, Cadeon is fine. He claimed that sword at great risk to himself." She tapped her chin. "He also wrecked your million dollar Veyron—"

"He did *what*?" That car had been Rydstrom's pride and joy. There were only three hundred of them in the world, and he'd expressly forbidden Cadeon and Rök from even touching it.

"Actually it was Holly, my niece, who crashed it. Which, naturally, has made her a hero among Valkyrie everywhere. Totaling the demon king's seven-figure ride? She'll never pay cover again—"

"Why did you let Holly go with Cadeon in the first place?"

"Because I'm *impish*?"

"Did Cadeon . . . give Holly up to Groot?"

"Yep. Cadeon chose bro's before ho's. But Holly, the little trooper, managed to get free all by herself. Don't look so astounded. She *is* my niece." Nïx fluffed her hair. "And then Cadeon rubbed out Groot."

"So Cadeon and Holly are together, then?"

"Cadeon gave her up to a psychotic murderer. She's not exactly chipper with him. But don't worry. She'll come around when she finds out he always planned to come back to save her."

Rydstrom was relieved to hear that, but he was still tense about his own situation. *Six days to win Sabine.* He'd taken his woman to his home, where she lay naked in his bed. He believed she would receive him tonight.

And he was nervous. *I want to make love to her . . . to get it right for her.*

"You're going to do fine tonight, tiger. Relax."

He hated that Nïx could read him so easily. "Are you saying that as a soothsayer?"

Nïx shook her head. "More as a female who's lived three thousand years. So I have to skedaddle now."

"Contact me if you hear anything else about Cadeon."

"B'okay. Will do." Over her shoulder, she murmured, "There's a thunderstorm brewing, Rydstrom. A bad one. Better be ready."

He surveyed the sky. Not a single cloud marred the blue.

❦ 37 ❦

Wake the hell up!"
    Sabine shot up in the bed, blinking around her.
"Is someone here?" she murmured, seeing no one in the
luxurious room with her. How long had she been out? It
was already dark outside.

"Are you up yet?" a voice said, laying words in Sabine's
mind.

"Lanthe?"

"Ah, gods, Abie, I've been searching this city for you!"

Sabine swung her legs over the side of the high bed.
"You're . . . here?"

"I got your message at Tornin and opened a portal here.
I've been scouring this place hour after hour."

"The Vrekeners—"

"Are everywhere. But you have to get back for your
dose—now! Where are you?"

"With the demon. In his home." In our home.

"Can you escape him?"

"*Things are different between us,*" Sabine admitted. "*We've kind of reached an understanding.*"

"*Good! I'll make you another portal in six days, and you can return then. But for now, you have to come with me!*"

"*What has happened?*"

"*Omort lied—the morsus will hit you a week before you'd thought.*"

"*He did what?*" That bastard! When she faced him again, she would make him meet his nightmares, would show him scenes that even he couldn't bear.

"*It's true. He admitted it to me himself. Abie, it's a mess at Tornin. The vampires bailed. The fire demons are squirrelly. And Omort nearly took my power and killed me.*"

"*Then you can't go back there!*"

"*I convinced him that you would never accept him if he harmed me. Omort still believes the two of you will wed. Now, find your way out of the house, and follow my voice to the portal. We can't waste any more time.*"

"*I can't just leave Rydstrom without a word,*" Sabine said.

"*Are you jesting? As much as I hope it works out for you kids, now is not the time to start confiding in him.*"

When Sabine heard the paneled bedroom door creaking open, she quickly cloaked herself in invisibility, then cast an illusion of herself sleeping soundly.

Rydstrom looked in on her, gazing at her sleeping form with an unmistakably proud expression. She probed his mind, just a touch.

—*My woman . . . in my bed. At last.*—

Then his expression changed once more, that line between his brows deepening.

"Oh, my gods, Lanthe. Rydstrom is looking at an illusion of me—and he appears to be . . . in love."

"You saw that look?" Lanthe sounded wistful. *"Did he have his brows drawn with feeling?"*

"Yes. And as he walked out of the room, he kind of rubbed his chest a little."

"Like his heart hurt?"

"I've only ever seen that on TV before!" Sabine said. *"Lanthe, I have to tell him—about everything."*

"So he can do what exactly?" Lanthe demanded. *"And while you're informing him that you are going to a place he will never let you go, I'll be Vrekener bait."*

If Sabine explained the poison to Rydstrom, he wouldn't likely allow Sabine just to waltz back to Omort. And if she told him that she would probably die if she didn't make it through this portal, he'd insist that he could find help for her here. But there was no one on this plane who could prevent the morsus from striking.

Even knowing this, Sabine bit her lip, torn about what to do. *"Sneaking out of his house seems so wrong."*

"You are without a doubt one hundred percent in love, because it's making you stupid! It's not reasonable even to consider this. You can come back in mere days."

"I could write him a let—"

"Abie, I just heard wings."

Sabine was on her feet in a second. *"I'm coming!"* She hauled on her boots, then snatched up her clothes. Leaving the illusion on the bed, she kept herself cloaked in invisibility and slipped from the room.

She heard Rydstrom walking the house and eluded him to find her way out of a back door. As she hurried off the property into the night, she hastily dragged on her top and skirt.

The demon would follow as soon as he discovered her missing—she could only hope to make it to Lanthe's portal before then.

"*Lanthe?*"

"*Sabine, just follow my voice. I'm in a park somewhere.*"

The streets all looked the same, like a labyrinth. Rain began to fall, lightly at first, then intensifying. Soon, lightning fractured the skies. Thunder quaked. As though poured from a bucket, rain pounded down.

"*Lanthe?*"

"*I'm here. This weather blows.*"

Sabine caught sight of a park in the distance. "*Talk to me.*"

"*You're close.*"

"*I can see a—*" Sabine stumbled when she heard the demon roar her name, the sound echoing like a cannon's boom.

He'd started the chase. And he sounded enraged.

"*Lanthe, he's coming for me!*" No answer. "*Lanthe? Where are you?*"

When she answered, her voice was fainter. "*Kind of had to make a detour.*"

"*You're getting farther away from me? What are you doing?*"

Her voice was a scarce whisper. "*Right now I'm running from winged monsters. You?*"

"*Fleeing a seven-foot-tall rage demon. . . .*"

❧ 38 ❧

When Rydstrom had gone to check on her again, he'd reached down to brush her hair.

And found nothing but illusion. He'd stared for long moments, disbelieving.

She tricked me. She'd obviously never intended to stay. Another lie. She'd . . . *deserted* him.

Why? He'd charged from the house into a storm, bellowing her name. *Where in the hell is she?* He caught her scent from what must be miles away.

He tore off after her, tracking her, following his instinct. He sprinted down sodden streets, rage overwhelming him with every step. The frenzied need to mark her consumed him.

She doesn't carry my mark . . . we're not wed.

He caught sight of her nearing a small park, darting through puddles. He squinted through the rain. In the distance, he saw an area of diffused air—a portal. And she was heading directly for it.

Can't lose her. He pumped his arms for speed until he was on her heels, then lunged for her. Seizing her by the hips, he took her down into the muddy grass.

"You told me you wanted to stay with me!" With his breaths heaving, he tossed her to her back. "You made me believe you. And you were running *back to Omort!*"

"No . . . yes . . . Rydstrom, you must listen!" She blinked up at him, the pouring rain hitting her face.

He hauled her beneath him, digging his claws into her thighs. "Why? Every word out of your mouth is a lie! How many times will I let you deceive me?"

She'd thought to escape him? The lying sorceress would pay.

His eyes glowed in the night, cruel obsidian. Rain poured down painfully—never had Sabine felt it like this. The drops pelted her eyes so hard, she could barely see, could scarcely hear herself.

"I'd planned to be good to you," he grated. "To make love to you. But no longer."

When he began unbuckling his belt, her eyes went wide. "Not like this!" she cried, raking her nails over his face and chest.

He roared with fury, then seized her wrists, fettering them behind her back with his belt.

"Rydstrom, no! Something has happened! Demon, *listen* to me. My sister's here—"

"Your sister's not here, she's in Tornin! In *my* castle! My home!" His horns were dark and flaring. "I don't want to hear any more of your lies!"

"Please, Lanthe's in danger. . . ." Her words tangled on her tongue as she tried to explain to him, while listening for Lanthe's voice or the sound of wings. "And the Vrekeners are everywhere!"

Rydstrom finished her binding and flipped her back over to face him. *He isn't hearing me.* "I have to go to her!" she said, trying again, but there was no talking to him, no reasoning. *I broke him.* The demon who had been so rational, so reasonable. "If anything happens to her." Her heart was about to explode with fear for Lanthe. That fear turned to nausea, then fury. "You have no right to keep me," she cried. "No right to attack me, tackling me into the mud!"

"You lied—you'll pay for it."

"Get off of me, you animal! You have to release me, now!"

"Never, Sabine. *Never.*" He snatched her up into his arms then over his shoulder, storming back to his home.

"No!" she screamed as he forced her away from the portal, away from Lanthe. "Don't take me back." Though the rain was easing, she still couldn't hear her sister.

"I'll keep her any way I have to," Rydstrom muttered to himself. "Chained to the bed if I have to. The demon in me will be satisfied this eve. . . ."

She gazed back over his arm, shuddering. Where was her sister? Sabine had to get back to her, had to escape Rydstrom.

When the gale ended, she attempted once more to tell him about Lanthe. But it was like talking to a wall. He wouldn't listen, not even when they returned to the house, not even when he stripped her. Not even when he stalked outside and found chains to trap her body to his bed.

One way to deal with a woman like her.

Rydstrom heard little of what she was saying. He didn't need to hear any more of her lies. *Just need to mark her.*

She lay on the bed with her damp red hair in a fall all around her head, her pale body spread and trembling. He shoved his pants off, then climbed over her.

Her eyes went wide. "You've got to let me go!" she cried. "I have to get back."

Do nothing irrevocable. . . . But he had to, because she wouldn't stay anyway. *Mark her.*

He knelt between her legs. "I was going to take you slow." When he lay over her, he clasped the sides of her face. His cock pulsed against her hot sex.

Get control. She makes me crazed! Got me so twisted inside. . . .

"Don't do this to me, demon!" She gazed up at him with beseeching eyes.

"You told me you would stay. I believed you."

"Rydstrom, I have to help Lanthe, my sister. If I don't get back, they'll kill her. Trust me to return to you, and I will."

"Did you think it would have ended between us when you went back to Omort? I'd come for you." As he ground his shaft against her, he said at her ear, "*Cwena,* if we are apart, it's only because I'm not done fighting my way to you."

"If we do this, will you let me go?" she asked desperately. "Then take me, claim me, do whatever you have to, but just release me."

"You must bear my bite."

"Then, yes! Do it!"

"You know what you have to say, sorceress."

"You want me to beg, demon? I will! I beg y—"

"No!" He shoved his hand over her mouth. He didn't want this. Didn't want her to break. When she grew quiet, he removed it.

"Th-that's what you wanted, isn't it?" she asked.

"Yes . . . no!" He eased off her, sitting on the edge of the bed, pinching his forehead. *Just think.*

"Then what?" she cried, writhing in her chains.

He rose, pacing. *Think . . .*

"What do you want me to do, demon? What do you want?"

"*I don't know!*" he bellowed, putting his fist through the wall. "I want you to *feel* something. For me." And then he was above her again, clutching her nape. "Because you're clawing my bloody heart from my chest!"

"I do feel something for you, demon. Take me, mark me as your own. Forever."

Words from a dream. He couldn't decipher the subtexts, couldn't foresee what trickery this was. Her silken tongue was telling him exactly what he wanted to hear, the sorceress soothing the beast inside him.

"But then you have to let me go. I will return to you!"

Can't think . . . nothing irrevocable . . . He rose once more, then staggered to the bathroom. Inside, he rested his forehead and palms against the wall, digging in his claws as he grappled for control—

He heard the unmistakable sound of Cadeon's old truck in the drive. With a curse, Rydstrom slung on some jeans, then went to head him off before his brother could use a key.

When Rydstrom cracked open the side door, his mind was seized on Sabine, but he vaguely noted Cadeon appeared . . . tired.

"Rydstrom?" Cadeon bit out incredulously.

He could only imagine what he looked like. He wore no shirt or shoes and had been buttoning up his jeans. Cadeon's gaze flickered over his clenched jaw, his shoulders bunched with tension, and the thin lines of blood running down his chest and across his cheek.

"Are you going to make me stand out here? Open the door."

Rydstrom glanced back into the house. *That dream.* She'd been about to take it away from him. He could hate her for that.

"You're worrying me, man. Let me in, and tell me what happened. The last I heard was that you'd been captured by Sabine."

When Rydstrom didn't answer, Cadeon said, "You were taken to Tornin, weren't you? Did you fight Omort to escape?"

Rydstrom finally shook his head.

"Then how the hell did you get free? No one escapes Tornin."

"I had an ace in my pocket," he said, his voice rough. *What will I have to do to make her want to stay?*

"You don't sound good. Are you all right?"

"I will be." Rydstrom looked back over his shoulder again. "Soon."

"I got the sword." Cadeon offered it to him. "Killed Groot, too."

Rydstrom accepted the weapon, barely sparing it a glance. *She'd been running from me. After making me believe she wanted to be with me.*

Cadeon was baffled, saying slowly, "That's the *sword* that will defeat *Omort*."

"We go to war in the spring. Be ready."

"That's all you've got to say? So much for abject gratitude, or even a pat on the back." Cadeon's tone grew louder with each word. "If you knew what I went through to get to that goddamned thing, what I put my female through . . . Oh, and for the record, your Veyron's missing, and it's never fucking coming home—"

"*Is someone out there?*" Sabine cried. "Oh, gods, help me!" She rattled the chains. "I'm being held against my will!"

"Is that *Sabine?*" Cadeon bit out. "Was she your ace?"

"*Please help me!*"

Rydstrom peered at him hard, daring Cadeon to do something.

Clearly striving for a casual tone, Cadeon said, "So, you've got an evil sorceress chained up in your bed, then?"

Rydstrom knew what his brother believed. "She's *mine*," he seethed. "I'll do whatever the fuck I want to her. And it's nothing that wasn't done to me," he snapped, recalling the humiliation she'd subjected him to. The memories burned worse, because he'd intended to be so *good* to her, had planned to completely forgive her for her treatment of him. His fists clenched.

"Hey, hey, no need to slug me, brother. To each his own, yeah?" But he was studying Rydstrom.

"Once I'm done with her, I'll contact you."

As he closed the door, he barely heard Cadeon mutter, "*Fuckall, does this mean I'm no longer the bad brother . . . ?*"

Before Rydstrom locked the sword in the armory, he took it to the bedroom to show Sabine his prize. "This is the sword that will kill Omort."

It glinted in the light, and her eyes followed its every movement as he checked the weapon's balance, swinging it in a circle by his side.

"Soon, I'll return to Tornin for his head. Would you like that? How does the idea of your brother's death make you feel?"

"Like I'm hearing a weather report for a town I don't live in."

"I almost *want* you to have loyalty to him."

"Don't you understand? You'll never get close enough to use that weapon on him. He rarely leaves Tornin. He has guards and mystickal traps surrounding him at all times. Damn you, Rydstrom!" Her wrists were bleeding. "Let me go!"

He turned from her and left the room. As he headed to his study, he gazed down at the sword—the most remarkable one Rydstrom had ever beheld. The weapon felt like an extension of his arm.

This was all he'd wanted, and he'd barely spared a glance at it. His brother had risked his life to claim this for him, and Rydstrom hadn't said a word of thanks.

Just now, Cadeon had looked at him like he'd lost his mind.

I think I have.

❊ 39 ❊

bie?"

She sagged with relief. *"Lanthe, where are you?"* Her sister's voice had come to her once before when Sabine had screamed for help, but then it had faded again.

Dimly Sabine heard, *"Dodging really big birds. What happened to you?"*

"The demon caught me and chained me to his bed."

"He did what? As soon as I lose these assholes, I'm coming after the demon."

"What are you going to do? Portal him to death?" Sabine said. *"Can you evade the Vrekeners for much longer? Wait, I hear him coming . . . just stand by!"*

Rydstrom returned to her then, gazing at her with pain and confusion in his dark eyes. He reached for her, but instead of touching her body again, he began to free her bonds.

She held her breath. Was he letting her go?

"Do you know what I saw when you told me to dream of what I needed most?" His voice was hoarse as he unchained her ankles. "I dreamed of you and of our son. We were happy, Sabine. I was able to make you happy—and to protect you. The feeling was indescribable."

"Lanthe, he's freeing me—just hold on a little longer!"

Rydstrom continued, "But now I know that will never happen."

Once he'd released her, she shot to her feet and scrambled back from him, but he just sank onto the side of the bed, his face exhausted, his cheek marked from her nails.

"Lanthe, are you still there?" Sabine took only enough time to snatch up the undershirt he'd left out for her and drag it over her head, then she headed out.

At the doorway, she said, "Look, Rydstrom, I'll be back in six days. I promise you."

"No, you won't. I'm done, Sabine."

She whirled around. "What? Rydstrom, no—"

"I'm not like *this*. You bring out the worst in me." He was holding his head in his hands. People did that in grief, or in the realization that something they'd wanted was forever out of reach.

He'd given up on her. And she wanted to ask him not to. Even give him reasons why he shouldn't. But Lanthe was out there alone, defenseless.

"All we're going to do is continue hurting each other. I don't want you to return," he said quietly, but with steel in his tone.

"Demon, wait. . . ."

He met her gaze. "Do not come back here."

When she felt her bottom lip trembling, she made herself invisible. Casting another glance at him, she ran from the room.

"Abie, are you there? What's happening?"

"I-I just got broken up with."

"What? Well, you don't need him anyway!"

"Ah gods, Lanthe. I think I really do."

Lanthe sprinted, out of breath, getting herself more lost. She and Sabine both had zero directional skills. Hadn't she just passed those tennis shoes strung over the power lines?

All the while she was craning her head around to scan the skies and trees for the Vrekeners. But she thought she'd ditched them.

There'd been at least two dozen. And when she'd first seen several of them crouched on the limbs of an ancient oak, she thought she'd spied the scarred face of Thronos among them. . . .

"I'm out of the house now."

Lanthe was so relieved she nearly tripped. *"Then let's get the hell out of here. I've lost the Vrekeners, so all we have to do is find our way back to the portal. Do you remember where the park was?"*

"Are you kidding?*"*

"One would think, huh?" Alley after alley opened up like doors to choose from. She sprinted headlong down the wet steaming pavement of one, then turned to follow another.

"Wait! I think I see it." Lanthe sprinted toward a clearing ahead—it would have to be the park. *"I'm*

here!" She could see the portal not even fifty yards ahead. "*Follow my . . .*" She trailed off, the tiny hairs on the back of her neck standing on end.

Lanthe gazed up with dread.

Vrekeners everywhere. Dotting the tree limbs, surrounding her on the ground. They'd trapped her, using the portal as bait. "*Ah, gods, it's a trap! They've been waiting for us. Driving me, so I'd draw you out.*"

If Sabine hadn't been tackled by that demon, she would've been seized by them. "*Abie, don't come here. This place is crawling with them!*"

"*I'm on my way!*"

Lanthe caught sight of Thronos once more. Crouched on a limb in his black trench, he looked like the Reaper. He smirked, stretching the raised scars across his face. Then he dropped effortlessly to the ground.

The asshole thought he had her.

A perilous incident was supposed to reignite her power of persuasion? It didn't get much more perilous than this. Why not try?

He gave a hand signal, and in a flash, they attacked as one. She gulped in a breath and sprinted for the portal.

Some flew overhead as she hunched and darted, some chasing her on foot. "Leave me alone!" she cried. Had she felt a twinge of power?

Never slowing, she glanced over her shoulder. The ones on the ground had stopped. Those in the air flew in place. All except for Thronos, who appeared to be gnashing his teeth, straining to resist her command.

He continued limping toward her with malice in his

expression, his wings unfurling with hostility. Stalking closer. . . .

Should Lanthe try to find Sabine? Or attempt to lead them away again so her sister could get through the portal—

One by one, they began to throw off her command, charging once more. In a panic, she scurried forward, diving headfirst into the portal, landing halfway into her room in Tornin.

Thronos was right behind her, catching her foot at the threshold. She gave a mule kick, connecting with his mouth. "Get back," she commanded.

The battle within him was clear as he resisted, but he took a step back.

Sabine said, *"Where are you?"*

"I'm at the portal door."

"Then close it!"

"What about you?"

"I can make it six days!" Sabine cried. *"But if you get caught now, I don't have a chance."*

"But—"

"You have to do this!"

"I'm coming back for you!" Gritting her teeth with effort, Lanthe began sealing the portal, closing the rift she'd created. The edges of the threshold were like the seams of a wound, easing together to heal. "Abie, hold on till I return!"

Just before she'd sealed the sides, Thronos shoved his boot inside. He gazed down at her with silvery eyes, his wings spread wide.

Lanthe cast him an evil smile. The wound of the portal was healing—nothing could keep the edges open now. She heard the echo of his roar as his foot was severed, then she fell back onto the floor of her room, gasping for breath. *I've got to find a vampire, someone who could trace me back to Sabine.* But they'd all bailed. . . .

She stood in gradual degrees, shoving her hands to her knees as she heaved for breath. She glared at Thronos's booted foot. Because of him, Sabine was stuck in that plane.

Lanthe yelled at the foot, "I'm so sick of you fuckers coming down on us! Five hundred years of this!" She punted it across the room.

It sailed past Omort in the doorway. "And you dare return without her."

Sabine sensed quiet and felt her sister's absence, which meant she'd gone from this plane. Through the portal. She was likely safe.

But now I'm screwed. She had six days till her rescue would come. Could she last that long? Damn Omort for his lies!

She had no idea where to go to hire a vampire to trace her back. She had no clue where to stay. She could weave illusions of money to get a hotel room, but the Vrekeners would just home in on her sorcery.

Why am I so despondent? I've been in much more dicey situations.

Maybe because she might be dying soon.

No! She refused to believe that. She'd heard the morsus attacked in waves. She could withstand the first episodes of pain. Hell, she might wean herself and tell Omort to go bugger himself.

Her eyes went wide. *Yes, I'll beat this thing!* The accounts of people dying from pain were about victims who'd never known agony like Sabine had. *I've died dozens of times. This will be old hat.*

She felt better about the morsus, almost looking forward to the challenge.

So why am I still despondent?

I miss the demon. She'd had a good thing and hadn't realized it soon enough. The odds were slim that she would find another male like him: a gorgeous king who would press her head down to kiss her nape, who was usually considerate and fair—except when he went demonic because she ran from him—and who was also her husband.

She wanted the demon. *But he no longer wants me. And it's all my fault.*

This hurts. Sabine felt her bottom lip trembling once more. *Not again!* Crying was something for weak women—the hand-wringers and the hopeless.

And still the tears came streaming down, the unfamiliar feel of them shocking her.

❧ 40 ❧

What have I done?

Rydstrom cursed himself bitterly.

I actually let her go.

At the time, he hadn't felt like he'd had a choice. He'd been appalled by his behavior. In that park in the storm, he'd come close to shoving himself inside her, and then again later in the bed.

Yet now that he'd calmed enough to think, he believed he might have detected some truth to her words when she'd told him she would return in days. She might in fact want more with him.

If she brought out the worst in him, then he would just have to work harder to become a better man for them. No male would work harder. And more, he was going to *ask her* what she thought he should do, putting everything out there for her: *I'm not interested in a life that doesn't have you in it. You make me crazed. I would give anything for you to grow to care for me.*

But he would demand that she meet him halfway.

And he would have to find her.

With that thought, he ran for her again. *She might have crossed that portal.* Yet he sensed she hadn't, still perceived her nearness. . . .

He found her not even a block away from the house, sitting on a curb.

As he approached, he saw her wiping her face with her forearm.

Sabine was . . . *crying?* "What are you doing out here, *cwena?*" Over the last week, Rydstrom had been pleased when she'd worried about him and gratified when she'd felt the sting of jealousy. Was he a terrible man to hope she was crying about him?

She glared at him with her bottom lip quivering, allowing him to see her like this instead of using a mask. "I d-don't have anywhere else to g-go." Another swipe of her forearm over her eyes. "Lanthe's gone, and I c-can't get to her for six days. And I'm in a strange t-town and land, and Vrekeners are everywhere."

Sabine hadn't even mentioned what they'd just gone through—

"And you br-broke up with me!" she said, her tears falling faster. "Is that supposed to make me happy?"

"Come inside, Sabine."

"No! You t-told me not to." She sniffled. "You don't want me at your house."

He swooped her up in his arms. "Will you shut up?" With his free hand, he brushed her tears. "I made it ten minutes before I came after you."

She buried her face against his shoulder. "I'm glad you did."

He swallowed, never imagining this night would turn around like this. "We have a lot of things we have to get sorted out. I'll put you in the shower, and then we'll talk about what we're going to do."

"Talk o-over wine?"

"The sweetest I can find."

"You still w-want me?"

He rested his forehead against hers. "I always will."

"Demon, I understand why you would think the worst about me tonight. I've given you no reason to grant me the benefit of the doubt. But I know now that you have to be able to trust me."

"Sabine, that's not reasonable—"

"Wait. J-just hear me out. There's something I can do that will let you know when I'm being untruthful to you. Something the bad guys use to keep each other honest. I want to do this for you, demon."

He had no idea what she was talking about, but he savored even the idea that she wanted to take a step for him—

"All I need is clay, picture hangers, an oven, and your blood."

"How can I be sure these covenants are going to work?" Rydstrom asked over his shoulder as he nailed three picture hangers to the wall.

"I made extras so we can test them," she said absently, gazing at his uncovered back as she tied twine through the hole of the third covenant.

The muscles, the tattoo, his smooth skin . . . *Gods, this male is too fine—*

He abruptly turned, catching her ogling him. She shrugged as if she was helpless not to ogle. Because she was.

"Are you ready with those?" he asked, his voice a touch rough.

"Oh. Yes." She had three covenants baked and ready to be hung. She carefully handed them to him.

He was clearly still dubious about this whole process, but he was going along with it as if hoping it would work.

When they'd returned to the house earlier, he'd trusted her to stay and shower while he located clay somewhere on the grounds. They'd met back in the kitchen, with Sabine dressed in another one of his undershirts. He'd showered downstairs and wore a clean pair of jeans—with *no* shirt.

His kitchen was ultra-modern, and she didn't exactly know her way around even a medieval one, but she'd managed to find a bowl to mix a small sampling of their blood with the clay. "Your blood will bind you to the spell," she'd explained as she made a small cut in his arm. "My Sorceri blood acts as the catalyst, the battery that gives this power."

Once she'd rolled the clay out flat in three baking dishes, Sabine had used an ice pick for a stylus. In the first tablet, she'd carefully inscribed, "I will never lust after Rydstrom." In the second, she'd written, "I will never kiss Rydstrom." The third read, "I will never lie to Rydstrom."

As he hung the tablets, she hopped up to sit on the granite counter top. "Covenant time! Sacred even among the bad guys."

While Sabine had worked, she'd been drinking a nice dessert wine from his collection. He'd been leaning against the counter with his arms crossed over that broad chest of his, watching her every move.

The sexual tension had been palpable.

When they'd had to wait for the tablets to harden, she'd reasonably suggested that they *occupy themselves*, but he wouldn't, instead keeping this all business, seeming very serious about getting things "sorted out."

Now he approached her spot on the counter. "What do we do?"

"Ready to test? Then, be so kind as to undo your pants and give me a peek."

"Sabine? Very well." He unbuttoned his jeans, pulling the fly open wide.

As soon as she laid her gaze on his shaft, she bit her bottom lip, wanting to touch him there, to run her lips over that flesh—

The first tablet shattered into pieces, plunging to the ground.

His eyes widened briefly as he refastened his jeans. "Kiss me," he told her, leaning in closer to her.

She pressed her lips to his firm, delicious ones, and her eyes slid shut. But when the second tablet splintered and dropped, he broke away. "It's bloody working."

"You married a sorceress, demon. I know what I'm about."

He abruptly turned, inspecting the tablets.

"You can ask me anything, and I'll have to answer honestly. But before you get to your questions, I have one for you." He waved her on in that kingly way. "If I had told you I had to get back to Tornin because of a life-or-death situation but I would return to you, would you have let me go there without you?"

"No. We do *not* separate, Sabine." As if to illustrate this, he returned to the counter, standing before her, wedging his hips between her legs. "I've found you after fifteen hundred years, and I'm not keen to part from you for any reason."

"I see." She hadn't expected him to answer differently, but his vehemence reminded her that she would have to tread carefully with him.

No matter how badly she wanted to trust him completely, she couldn't. Like Lanthe had predicted, the demon wouldn't be apt to let her go poison herself. In six days, she would have to. "Ask your questions."

"Where were you going tonight? And why did you run from me?"

Tread carefully. "My sister opened a portal to come get me. She and I can speak telepathically when we're close enough to each other, and she woke me up. I explained to her that it didn't feel right not to tell you that I was leaving, even if only for a few days. I told her we had an understanding. That we were together."

At that, he gazed over at the last covenant, likely expecting it to fall, even as he so obviously wanted it to stand.

Some unfamiliar feeling bloomed in her chest. *Lonely demon. Yearning so much for his loneliness to end. . . .*

When the tablet didn't break, he said, "Go on." His tone held a note of excitement.

"Lanthe's portals require a lot of power, and soon it attracted the Vrekeners. She was telling me that she was running for her life. Rydstrom, she doesn't have any defensive sorcery. She can't fight them. I raced from your house to help her."

"Were you planning to return to me?"

"Yes."

He laid his hands on the countertop on each side of her thighs, seeming stunned by these revelations. Then his eyes narrowed. "Are you working with Omort on some plot now? Working against me?"

"No."

"Are you not on his side?"

"No. I'm on my side and my sister's side."

He took that in. "Could you want a future with me?"

She hesitated. *Do I for certain?*

"Yes?" she finally answered, peeking over at the covenant. When it remained in tact, she gave him a well-what-do-you-know expression. "Rydstrom, if I were going to want anyone, it would be you. I just don't know if I'm what *you* need. I'm not . . . *like you*."

"You know what, Sabine? You were right when you said I've lived an ordered life. Before you, I kept everything around me rational and reasonable. And yet everything about you defies reason. I *like* your devious mind and your inappropriate humor. I like that it doesn't make *sense* for me to feel this strongly about you—but I still do."

In response to that heartfelt declaration, she met his gaze. "Rydstrom . . . you look *really* sexy in jeans."

He collected himself after a moment of obvious bafflement. "I *know*," he finally said, appearing to be stifling a grin. "Can I get a little more than that?"

She grew serious once more. "I like that people respect you. I like that your chest is warm and that you make it available to me. And I love that you came after me tonight."

"Then you will stay with me?"

"For now, I can only promise you six days."

"Six days again?"

"Lanthe can only create a portal every six days."

"Ah. Now I see. Are you planning on leaving me when she returns?"

"I'm trying to make you a promise I know I can keep. I have six days I can give you. After that, the future might not be my own. We could reconvene on the last day."

He looked like he would question her more about this, but then he let it drop. "Why didn't you tell me you'd begun to feel something for me? I've been flying fairly blind here."

"I wasn't certain about it. And how would I know that I should? I've never been in a relationship, and it's not as if I see declarations of feeling everyday in Tornin." Her arms twined around his head. "I've been flying fairly blind here."

"There's still much you aren't telling me."

"Yes. But I'm trusting you more than I have anyone except for Lanthe. Can't we take this in steps?" His scent was making her melt, and she felt herself easing closer to him. "Maybe it could be enough for you to know that I didn't want to leave before, and that I won't *want* to in the future?" she asked, their lips now inches apart.

He rasped, "Do you want me to make love to you?"

"Right now, I want that more than anything."

The last covenant remained.

❄ 41 ❄

The demon clutched her in his arms, hastening toward their room. He bounded up the stairs two at a time, breathing hard against her neck.

Inside, he dropped her on the bed, stripping the shirt from her. She'd thought this would be a frantic joining, but again, he eased the pace.

"Need to slow down." He leaned down to kiss her, grasping her nape in that possessive way. "I want to savor this."

His lips slanted over hers, and he slipped his tongue in her mouth, but not to flick it against her own. He thrust it wickedly, deepening the kiss into a thorough taking.

He means to claim me, all of me.

Once he broke the kiss, she found herself lying back on the bed under the firm press of his hands. Those obsidian eyes roamed over every curve as if he was making love to her for the first time.

Already, she was trembling, needing her demon's touch.

He finally reached down to graze his callused palms over her hips, her belly, her breasts. He unhurriedly explored every nuance of her flesh, rasping to her, "*So fair.*"

When he rolled her nipples between his fingers, pinching, then soothing them, illusions of flames smoldered all around them. "Rydstrom," she breathed. "I need you."

With a nod, he stripped off his jeans, then lay beside her. "Have to make you ready for me." His muscles were tense, his eyes black, but his appearance was somehow different than before. Not as mindless. His eyes were burning with *intent.*

Her demon looked very focused on what he was after.

Once he guided her legs apart, she let them fall wide in blatant invitation. He teased her flesh with seeking fingers, caressing her so sensuously. Then he worked one inside her. She moaned as he withdrew his finger and returned with two.

Bliss welling up, strengthening.

He cupped her sex, pressing the heel of his palm against her clitoris, stirring those fingers so deep within her. "Demon, please!"

"*Come for your male.*" He gave a thrust of his fingers to punctuate his words.

Need mounted, building . . . building . . . until it peaked and finally shattered.

Her fires soared as she came, her blue eyes reflecting the light. Her flesh was hot and wet in his hold, her sheath gripping his fingers hungrily, making his cock ache to replace them.

But he had to take this slow. He had to make this into something she couldn't live without. The look he'd just seen in her eyes said he could.

Once he'd wrung every last shudder from her, he knelt between her thighs, then fisted his cock to run the crown up and down her plump folds. He placed the swollen head against her entrance, but stopped there. "Relax, *cwena*. I will go slow."

She nodded up at him.

Leaning over her, he rested his elbows beside her head. With every ounce of will he possessed he made himself inch into her tightness, holding her gaze as he entered her. Her breath hitched in, but she never looked away.

He went awash in feeling as he seated himself deep inside his woman. "Did I hurt you?"

She shook her head. "No, Rydstrom, no."

He let her get used to him, holding himself still, sweating from the effort it took not to thrust into her lush little body. He had to make this last, but already his seed was climbing for her.

"It's different this time, so perfect. . . ."

Once she began to rock her hips, he rasped, *"Give you more?"*

"I'm ready . . . I need more."

He rose up on straightened arms. Sweat dripped from his forehead, splatting hard onto her breasts. She arched her back in delight.

He couldn't help stirring himself in her, savoring all her wetness around him. She moaned when he withdrew, then cried out as he drove inside for the first time.

The pressure . . . her tight heat.

"Deep inside you." He tilted his hips up, plunging home. "So *hot!*"

"Rydstrom . . . yes!" She was already close again. He could feel her body quivering beneath him, her thighs tightening and relaxing around his hips.

Another exquisite thrust made him shudder violently over her. When he withdrew, her flesh squeezed his cock like it'd never let him go.

Once more, he drove inside, needing to bury himself to the hilt. He ground against her, wanting in deeper, needing to possess her completely. . . .

When Rydstrom had first entered her, she'd tensed. *So big, the fit too tight.* Yet there was no pain this time—only pleasure.

Now he laid his body over hers, pressing every inch of his skin that he could against hers. He guided her arms over her head, covering them with his own as he threaded his fingers through hers.

His chest was slick and rubbed over her aching nipples. When he slowly rocked into her like this, she was bombarded with sensation, shivering with wonder at what he was doing to her.

Another rapturous thrust, more of his rumbling words in her ear, "*Couldn't please me more. . . .*"

Like this, the friction against her sex was delicious,

every movement of his hips intensifying it. She arched beneath him, gasping, "I need you, Rydstrom."

His fingers tightened around hers. "Say it again."

"I need you."

He lifted his head, his dark gaze rapt on her neck. "Then take my claim."

Ah, gods, he was going to mark her. She knew it was coming, and still her body strained toward the orgasm he was building with each measured thrust.

With his arms capturing hers over her head, he kissed her neck, his tongue flicking over her skin, lulling her. *"Waited so long . . ."* In a flash, he bit her, his upper and lower fangs piercing her flesh.

Her body fell limp beneath his, powerless to do more than come for him and accept his hot seed as he marked her.

When her climax hit her in blinding waves, she screamed from the strength of it. Over and over, her sex clutched the girth of his thick shaft, demanding what it had to give her.

He snarled against her, driving harder, deeper. Finally he released her neck, licking her there before he drew his head up. With his voice ragged, he said, *"Mine now."* He pressed their entwined hands down, pinning her to the mattress as he bucked between her thighs, sending her spiraling toward another orgasm.

"Rydstrom, don't stop!" Her head thrashed with every surge of his hips. Closer . . . closer . . . *need.* And then it crashed over her, so fiery and wet that she screamed, her back bowing, grinding the front of her body against his.

"Sabine! I'm going to come in you, *come so hard.*"

His muscles tensed, rippling with strain, then he suddenly froze above her, his cock throbbing inside her. His eyes met hers, glowing black with anguish, his body wracked with pressure, not yet released. "My *Sabine*—"

He threw his head back to roar to the ceiling. With his neck and chest flexed with corded muscle, he pumped his hot semen into her with such force, she could feel it . . . again and again, searing and palpable as he emptied himself. . . .

Once he was spent, he collapsed over her, still softly thrusting as his heart thundered against hers.

Between hoarse exhalations of breath against her damp neck, he kissed her marked skin, and it was soothing. "*Cwena,* you were worth every minute of my wait. . . ."

❧ 42 ❧

I would say something nice," Sabine began when she first spied the rickety shack, "something like 'I'm sure it's a really nice place inside.' But my covenant would just break."

"You wanted me to take you out on a date to a Lore bar," he said, sliding her a grin. His smiles were coming more frequently, but they still made her go soft each time. "We're on a date, and here it is."

She *had* wanted him to take her out on what would essentially be her first date. After all, they'd spent the last four days in and around the house, mainly in bed. But she also had ulterior motives. . . .

"It's packed tonight," he said as his new sports car prowled the shell parking lot for a space. They were out in the middle of a swamp—how could this place be so crowded?

When he finally parked, she said, "I still think you should have let me drive."

"Not a chance," he said, as he exited the car.

Once she'd woken the morning after their first night of lovemaking, he'd had a surprise for her. He'd bought a new vehicle for himself and had one delivered for her as well. But she'd just blinked at the shiny red convertible in confusion. "I can't drive."

"I'm going to teach you," he'd said confidently.

At the end of the lesson, he'd declared her the most aggressive and dangerous driver he'd ever encountered. Which meant . . . *number one!*

And after that, Rydstrom had arranged for Lore vendors of the finest clothing and jewelry to come to the house and supply her with everything she could need. She'd asked him, "Are you trying to buy my affection?"

"Is it working?" he'd answered.

Now as he opened her door, she was assailed by damp air and the sound of music and raucous laughter.

Gods, he looked good. He wore dark jeans, and a black button-down shirt, with an expensive leather belt and boots. His overall air said, *"Money, power, and I know it."*

When he helped her out, he bent down and briefly kissed her lips. "Are you sure you don't want to go back to bed?" Her lusty demon seemed insatiable. In fact, they both were.

He was so fascinating, loving it when she brushed kisses over his face to show affection—and shuddering in bliss when her nails raked down his back. This morning, she'd caught him twisting in front of a mirror to inspect the scratches. "Sign of a job well done, then?" he'd said proudly, flashing her a sexy grin that made her toes curl with delight.

She would have been more than happy to go back to their bed. But this evening she'd experienced a twinge of discomfort—not pain, just a feeling that seemed out of place in an immortal. The old Sabine had roused, the one who held survival paramount. Though she'd grown confident about defeating the morsus, she always had a plan B.

Tonight she was scouting for a vampire who could trace her back to Rothkalina just in case things got bad. . . .

"You look stunning tonight," he said. "I'd have told you earlier, but you robbed me of speech." Earlier, when he'd spotted her coming down the stairs, he'd done a stutter step.

"I thought you'd be more resistant about my attire." Though she'd worn her hair as wild as ever, she'd donned a simple headdress, and her navy blue kohl was drawn more conservatively for him, only streaking back to her temples. But her skirt was short, her boots were high, and her top was a metal mesh bandeau held in place by chains connected to her choker, two in the front and four climbing up her back.

"I refuse to have you deem me old and stodgy again." As he ran his eyes over her, he took her hands and spread her arms out at the sides. "Will I be jealous that other males see you like this? Without doubt. My horns will go ramrod straight from the first double take. But it also makes me proud."

He wrapped his arms around her, pulling her closer to him, his warmth and scent making her lids grow heavy as she gazed up at him. "People have pitied me for going so long without finding my female. Now I want to show you off, and I want to be so bloody smug because it was always going to be you for me—I just had to do my time."

Over the last four days, when he'd said things like this with his tone gruff and his eyes so piercing she almost feared he was *too* wonderful—too handsome and good and considerate to possibly be hers.

This time with Rydstrom had been blissful. But in all fairness, it hadn't always been perfect. For one thing, he'd insisted she learn how to swim, teaching her in his luxurious pool. Though she was already getting better, she spent more time attached to him, arms wrapped around his head.

And he still drank demon brew, ate steaks, and sucked on little buglike creatures called crayfish. But he did make sure she had vegetables to eat and sweet wine to drink. He'd even brought a bottle in the car for her tonight, in case she couldn't find a drink she liked inside.

With that thought in mind, she turned her attention to the ramshackle tavern. A battered neon sign glowed, but the lettering was illegible. "So what's this place called anyway?" It was situated over the water, nestled among cypress trees and looked like it would blow apart with a strong wind. A precarious-looking pier led out to it. "The Thirsty Thistle or something like that?"

"It's just called Erol's. Now if anything goes south inside, just stay behind me. Promise me."

He was overprotective to a fault. "I can't promise you that, or there's going to be clay all over your kitchen floor."

"*Our* kitchen floor."

"Demon, if anything goes south in there, I won't need you to take care of me. I'll need you to help me take care of us."

That seemed to throw him. She turned and sauntered onto the pier, leaving him with a bemused expression on his face. The big demon male was having to learn some new tricks with her.

When she began tip-toeing so her stiletto boot heels wouldn't get stuck between the planks, he asked, "Why don't you wear flats and just make them look like boots?"

"Because wearing these makes me feel sexy."

"Would being carried by your man make you feel sexy now?"

"I can manage, King Charming," she said. "So, if it's really packed inside, will you see anyone you know? Perhaps one of the thousands of demonesses you've bedded, like Durinda," she said, teasing him.

When he fell silent, she faced him. "I was just joking— I know you weren't with her. Wait, why do you look so guilty?" Why would Rydstrom appear guilty at the mention of the female— Suddenly she felt like she couldn't get enough air. "You didn't . . . in the camp . . . you weren't with her . . ."

"Gods, no! But I told you I hadn't slept with her. And, apparently, a millennium ago or so, I did."

Relief sailed through her, but then she said, "You told me you hadn't."

He ran his hand over the back of his neck. "I'd . . . forgotten."

"Did she have to remind you?" When he reluctantly nodded, she burst out laughing.

"It's not funny," he said gruffly. "It was embarrassing as hell," he added, looking like he'd begun fighting a grin.

Still laughing, she said, "I would have given gold to hear that conversation!"

"I'd thought you'd be angry."

After another chuckle, she said, "Not at *funny* things. Hey, I have an idea! Maybe we should start a database and enter all the names of females you tagged, so you can keep up with them—"

"You think so, smart ass?" He swooped her up in his arms. "All I care about is the last entry." He charged down the pier, with her laughing the whole way.

At the entrance, he let her slide down his body. As they walked in, Rydstrom had his hand on her hip and his shoulders back, looking arrogant and every inch the king. She loved it.

The interior was dimly lit and crowded. In the corner, an old-fashioned juke box played twangy songs. On the back wall, skulls framed a mirror, their eye sockets laced with Christmas tree lights.

The place had its charm.

They passed the bar where a pair of startlingly good-looking twins sat. She suspected the two males were Lykae, and was proven right when they spoke with a thick Scottish accent.

"Damnation, Rydstrom, where'd you get *her*?" one said as he shot to his feet off a stool. "And she's dressed up like a sorceress of yore." He whistled low.

The brother added, "Does the lass have a sister?"

Rydstrom acknowledged them with a cool nod, then said, "Sabine, this is Uilleam and Munro, Lykae soldiers."

"I do have a sister," Sabine eagerly said. "You'd love her, and she would *certainly* adore you—"

But Rydstrom steered her away before she could finish, heading toward the back to the only empty table. Raucous females sat nearby, playing dice. All looked intoxicated on drink or intoxispells.

When Rydstrom muttered, "More witches," Sabine put out a light probe for powers. Again, finding nothing she'd get out of bed for. But one of the females with them had pointed ears and glowing skin.

"And Regin the Radiant," he said, shaking his head. "She's often Nïx's partner in crime."

Once they reached the table, and he'd pulled out her chair for her, he was clearly reluctant to leave her to go get drinks. "Go, Rydstrom, I'll be fine."

He leaned down to say at her ear, "Just don't tell anyone your full name or your sorceress title, and we ought to be fine."

When Rydstrom hesitantly left her, Sabine glared at all the females sighing over him as he passed, though he seemed oblivious to their notice.

At the bar, he turned back to her, checking on her, those green eyes watchful.

Taking one on the chin for Team Evil? Try scoring one for Team Sabine.

He was so incredibly masculine. A dynamo in bed, on the couch, and in the shallow end of the pool. And he was good to her.

She'd been good to him for the most part, striving to be so for him. But old habits died hard. Whenever Rydstrom had unlocked his armory to view that sword, Sabine had made herself invisible.

And now she had the combination. . . .

This could get dicey. He'd brought Sabine here because she was going to have to get used to being in this society sooner or later. And the Lorekind were going to have to get used to seeing her.

But he also had another reason for coming here. Erol's was an excellent place to get information. And Rydstrom wanted Lothaire's whereabouts.

When Rydstrom had admitted to Sabine the terms of the deal struck with the vampire, she'd been understandably worried. Lothaire could ask him for any one thing. At any time. "What if he wants your firstborn? We've got to kill him!"

"*Our* firstborn. And I'll take care of it. . . ."

At the bar, Rydstrom asked a nearby storm demon and then the barkeep for information, but the mere mention of the Enemy of Old had them shaking their heads.

As he waited for drinks, Rydstrom gazed back at Sabine. She was sitting with an innate grace, casually surveying the room with those amber eyes.

So bloody beautiful. And of course he wasn't the only one who thought so. Males were craning their heads to get a glimpse of her. Just as he'd predicted, Rydstrom's horns were flaring. He cast killing looks at some of the bastards, letting them know that the female was his.

But was she? According to Sabine, he had only two more days with her—then they would *reconvene*. He hadn't pressed her about it, because he'd simply assumed keeping her here was a function of making her want to stay with him. He was doing everything he could think of, and still he felt her slipping away. . . .

Just as he accepted her wine and his brew from the barkeep, Regin yelled across the tavern, "Yo, demon, who's the tartling?"

Rydstrom exhaled, turning to stride back to the table. He saw that some of the witches in the back were from the pool party. They must have recognized Sabine, because they were urgently trying to shut Regin up.

Though they whispered to her, Regin responded loudly, "Sabine? Who the hell is she? Still looks like a tartling to me."

When Sabine slowly turned toward Regin, Rydstrom hastened back to her, dropping the drinks at a random table—

"I am not a tartling. I am the Queen of Illusions," Sabine answered with silky menace, her palms at the ready.

Ah, fuck.

"Sister to Omort?" Regin shot to her feet, knocking over her chair. As lightning streaked the sky outside, the Valkyrie snatched two short swords from holsters across her back. "How'd you like those no-handed fire demons that Nïxie and I sent back to you? Did you get her note?"

At the mention of Omort, beings in the crowd began comprehending exactly who Rydstrom had brought to this bar. He heard mutters and whispers about the sorceress, and people began filing toward the door.

As the Lykae twins reached the exit, one of them called to Rydstrom, "Damn, demon, that filly's no' yet been broken."

The other added, "Talk about goin' out and gettin' some strange."

Rydstrom stepped between Sabine and Regin. "Valkyrie, she's with me. Nïx wouldn't want you to fight with Sabine." Because Sabine would destroy Regin.

Regin frowned in confusion. "She must be the sorceress Nix *specifically* told me not to off tonight." The Valkyrie shrugged, expertly holstering her swords behind her back. Her ire had left her as readily as it had arrived, and her attention drifted from Sabine and Rydstrom. "Hey! Where's everybody going? *Rocky Horror Picture Show*'s playing downtown!" Regin brushed past them toward the exit, her friends following.

In minutes every being in the entire tavern—including the barkeep—had cleared out.

Sabine regarded the empty area with an unreadable expression.

He wrapped his arms around her, curling his fingers under her chin. "Baby, I'm sorry. It'll take time."

"Are you kidding? I was very flattered." When he gave her a doubting expression, she said, "Rydstrom, don't forget that I was raised to equate fear with respect. All those people just showed me an enormous amount of respect."

He still must have looked unconvinced because she added, "Demon, I didn't come here expecting to make friends. Now, is this still a date?"

"Of course."

"And we're still in a Lore bar?"

"That we are."

She crossed to the bar and hopped over. "So what will you have?" she asked with a grin. "Drinks are on the house."

They sat in companionable silence on the way home, both lost in their own thoughts.

Rydstrom had told her that demons loved nice cars, were fascinated by them, and now she could see the appeal. The scent of new leather surrounded her, the seats were toasty warm, and the lights on the dash illuminated his handsome face.

And there was a marked confidence about the way he drove. He was good at this, and he knew it. Gods, there was something about a male who drove well that was so sexually attractive, though she'd only really seen it with horses and carriages before.

At every red light, he took his hand off the stick shift and rested his palm on her knee, as though he couldn't stand not touching her for even a few moments.

The anticipation of knowing that they were going back to their house to make love all night took her mind from any worries she might have harbored. And she *felt* his strength, palpable and reassuring. He'd vowed to protect her, had *wanted* to.

After they made love, she was going to tell him about the poison. . . .

"You looked beautiful tonight," he said, his voice rumbling.

"You didn't look too bad yourself."

"I made the podium?"

"Demon, you'd get my gold. I was proud to be on your arm. For as long as it lasted." With the place all to themselves, Rydstrom had taught her to play pool. "And I had fun."

He grinned over at her. "Even though we didn't leave any bodies behind?"

"Maybe you're wearing off on me," she said absently, gazing at his curling lips and intense green eyes. That feeling came over her again, so sharply that realization struck her like a stray punch.

I think I'm in love with the demon.

❧ 43 ❧

Later that night, Rydstrom sat in his den, staring into a glass of demon brew. He'd left Sabine sleeping soundly, after taking her more times than he could count.

She'd said she had something she wanted to talk to him about later, but she'd drifted off. He'd noticed her face had been pale, and he feared he'd exhausted her.

Sometimes when she was digging her nails into the backs of his thighs as he took her from behind, he forgot that she didn't have the strength of a demoness.

It was as if he were trying to bond her to him through bouts of sex—because his other efforts appeared to be failing. Though she'd seemed genuinely happy to be with him, like tonight at the bar, he'd sensed an underlying urgency in her. And he had only two days left before her sister would return for her.

Rydstrom needed Nïx's advice, but she'd been impossible to locate over the last few days. He had the sword, and it was time to strategize and to act. Yet he felt like he could do nothing until he'd solidified things with Sabine—until he'd wed her and truly made her his queen. Which meant he had to come clean with her first. . . .

Filled with doubts, he sat pounding demon brew as his brother often had—to Rydstrom's past censure.

As if any of that mattered now. He'd been so damn hard on Cadeon. And for what?

The side door opened then. *Speak of the demon.*

Shortly after, Cadeon strolled into the room. "You still look like shite warmed over. But better than that last time at least."

Though it had always been uncomfortable between the two brothers, now everything could be different. The past wasn't what they'd believed, and Cadeon had redeemed himself.

When Cadeon dropped onto the couch across from him, Rydstrom held up the bottle in offer.

"A dram, but not more."

Once Rydstrom splashed the dark brew into a glass, he accepted the drink, inhaled, then took a sip. "You alarmed the piss out of me the other day."

I alarmed myself. "I've tried to contact you since then."

"I've been MIA," Cadeon said simply. "But I've been left to my own recognizance tonight, so I thought I'd stop by." He studied Rydstrom's face. "I think this is where I'm s'posed to ask if you want to talk about it."

Rydstrom gave a bitter laugh. "Maybe after another bottle."

"When did you start pounding demon brew?" Cadeon asked.

"When did you stop?"

"No more getting blotto. I'm responsible now, didn't you hear? I got hitched."

Rydstrom raised a glass. "Congratulations, brother," he said, relieved that things had worked out between Cadeon and his female.

"That's why I haven't answered. Been keeping time with the missus at the new estate I just bought her. Nïx informed me that I couldn't keep living in my 'pool house man-cave' I shared with Rök, not if I was going to have Holly."

Rök was a smoke demon, Cadeon's second in command, and a fine soldier—except for the fact that he continually disappeared. "Where is Rök? I haven't seen him by."

"Told me cryptically that I might not be the only one settling down, then he blazed. Haven't seen him since."

Rydstrom would relish seeing the bed-hopping demon domesticated.

"I want you to officially meet Holly," Cadeon said. "So I figured I'd come by to see if you were up for company. It looked like you had some things to work through."

No kidding. "Why don't you tell me what happened when I was . . . gone."

"All right then." With his usual excitement, his brother told him of the journey to Groot's, details about checkpoints and near-death escapes, battles with revenants and fire demons.

But when Cadeon talked about his new wife, his entire demeanor changed. His glass of liquor went forgotten on the table. "We knew how smart she is. But who knew how sexy a mathematician could be?"

"How did you get the sword?"

"I had to give her to Groot for it. Thought you'd be proud of me for making a sacrifice for once in my life. I thought of you, of the kingdom, and the people. Still, I was planning on taking her right back, but the bastard tricked me. . . ."

After Cadeon relayed everything that had happened. Rydstrom could hardly imagine how painful it would've been to see the betrayed look on the face of the woman he'd fallen for so completely.

Even though Cadeon had a plan to save her, Rydstrom didn't know that he himself could have done the same.

Cadeon said Holly had . . . cried.

My brother's a stronger man than I am. It was difficult to swallow that truth, but Rydstrom was craven with his need for Sabine—the thought of even parting from her for a day made his fangs grow. "Holly's forgiven you?"

"Almost mostly. But she still gives me slack about it when she's sick. I take it as a husbandly badge," he said, puffing out his chest.

"Sick? You told me she was fully immortal."

"Yeah, but she throws up some, because, well, the thing of it is . . . Ah, fuck, Rydstrom, I knocked her up."

"You're going to be a father?" Gods help the world. *I'm going to be an uncle?*

"I got Holly, like, on the first shot. Nïx is calling me Bull's-eye and the Womb Raider."

"Nïx is nothing if not subtle." A month ago, Rydstrom would've been uneasy with the idea that his brother had gotten a babe on the Vessel. Now he felt confident the female would bear a warrior of ultimate good.

"That's why I'm on my own tonight—cause Nïx and Holly are out shopping for baby swords or something." He scratched his head. "I'm kind of hoping they were joking about that, but with Valkyries, how can you know?"

"How do you feel about having a babe?"

"At first, I was happy, because I thought it'd mean Holly'd have to forgive me, like I'd smuggled an ally on the inside who'd help me," Cadeon said, still every bit the mercenary. "Then I got excited. If Holls thinks I drive her crazy, imagine little Cadeons running around all over the place."

"I have firsthand experience with one. And that was plenty."

An awkward silence fell over the room. Rydstrom took a drink, muttering over the rim, "Make sure you have wainscoting."

"What?"

Rydstrom shook his head. "Nothing."

"No, tell me."

"When you were little and your horns were molting, they itched so bad that you'd run them against the walls. Nylson and I used to burst out laughing to see every new three-foot-high gouge running the length of a hall. We wouldn't let anyone repair them." His lips curled until he noticed Cadeon's expression. "Why are you looking at me like that?"

"You're talking about *me*. And it sounds . . . fond."

What the hell did Rydstrom have to lose? "It nearly broke me to send you away."

Cadeon scowled. "So much that you visited all the time?"

This much resentment? "I did every chance I could. At least once a week in the beginning." At Cadeon's disbelieving look, he said, "I was there watching over you, making sure you had everything you needed. I stayed out of the way because Zoë and Mia said I would interrupt your bonding with your new family."

"How about not sending me away at all?"

"After Nylson and our father had just been slain? Because they broke the custom? When you were little, I was still adjusting to being king. I'd just lost my older brother, who was my best friend. And my father, as well. Then you were to be in jeopardy, too? I couldn't stand the thought of it. I was tempted to take you and our sisters and start anew, turn our backs on wars and killing."

Cadeon gaped. "You considered giving up the crown?"

"If there'd been a worthy replacement for me. Yes. Then, just a few years later, I lost the kingdom to a vicious murderer. I'd wondered if I'd fought hard enough, or if I'd let go too easily. The guilt was unrelenting, *is* unrelenting."

"But the crown was everything. That's why you've hated me all these years."

"I never hated you. And the crown had nothing to do with why I've been hard on you." At Cadeon's raised brows, Rydstrom said, "All right, that was part of it.

But I was also angry because of the way you were living your life. You were selfish and uncaring." Rydstrom knew Cadeon wouldn't argue that. "Sabine's since told me that you would've been assassinated if you'd gone to Tornin. Omort had five hundred troops waiting for you."

"Sabine told you that?"

"She wanted to ease some of the strife between us."

"Kind of nice, for an evil bitch."

"Guard your words carefully, brother, that woman is going to be your queen." Just when Rydstrom thought they'd have another row, Cadeon raised his palms.

"Yeah, you're right. Sorry. But don't forget that she's part of the reason I gave up Holly. I thought if I got the sword, I could free you. It ate at me, thinking of you in a dungeon. Nïx told me the sorceress would . . . *use* you."

The sorceress did.

With a nod at the now empty bottle, Cadeon said, "You've finished it—something I never thought I'd see—so are you ready to divvy what happened?"

Rydstrom exhaled. Then he told Cadeon almost everything, leaving out his false vow, ending with, ". . . I'm not making progress with her as I'd hoped. And I've only got another two days."

"Look, I know I'm the last person you want to take advice from, but you can't force this. You can't *make* her love you."

"Then what would you do?"

"You know, do nice shite for her. Buy her things. Really think about what she likes and what makes her happy and make it happen. She'll come around. And if she doesn't, you can cut off your horns for her. Chicks dig that."

Rydstrom's gaze shot up. Sure enough, Cadeon's had been shorn. "What the hell did you do that for?"

"Holly wanted a normal life, so I was trying to give her normal. She's since berated me, and forbidden me from ever touching my 'rock-hard, sexy horns' again. Then she outlined what she was going to do to me when they grew back. Gods, brother, that woman quicks my wick." Then he frowned. "Wait a minute. Did you say Sabine was *going* to be my queen? What the hell is she now?"

Deceived.

A storm was coming, outside the house and within it as well.

Rydstrom was going to confess to Sabine about his sham vow. With a heavy heart, he made his way upstairs to their room, leaving Cadeon to finish his drink.

Though he'd been working to earn her trust, Rydstrom was about to destroy it with one blow. But he had no choice. Every time she called him her husband was like a knife to the chest.

He sat beside her in the bed. "Sabine, there's something I must confess to you."

She didn't answer, didn't turn to him, but her slim shoulders tensed, letting him know she'd awakened.

"All I ask is that you try to understand the circumstances. Can you do that?"

No response. He laid his hand on her shoulder and tugged her over to face him. She opened her eyes.

They were filled with blood.

"What is this? Sabine, what's happening?"

"It's . . . *here*." Her words were slurred, her skin waxen.

He gathered her up in his arms. Her heartbeat was racing.

When a line of blood tracked from her nose and another from her ear, the sharpest fear he'd ever felt came over him. "Ah, gods, what is happening to you? Tell me, *cwena*!"

"Poison," she gasped.

"What are you saying? How? Who did this to you?"

Her back arched sharply, her hands fisting in Rydstrom's shirt. When she coughed, blood misted from her mouth.

Have to get her help . . .

"Cadeon!" Rydstrom bellowed.

His brother came bounding up the stairs, barreling into the room with his sword drawn. "What the hell?"

"Sabine's sick—where is Nïx?"

"I can go get her."

"Do it, and then meet us at the witch's coven—"

"Nooo!" Sabine screamed, thrashing in his arms. "No . . . coven."

"Easy, baby, we'll stay. Easy . . ." To Cadeon, he snapped, "Bring Nïx here. If you can't find her, then hunt for Mariketa the Awaited. Or even Tera the Fey. She knows poisons."

Without a word, Cadeon bolted from the room. Rydstrom heard the side door slam shut, then Cadeon's truck peeling away.

Rydstrom laid his palm on her cheek, wincing in confusion as pain suddenly shot through him, as if he'd laid his hand on a flame. But then her nightgown and the bedclothes were *cold*.

"Hold on for me, Sabine. Help's coming."

Pain razored through her body, making her muscles knot. The coppery tang of blood flooded her mouth. *Feels like blades are slicing through my veins, and pumping into my heart.*

Rydstrom kept demanding to know what was wrong, staring down at the blood in horror, rocking her in his arms.

She panted in anguish, her eyes squeezed shut. She'd been wrong. There was no way she could withstand this. So stupid, so arrogant to think she could live through this.

And now she'd pay for it. *Unless Rydstrom can bring himself to do what needs to be done.*

Her body twisted as the excruciating waves built, her mind overrun with visions of drinking her poison. Yes, downing glass after glass of it . . . just dripping the searing black granules straight onto her tongue, then swallowing them dry.

Ah, gods, she could accidentally poison Rydstrom with her skin, her blood. *Must warn him.* "Can't . . . touch me."

"Sabine, I have to get you to someone who can help!"

She shook her head violently. "No one here . . . can."

Another wave hit. Unthinkable . . . unearthly *agony*.

Her eyes flashed open when the manic pounding of her heart *stopped*.

Their gazes met. "*Cwena?*" he rasped, "your . . . heart?"

Over. Her mind went blank. Her lids eased shut.

His unholy roar shook the room.

❧ 44 ❧

Her fucking heart had stopped . . . she'd almost died. He'd never forget how he'd felt when he'd heard that first dogged beat as her heart struggled on.

He sat with his back against the headboard, squeezing her in his arms, rocking her as they both sweated from pain. When she moaned, he murmured, "I'm with you, baby. I'm with you."

Whenever he touched her skin, he felt eviscerating pain, so he continually smoothed his palm over her forehead and face, hoping to draw it from her.

Her bloody coughing had subsided, but he sensed this was in no way over. He was grappling to keep the rage reined in so he could take care of her.

A storm had descended on them, with lightning streaking all around the house, thunder rattling the glass doors. With each lightning bolt, Sabine's face looked even more deathly pale.

When Cadeon squired Nïx into the bedroom half an hour later, the Valkyrie's gaze flickered over Rydstrom's face, as if gauging his sanity. His horns were straight, and he knew his eyes were black, but he was holding on.

"What is going on here?" she asked. "All Cadeon would say is, 'Have you ever wanted to see a scene from *The Exorcist* in real life?'"

"She's sick," Rydstrom said. "She told me it was a poison. You know poisons. Tell me what to do."

In the darkened room, figments of Sabine's illusions began flashing in a delirious procession, like words babbled.

Nïx approached the bed, tilting her head. "There's a blue tinge to her lips." She turned Sabine's arm over.

Streaking down the pale skin was a jagged red injury, like a burn. It ran all the way to her palm, where it made an X.

Nïx abruptly dropped her arm, wiping her hand on her pants. "She's been condemned."

"*Condemned?* What the fuck are you talking about?"

"This is the morsus, the cruelest poison—because it causes inconceivable pain upon the withdrawal. Sabine would have had to take a regular dose of this poison to keep it at bay."

"Ah, gods, she'd been trying to get back to Omort days ago. I . . . stopped her."

"Then he's the one who has done this to her. It makes sense that he'd use this to control her for all these years."

"What will happen to her?"

"Have you touched her skin? Did you feel that pain?" When he nodded, she said, "You're experiencing possibly a percent of what Sabine is. There's supposed to be no greater agony. It feels like being scalded and stabbed, as if your skin is being pincered from your body. Demon, this will get a thousand times worse. The pain will become so great, it will prove a shock to her body, so intense that her heart will stop."

"It already *has!*" Inhaling deeply, he tried to calm his tone. "What can I do?"

Nïx shook her head sadly. "Absolutely nothing to help her. The only person who can save her is the one who poisoned her. Rydstrom, you need to prepare yourself. Sabine will have one heart attack after another until . . ."

"No! No, someone has to be able to help her," he said, his voice breaking. "Tera, Mariketa—"

"Will only confirm what I've said."

"What about Sabine's sister—she's saved her before!"

"Ah, Melanthe, the potential Queen of Persuasion. Healing another is one of the hardest processes to effect. And her power is weak, only manifesting itself in unpredictable fits and spurts."

Rydstrom rested his forehead against Sabine's, desperate to take this pain from her. "There has to be *something* I can do for her." He gazed up at the Valkyrie, unashamed to beseech her. "Nïx, please . . ."

"There is something you *must* do. Rydstrom, if you care anything about Sabine," she said, "you will kill her now."

In between fevered waves of agony, she'd heard Rydstrom speaking to her.

With his voice growing thick, he'd pleaded, "*Cwena, fight this for me.*" He'd threatened, "What am I supposed to do without you? You can't leave me like this! I'll follow you to the gods damned grave, Sabine."

And when another wave had crashed down and she'd thrown back her head and shrieked, he'd roared with his own pain and confusion, clutching her so tightly, until her screams died down. . . .

Sometimes, she heard other voices. The brother was often here. Two females came and went.

Now she perceived Rydstrom sitting beside her on the bed, stroking her hair. But another wave was building . . . building . . . And each one was worse than the last.

"Rydstrom . . ."

"I'm here, Sabine." He kissed her palm, then rubbed his face into it. "I'm right here."

"*Kill me,*" she begged as residual pain seared through her body. "Please . . ."

His dark eyes were frantic. "Never!"

"You say . . . you care about me," she whispered. "But if you did . . . you would kill me."

"I don't fucking *care* about you! I'm in love with you, Sabine. You told me I needed you," he said desperately. "I do. Freely, I admit it." He held her face, seeming to grit his teeth against the pain of the contact. "We'll fight this together."

"You . . . love me?" She'd known, had felt it every minute with him. But to hear him say it . . .

"Ah, gods, *cwena.* You have my heart. Anything that I possess is yours. Just heal. Just feel no pain."

* * *

"Then let me go." Damp tendrils of red hair framed Sabine's pale face. "Please . . . I'm *begging* you . . ."

He couldn't hear these words, couldn't imagine the pain that would drive her to speak them—

She seized again, her back arching, more blood gurgling from her lips as she screamed again and again. Nïx and Cadeon rushed inside just as her body fell limp.

But her eyes were open.

They were sightless, staring at nothing.

Nïx said, "She takes no breath, demon. She's gone."

"No!" Rydstrom roared, clutching Sabine's shoulders, shaking her.

"Rydstrom!" Cadeon gripped his arm. "She's gone, brother. She wants you to let her go."

"Never!" More shaking . . . *"You come back to me, Sabine!"*

Sabine's lids twitched, her muscles visibly knotting. *She lives.*

"*No . . . no more,*" Sabine moaned in despair, realizing she hadn't died. She gave Rydstrom a look of utter betrayal then fell unconscious in his arms.

"You've only saved her until the next wave hits," Nïx said. "Demon, next time, you must let her go."

No, there is another way. "There won't be a next time." He narrowed his eyes at the Valkyrie. "You knew this would happen. You knew all those nights ago when you asked me if I could pick one, which would I choose—my kingdom or my queen. And you asked for a reason. I can sacrifice all hope for one to save the other."

"You answered your kingdom so easily back then. I was amused."

"Whoa, whoa," Cadeon said. "What the hell are you two talking about?"

Rydstrom asked Nïx, "How do I get to Tornin tonight?"

"It's being, uh, taken care of."

"If you've seen all this, then tell me—will she live?"

Nïx gazed at the ceiling, then back. "I don't know about her. But you might want to have a talk with your successor here and let him know what's about to happen."

Rydstrom nodded, accepting death—or worse.

"Yeah, let me know what's going on!"

"I'm going to Omort for the antidote. The sorcerer will likely kill me this time," he said matter-of-factly. "Cadeon, you're my heir. Nïx said this was my last chance to claim my crown. She didn't say you had no chance."

"*What—the—fuck?*" Cadeon thundered. "No way! No goddamn way!"

"This *will* happen, brother," Rydstrom snapped. "I wasn't *asking* you—I was informing you."

"Okay, then, so we make this a trap," Cadeon said, plainly wrestling with his temper. "You can't go there without a battle plan."

"You told me Groot hit at your mental blocks like a sledgehammer. Omort will demand I open my thoughts to his probes. I have to be utterly free of conspiracy, else I risk her."

Cadeon ran his hand over his face. "If you do this, you'll be committing suicide."

"I understand. If I can save her from this pain . . ." *Then mine was a life well lived.*

"Nïx! Tell Rydstrom this is a suicide mission."

She sighed. "If he wants to go all Aslan the Lion on us, who are we to stop him?"

"I won't let you do this!"

"It's done," Rydstrom said. "Nïx, tell me how to get to Tornin."

"The way to get to Tornin is already on her way to New Orleans. And she's *pissed*."

❊ 45 ❊

"So how are things with Mike Rowe?" a woman's voice said.

Consciousness gradually returned to Sabine, and she found herself between waves of pain—in that harrowing lull between remembering agony and anticipating it.

"Mike Rowe? Who exactly are you talking about, Holly?" another female answered. *Is that Nïx speaking? Yes. What is she doing in my dream? Or am I waking?*

"The actor?" this Holly said slowly. "From *Dirty Jobs*. Who took out a restraining order against you?"

A pause, then Nïx said, "Ah! Yes, well, Mikey and I broke up after I finally got him to fool around with me."

"In the week since I saw you last?"

"Yes, last night if I recall correctly," Nïx said. "He was quite *adroit* for a human, very tempting. But then I had to forget the phone number he pressed on me."

As if she couldn't help himself, Holly asked, "Why's that?"

"I remembered I'm a rake."

Sabine blinked against her hazy sight and spied Nïx in the sitting area of the bedroom. Sabine squinted at the Valkyrie's T-shirt. It read, BORN TO BLOSSOM, BLOOM TO PERISH—G.S.

The other female, this Holly, had glasses and a prim demeanor. She looked to be *folding clothes*?

"Besides," Nïx said, "I needed to break it off with Mikey, since I'm leaving town."

"What do you mean you're leaving?" Holly demanded, folding and refolding the same towel. "I still don't know my way around this world, and you're taking off—yet again?"

"Cadeon can show you about."

"Where do you have to go that's so important you can abandon me?"

"Auntie Nïxie's taking a TO. I'm heading to Budapest, to investigate this band of immortal warriors," she explained. "They're called the *Lords of the Underworld*. If that doesn't make you want to mate . . ." She growled and clawed at the air. "Anyway, they're supposed to be excessively hawt."

"And by *investigate*, you actually mean *do*."

Nïx made a scoffing sound. "Holly, how else is one supposed to investigate a male? Really?"

Holly sputtered, but Nïx talked over her. "Just between us—if they can handle what the Nïxanator's bringing, I might not ever leave. . . ." Her vacant gaze skittered over to the bed, and her eyes widened. "She's awake."

Nïx strolled over to the bed with Holly following. "Remember me? Nïx, the Ever-Knowing? And this is my niece, Holly." Nïx indicated the pretty blonde who gave her a weak wave. "She's Cadeon's wife."

Nïx put a glass of water to her lips, but Sabine turned away to gasp out the words, "Where's . . . Rydstrom?"

"We finally peeled him away from you. We'll be your sitters this eve. Rydstrom, Cadeon, and myriad demons are out searching for your sister, so they can poach her portal." She laughed abruptly. "I'm sorry, this is not a funny situation, but 'poach your sister's portal' really sounded *raunchy*."

Holly rolled her eyes.

"He's bringing Lanthe back here," Nïx finally continued. "And then he intends to take you to Omort and beg for the antidote."

Sabine's heart stuttered—this time from emotion. "He can't . . . go through with this!"

Nïx said, "He's decided to sacrifice himself for you."

"Omort will kill him this time . . . will read his mind . . . discover any of his plans of attack—"

"There won't be any," Nïx said quietly. "Rydstrom's counting this as a one-way trip, sorceress."

Sabine shook her head sharply. "You can't let . . . him do this!"

"You try stopping a nearly seven-foot-tall demon who's hopelessly in love."

"Nïx," Holly murmured, "Sabine needs some clean sheets. They're dirty with all the blood . . . blood—" Her hand flew to her mouth, her face paling even more.

"Are you having morning sickness again?" Nïx asked. When Holly darted from the room, she called, "My gods, Holly, way to steal Sabine's thunder!"

To Sabine, Nïx said, "I'll be back shortly. Yell if you need anything." She heard Nïx mumble at the door, "Poach her portal. *So* going on a T-shirt."

Sabine lay quaking and stunned. Rydstrom planned to sacrifice everything for her.

An idea arose, a plot. Could it work? She had little time before the next wave hit—did she have the strength?

She would find the strength, because if he was going to save her, she was going to protect him. Or at least give him the means to protect himself.

Gritting her teeth, she rolled off the bed, collapsing onto the plush rug. She could hear Holly retching in the guest bathroom and Nïx running water for her. Sabine had no strength to hide herself with illusion, but as long as she could hear them, she'd be clear.

She crawled on her belly from the room, sometimes digging her nails in the carpet to pull herself forward. When she reached the hall at last, it looked interminable, the distance to his study impossible.

So weak . . . But she pressed on through the pain. One elbow in front of the other, her legs trailing uselessly behind her.

Ever listening for the Valkyrie, crawling, crawling. Only her love for that demon kept her going.

She spit up blood, choked back a cough, crept another foot. Just a few more to the study door . . . then finally inside.

She'd made it to the armory! With effort, she craned her head to gaze up at the combination lock she'd have to reach. From her place on the floor it looked as attainable as the moon.

Rydstrom will die if you don't do this!

With that thought spurring her, she wobbled to her knees, then began dragging herself unsteadily to her feet. *Have to reach it.* She was about to crumple to the floor. *Can't . . . can't do this.*

A shadow loomed behind her. Sabine twisted her head around. She cursed fate to find Nïx standing behind her.

"Did you need something, sorceress? Hmm?" She had blankets thrown over her shoulder and was fiddling with something in her pocket. *A weapon?* "Perhaps a Vicodin?"

Sabine felt like weeping. "What do . . . you want?" *She'd been so close.*

Just as Sabine heard the front door opening, Nïx said, "Rydstrom's back with your sister."

He'd already returned? "Nïx, I . . . need . . ."

"And he's about to find you out of bed—"

"*Sabine!*" Rydstrom's voice shook the walls of the mansion.

Sabine's heart was about to seize again. She collapsed to the floor, dazed.

"Do you want the sword, sorceress? Isn't that what you came here for?"

Speechless, Sabine gave a weak nod in answer.

Nïx pulled a giant syringe out of her pocket, holding it up. As Sabine stared in astonishment, Nïx blinked at it, as if she didn't understand where it had come from.

The Valkyrie scratched her head with her free hand. "Ah!" She smiled, her face lit with realization. "I knew that I'd come here tonight to do one of two things: shove this into your heart or to play Wii. And I forgot my Wii!" She shrugged—

Then plunged the syringe directly into Sabine's chest.

Eyes wild, Sabine sucked in a desperate breath, grasping at the needle jutting from her chest—gaping at Nïx as she busily worked the combination on the armory.

"The adrenaline will keep you conscious for a few more minutes, but not much more."

Just as fits of energy began flowing through Sabine's body, Nïx unlocked the armory and whistled in a breath at the sword.

❧ 46 ❧

Panic was about to overtake Rydstrom as he tore through the house, yelling for Sabine.

Lanthe was trailing him, crying, "You *lost* my sister!"

His breath rushed out when he found Nïx in the main hall upstairs with Sabine in her arms. The Valkyrie blinked at him. "What? A sorceress can't go check her mascara?"

He was about to yank Sabine from the Valkyrie, but Nïx said, "Easy, demon. She's hurting. Don't squish her all up."

With a nod, he took Sabine, gently cradling her.

Sabine gazed up at him. "Rydstrom, please don't—"

Nïx interrupted her. "Enough of that. He wants to take you. Count yourself fortunate, Sabine."

"Ah, gods, Abie!" Lanthe rushed to her side.

Sabine weakly reached for her sister, then drew back her poisonous hand. "Lanthe . . . stay beside me . . . no matter what Omort says."

Lanthe shook her head. "But he'll make me leave."

"You can be . . . persuasive."

For some reason the sister went wide-eyed. Rydstrom didn't have time to consider her reaction because another wave was building in Sabine, and she stiffened in his arms, her eyes sliding shut.

"Lanthe, we've no time to spare," he said. They'd lost hours before they'd found her wandering the streets, looking for Sabine. "We leave for the portal right now."

At the front door, Cadeon was waiting with Holly, his wife, who Rydstrom only saw briefly before. Rydstrom was reassured to see that she gazed up at Cadeon with concern and obvious love in her eyes.

Cadeon moved to block Rydstrom's way. "Let the sorceress's sister take her. There's no reason for you to risk yourself like this."

"I've told you," Rydstrom said, "that I will not be separated from Sabine."

"I've got my crew meeting here in just minutes. We're following you in."

It struck Rydstrom that he might not ever see Cadeon again after this. "No. That's not the mission for tonight," he told him solemnly. "Cade, you can take up the fight in the future."

"This could be a trick—the sorceress can make us see things. She's trapping you for Omort. *Again!*"

Lanthe said, "She's dying! Can't you smell the blood?"

Cadeon ignored her. "Rydstrom, give me the combination to the armory. I'll use that sword tonight!" At his unbending expression, Cadeon said, "Then you take it. Conceal it—"

Nïx impatiently said, "That won't work. Omort will know if Rydstrom is hiding anything."

Cadeon shook his head. "There has to be another way."

"Put yourself in my shoes," Rydstrom said. "Imagine if this were Holly, about to die from pain."

At that, Cadeon clenched his jaw. With a harsh curse, he stepped aside, slamming his forearm against the doorway in frustration.

Heading to the drive, Rydstrom looked back over his shoulder. "You'll be a great king."

Cadeon faced him with his eyes wet. "I don't want to be bloody king! And I don't want to lose my brother, just when things . . . just when you don't hate me."

"I *never* hated you." Rydstrom gruffly added, "I love you, brother. And I'm proud of the man you've become."

With Sabine in his arms and Lanthe trailing him, Rydstrom stepped through the smooth portal directly into the court of Tornin.

Immediately, he spied Omort upon his throne.

"What is this, Melanthe?" the sorcerer snapped.

The court was nearly empty—and even more revolting than it had been before. Bodies were piled up, flies buzzing in the stench. The walking-dead revenants lined the walls.

Rydstrom forced himself to ignore it all; only one thing mattered to him. Without hesitation, he strode toward the dais. Sabine writhed in his arms, her fingers clenched in pain.

But Omort halted him with a flick of his hand, freezing him where he stood. "The demon comes to me?" Omort smiled, his eyes maniacal. Then to Lanthe, he said, "You leave! Now!"

"Brother, look at her!" Lanthe sobbed. "She's dying. You can't let her die! Please!"

"Her heart has already stopped," Rydstrom said. "She'll perish in minutes—"

Omort leaned forward in the throne. "Open your mind to me, demon. Now!"

Rydstrom did, willing the sorcerer to see the truth—that all he wanted was for Sabine to be safe. "I'm told you have an antidote that will heal her. That's all I seek."

"You truly have no plan? There is no trick. You merely want your *little female* to be well. Because you're in love with her?" He gave a bitter laugh. "I could not have punished you more, since loving her has brought me nothing but misery."

"If you love her, then help her—"

"Wait . . . there's more in your mind. Sabine, open your eyes." After a moment, she blinked them open. "You've been dealt treachery from one sworn never to give it. The demon tricked you. You are *not* wed. He lied about the vow. Instead of swearing to protect you, he swore to hurt you."

Sabine gazed up at Rydstrom, bloody tears gathering.

"By the look on your face, sister, I think he kept his word."

Rydstrom wasn't denying it.

Ah, gods, no! She wanted *to be his wife. . . . And she* wasn't? *He'd lied?*

No, focus, Sabine!

She would deal with this grief later. Right now she was in deep with a plot, and another wave of pain was coming. Once the shot wore off, she wouldn't be able to hold on much longer.

Sabine knew this wave would be her last. . . .

Omort continued, "Your treachery's fitting, demon, since Sabine was going to murder your babe. Her own child. Weren't you, Sabine? She and I planned to sacrifice it to the well to unlock its power. That's why she was working so tirelessly to seduce you."

"I don't believe that," Rydstrom said. "And you'll never convince me of it."

"Omort, we can do this later," Lanthe cried. "She needs the morsus now!"

"And I'll give it to her when the demon's dead and you are gone! Now leave before I finish you."

Lanthe's tears ceased. Her eyes went cold. "No."

"What did you say to me?" His words were dripping with malice.

"I said . . . *use—no—sorcery.*"

At Lanthe's command, Sabine silently begged, *Please let this be the time. Everything rests on this . . .*

Sabine's amazement matched Omort's—because when he raised his hands to punish Lanthe, his palms were cold.

Rydstrom tensed against her.

"What is this?" Omort bellowed, that vein pulsing in his forehead. His eyes darkening to a metallic yellow, he stalked after her. "I will make you burn, Melanthe!"

"Come no closer to me."

Omort stopped abruptly, staring at Lanthe in bewilderment. "Guards!" he called for the mindless revenants. They marched from the perimeter as one, surrounding them with swords raised.

Lanthe faced them, and with her voice ringing out, she said, "Fight only each other."

When they began engaging each other, clashing swords all around them, Lanthe ran for the double doors of the court, barricading them with their locking bar, buying time.

Sabine thought, *That's my sister.* . . .

"No!" Omort yelled. "Demons!"

"Don't call them!" Lanthe hissed, and Omort fell silent. But with that command, Sabine sensed Lanthe's power was depleted once more.

Rydstrom appeared stunned, even more when Sabine whispered, "I have something for you, demon." She shakily tugged open the edge of one of the blankets that Nïx had bundled her in, presenting him with the sword that lay along her body. She'd asked the Valkyrie, "*Why are you doing this? For your army? Or for Rydstrom?*" Nïx had answered, "*Maybe I'm doing it for you.*"

"Sabine, I don't . . . you are sick?"

"I am, but Nïx gave me a shot . . . so I could have the strength to give this to you. But it's starting to fade. You have to use this to kill Omort—"

"Then who will give you the antidote?"

"The Hag will help . . . but only after Omort dies. There's not . . . much time, Rydstrom. Lanthe's powers are weak. . . . Hettiah might come and erase her commands."

"Then if I fight Omort, I risk you. There's not *enough* time—"

"You can do this. You must. Destroy him forever. It's your due. . . ."

❈ 47 ❈

This was all a trick?

Sabine had warned him again and again. *I always have a plan*, she'd said. *Nothing is as it seems with me.*

Here was his chance to destroy Omort, and as he took the sword from her, all he could wonder was if she had feigned her feelings for him.

No. He knew his woman, and with everything in him he felt that she returned his love. "Sabine—"

"Kill first . . . talk later. *Please.*"

He gave a grave nod, then turned to Lanthe. "Come, take Sabine."

She hurried over, clasping Sabine in her arms.

"If you've gotten your powers back, then heal her," Rydstrom said.

"I'm out, demon. I'm tapped. I can't help Sabine, I can't stop the fire demons from eventually busting down that door, and I can't freeze Omort for you to simply behead him. I forbade him to use sorcery, but he can still fight you."

Rydstrom grasped the sword, rising up to slay a sorcerer. Omort's yellow eyes seemed to bulge at the sight of the weapon.

"How did you get that inside here? *Sabine?*" He briefly appeared devastated, before his crazed look returned. To Rydstrom, he said, "You forced her to do this. She would never willingly betray me."

From his scabbard, Omort drew a sword with a mystickal blade of concentrated fire. "Even without my sorcery, I will still take your head! I look forward to meeting you once more in battle—and I fight for her."

I do, too. "In any other circumstance, I'd want to savor killing you," Rydstrom said, advancing on Omort. "But as much as I've envisioned this fight, I just don't have time for it." Never would he have imagined he'd be fighting Omort, not for his crown, but for the life of the woman he loved.

They began circling each other. Omort struck first, but Rydstrom made an easy parry, his sword sparking off Omort's blade.

"My brother Groot forged that sword true," Omort said. "Mine usually cuts through metal." He charged once more, striking with a blinding speed.

Rydstrom blocked again. Omort was surprisingly good—just as he'd been nearly a millennium ago. He was fast, his eyes revealing nothing. He telegraphed no move.

Again, they circled, assessing each other for weaknesses. Omort surged forward, flying to get to his back. Rydstrom pivoted around with his sword for a clean block.

The sorcerer had skills and technique, but so did Rydstrom. And he could beat Omort's speed with his strength.

When Rydstrom's sword connected with Omort's, he followed through with all the power in his body, making the sorcerer's weapon quake in his own hands, jarring him with the merciless strike.

Again and again, their swords clashed. Then Rydstrom feinted, catching Omort off-guard, and delivered a particularly punishing blow against his sword. Omort staggered, his body growing weaker.

Just when Rydstrom made a charge to end this, Omort snatched off his cape, throwing it over Rydstrom's head.

His vision obscured, Rydstrom leapt back, snatching at the material, just dodging the worst of Omort's next blow. The blade of fire cleaved through Rydstrom's shirt, searing a line across his chest.

The sorcerer came in for the kill right as he was able to see once more. Rydstrom switched sword hands as he twisted around, then swung a backhanded blow.

It landed true. Omort's head thudded to the floor. His corpse dropped to its knees before slumping to the ground.

Need to get to Sabine. But Rydstrom couldn't repeat the mistake he'd made the last time he'd faced this foe. He forced himself to wait for the space of several heartbeats.

These moments feel longer than the nine hundred years I've waited for this. . . .

The sorcerer did not regenerate. A wall of hanging tablets came crashing down, splintering across the floor. With the death of their master, the revenants dropped all around them.

Rydstrom clutched the hilt of the sword in thanks as he charged for Sabine. The weapon had fulfilled its fated task.

Lanthe murmured, "No longer deathless—"

Suddenly, the great doors of the court began bowing as fire demons fought to get inside. Rydstrom skidded to a stop, swinging around, readying for battle once more.

Over his shoulder, he said to Lanthe. "Still nothing?"

"No, but if we can make it out of here alive, we can get to the Hag—"

The doors began to smoke, then burn. Soon the remaining warriors of the Pravus, mainly fire demons, rushed in. The tide slowed when they spied Omort the Deathless, sprawled beheaded by his throne.

The call arose among the fire demons to take the castle. They surrounded Rydstrom, raising their palms alight with flames. With this many combining fire, they could kill him. *Too many . . .*

Rydstrom heard Sabine scream again as the pain hit—

Suddenly, the fire demons' attention shifted from Rydstrom to something behind him.

"Need some help?" Cadeon called.

When Rydstrom twisted around, he found his brother—and Cadeon's entire crew of mercenaries—here and looking bloodthirsty.

It hit Rydstrom then—with Omort's death, Cadeon could trace once more. And he'd led his men here.

Just as the mercenaries attacked, Sabine screamed again. Rydstrom charged for her, battering any opponents in his way. When he reached her, he shoved the sword in his belt, then cradled her in his arms. She'd gone unconscious.

Lanthe said, "We have to find the Hag! She's the only one who can cure her."

Rydstrom whisked Sabine up, storming from the court. Over his shoulder, he yelled, "Cadeon! Taking her for help!"

"I've got this!" his brother called back as he slashed at opponents with abandon. "I have some experience against these fucks! And I'm out for fire demon blood."

Lanthe was right behind Rydstrom as they rushed for the exit. "Demon, head for the base—"

She was abruptly cut off. When Rydstrom swung around, he saw her skidding across the floor.

A wild-eyed Hettiah had tackled her, blocking her way to the door. "You and your sister will pay!"

Lanthe snatched up a sword from a fallen revenant. "Take Sabine! Go!"

Rydstrom turned, barreling down the corridor stairs, before remembering he could now teleport as well. He traced Sabine into the bowels of the castle. But there were chambers everywhere, connected by a twisting labyrinth of passages. He turned in a circle, bellowing, "Hag, where the hell are you?"

"In here," she called. He followed the sound of her voice to a chamber that was exactly like he imagined a poisoner's laboratory. Atop long tables were dissected creatures, fermenting potions, bubbling brews. Bats' wings and frogs' legs hung from the ceiling.

The Hag, however, was *not* what he was expecting. Instead of the crone, a pretty elven brunette stood before him, the woman he'd glimpsed before.

And she was packing.

"Save her . . ." Rydstrom rasped. "You have to save her."

Without glancing up, she said, "And why should I?"

"Because I defeated Omort. I think his death has freed you."

"Well, there is that." She met his gaze. "For five hundred years, I've waited for the sorcerer's curse to end. Lay Sabine on the table." Rooting through a safe, she withdrew two wooden cases, opening the first one. Within it lay a vial of black liquid.

When the Hag offered the antidote, Rydstrom accepted it, then propped Sabine up, holding the vial to her pale lips. He glanced at the Hag. "Do you vow this will cure her?"

"Cure her of the morsus? Yes, I vow it. But I can't help her with the bitchiness."

He scowled at her, then dripped the contents between Sabine's lips.

Waiting . . . nothing . . . "Why's it not doing anything?" he snapped.

She shook her head, baffled. "It should have worked by now. It must be too late."

❧ 48 ❧

re her cheeks pinkening? Is she healing?"

Sabine heard Rydstrom's harried voice as she woke by degrees.

"They are." Was that the Hag? "It figures the sorceress would milk the tension for all it was worth."

When Sabine murmured Rydstrom's name, he exhaled. "Ah, gods, *cwena*. I'm here with you."

When she opened her eyes, she found his were fierce but tender as he gazed down at her. He brushed the backs of his fingers against her cheek.

The Hag muttered, "I'll leave you two alone."

"Wait," Sabine said. Who was this female that sounded like the Hag? *Was* this the Hag? "Where's Lanthe's cure?"

"I left her vial on the table beside the rhinoceros testicles."

"Oh." *Free.* They were finally free of Omort. Of the poison that had befouled their blood. And the Hag was apparently free as well. "How is it that you are . . . different?"

"Omort stole my foresight, cursing me to live as a crone in this hellhole. All for a foretelling I gave about a sorceress Omort would fall in love with. At least, as much as he was capable of it. Sabine, your brother didn't seek you out for the demon—he sought you for himself. But as soon as I saw you, the prophecy came to me that you and the demon king would wed and have a son who would unlock the well's power."

"But not in the way Omort said?" Sabine asked.

"Not in the least. Omort used the prophecy, embellished on it, until even he believed his own lies. Now, if you don't mind, I've got a portal to catch. And I'm five hundred years late for a date."

"But wait—"

"The battle's still going on upstairs, sorceress." She swept out of the room.

Sabine turned to Rydstrom. "Trace me to my sister!"

In an instant, he traced her to the court. But Lanthe had already felled Hettiah and was kicking her lifeless body, telling it, "For centuries, I put up with your shit! Day after day!"

That's my sister. . . .

Sabine saw Rydstrom gazing at his own sibling in the melee, looking torn, clearly wanting to be with her but needing to help his brother. "I need to get Cadeon's back."

"Oh no, you don't, demon!" With an angry flick of her hand, Sabine made the mercenaries invisible to the fire demons. "We have things to discuss."

Cadeon roared, "Hell, yeah!"

After a few moments observing Cadeon's joyful slaying and Lanthe's therapy, Rydstrom said, "I think they've got it." He shoved his sword under his belt again, then traced Sabine from the court to her room in the castle, to the balcony overlooking the sea.

Once Rydstrom had steadied her from the teleportation, she said, "You didn't believe Omort about the well and the sacrifice? That I was a part of that plan?"

"Of course not. Just as I don't believe this was all some plot you concocted ahead of time. The last week between us was real."

"Like our marriage?"

Sabine's expression was inscrutable, eyes glowing blue with emotion. He couldn't predict what she would do about his deception, had no idea . . .

To be this close to all he'd ever wanted.

"Did Omort lie?"

He ran his hand over his mouth. "I—*cwena* . . ."

"You can't call me that, can you? I'm not your queen. What had you promised that night? What did you say to me so solemnly?"

"That I would exact my revenge on you."

Her brows drew together, and her bottom lip trembled.

Rydstrom's heart fell. "Ah, gods, Sabine." She was crushed. She should be. To act as if he'd wed her. . . .

"Demon. I. Am"—she shook her head and swallowed hard—"so proud of you." Her eyes were misty. "You got one over on me."

He parted his lips with astonishment. "You're not . . . you—" He swept her up in his arms.

"Well, it did anger me at first. But luckily for you, I'm not a tool. When someone decides to sacrifice his life for mine, I can be forgiving."

"I'd do it gladly, Sabine. Always."

"Yes, well, I also realized that I can hold this over your head—*for eternity*. Think of the leverage, demon!" In a feigned innocent tone, she said, "But whatever do you mean we're not instituting a kingdom mini-skirt day? Don't you remember when you deceived me about our marriage vows?"

He cupped her nape. "Do it, hold it over my head. Wear me out on it. Just as long as you stay with me."

"I don't have a choice, since I seem to have accidentally fallen in love with you."

That line between his brows deepened. "I love you, too, sorceress. I want to remedy this lack of a marriage right now."

She laid her palms on the sides of his face. "Good, because I need the authority to make some serious changes around here. Oh, and this time, make it in English."

❧ Epilogue ❧

Two months later
New Tornin, The Kingdom of Rothkalina

Like taking candy from a baby!" Rydstrom's wife cried as she swung her bag of stolen loot over her shoulder.

Lanthe answered, "Shooting fish in a barrel!"

Sabine and her sister still hadn't seen Rydstrom sitting quietly on his throne in the empty court. Lanthe had created her portal in here—the one place no one was supposed to be today. But Rydstrom had finished up with a construction project early, and had come here merely to relax and enjoy the renovated court until his wife returned from "shopping."

"Your shopping went well?" he said, his voice booming.

Sabine and Lanthe froze midstride, then slowly craned their heads to him.

"I hope you paid for all that."

"Busted," Lanthe muttered. "I'll be in my tower." She scurried out.

Sabine recovered from her surprise and sauntered up to him. "We didn't pay for these with money *per se*. But we paid back some karma."

"Who did you steal from?"

"This half demon Nïx told us about. A drug lord down in Colombia."

Rydstrom steepled his fingers. "And why would you do this?"

"She said we should 'have at him.' Since I owe her for helping me in a tight spot, I thought I should be accommodating to her. This one time. And we didn't think you'd be mad if we stole from a bad guy."

"I'm not. But I'm furious that you put yourself in danger."

"No one ever saw us! And Lanthe even managed a tiny bit of persuasion, just to make sure we were extra safe."

Rydstrom sighed. "Then let me see what you got." He could never stay cross with her, not when she was so happy here with him and with their new life together.

When she settled on his lap, he wrapped his arms around her, and she proudly showed him a bag of gold coins of an ancient cast.

Of course, this wasn't his little queen's first heist since they'd wed. He knew it wouldn't be her last.

But then, she could get away with anything. All of Lorekind knew that if anyone harmed a hair on her head they'd be dealing with a maddened rage demon out for blood. Sabine took full advantage of that fact.

"This is a respectable take," he said.

"Lanthe and I are *exactly* like Robin Hood." She nodded winningly with laughing amber eyes. "Except we don't give to the poor."

"You will be now. I'm seizing forty percent of this." When she grumbled, he said, "Or we could use that percentage for another new road project."

During the days, the sound of hammers, building, and restoration rang out over the kingdom. His people were thriving once more. "Just think, you'll be helping us ease out of medieval times." Into the sixteen hundreds. But they were taking it slow. "And we could even name a major thoroughfare after you."

The people certainly wouldn't object to that. They loved their merry and clever queen, who'd helped her king defeat an evil tyrant, and who only wanted a *bit* of gold.

She nibbled her bottom lip. "And one after Lanthe, too?"

"Of course."

"Do you think I don't know you're managing me?"

"I do. But I think you like it." He drew her in closer, savoring the smell of her hair. "By the way, Puck came by just after you'd left this morning."

The boy had been fostered with Durinda and her new husband, but Sabine got to see Puck whenever she liked because he and his new family had returned to Rothkalina—many refugees had, as well as families from other factions of the Lore. "Puck was sad you weren't here, so I showed him the presents you're having sent to Durinda's."

A full drum set and a year's supply of sugary candies. The demoness was going to love that.

Since Rydstrom and Sabine had officially moved back into the renovated castle, they'd continually had guests. Old friends and trusted allies visited often. Even Mia and Zoë, Rydstrom's younger sisters, were coming to stay with them in the spring.

"And Cadeon dropped by the work site today," Rydstrom said. "I invited him and Holly to dinner."

"Tonight?" Sabine sighed, though Rydstrom knew she grudgingly liked her in-laws. "Great. I get to watch Holly battle all through dinner to keep her meal down."

Holly's unrelenting queasiness wasn't surprising since they'd learned she was carrying Cadeon's *twins*. Two warriors of ultimate good.

Sabine continued, "The last time they were here, Cadeon followed her around like she'd break. He carried her down a set of three steps. You better not do anything like that once we decide to have a kid."

Rydstrom and Sabine were waiting to have their own son until they'd gotten the kingdom settled. They'd decided the power of the well had gone untapped for eons, so a little while longer wouldn't make a difference. Especially when Rydstrom was savoring the indescribable satisfaction of protecting his little queen, spoiling her.

"Sorceress, you know I'll be worse."

"Then expect me to make fun of you. It won't be avoidable."

There was another factor in their decision to wait. As Sabine had put it, "We'll be having no firstborns, demon, until that vampire Lothaire is contained." As a surprise castle-warming gift to Rydstrom, Sabine had used a good deal of her own personal jewelry to pay Cadeon's mercenaries to hunt down the Enemy of Old.

The crew had strong leads already, and it was only a matter of time before they found the cunning vampire. . . .

When Rydstrom dropped Sabine's bag of gold on the floor and turned her in his arms, she said, "Earlier, I was thinking about the first night we met. You'd had no idea what was about to hit you when you saw me on the road that night."

"You wrecked my car, my life as I knew it."

"But now you have me, and your crown. You look very kingly on this throne, by the way."

"I practice in the mirror every day."

She grinned. "No, you don't. You're too busy staring at the scratches running up and down your back." Then she said with a purr, "I could add to them, my liege."

He inhaled sharply—and had her traced to their bed before he'd released that breath. As he began the pleasure of undressing her, the sea winds rushed in over them, and she stretched her arms over her head with a languid smile.

He dipped a kiss to her neck while he unraveled the laces of her top. With approval in his tone, he murmured, "This one's complicated."

Sabine sighed, "I'll be worth the wait, demon."

Rydstrom met her gaze, needing her to see all that he was feeling for her.

She did. Her expression grew soft when he grazed the backs of his fingers along her silky cheek. *"Cwena, you always are. . . ."*